The Riptide Ultra-Glide

ALSO BY TIM DORSEY

Florida Roadkill

Hammerhead Ranch Motel

Orange Crush

Triggerfish Twist

The Stingray Shuffle

Cadillac Beach

Torpedo Juice

The Big Bamboo

Hurricane Punch

Atomic Lobster

Nuclear Jellyfish

Gator A-Go-Go

Electric Barracuda

When Elves Attack

Pineapple Grenade

The Riptide Ultra-Glide

Tim Dorsey

HARPER LUXE

An Imprint of HarperCollins*Publishers*

THE RIPTIDE ULTRA-GLIDE. Copyright © 2013 by Tim Dorsey. All rights reserved. Printed in the United States of America. No part of this book may be used or reproduced in any manner whatsoever without written permission except in the case of brief quotations embodied in critical articles and reviews. For information address HarperCollins Publishers, 10 East 53rd Street, New York, NY 10022.

HarperCollins books may be purchased for educational, business, or sales promotional use. For information, please e-mail the Special Markets Department at SPsales@harpercollins.com.

FIRST HARPERLUXE EDITION

HarperLuxe™ is a trademark of HarperCollins Publishers

Library of Congress Cataloging-in-Publication Data is available upon request.

ISBN: 978-0-06-222285-5

13 14 ID/RRD 10 9 8 7 6 5 4 3 2 1

For Dave York

It would be a bitter cosmic joke if we destroy ourselves due to atrophy of the imagination.
—MARTHA GELLHORN

The early bird gets the worm, but the second mouse gets the cheese.
—STEVEN WRIGHT

The Riptide Ultra-Glide

Prologue

FLORIDA

The hookers were slap-fighting a Hare Krishna up at the intersection when the bullet came through the windshield.

Until then, the tourists' rental car didn't have a mark and would have passed the damage inspection back at the airport, but this was unusually hard to overlook.

It was shortly after eleven on a hot Thursday morning, and the hole in the glass was neat and small, just above the steering wheel, with a tiny circle of cracks indicating a high-velocity round. The Chevy Impala continued straight for almost a block before the horn blared from the driver's forehead. Then it veered over the centerline and clipped an oncoming Nissan. Both cars spun out in opposite directions, sending other traffic screeching toward curbs and sidewalks and hookers.

Finally it was still.

Two surviving tourists in the Impala stared at each other in shock. "What just happened?"

Then it was unstill.

The driver's-side windows exploded from more gunfire, this time a MAC-10 submachine gun preferred throughout the metropolitan statistical area. The tourists ducked in a spray of glass. A twelve-gauge blasted open the trunk. The pair spilled from the passenger door, onto the burning pavement, and scrambled on hands and knees up the middle of U.S. Highway 1.

More bullets raked the car; others took chunks from the street around the fleeing tourists. The attack came from a black Jeep Cherokee with all the fog-light trimmings. It had skidded up sideways behind the crashed Nissan. Overloaded with passengers, an armed clown car, leathery men in cowboy hats and plaid shirts. Jumping out and firing as they advanced, as if it were completely normal behavior in South Florida. They had a point.

They were along a stretch of U.S. 1, also called Federal Highway, between Fort Lauderdale and Miami. No-man's-land. A gritty corridor of strip malls, service stations, old mom-and-pop motels and new bank branches.

Calls flooded 911 operators. Stray rounds shattered glass at a pizza place and nail salon. Another vehicle arrived. A silver Ford Explorer with Kentucky plates cut the corner through a Citgo station and stopped half over the curb at a Walgreens. More men with guns. Blue jeans, T-shirts, boots. The newcomers began firing on the gunmen from the Jeep Cherokee. Two immediately got hit, MAC-10s twirling and shooting the sky as they went down. The rest ran back behind their car and returned fire on the Ford. Both groups occasionally turned to squeeze off shots at the Impala and the tourists.

A police helicopter swooped over the scene, looking down at the geometry of a Wild West corral: the Jeep on the east side of the street, the Ford on the west, and to the south, the Impala, forming a tight triangulation of fire. The tourists were on the far side of their car, desperately crawling low down the centerline. They would have headed for the side of the road, but the positions of the other vehicles was placing fire along both edges of the street. The helicopter saw them and got on the radio.

The first patrol car screamed north up the middle of the highway. He saw the tourists and swung around the couple, placing his cruiser between them and the bullets. The officer jumped out and opened the back door. "Get in!"

The tourists began standing up.

A concentrated salvo from the Jeep blew out two of the patrol car's tires and most of the windows.

"Get down!"

The officer joined them on the pavement.

"What do we do?" asked the woman.

"See that copy shop?" said the officer. "We need to get around the corner."

"I feel safer here," said her husband.

The cop shook his head. "Some of those rounds are armor piercing."

The woman couldn't command her shaking legs to move. Tears. "I can't do it."

A bullet came through the door of the police car and chipped the pavement near her head. She took off like a track star, shots pocking the street around her feet. The men were right behind.

They made it around the side of the building and flattened against a wall, plaster from the storefront spraying behind them. The officer grabbed his shoulder mike to radio their position.

"What on earth's going on?" asked the man.

"Probably find out on the news tonight," said the officer. "Do you know any of those people?"

Two heads shook. "Never seen them before."

"What about the dead driver in your car? . . ."

A thin, wiry man in a tropical shirt stood on the second-floor balcony of one of the mom-and-pops.

A shorter, plumper man hid behind him and peeked around his side. "They're shooting down there!"

Serge smiled and continued filming with his camcorder. "I love the beach season."

"Where *is* the beach?"

Serge aimed an arm east. "About a mile and another world away, magnificent sand and surf, with the postcard-ready Highway A1A running along the shore. Most tourists take root out there and never get dick-deep into the underbelly. That's why I *love U.S. 1!*" Serge shouted the last part loud enough for one of the shooters to look up. Serge waved back. "Humid yet dusty at the same time, harsh egg-yolk tints, devoid of vegetation except for the most determined wild palms fighting their way up between the pavement and concrete blocks. And the foot traffic, a rudderless rhythm of the same bad choices and narrow appetites, trudging the streets at all hours like the undead . . . But every now and then, a fortunate tourist will confuse U.S. 1 with A1A, and accidentally book a room out here and get to dig it like a native!"

A bullet clanged off the balcony railing near the stairs.

Coleman tugged Serge's shirt. "Maybe we should go back inside."

"And miss this great footage? We're going to be famous!"

"But you're already famous, sort of," said Coleman. "All those murders. The cops call you a serial—"

"Shut up." Serge winced. "I hate that term. Serial killers are losers."

"How are you different?"

"A victim of circumstance." Serge zoomed in on the Jeep. "What are the odds all those assholes would cross my path?"

"So you're filming another documentary like the one you shot at spring break?"

"No, I've got a new hook." He panned to the Explorer. "I misjudged the market for that last project. I went for the non-market because nobody tries to reach them."

"Non-market?" asked Coleman.

"The people who never watch TV or movies, so I figured it was wide-open territory. But no takers, not even a nibble."

Another bullet hit their building two rooms down. Coleman took a swig from a pint of Jim Beam. "But

I liked your spring-break documentary. It had topless chicks, frat boys funneling beers and me burying my vomit in the sand."

Serge shrugged. "Documentaries are too intellectual for the general public."

"Then what's your new hook?"

"I already explained it to you, and we've been filming for over a week. Were you high?"

"Yes, tell me again."

"A reality show," said Serge. "I was surfing the channels, and you wouldn't believe the dreck the cable people are putting out these days. Not even good reality. We come home at the end of the day and turn on the tube and watch the bullshit parts of what we just came in from: people cooking, working on motorcycles, trying to lose weight, getting fired, getting tattoos, getting their car repossessed, going broke and pawning World War One gas masks, suing ex-boyfriends in small claims over the power bill, couples stressed out because they had ten kids, speeders making excuses to cops, truckers driving on bad roads, guys rummaging through abandoned storage units, a dude who does a bunch of jobs that cover him with filth, a game show in a taxi, interventions for people who hoard trash, families getting their kitchens remodeled against their will."

Coleman took another slug of whiskey. "What about *Cupcake Wars?*"

"That one sounded promising," said Serge. "So I tuned in one night, and no fighting at all. Just a lot of frosting. What the fuck?"

"Who do you think will buy your show?"

"Probably MTV." Serge swung his camera toward more arriving police cars. "Our reality show will beat those *Jersey Shore* mooks like a gong. They even had the gall to set their second season on South Beach, but that was an antiseptically controlled environment. They'd never survive the real Florida. Inside a week, Snooki would be blowing winos for cigarette butts."

"I'd watch that," said Coleman.

"And that's why everyone will definitely watch *our* show."

"I've got the title," said Coleman. *"Scumbag Shore."*

Serge nodded. "I'll run it by the suits."

"The only thing I don't understand is you're just filming other people at a distance." Coleman killed the pint and fired up a jay. "If it's our reality show, aren't we supposed to be in it?"

Serge pulled a nine-millimeter pistol from under his tropical shirt and headed for the stairs. "That's what we're going to do now."

"But they're still shooting."

"Good, I was afraid we'd get left out." Serge waved his gun vaguely at the street. "Let's go down there and interact with our peeps."

Coleman tossed the nub of his joint off the balcony and jogged to catch up. "Who are we going to interact with?"

"Thought we'd start with those two tourists who were crawling on their hands and knees through gunfire up the middle of U.S. 1." Serge racked the chamber of his pistol. "Most visitors could stay here for days without experiencing that kind of genuine Welcome-to-Florida zeitgeist. Since they're probably thrilled with their beginner's luck, we'll hook up and I'll take them on a behind-the-scenes tour of the Sunshine State that will trip their minds. I have a hunch they won't forget this vacation."

Chapter One

ONE MONTH EARLIER

Afisherman found the body in the mangroves just before dawn. Actually, tiny crabs found it first. The tide had ebbed from an inlet near the top of the Florida Keys, and the muck began to give off that funk. The homicide was what authorities like to call a classic case of overkill. But they were still stumped about the specific cause of death because of the way . . . well, it's complicated. And all this didn't happen until tomorrow. Right now the victim was still very much alive, and the residents of Key Largo had their attention on something else . . .

At the very bottom of the state—below Miami and the zoo and the Coral Castle and everything else—sits the tiny outpost of Florida City. Last stop. Nothing below on the mainland but mangroves and swamp.

There was some agriculture and migrants on the outskirts, but mainly it was just a short tourist strip where the end of the state turnpike dumps motorists into a cluster of economy motels and convenience stores: a final gas-up, food-up and beer-up before the long, desolate run to the Florida Keys.

Sportsmen bashed bags of ice on the curb in front of a Shell station, college students toted cases of beer, and a '72 Corvette Stingray flew south doing eighty. It ran a red light and was pushing a hundred by the time it passed the last building—the Last Chance Saloon— and dove down into the mangroves.

The driver looked in the rearview. Faint sirens and countless flashing blue lights a mile behind. He floored it.

Coleman leaned back and shotgunned a Schlitz. "Serge, do you think we'll ever be caught?"

" 'Caught' is a funny word," said Serge. "Most criminals catch themselves, like getting stuck at three A.M. in an air duct over a car-stereo store, and the people opening up in the morning hear crying and screaming from the ceiling, and the fire department has to get him out with spatulas and butter. If your arrest involves a lot of butter, or, even more embarrassing, I Can't Believe

It's Not Butter, then you actually need to go to jail, if for nothing else just some hang time to inner-reflect."

"Those cops are still chasing," said Coleman, firing up a hash pipe.

"Where did they all come from?" Serge leaned attentively. "There was nobody following, and then, *bam!* The road hits Florida City and suddenly it's like a *Blues Brothers* chase back there."

"Florida City?" Coleman dropped a Vicodin. "So that's what that string of motels is called?"

Serge nodded. "Actually a funny story. Used to be called Detroit."

Coleman swigged a pint of Rebel Yell. "Now you're making fun of me because I'm wrecked."

"Swear to God. You can look it up," said Serge. "I wouldn't shit you."

"I know," said Coleman. "I'm your favorite turd."

"And naming it Detroit wasn't even an accident, like the other times when two pioneer families set up shop in the sticks and there's no one else around to stop them, and they're chugging moonshine by the campfire, 'What should we call this place?' 'Fuck it, I already spent enough effort today running from wild pigs,' and then you end up with a place called Toad Suck, Arkansas—you can look that up, too. Except modern-day Florida City started as an ambitious land development with hard-sell advertising and giant marketing geniuses behind the project. Then they had the big meeting to concoct a name: 'I got it! What do people moving to Florida really want? To be in Michigan!'"

"Bullshit on Michigan," said Coleman.

"That was pretty much the universal consumer response back in 1910," said Serge. "But I still can't wrap my head around that management decision to name it Detroit. The brain wasn't engineered to deal with that rarefied level of dumbness."

"Sounds like they were all on acid," said Coleman.

"Exactly," said Serge. "So here's what I think really happened: The top guy mentioned the name, and everyone else obsequiously nodded and went along with the idea like they do around Trump, and then months later they take the train south, and the main cat sees the signs at the city limits: 'You idiots! That was sarcasm!'"

"The cops are still back there," said Coleman.

"Chasing is in police DNA memory, like Labradors running after sticks," said Serge. "They probably don't even know why they do it. They just put the lights on and go, and a while later the partner who isn't behind the wheel says, 'Why are we stopping?' 'Something inside just told me to because there's a really cool crash up ahead. It's weird; I can't explain it.'"

"I hope we never get caught," said Coleman.

"That would be my choice," said Serge. "Unfortunately, a lot of people are looking for us, and heading down to the Keys is never a good call when you're on the run."

Another Schlitz popped. "Why?"

"Geography. There's just one road in and no way out, so it's a fool's move," said Serge. "Except in our case, because I can line up some boats. I know these guys."

"The cops are getting closer."

Serge gestured with the book he was reading. "Turn up the volume on the TV."

Coleman twisted a knob. "That Corvette is really flying."

"I love watching live police chases on TV," said Serge. "You usually have to live in California."

"They have more helicopters out there," said Coleman.

"But our Channel Seven whirlybird is staying right with him," said Serge. "Down the Eighteen Mile."

"What's that?"

"The name for the empty stretch of road through the limbo of mangroves from the bottom of Florida City until the bridge to Key Largo."

Coleman pointed. "He's crossing the bridge . . . The cops are right behind."

"It's the big new bridge," said Serge. "Takes you right across Lake What-the-Fuck."

"Is that another real name?"

"No," said Serge. "That's what I call it. It's really named Lake Surprise. But surprise is usually something good that provides delight, like winning the lottery or reaching in the back of the fridge and finding an unexpected jar of olives. But this lake got its name because it pissed people off."

"How'd it do that?"

"Another funny story. When Henry Flagler started the Overseas Railroad down the Keys, he looked for the route with the most land, because bridges over water cost more. So he sent out surveyors, and they began laying tracks south from the mainland of Florida, across some little islands and an isthmus to Key Largo. And I can't believe they built that far before realizing that right in the middle of a big chunk of land was this giant lake, and now they have to build an *extra* bridge that wasn't in the budget."

"I guess the guys at the lake didn't yell, 'Surprise.'"

"That's why history gives me a woody." Serge nodded toward the television. "Even recent history. Like this bozo heading our way."

"The TV people said the Corvette was stolen in Coconut Grove."

"He's coming off the bridge," said Serge. "The rocks will start soon."

"Rocks?"

"It's local tradition, and another reason I love the Keys." Serge stood and put on his sneakers. "It's our version of when those people went out to the overpasses and waved at O. J. Simpson during the slow-motion chase. Except in the Keys, when there's a high-speed pursuit on TV heading south, the locals line the road and wait for the car to come off the bridge to Key Largo. Last time was around Christmas."

"You're right." Coleman pointed at the TV again. "They're lining the side of the road. They're throwing rocks."

"And we're at Mile Marker 105, so that gives us about three minutes." Serge tightened the Velcro straps on his shoes. "Let's go throw rocks."

"Cool."

They went outside.

"Is this a good rock?" asked Coleman.

"I think that's a hardened piece of poo."

"Righteous," said Coleman, tossing the brown oval up and down in his palm to gauge heft. "I'll bet nobody else is throwing this at the car."

"My wild guess is you're probably right," said Serge. "Man, look at all the freakin' people out here. There's barely room for us."

"It's like a parade, only better."

A drumroll of pinging sounds came up the road toward them. Pieces of gravel and brick ricocheted off the Chevrolet frame.

"There he is now," said Serge.

"He's swerving all over the place," said Coleman. "And the car's completely beaten to shit."

"That's why it's always better to be at the front of the rock line." Serge fingered a smooth stone in his pitching hand. "Here's the secret to enjoying this moment in history: In World War Two, ten percent of the pilots got ninety percent of the kills, and most were from southern states where they did a lot of hunting."

"What's that got to do with it?"

"They learned to lead their targets," said Serge. "But you're inexperienced. So stand ten yards on the far side of me, and when you see me throw, you let her rip. Your marijuana reflexes will build in the necessary time lag."

The pinging sounds grew louder.

Serge stretched his right shoulder in a circular motion. "People in the Keys don't hunt, so even if you're not at the front of the rock line, they usually still leave you the prize."

"Which is what?"

"The driver's window."

"Here he comes!"

"*Readddddddyyyyy . . .*" Serge wound up. "Now!"

Serge let fly.

Coleman did, too.

Smash.

"You got the window," said Coleman.

"And I think your shot went through the opening I created. Good teamwork."

"He's fishtailing," said Coleman. "He's losing control."

"And now the other rock people are scattering to make room for him sliding sideways into that mailbox."

"The police are slowing down," said Coleman. "But they don't seem to know why."

"Here's where they pull him out through the window by his hair. Let's listen . . ."

"*Ow! Ow! I'm not resisting . . . Someone hit me with poo. Who throws poo?*"

"Welcome to the Keys," said Serge.

"It's hot," said Coleman. "Let's go back inside."

MEANWHILE . . .

A blistering afternoon on U.S. 1.

People fanned themselves under the shade of a bus-stop shelter. Several had inexplicably massive amounts of worthless possessions in a variety of unsturdy containers that symbolized the earth's history of evolutionary dead ends. The bus finally came, and the driver wouldn't let someone on because he had a George Foreman Grill, even though it wasn't lit. Alongside the bus, someone else in a safari hat drove a riding lawn mower through a thin strip of grass in front of an outreach ministry. The bus pulled away. A man stayed behind on the bench and considered the downside of being able to suddenly barbecue with little warning.

But it was best not to think too hard about this strip of hot tar below Deerfield and Pompano. Which put it in Broward County, between Palm Beach and Miami-Dade. Shop after shop in endless miles of scrambled economy: ceiling fans, patio furniture, Oriental rugs, barbers, psychics, Pilates, a massage parlor on the up-and-up, herbs for the pretentious, used car lots for customers with radioactive credit, carpet remnants for people who didn't give a shit anymore, a karate studio run by a prick, and one business that simply said LASER.

The traffic was typically heavy and frequently slowed by countless school zones. People in orange vests escorted children across the street. A school bus drove by. A man in a gorilla suit stood on the corner, twirling a sign advertising divorce representation.

More school buses. Regular ones, short ones, public, parochial. And one that looked like the others, except upon closer inspection. All males, all adults. The license plate read: THE BLUEGRASS STATE. The bus cleared a school zone and accelerated a few more blocks before pulling into a shopping center that was busier than the others. A lot busier, cars everywhere, no parking at all on the south end. A psychic came out of her shop and wondered what was going on. The bus pulled around back.

Inside, a waiting room spilled into another waiting room, every chair taken, overflowing outside onto the front patio, where people fiddled with cheap radios and cell phones. Except the wait was surprisingly short, and people moved chair to chair like they were turnstiles. A platoon of nurses called names from manila folders and continuously funneled the clientele into a series of individual examination rooms that ran the length of a hall. A single doctor emerged from the last door, came down the hallway and started again at the first. The loop took twenty minutes, even if someone was chatty. Because most of the patients spoke Spanish, and the doc had no idea what they were saying.

"What seems to be the problem?"

"¿Qué?"

"Sounds like gout. Take this and see the nurse out front."

Patients stacked up again at the checkout window. But not to settle accounts. This was exclusively prepay. And one size fits all. Each person picked up an identical single small square of paper that the doctor had filled out ahead of time and stacked in a tall pile. The only chore left was for the nurses to fill in the names. Back pain, knee pain, migraine, toothache, general blahs, didn't matter: The nurse handed over a script for ninety tablets, eighty-milligram oxycodone, the greenish-blue ones.

"And here's the address of the pharmacy. Make sure you go to that one . . . Next, please! . . ."

Palm Shore Pain Associates, Inc.

The back door opened and the men from the school bus filed in. They had an express-line arrangement; nurses took them directly to the doctor's personal office in groups of fifteen. And they didn't look too good. Missing front teeth and that sallow, ruddy complexion that says *no permanent address*. As the men filed past the reception desk, the driver forked over four hundred dollars a head, which was a hundred more than everyone else waiting behind them.

An hour later, the sixth and last group of fifteen left the office and climbed back on the bus. The driver collected a prescription from each, just as he had done on all of their last eight vacations to Florida. Of course, they would get them back at the pharmacy, but then they'd have to turn over their pill bottle upon rejoining the bus, or it would be a long walk back to Kentucky, and no three hundred bucks for their trouble.

The driver started up the bus and pulled out of the alley behind the pain clinic.

Suddenly: "What the hell?"

A single whoop of a siren. Before anyone knew it, the SWAT team was everywhere, black helmets and Kevlar vests, M16 rifles pointed at the windshield, storming aboard.

Patients waiting on the patio in front scattered across the shopping-center parking lot and were tackled under running sprinklers.

The shrill yelling outside brought nurses running into the waiting room, just in time for more officers to crash through the doors. Someone in the bathroom stopped up the toilet trying to flush prescriptions.

More M16s. "On the ground! Now!"

Every chair emptied in the waiting areas. Officers pulled others from examination rooms. Another member of the tactical unit came in the back door, pushing the doctor ahead of him. "Tried to climb out his window."

Another pulled a nurse with wet arms out of the bathroom. The crackdown required several bags of those plastic wrist cuffs. Finally, everyone was lying stomach down and heard their Miranda rights in two languages.

"Secure," said the officer in charge. "Let 'em in."

Lights! Cameras! . . . The TV gang from all the local affiliates poured through the door.

"Can you hold up the money and those prescription pads again? . . ."

One of the stations went live from the parking lot as officers paraded suspects toward corrections vans.

"In a highly coordinated and dangerous operation, authorities have just raided one of the largest South Florida pill mills illegally dispensing oxycodone, which has contributed to record numbers of overdoses not only in Broward County, but as far away as West Virginia. Officials report they even seized a bus that out-of-state traffickers were using to transport home- less people from Kentucky, and today's arrests should seriously disrupt the Interstate 95 pipeline of so-called Hillbilly Heroin . . ."

Behind the TV correspondent on U.S. 1, dozens of weary street people stared out the windows of an unno- ticed school bus that had just left a different medical clinic three blocks away and was headed back north on Interstate 95.

Chapter Two

KEY LARGO

"Throwing rocks at cars is cool!" said Coleman.

"Another quote for the ages," said Serge.

And another typical afternoon in paradise in the Florida Keys. Empty, bright, baby-blanket sky. Shimmering emerald water all around the Long Key Viaduct with its century-old arches. Heavy, happy traffic heading both ways, including a clown-fish-orange 1976 Ford Gran Torino SportsRoof, with the Magnum 500 wheels, laser stripe and 429 cubic inches of V-8 madness.

A foot hit the clutch, and a hand slammed the shift into top gear. The Torino swerved across the centerline and passed six cars, swinging back at the last second as a van full of sheet-white people passed in the other direction.

"Hot damn!" Serge reached over from the driver's seat and punched Coleman in the shoulder.

"Ow."

"I'm so jazzed!" Serge bobbed in his seat. "I love the beach season!"

"What's the beach season?"

"Comes right after *the* season, otherwise known as tourist season or snowbird season, starting after Christmas, when people migrate to Florida to escape the cold. Then they walk along the beach at sunset with sweaters tied around their waists. I respect the lifestyle choice, but I can't hang with it. What's the point of Florida if you don't get in the fucking water?"

"I remember on New Year's Day, you were the only one splashing around out there."

"That was my annual polar-bear plunge," said Serge. "But how can it count if you're living in Florida? Except in Jacksonville, where the Parrot Head Club makes it interesting by drinking tequila before sunrise. And I mean way into the bottle, before jumping in the surf at a sunrise that is blocked by a frigid gray sea mist, and they leap back out with half of their wacky foam hats left drifting out to sea, then finish the tequila, sleep twelve hours and dance that night at the local moose lodge. They're very focused."

Coleman lifted a cheek to sneak one. "The time I'm thinking of, you were yelling at the people on shore."

"What was I yelling?"

" 'Get in the fucking water!' " Coleman dropped a tab of ecstasy. "But they ran the other way instead. Oh, you were also waving a gun. Then the beach was empty and covered with sweaters."

"It was probably getting late for them anyway."

"Then you came charging out of the water," said Coleman. "At first I thought you were running after them like the other times, but you jumped in the car and turned on the heater."

"Because the water was way too goddamn freezing to get in." Serge shivered at the thought. "What was I thinking? That's why I love the beach season! Instead of fleeing the cold, people get in the water to escape the heat. That's my crowd, keeping it Coppertone real. And it all builds to the huge climax on the extended Memorial Day weekend. I can't wait! I love the beach season! That's why I bought a ton of toys at that Home Depot on Vaca Key."

"Home Depot has beach toys?"

"Better." Serge reached for a bag in the backseat and pulled it onto his lap. "Hurricane toys! Hurricane season starts the first of June, which means hurricane *preparation* begins the same time as beach season . . ." Serge glanced back and forth from the road to the bag, steering with his knees and pawing inside. "Here's the crank-powered emergency weather radio and compass, the floating diode flashlight that needs no batteries and runs on the Faraday Principle, a laser-guided compass with GPS, the solar survival blanket developed by NASA, a big-honkin' all-purpose tungsten hunting knife with compass *and* flashlight . . ."

"All this stuff will help us survive a storm?" Coleman asked nervously.

"Heck no." Serge flicked the laser on and off at approaching traffic. Someone in a Mazda skidded down the shoulder into sea grapes. "There ain't going to be any hurricanes this year. I just like to play with this crap during beach season. Did I mention I love it?"

"Where have I seen those other boxes before?" asked Coleman.

"Military MREs, or Meals Ready to Eat, distributed by the National Guard to storm victims. Got them at a surplus sale this morning. The cool part is the heating element: This clear plastic pouch with what looks like a tea bag in the bottom, and you add just a *little* water to start a chemical reaction that generates a ferocious amount of heat. I'm going to have some fun with those."

"Now I remember," said Coleman. "You used the heating pouches on that price gouger we captured a few years ago after that hurricane. But you never like to use the same thing twice. You said it shows lack of imagination and disrespect for your contestants."

"That's right!" Serge opened one of the boxes on his lap. "But true imagination is squeezing a second, totally unrelated use from the same item. This time, an ignition source."

"Ignition?"

"Read about it on the Internet." Serge pulled a plastic bag from a meal, containing plastic utensils and condiments. "Here's the key . . ." He pointed at a tiny, one-serving foil packet of Tabasco sauce.

"Why do soldiers have Tabasco sauce?"

"Because war requires spicy food." Serge stowed the bag. "Anyway, back to the plot: Some cadets from West Point were on survival training, and one of their tasks was to start a fire."

"How hard can that be?"

"They took away their lighters and matches."

"Oh."

"So this one cadet gets the idea to substitute hot sauce instead of water in a heating pouch and—*shazam!*—fire.

Who would have thought? . . . But I still haven't figured out how to use it as an instructional aid."

"Can I have some of the freeze-dried ice cream?"

"Knock yourself out." Serge tossed a foil packet sideways across the front seat. "But the most excellent purchase of the day is in the trunk, courtesy of the construction wholesaler I hit after Home Depot."

Coleman sucked foil. "When I was in the bar next door?"

Serge nodded and spread his hands. "Been looking all over for these ever since I first saw them on the Internet when Hurricane Wilma slammed Fort Lauderdale: instant sandbags. Just add water."

Coleman stopped sucking. "I thought sandbags were supposed to *stop* water."

"These are special. Each bag weighs only two pounds dry because they're filled with these lightweight, scientifically developed crystals. But soak them in water, and a half hour later each feathery sack has inflated into a thirty-five-pound rock-hard bulwark of flood protection. Perfect for the hurricane survivor with a hectic schedule." Serge jerked a thumb back over his shoulder toward the trunk. "Picked up thirty of 'em for hours of entertainment and education."

They came off the bridge into Islamorada.

"Serge." Coleman aimed his joint out the window. "You're passing the Hurricane Monument. You never pass the monument; I always have to stop and wait for your photos."

"No time." Serge hit the gas. "I need to find a shopping center on Key Largo with a Target or Kmart."

"What for?"

"It's the beach season! I need to buy a ton of surfing music and every beach-movie DVD they've got." Serge reached under his seat and pulled out a camcorder. "I've totally rededicated my life to complete immersion in the beach culture. We'll get jobs raking sand before dawn behind the resorts, rubbing lotion on aristocrats and selling tropical snow cones behind the boardwalk."

"What boardwalk?"

"We'll build one. That's how dedicated I am." Serge turned the camcorder toward Coleman. "And through it all, we'll record every last second for my new smash-hit reality show. We'll be famous! . . . Let's rehearse."

Serge began filming his pal as they drove.

"Okay," said Coleman. "What am I supposed to—"

"Shut the fuck up!" said Serge. "You do this every time! You ruin every single vacation with your bullshit!"

"But I didn't do anything."

"Oh, right!" Serge turned the camera around to film his own face. "Act all innocent, like I don't know what you've been up to behind my back! Pitting one side against the other so one day you can rule the whole beach. You're a scheming little bastard, and I'm here to stop you! Your glory days in the sand are over!"

"Serge, you've never talked this way to me before." Coleman was on the verge of tears. "I thought we were best buddies."

Serge put the camcorder on pause. "We are. But we have to pretend there's all kind of brooding tension on the beach about to boil over any second."

"Why?"

"Because it's a reality show. You have to fake a lot of stuff."

Serge resumed filming out the driver's window at a giant roadside mermaid, a giant lobster, a giant conch shell.

Coleman settled his nerves with a flask of Early Times. "You mean reality shows aren't real?"

"Of course not," said Serge. "Reality's boring. Especially the realities they pick for these shows. People repairing stuff or the daily life in a tattoo parlor. You know what daily life in a tattoo parlor is? Sitting around and smoking with no customers. Then, after five hours, bells jingle at the front door and someone finally comes in. 'Yeah, give me something on my face with a flaming skull, an inverted pentagram and lots of swastikas. I want to impress my boss.'"

Coleman emptied the pint. "That *is* boring."

"But easily fixed, and always with a feud. Reality shows are required to have them," said Serge. "Take the most painfully mundane situation, add some nasty spats, and everything is forgiven. In the middle of a five-hour dry spell with no customers, the hotshot new tattoo artist walks over to the minifridge. 'Okay, who the fuck took my pudding cups?'"

"Now I'm into it," said Coleman.

"Me, too," said Serge. "Feuds have a way of cheering up the viewing public. Or humiliation."

"Humiliation?"

"The new tattoo guy can go next door in the strip mall to the health spa where they're filming the reality-show contest on people trying to lose a hundred pounds. 'Oh, so you like pudding, eh? Then take this!'—mashing tapioca up the nose of a fat chick."

"Who could not watch that?" asked Coleman.

"We are a proud people."

"The sign said 'Key Largo.'" Coleman pointed with a cocaine tooter. "And there's a shopping center up ahead."

Serge cast a glare sideways. "You still into that stupid crap?"

Coleman flicked open the access hole on the small plastic tube for a quick snort. "Just on Tuesdays."

"It's Wednesday."

"Then I'm late." Another snort.

Serge rolled his eyes. The shopping center came into view, and a turn signal blinked.

Coleman hung his head out the window. "I don't see a Target or Kmart."

"But there's another big place near Winn-Dixie that's sure to have everything we need."

They parked, and Serge fleetly went inside to canvass the media section, filling his arms with a harvest of Beach Boys and Annette Funicello.

"There's a *Gidget* movie," said Coleman. *"Gidget, Gidget, Gidget . . ."* Uncontrolled giggling. "That's messed up. *Gidget, Gidget, Gidget . . ."*

"Coleman, you're acting really weird." Serge grabbed a *Baywatch* boxed set. "What the hell's wrong with you?"

"Nothing." He turned and bent over. Snort.

"Jesus!" Serge's eyes shot around for any onlookers. "We're in a big store. You can't be doing coke!"

Another giggle. "Coke, blow, flake, fluff, snow, marching dust, weasel powder, white death, white lady, wings, yeho, nose-candy, donut glaze, gutter glitter, Charlie, Chippy, Belushi, Foo-foo, Merck, mojo, movie star, Mayan mist, Bolivian blizzard, Inca telegram, California cornflakes, lay lines, cut rails, hitch the reindeer, chase the dragon . . ."

Serge slapped himself on the forehead.

Then a lightbulb went on. Serge reached in his shoulder pouch for the camcorder. "From the top!"

"Coke, blow, flake . . ."

A few minutes later, Serge finished checking out at the registers and paid with fresh twenties.

" . . . Roxanne, pimp, sugar, thing, cotton, girlfriend, Big C . . ."

Serge gathered up his bag. "Come on, Coleman, follow me."

"Where are we going?"

Serge led him over to the back of a long line stacked up at the customer-service desk.

"I don't understand," said Coleman. "You just bought those and now you're going to return them?"

"No," said Serge. "I just need some customer service. Except for some reason, I always have trouble at customer service. Even though it says 'Customer Service' on the sign, it usually feels like I'm getting the opposite. I'll give it one more try, because I'm into hope . . ."

ON THE OTHER SIDE OF THE STATE

Arnold Lip was an ordinary doctor in Tampa who ran a modest private practice that had fallen on hard times because he wasn't a very good doctor. He was forced to move his office several times, down descending strata of square footage and facility maintenance. Until he ended up in a professional building that was a two-story converted crack motel. He specialized in diseases that medical journals described as the most likely to go away on their own.

One day just before lunch, he walked through his ✓ empty waiting room. The only receptionist had been let go. He stepped outside and looked over the balcony railing, wondering what he was going to do. He looked around the office complex. No cars in the parking lot. None of the other professionals doing any business either, not the forensic accountant, maritime insurance agent, empty office-space broker, Ventures Limited, or something called the Lone Wolf Group. The outsourcing firm next door had been replaced by an office in a converted motel in India.

He strolled toward the end of the balcony with the stairwell, thinking of the sandwich shop across the street. He stopped. What were all those cars doing on the other side of the parking lot? He watched throngs of people flowing toward one particular office on the first floor. He jogged halfway down the stairs and read the sign by the door. What was a personal injury attorney doing in such a run-down business complex? Those guys can afford full-page ads on the backs of phone books.

At the end of the day, Arnold made a point of taking the same stairs. And waiting. All the cars were gone except a Porsche 955. A young man with German features and a Lance Armstrong haircut was the last to leave the building. He folded his jacket neatly in the backseat of the coupe and sped off, punching the car through its gears.

A week later, Arnold Lip sat in his empty office. He was behind the reception desk, eating a tuna-salad sandwich that he had made at home with extra chopped celery because he liked the crunch. The sliding translucent window to the waiting room was closed.

The office's front door opened. Arnold observed a silhouette approach and stop on the other side of the pebbled glass, like a priest hearing confession.

A hand knocked.

Arnold slid the window open, still chewing. "Yes?"

"Is Dr. Lip in?" asked a young professional with a short haircut. He leaned slightly through the window, looking around for other signs of life in the office.

Arnold wiped his mouth with a napkin. "I'm Dr. Lip."

"Oh." A gaze that had been straining down the hall dropped down to the man behind the desk. "My name is Hagman Reed . . ." He pointed generally toward one of the walls. "I'm an attorney from the other side of this building."

Arnold took another bite. "I recognize you from the parking lot. Porsche 955."

Hagman looked around the office again at stacks of old *US* magazines. "But you are a doctor, right?"

Lip nodded. "How can I help you?"

"I have a business proposition . . ."

THE NEXT DAY

Arnold opened the door to the waiting room. He looked down a clipboard with a grid full of names and times. "Mr. Euclid?"

He had to raise his voice because the waiting room vibrated from a loud din of conversation, mostly on cell phones. The rest of the overflow clientele flipped through magazines and photo spreads of Angelina dragging Brad Pitt around the third world. The new patients sported a variety of neck braces and casts.

A man with crutches got up and did a three-legged stroll behind Arnold and into an examination room. He was out in two minutes.

Lip stood in the door again. "Mrs. Lambright? . . ."

And so it went the rest of the day. And the week. And the month. You could almost see the waiting line picking up speed.

The attorney's business proposition had kicked in.

The reason lay on the unattended reception desk, the morning edition of the *Tampa Tribune*. A small article below the fold on page fifteen. Physician arrested for insurance fraud.

It wasn't unexpected. Florida had long been plagued by a burgeoning scam industry, making the state the national leader in staged auto accidents. The faux-fender-bender capital was Miami. Until law enforcement cracked down in a big way. And like any other species of scheme in Florida, it was simply a game of Whac-A-Mole. Those who escaped the dragnet just pulled the tent stakes and drove three hundred miles up to the west coast.

Tampa officially became the new U.S. capital of insurance rip-offs. We're Number One!

Authorities rolled up their sleeves and clamped down again. The arrest that was announced in that morning's paper was the sixth in less than a month. But this one was different. He was the physician in league with Hagman Reed.

The doctor faced an eighty-six-count indictment, but Hagman was in the clear because he was a lawyer.

Except it still left him without a conspiring doctor. And twenty more cars had already been smashed up. What about those people? It wouldn't be fair to them. So Hagman had paid a visit to Arnold Lip, because Lip wasn't a good doctor. He could have gone to a good doctor, but that would mean no kickbacks and, most lucrative of all, no documentation for imaginary pain and suffering.

Which brought us to today. Mrs. Lambright sat on the edge of an examination table.

Lip stood over her with a manila patient file. "Where does it hurt?"

"It doesn't."

He hit her in the leg with a triangular rubber hammer.

"Ow."

Lip talked to himself as he wrote: "Hyperextended knee."

Then he set down his folder and got her in a head-lock. He twisted.

"Ow." She pushed him away. "Stop that."

He picked up the folder. "Delayed neck pain . . ."

Chapter Three

KEY LARGO

In the back of a crowd at a customer-service desk:

"Look at this line," said Coleman. "Why isn't it moving?"

"Because the customer at the counter is telling her life story from the delivery room," said Serge.

Five minutes later: " . . . Now, this other person doesn't have ID or a receipt, but wants cash . . ."

Another five minutes: " . . . He's explaining that he only wore the underwear a single time on a camping trip . . ."

Five more: " . . . She's holding up a finger for the service rep to wait while she takes a cell-phone call . . ."

"Serge," said Coleman. "I'm impressed."

"By this parade of rudeness?"

"No, by your reaction. Don't take this the wrong way, but you can be a little impatient."

"A little? I'm *super*impatient," said Serge. "But trying to improve. That's the whole problem with society: We detect countless faults in others, but never work on ourselves. And behavior in long lines brings out the worst. Take the nicest people you'd ever meet, stick them in an ultralong line that's moving like molasses, and it's as if they were bitten by a werewolf. Some sweet old lady who volunteers to read to the blind: 'Look at this dickhead with *eleven* items in the express lane.' Supermarkets bring out the worst."

"Supermarkets?"

"I've spent hours with calibrated instruments charting the phenomenon. When the national fabric finally tears itself apart, they'll trace the first rips to grocery checkouts, where all registers are jammed, and suddenly two shoppers with overflowing carts spot the one register with a slightly shorter line. And the rival customers are exactly the same distance away from the register in opposite directions. They both want to get there first, but need to maintain the social facade of not rushing to cut the other one off, so they do the supermarket dance. Happens a million times a day."

"What do you mean, 'dance'?"

"They both speed up, but in a special, highly trained way that creates the illusion they're actually slowing down. It's an amazing thing to observe in nature, like the moonwalk. And the key is to deliberately not look at the other shopper, but track their progress with peripheral vision, and responding appropriately by speeding up or slowing down, depending on their velocity and how many people are around who might recognize you from church.

"And this whole pas de deux continues with one woman tracking the other out of the corner of her eye, thinking, 'She's deliberately not looking at me and watching out of the corner of her eye, so under the rules I'm allowed to speed up and cut a tighter angle past the promotional pyramid of Honey Grahams.' And it goes back and forth like this until they arrive at the same time, and suddenly it's the biggest surprise: 'Oh, I didn't see you.' 'I didn't see you either.' 'Go first.' 'No, you go first.' 'No, you.' 'No, you.' 'Okay . . .' And the second one is like, 'She took advantage of me because of all these people that I know from church, goddammit.' "

"And you're going to change all that?" asked Coleman.

"It only takes one person to begin," said Serge. "As of this moment, I'm rededicating my entire life to patience. It's the least I can do for the common good. From now on, I'll always let the other person by first, like this woman behind me with her arms full and a crying kid . . . Excuse me, ma'am? Please go ahead of me, and I don't even go to a freakin' church, because *this* is my church. I mean, not this store specifically, but I just rededicated my life a few seconds ago. The evangelicals say good works can't get you into the Kingdom, but then they go telling *you* what to do. What's that about? The devil tempts me not to let you ahead in line, but I tell Satan to get the hell out of my happy place and pound sand . . . Please, go ahead of us . . ." He turned and smiled big at Coleman. "You've just witnessed the start of the country turning around."

"But, Serge, she's not going ahead of you," said Coleman. "In fact, she went to an entirely different line."

"And cut another shopper off in the process." Serge sighed. "Fixing the country will take more time than I thought. Screw it, life's too short."

"Dedication to patience only has to last a minute?"

"You're right," said Serge. "I need to adopt coping mechanisms for stress. I'll control my breathing and think Hindu thoughts."

"Like what?"

"I'm not sure," said Serge. "I don't know any Hindus. So I don't know what they're thinking about when they're in long lines and trying to get their heads centered. But I'm guessing they're imagining round things . . . I'm going to think about circles."

"We're number two in line," said Coleman. "That woman's still on her cell phone."

"Must be an important call, too, because she's not conducting any business. Let's listen . . ."

Coleman stuck his head forward next to Serge's. "I think she's mad at her sister-in-law for stinking up the trailer with burned possum . . ."

"I'm thinking of ovals now."

Coleman strained to hear more. " . . . And Bobby Jean's new hairdo caught fire in the bug zapper."

"That's it," said Serge. "Time for action."

"I thought you were working on patience."

"Oh, I'm not losing patience," said Serge. "It's another way of contributing to the common good. This woman clearly needs help. But how many times have you seen someone in distress and everyone else just stands around doing nothing. It's not neighborly."

Serge tapped the woman on the shoulder.

She turned around. Into the phone: "Hold on a second, some jerk . . ." She looked up: "What?"

"I couldn't help but overhear," he said. "Because I was placing my ear real close trying to overhear. My name is Serge Storms, and I wander from town to town helping people. I don't do it for the thanks, just the satisfaction of seeing a person tearfully realize that someone else out there truly cares. But how do I help? you ask. By sharing invaluable pointers that will revolutionize your life! Could be as simple as which technical college fits your strengths, or a slight fashion correction that will land you the big promotion. Friends and relatives could easily do the same, but they'd be jealous of your success. In your case, I've already customized my program to pinpoint everything that's holding you back from the cover of *Fortune*. Ready? You shouldn't spend so much time on the phone if you're shaped like a hippo."

Serge stepped back with a giant grin.

An astonished gasp. "How dare you!"

"Because I care," said Serge. "And if that tube top ever gives way, you're going to kill at least five people."

A shorter man next to her stepped forward. "Who the hell do you think you are, talking to my wife like that?"

"An at-large life coach, just trying to help," said Serge. "And while I'm at it, lose the diamond earring. You look like a prick and definitely don't want to attract attention to your face."

The couple rushed away from the counter and toward the door.

Coleman whistled. "Look how fast they're moving."

"They're chasing success," said Serge.

"We're next up."

Serge stepped to the counter and dumped out his bag of CDs and DVDs. He smiled at the employee.

She smiled back. "You want to return those?"

"No," said Serge. "I want you to open them."

"Excuse me?"

"Open these, please." Serge picked up one of the movies and clawed at it like a squirrel. "These things are friggin' impossible to open. And my futile attempts have now passed sleep as the largest time slice of existence."

"Sir, I just handle returns and exchanges—"

Serge pointed up. "Does the sign say 'Customer Service'?"

"Yes?"

"Please open these."

"I can't."

"Neither can I," said Serge. "Especially because I bite my nails. I bite other people's, too, but they always had it coming. So I really need you to open these because I don't have the time, but who does if you have a job? I don't have a job, but I participate in current culture, which is like three jobs, not to mention constantly writing letters to the president to keep his spirits up. I recently sent him one saying *Illegitimi non carbo-rundum.* That's Latin for 'Don't let the bastards grind you down.' Except my Latin was rusty and I think I wrote, 'The organ grinders are bastards.' Hoo-wee, they must think I'm crazy up there, so I wrote him a corrected letter." Serge pulled an envelope from his back pocket and flapped it energetically in front of her face. "I'm going to stand in line at the post office next. Even if you're into patience, that's hard-core. Which is why you can surely understand that I need you to open these."

The woman maintained a professional gaze. "Sir, I'm going to have to ask you to step away from the counter."

Serge pointed at a male employee walking behind her. "What about you, sir? Can you open these?"

"No, they're too hard to open." He kept walking.

Serge turned to face the line behind him. "Can any of you open these fucking things?"

They all shook their heads.

"Sir!" the woman said sternly. "Your language! This is a family store."

"Oh, I get it," said Serge. "You're one of *those* customer-service people." He slowly twirled a finger in the air. "You like to twist the meaning of words to your advantage. If anyone in this discussion has family values, it's me. I just bought Beach Boys and Annette Funicello, but do you have any idea how many R-rated movies and CDs with explicit-lyric warnings are on the racks back there? *You're* the ones peddling pussy, bitches, and ho's."

She picked up the phone. "I'm calling security."

"Really? You think they can open these?" He turned around to the line again. "Am I right or am I right?"

Three large guards arrived. "What seems to be the problem here?"

Serge pointed behind the desk. "Her . . . I'm just trying to buy some wholesome family entertainment while this establishment is trafficking in cocksucker and cunt." He began filming the guards with his camcorder. "And could you give me a little more anger for my reality show?"

Seconds later, the front doors of the store burst open. Serge and Coleman came flying out and tumbled on the pavement.

A deep voice. "If we ever see you around here again, we're calling the police."

Then a shower of violently flung CDs and DVDs that smashed on the ground.

Coleman crawled over with skinned palms and picked up the *Good Vibrations* disc. "Some of these broke open."

"I was right. I knew they could do it." Serge pushed himself up. "It just took me to show them their potential."

WISCONSIN

The winter was a long one. Patches of snow still covered the ground near the feet of the protesters, screaming and waving signs at the dome of the state capitol in Madison.

It was a new era of hope.

Across the nation, recent elections had swept fresh blood into office. They would reinstill fiscal responsibility. Among their first chores was to end wasteful collective-bargaining agreements for workers. Which made it a Right-to-Work State. Which cleared the way for layoffs. But the dismissals only trimmed the fat, you know, like police officers, teachers and firefighters.

All the jobs were eliminated by politicians who said their biggest campaign donors deserved tax breaks, because they called themselves job creators.

But you just can't please some people. And hundreds of them now ringed the capitol grounds, hollering and otherwise dampening the party. They'd been coming for weeks, setting up before dawn and rubbing mittens together. TV cameras from local morning shows broadcast the images between traffic reports and college basketball scores.

Twenty miles away, a cold gray light came through a kitchen window. The thermometer outside the window on the bird feeder said five. A red grain silo with a silver dome stood silently on a white hill.

Barbara McDougall glanced at the small television mounted under her cabinets and continued spreading fat-free mayo on a baloney sandwich. The sandwich went in a stack with three others, awaiting Saran Wrap and brown paper bags. Bar, as her parents called her, learned from TV that a dozen protesters had been arrested, Interstate 94 was clear all the way to Oconomowoc and the Badgers won in double overtime.

Bar heard footsteps from behind and smiled, but didn't turn around. A peck on the cheek. "Good morning." Her husband, Patrick. He started the coffee. The kitchen curtains were plaid, in a color scheme popular at bagpipe funerals.

"They laid off another five hundred," said Bar.

Pat sat down at the table with the paper. "*State Journal* says six."

"Charlie called last night. He just got word." Barbara set two paper sacks on the edge of the counter. "Jen's gone, too."

"Everything will work out," said Pat.

"I know," said Bar, pulling out her own chair at the table and placing a hand on top of her husband's. "It always does."

Their exchange wasn't just platitudes or keeping a stiff lip. They were among the few people who genuinely counted their blessings. You had to hate them.

They had gotten their own notices the previous week. Abrupt walking papers after seven years with the school district. And an awkward arrangement because it took effect at the end of the school year, which was three more months. Because the district needed the teachers.

The vast majority of their colleagues quit immediately. An option with a severance package. Who could blame them? Bar and Pat never considered it.

Theirs was an older wooden house, behind a dairy farm, with propane tanks on the side. The kind of extremely small place that Realtors call cozy. But it was ample room since there were only the two of them. Not their choice. The McDougalls desperately wanted children but couldn't have any, even though they were practicing Catholics and rabid Packers fans.

That's why they would finish the school year. And volunteer after that. Their students *were* their children. Corny, yeah, the premise for a schmaltzy network series, except these were not made-for-TV kids. The McDougalls volunteered for special-needs duty.

They were offered developmentally delayed. They turned it down, and said what they really wanted. The administrator stared at them in disbelief, then signed off immediately before they could change their minds.

Their classrooms had special, washable paint, floor padding, and no sharp corners. Three grades were combined, six-to-eight-year-olds, emotional disorders. Courtney cried all day, Jason had to wear a football helmet, Gary was permanently stuck making a beeping sound like a truck backing up, and Alex threw feces.

That was just Barbara's class. Patrick was stabbed at least once at the beginning of each day, even though it was only a Popsicle stick.

"*I stab you! Stab! Stab! Stab!*"

"That's nice, Jeffrey. Now time to sit down."

Then Harry's turn: "*Fuck! Fuck! Fuck!*"

And all the other kids in unison: "*I'm telling!*" "*I'm telling!*" "*I'm telling!*"

As he did every morning, Patrick picked up an acoustic guitar. The students magically settled down, more or less, and sang along.

The McDougalls were unflagging. First to arrive at school, last to leave. And every single student got extra attention. They spent hours on the phone with parents and made house calls.

At the end of the first year, the children had become, well, a year older. Still the same by measurable test standards. But there was a difference only a parent could notice. They were more *reachable*.

At the PTA meetings, some parents had tears. Bar and Pat were nominated and heavily favored for teachers of the year, but the award instead went to someone whose family barbecued with the chairman of the school board. The principal put in for special merit-pay raises, but the district gave it to a phys ed teacher who turned the football team around.

A lot of people complained.

But not the McDougalls. They were happy as long as they were with their students.

So they were laid off.

Chapter Four

KEY LARGO

Two men sprinted frantically from a post office and jumped in the front seat of a '76 Gran Torino.

"I got to get the hell out of here." Serge turned the ignition and floored it. "I know I said I was into patience, but that was like waterboarding." He grabbed his camcorder and rewound the film. "All that footage was worthless. Just people standing around. It was too real."

Coleman's shaking hands cracked a beer. "Don't ever let me go back in that place. It's enough to make me give up pot."

"I thought you said you had a good buzz."

"I did. It was excellent weed," said Coleman. "That's the problem. I was totally grooving, and suddenly I realized I'm in a brightly lit place crowded with people that's super-quiet. And they all just *knew* I was stoned, man. Except they all acted like they didn't, which is how you know they can tell you're totally baked. Your pulse races, you can't catch your breath, and your face and palms get all clammy, which just makes it more obvious. There's nothing so terrifying as when they all know, man."

"Coleman, I really don't think anyone knew," said Serge.

"Of course they didn't know," said Coleman. "It was just the drug creating this horrible effect. That's how you can tell it's excellent weed."

"I had my own horror show back there," said Serge. "Like one of those bad science-fiction movies where an alien ray gun shoots a plasma beam at the town square, and it acts like a giant blob of glue."

"I thought it was only the pot that made them seem slow to me," said Coleman. "Could have sworn the guy working that one counter had died."

"No, it wasn't the pot," said Serge. "He actually had a near-death experience. His heart stopped and he was clinically dead while handling three or four customers, then when he came back from the tunnel of light, he's thinking: 'All this rushing isn't good for me. I'm going to smell the roses.' "

"Is that when we were almost to the counter, and he suddenly put out his 'Position Closed' sign and went backstage?"

"Must be where they keep the roses," said Serge.

"I thought your head was about to explode when he left," said Coleman.

"It was," said Serge. "It only fed my post office psychosis. Whenever I'm in one, and almost to the counter, I keep repeating to myself: 'Please don't put out the "Position Closed" sign; please don't put out the "Position Closed" sign; dear God, don't let him put out the sign; please, please, please, I'm almost to the counter! I made it! I finally made it! He didn't put out the . . . Wait, what's he reaching for? . . . Fuck!' "

"You did yell 'fuck' pretty loud back there."

"But I quickly apologized to the crowd and pointed at the sign," said Serge. "You could tell they had all been repeating the same thing."

Coleman fiddled with a lighter that was low on butane. "That was a brutal wait. There were only two people at the counter, but a whole bunch of guys in the back room. You could see them through the doorways. What were they all doing?"

"Standing in groups just out of sight behind the doorway. Then, one by one, they send someone across to the other side so we think that actual activity is happening. But they're just walking to stand in a circle painted on the floor until it's time to be sent back the other way. Except for the one guy who's assigned to come out of the back room every fifteen minutes and walk up to a 'Position Closed' sign, and all the customers joyously weep and praise Jesus, but he just opens a drawer for some scissors and goes back."

"How do you know all this?" asked Coleman.

"I don't," said Serge. "It's too easy to make fun of the post office. And ironic, considering their deceptively amazing efficiency. For less than the price of a newspaper, I can stick a small square on an envelope, and two days later my letter is a thousand miles away being dusted for prints by the cops. It's a modern miracle."

"But then why does everyone make fun of the post office?" asked Coleman.

"To feel good about ourselves," said Serge. "We used to brighten the day by shitting on ethnic and religious minorities. But that got ruined just because it turned out to be very, very wrong. So now the post office is one of the last prejudice sanctuaries left, like bad-mouthing airline food: Fire at will! . . . Except I genuinely like airline food because of the cool packaging, and it's not the postal employees' fault about the waiting lines. Management messes up staffing and sends a million people to one post office with no customers, and vice versa. The jokes are unfair and cruel."

"So you're going to stop telling them?"

"No, it's fun," said Serge. "Plus, there's a lot of responsible things you need to do while waiting, like reading the sign that says it's a federal crime to assault a postal employee. Okay, that's always good to be reminded of. Then I check the FBI photos to make sure I'm not up there. Now I'm free to kick back and enjoy checking out the photos of who *is* up there. What a bunch of losers! Those creepy mug shots are one of my very first memories as a tiny kid. Killers, kidnappers, people who assault postal employees. I was only four, and still thought logically: These pictures are up here, so it must be a system that's working. I mean, they're not asking us to spot people in Seattle; all these guys obviously live in my neighborhood. And they wondered why I was a jumpy child."

Coleman pointed his joint at the windshield. "Where are we going now?"

"To find an ATM," said Serge. "I'm low on cash."

"There's one," said Coleman. "But how do you get a bank account?"

"Most people think that if you're a fugitive, it's harder than it actually is, but establishments aren't as strict with ID when *you're* giving *them* money," said Serge. "Any kind of fake photo ID will suffice, like an annual pass at the zoo, and you rent one of those private PO boxes at a strip mall that appears to be a real street address. Does that answer your question?"

"I meant an account in general," said Coleman. "I've never had one. But I've heard about them. And I see people going in and out of banks. Just curious."

Serge parked at a slot right in front of the machine. "We're in luck. Only one guy in line."

They jumped out, and Serge took up a spot at the edge of the curb.

Coleman leaned sideways. "Why are we standing so far back?"

"Another tip to weld society together. Give the person up to bat at the ATM plenty of space so they're not nervous about you peeking at their PIN number or slipping a blade between their ribs the second the money spits out."

"You said that kind of loud," said Coleman. "I think he heard."

"Good," said Serge. "Then he's happy to know the knife isn't coming."

"What's he doing?" asked Coleman. "He's not even at the machine. He's standing to the side at the little metal shelf that's like a table."

"He's still at the ATM proper. It's his until he relinquishes the zone."

"But he's just playing with his wallet."

"I think he's looking for his card," said Serge. "And making a deposit in my patience karma."

"I don't think that's it," said Coleman. "I think he already used the machine and is now reorganizing all his shit. We may be waiting for nothing."

"Could be," said Serge. "But there's an appropriate social procedure to find out."

"How?"

"We clear our throats at super-high volume and then stare at him unflinchingly," said Serge. "As a courtesy."

"Then what?" asked Coleman.

"If he's into a wholesale spring cleaning of his billfold, he won't look back. But if he really is waiting to use the machine and can't find his card, he'll reflexively glance up. Then he'll hurry his search or wave us on. Either way, we'll know the score so we can make the polite choice . . . Ready?"

Coleman nodded.

"*Ahem!*" Cough, cough. "Clearing my throat now, *ahem!*" said Serge. "That would be my throat clearing, *ahem* . . ."

"Clearing my throat, too," said Coleman. "*A-hem!*" Cough. "And now a fart." *Pffffft* . . .

"Coleman!"

"What?"

Serge pointed. "He's downwind. The national fabric."

"He's still going through his wallet," said Coleman. "He's not looking up."

"There's our answer," said Serge. "But we give it another ten-second cushion as a fail-safe, and then move very slowly in case he misinterpreted what I meant about stabbing him."

. . . Eight, nine, ten. They crept forward. Serge slipped a magnetic card into the slot and began entering his pass code.

From the side: *"You are one rude motherfucker!"*

"Uh-oh," Serge said to himself. "A wild card." He tried to hurry the transaction, but that only made him mess up.

"You deaf, too, motherfucker?"

"What?" Serge turned. "But I didn't mean—"

The man crowded in from the left side, stretching to get his face between Serge and the machine. "Do you just cut in line whenever you feel?"

"I'm sorry," said Serge. "I thought you had completed your transaction and were reorganizing your wallet."

"That's what you get for fuckin' thinking!"

Serge thought: *What does* that *mean?*

The man tried to wedge himself farther between Serge and the machine.

"Please stop leaning against me," said Serge. "I'll just get my money and she's all yours."

"And then you just walk away, motherfucker?"

Serge got his money and walked away.

Ten minutes later, Coleman sat in the passenger seat as the '76 Gran Torino tooled down the Overseas Highway. "That guy was unbelievable."

"I still can't process what my eyes just saw," said Serge. "But you were there. I'm not imagining things, right?"

"No, man. That dude was off the charts."

"If you tried telling people this story, it would sound like bad fiction some guy wrote in a book," said Serge. "But it really did happen to me. And it was a nice shopping center; that's what threw me off balance."

"He just went on and on," said Coleman. "Still yelling even after you left."

"That's the nature of the twat-heads," said Serge. "The second I responded to his initial insult with patience, he took that as a weakness green light to unload all the emotional bile he brought with him to the ATM from breakfast. And I should know: I have the same perpetual loop spinning in my head of people who have fucked with me going back to kindergarten, running nonstop, over and over, driving up my blood pressure and pissing me off until I find myself muttering out loud and honing the absolute perfect comeback ten years later: 'Oh yeah? Well, you're wrong.' . . . That kind of pent-up rage will eat you alive unless you get your arms around it and recognize the problem."

"So by knowing that it's just inside your head, you've learned to turn it off?"

"Not exactly," said Serge. "Some jerk crosses my path and I beat the piss out of him for what all those other people did to me. *Then* I can turn it off." He turned to Coleman. "Is that normal?"

Coleman shrugged. "I thought everyone was looking at me in the post office."

Serge pulled over to the side of the road and opened the door.

Coleman got out his own side. "But you still didn't do anything to that ATM guy. That's progress."

"You know me when I put my mind to something. It's all about coping mechanisms." Serge stuck his key in the trunk and popped the hood. "Where's that tire iron?"

Coleman gestured with his beer. "Under those rags by the spare."

"Good eye." Serge reached for the metal bar. "What was I talking about?"

"Coping skills."

"That's right." Serge raised the iron high over his head and brought it down hard like a carnival mallet.

A curdling, muffled scream from under duct tape.

"Oooooo!" Coleman winced. "You got the ATM guy right in the kneecap."

"For some reason that always sounds to me like pottery breaking."

Coleman chugged the rest of his beer. "How do you feel?"

"Now I can turn it off." He reached in the trunk again. "Every day you spend sweating the small stuff is such a waste. Snatching dicks like this out of parking lots is much more constructive." He yanked hard.

Another ghastly, muffled scream echoed from the trunk well.

Serge stood back up. "You can't allow the jerks to get inside your head." He held out his hand.

Coleman looked at Serge's bloody palm holding a diamond-stud earring. "It's just like that other jerk in the store. Do all assholes wear those?"

"Only the ones who are overcompensating for a face that looks like a scrotum." Serge stuck his hand in his pocket. "Unfortunately for this guy, he ran right into my psyche without knocking, plopped down on the couch, and propped his dirty feet up in my Happy Place."

"You were more than patient."

CATFISH

Local evening news came on. Dramatic theme music that sounded like a loud, rapid-fire teletype, even though nobody had seen a teletype in decades.

"Good evening. Our top story tonight: A major crackdown has begun on the I-95 pipeline of OxyContin being dispensed from numerous South Florida pill mills that have sprouted like mushrooms in recent years. Utilizing strengthened laws passed by the legislature this session, various police agencies have been raiding the most brazen pain clinics operating with little more than a few bare rooms and ballpoint pens. But now state police have opened a second front on the war against the so-called hillbilly heroin, intercepting large vehicles of patients and pills . . ."

The televised image switched to earlier footage of a school bus, painted gray, stopped on the side of the interstate. Deputies led a single-file line of handcuffed passengers into a series of correctional vans. Then a live news conference at a nearby command post: a trophy table covered with pill bottles, cash and two .38

revolvers. A commander with the state police stepped up to the podium, holding the leash of a German shepherd. *"Today marks a new offensive on the scourge of prescription drug traffickers laying waste to South Florida. Taking advantage of just-passed laws, we're stepping up the fight against out-of-state couriers who have begun using sophisticated tactics that until now haven't been seen outside the cocaine trade, such as concealing contraband inside fuel tanks and swallowing condoms. This is just the beginning of the battle, but we will not rest until—"*

A thumb hit a button on a remote control. The TV switched off. Next to the television was a table not unlike the one at the news conference: pill bottles, cash, guns.

"What are we going to do?" asked someone in the background wearing a trucker's hat. He pointed at the dark TV tube. "They got our first two buses. And I'm sure they'll find the third we ditched after unloading all this stuff."

"I'm thinking," said the man with the remote control.

"But we just dumped all those guys at the beach and told them to wait. Most are wearing bib overalls and engine grease. It's just a matter of time before they connect them to the abandoned bus."

The first man massaged his temples. "You're giving me a headache."

"But, Catfish—"

"Shut up! For fuck's sake! You said we dumped them at the beach, which means they don't know where this motel room is . . ." He tossed the remote on a bed and eased down into a chair. "So just grow a pair and let me logically work this out like I always do . . ."

He was the leader. The gang loosely numbered forty. Six buses total, three going each way at all times. With Oxy tabs running up to eighty bucks each on the street, they'd made so much money so fast that they hadn't figured out the laundering end, and a few million dollars was buried in a scattering of ramshackle tobacco barns in Bourbon County and the horse country surrounding Lexington. The rest of the gang drove the buses, but he rode in a trail vehicle with no contraband, allowing him to monitor operations while remaining clean in case the cops stopped them. It was an old Dodge Durango. He could afford a Rolls, but this was his blood.

His birth certificate said Jebediah Alowishous Stump, but everyone called him Catfish. Because of the deep scars on the backs of his legs. Long story.

Short version: His dad, Cecil, ran stills from Bowling Green to Cumberland Lake. Clear whiskey. And on the boy, he was quick with the switch. During the war, which was number two, Cecil ran black-market rubber, stored the tires in the garage attic. Catfish was playing with matches. It wasn't that the garage burned down, but the rationed tires were worth more than the entire house. And if you've never seen a bunch of tires go up, well, it's a big black smoke signal for several counties. The police could have been blindfolded and just followed the smell. Those were the deepest of the scars on Jebediah's buttocks and thighs.

Next to that transgression—or even in front of it—the cardinal rule: Never, ever touch Dad's prized frog-darter fishing lure. It was Cecil's secret weapon for catching fish, passed down generation to generation from his great-grandfather. And if anything ever happened to it, there would be a beating that would make the Spanish Inquisition wince. Jebediah had seen photos of the record catfish his dad had landed at the lake cabin, thanks to that lure. The boy had never caught a catfish. The frog-darter became the forbidden fruit.

Just before dawn on a Sunday when his pa was running moonshine halfway to Drip Rock, Jebediah took the skiff out on the lake, manning the small motor till at the back of the boat like Bud from *Flipper*. He anchored at dawn and went to work. Casting and casting, nibble here and there, then thoughts of a big one when the hook snagged something monstrous, but it had just gotten caught on the bottom, and the boy pulled up weeds. Hours passed. The line snapped on another bottom snag. Jeb wiped his brow. He opened his dad's tackle box for a fresh hook. At the bottom sat the frog-darter. The boy glanced around the lake's distant shores. Nobody would ever know. He took a deep breath, then attached the lure and cast.

And you can't make this up: almost immediately a bite from a catfish larger than anything in his dad's photos. Jeb reeled with all his might. The fish hit the surface a couple times, getting closer to the boat. Suddenly something huge caught the edge of Jeb's eye. What the hell? A great horned owl swooped down and snatched the catfish in its talons and flew off.

The frog-darter still attached.

So now Jeb is reeling again, facing upward as the bird circled the sky over the boat. Finally, it released the fish, which splashed into the water next to the skiff. But something was wrong. The fish wasn't on the line anymore. The owl was. Somehow the lure had pulled from the fish's mouth and gotten caught in the talons. And the bird was trying to fly off with the darter. This wasn't about a trophy fish anymore; it was survival. Jeb reeled like never before.

The owl slowly came down, flapping spastically with all it had. *Come* onnnnnnn, *please don't break the line.* Forty feet, thirty, twenty . . . But how did you land an owl? Jeb freed his right hand to grab a paddle from the bottom of the boat. Frantic reeling resumed. Ten feet, five, three, then all hell broke out. Paddle swinging and missing, wings flapping, screeching, feathers flying. Then a brushing swat from the paddle clipped a wing and more feathers. Every few swings, Jeb began finding his mark. Nothing direct, just glancing blows with only minor effect. But after a while they began adding up. *Wham, wham, wham.* The owl didn't feel so good anymore, and not flying too well either.

Finally a smack to the head, and the bird spun down into the boat, running around like a chicken in the confined space. *Wham.* The owl staggered. *Wham.* It fell over, still. Jeb rushed to retrieve the lure, tugging and twisting. He pricked two of his fingers, drawing blood, but nothing like what awaited him back at the cabin if he didn't get this job done. No luck. It was in one of the talons good with a reverse barb, and Jeb didn't have the right tools in the boat. The task required completion back onshore. The boy pulled up anchor. From his vain work trying to free the lure, Jeb could tell the bird was only unconscious. He didn't need any more adventure. So to play it safe, he bound the owl's claws with rope and tied them to a spare, empty gas can that sat in the front of the vessel. He pull-started the motor and began heading home.

Roughly a half mile from the bank, an abrupt noise. Commotion. The owl was awake. It flapped its wings. And started flying.

At the other end of the boat, Jeb couldn't believe his eyes as the bird slowly lifted out of the skiff, can and all, and took off across the lake. It was a damn big owl, but how was the boy supposed to know it was that strong? "Now I've lost the frog-darter *and* a gas can." He considered running away with the circus. Then Jeb noticed something. The bird could get airborne, but the weight of the can prevented it from gaining any altitude. It flapped and skimmed its way low over the water.

Jeb gave the motor full throttle. The boat planed up and took off like a shot across Lake Cumberland . . .

About that time, his father's trusty Hudson pickup truck with the running boards returned empty from the last hooch run. He walked around the side of the cabin and reached for the screen door. He stopped and squinted into the distance.

"What in the jumping fuck?" He walked slowly down toward the bank and scratched his head. "Jesus,

Mary and Joseph, live long enough and you will see damn near everything."

Coming straight toward him, flapping for all it was worth, one of the largest horned owls he'd ever laid eyes on. Carrying a gas can. And right behind, his ten-year-old son, running the fishing skiff at top speed, one hand on the till, the other stretched out over the starboard side with a paddle.

Wham.

The paddle snapped. The bird fell in the water and the boy circled around to fetch it. He breathed the biggest sigh of his short life, in the clear. Then he saw his dad onshore.

Gulp.

Jeb docked the boat without speaking, and got out like everything was normal.

Cecil gazed down into the fishing skiff at a broken oar and a dead owl tied to a gas can. He looked up and studied the boy. "Son, what exactly have you been doing this morning?"

Jeb stuck his hands in his pockets and stared at the ground. "Nothin'."

"How'd my frog-darter get in that bird's foot?"

"I don't know."

Cecil shook his head. "This is some bizarre enough shit." He headed into the cabin.

Jeb stood in place and cringed. *Here comes the switch.*

Instead, Cecil came back out with a Kodak Brownie camera. "Hold up that owl."

Jebediah still kept that photo to this day. But he never did catch a catfish.

So they called him Catfish.

Chapter Five

KEY LARGO

An old Magnavox television flickered in the modest ranch house. Local news. The picture was a little snowy.

Coleman randomly tossed sofa cushions on the floor and glanced back at the tube. "Serge, do you think they'll chase another guy on TV today that we can throw rocks at?"

Serge ransacked the kitchen cupboards. "One can only hope."

Coleman strolled to the dining room and dumped a handful of change on the table. "Found this in the couch." A nickel skipped off and rolled across the terrazzo. "What about you?"

Serge closed a cabinet door. "Nothing." He dumped food containers into the trash. "And I was hoping to find drugs or weapons."

"Didn't you say this guy was ninety-three."

"He still could have a roll of hundreds stashed in the sugar bowl or Metamucil." Serge opened a box of spaghetti and watched thin sticks fall into the garbage. "Crap."

Coleman went through the cushions of a recliner. "More money." Seventy-eight cents went on the table. "Why are we going through this old guy's house anyway?"

Serge dug a hand into a large can of Folgers. "Because he's dead."

"Did you kill him?"

"No." Serge emptied a box of Tide. "I don't kill everybody."

A thumping sound from behind a closed closet door. Muffled whining.

Coleman fired up a joint and looked back over his shoulder. "What are you going to do with the ATM guy?"

Serge held a jar of olives to his eye. "Still on the bubble . . . Did you check those chairs?"

Coleman grabbed another cushion. "You sure this is legal?"

"Not only is it legal—it's our job. I already explained this to you. Twice."

"I was fucked up."

"We were hired to clean out dead people's houses."

"That's a job?"

"An excellent one." Serge pulled out a lower drawer full of real silverware and dumped it into a suitcase that already contained sterling candleholders. "It's this economy. To survive, you have to find the weirdest jobs that nobody else thinks of. And with all the retirees in Florida, there's a booming, under-the-radar industry of people who get houses ready for probate sales. And it pays a ton better than cleaning up the homes of the living. Plus the best part of this job: The boss is dead . . . I used to put that in my résumés. 'Seeking fifty-K-plus, flexible hours, dead boss.' But it never worked because I guess everyone else was asking for the same thing."

"Why does this pay a ton better?"

"Because the people we're working for don't give a hoot."

"I thought you just said the boss is dead."

"Actually we're working for his estate, the kids and all." Serge made room in the suitcase for a new food processor, which was a late-night infomercial impulse purchase that the deceased couldn't remember arriving. "It's all found money to the adult children. And that's why retiree-rich Florida leads this business: The heirs are a million miles away. Sure, they fly down for the funeral and the reception with barbecue-glazed mini-weenies and a casserole from a recipe on a bottle of Kraft ranch dressing. But then they can barely wait to rush back up north from where their loved ones retired."

"Michigan?" asked Coleman.

"Sometimes. And they definitely ain't sticking around the house to get it ready for resale. They hire lawyers and real-estate agents and tell them: 'Just get it done.' And then the people they hired hire *us* and pay ridiculous fees because nobody's counting. It doesn't come out of their end; they just want to turn the property. And most people are creeped out by this kind of job, especially if they didn't find the dude for a week and you have to deal with the mattress. It works out even better if they're like this guy and die intestate."

"They cut his balls off?"

"Coleman! . . ."

Coleman took a toke and giggled. "I see dead people's stuff."

"So how about giving me a hand with the stuff?"

"Okay." Coleman crouched down and reached under the couch. "I think I found one of the miniweenies."

"In case you're wondering, that goes in the trash."

Coleman leaned and reached again. "But I thought you said your personal code only allowed you to steal from other criminals."

"What I specifically said was I don't steal when it makes me feel guilty. Criminals are just the best example."

"Still sounds like you're ripping off innocent people in grief."

"Hey, I don't know from these kids." Serge held a gold pocket watch to his ear. "If they cared, they'd be in the room with us right now, helping out, and then I'd get to know them and feel guilty."

"And then you wouldn't rob 'em?"

Serge stopped to rub his chin. "Michigan's a tough call . . . I'd probably still do it but feel bad enough to put a couple bucks in the poor box, especially since I'd have to conk them in the head with the candlehold-ers because it goes without saying you can't have them follow you out to the car, yelling in front of all the neighbors, 'They're stealing forks and pocket watches and the Kitchen Pro Slice-O-Matic!'"

"I still don't know," said Coleman, lying on his side with his arm all the way under the couch. "What's that big word you use that means when you make excuses and fib to yourself?"

Serge opened a drawer on the TV stand. "'Rationalizing'?"

"That's it. I think that's what you're doing."

"Of course that's what I'm doing." He grabbed a silver-dollar cowboy belt buckle handcrafted by Indians. "And here's how I rationalize my rationalizing. God gave us the ability to rationalize so we can stomach all the horrible things we're required to do every day just to survive the concrete jungle. 'Yeah, it was shitty for me to eat some of his pudding cups from the employee refrigerator, but I was hungry. And he's a jerk.'"

"Do animals in the real jungle have to rationalize?" asked Coleman.

"No, some predator sees food or an enemy, they rip its face off without a second thought," said Serge. "But when we humans vote for candidates to take away the other guy's benefits—'but keep your fucking hands off my Medicare'—we need to lie to ourselves. It makes us special."

Coleman pulled his arm out from under the couch again. "How'd you learn about this job in the first place? . . . Here's a button."

"From probate attorneys. They're recession-proof. They're *everything*-proof. Nothing can touch them. Why? Because people will always die, and heirs will always like to receive found money." Serge's hands fanned through an invisible stack of currency. "When Armageddon reigns, and survival on this planet gets down to brass tacks, the last three left standing will be cockroaches, viruses and probate attorneys. Fade to black, check please."

"I've never heard about this," said Coleman.

"They don't teach it in business school, but whenever the economy comes unglued like House Speaker Boehner watching *Brian's Song,* we can survive and even prosper just by imitating exactly what probate attorneys do. Except we can't because we're not probate attorneys. The attorneys made that rule. So here's what you do. Let's say you're approaching middle age and suddenly remember you forgot to go to law school. Not the end of the world. Probate attorneys can't do it alone. They have to farm out the dirty work, and there's a whole, invincible, ambient economy surrounding them like a holy aura as they walk down the street. The answer is to study them and pick up tips for sidestream income in a down market. Or even better, follow them. Twenty-four/seven. That's what I do. They don't really like it. And that's why selling yourself is so important. My guy's name was Steve. I introduced myself real polite: 'Can I call you Steve? I mean since I'll be following you. Or actually *have been* following. I got your name when I peeked in your mailbox, just before I peeked in your windows last night. But only the kitchen and your home office while you were licking stamps. But definitely not the bedroom, because personal privacy is number one with me! Let's get that out of the way from the get-go, in case you've heard the talk. Want some of this coffee? No? Good, 'cause I want it all. Excuse me while I kill this. *Glug, glug, glug.* So, anyway, I'd like to hear all your invaluable tips on secondary recession income . . . Why are you backing up on the sidewalk? Wait, slow down. Stop running . . . Face it, Steve, you can't outrun me. See how I'm easily keeping stride, and you're breathing and sweating like Rush Limbaugh being whipped by a jockey up a pyramid? I can do this all day. You don't want to turn down that alley; there's only the parking garage . . . Okay, you did it anyway. And you just made another careless error, running the wrong way on level one. I know this garage—you've just boxed yourself in. But since I now have you cornered against those walls, a few golden drops of your wisdom, please . . . Man, Steve, you're really shaking; dress shirt all stuck to your chest and shit. Are you trying to kick H? If you are, I know these cats. Revolutionary new technique. Forget nine to twelve weeks in a mountain chalet with Liza Minnelli. One week, *pow!* You hire them, and they grab you off the street without warning, sack over your head and into the back of a van. Variation on tough love, but incredible success rate . . . Steve, I'm trying to talk to you, but you've got your cell phone out. Am I not giving you *my* undivided attention? Don't call the police . . . You're still calling them. Gimme that thing. I'll give it back when we're done. You know those fantastic nature documentaries in high def where they get stupid-close to those big fuckin' sharks, and the one fish the sharks don't tear to a bloody mess are the little guys that clean their skin and eat the sidestream chunks of flesh that get stuck in their teeth? Get it? Sidestream income, sidestream flesh? *I want to be your skin cleaner.* That melody is Peter Gabriel's 'Sledgehammer.' What ever happened to him? . . . Steve! You're fainting! . . . God*damn,* that's the biggest forehead gash I've ever seen.' . . . And then *I* had to call 911 . . ."

"Guess you didn't get any of his money tips," said Coleman.

"Just the opposite," said Serge. "It's how we landed this job."

"You mean the place where we are now?"

Serge nodded and pocketed cuff links. "And the six houses before this when you weren't around. After the parking-garage mishap, I called Steve at home."

"You had his number?"

"No, I was calling him through his bedroom window," said Serge. "I promised no bedroom windows, but he wasn't answering the phone. And I'm standing there in the bushes saying I think his phone is broken, and his wife turned out to be a real screamer, and he motions for me to meet him at the front door. I finally see his face in half-decent light from the street, and I'm like, 'Jesus, that's one big-ass bandage over your stitches. Couldn't the doctors have used anything smaller that doesn't tell everyone you faint for no reason?' . . . And he begs me to leave him alone, and to call his office in the morning. Of course I do, and his secretary explains this job about cleaning up after the dead and gives me an address, and then a few days later, a check from the real-estate agent arrives at the same address. Since then, whenever I need some extra cash, I just call Steve's office, and the secretary immediately gives me another address. It's almost as if she has a list taped to her phone. Steve's polite like that, respecting my time . . ."

Banging and whimpering from the closet.

"Serge," said Coleman. "The ATM guy . . ."

"He'll get tired of doing that."

Coleman herded dust bunnies on the floor. "But where'd you learn how to do this job?"

"What's to know?" Serge shrugged. "I don't even think they care how well I perform, because once I did a really crappy job. Showed up for an hour but got distracted by Fantasy Fest in Key West and didn't come back for three weeks, and when I finally remembered, I went to the real-estate agent's office to apologize, but her secretary says she's not in, and then I see some woman running out the back door and speeding away in a car. And the secretary suddenly hands me a check, full payment."

"That's weird," said Coleman, staring at the banging closet.

"Steve must have talked to that agent about me," said Serge. "Put the ol' probate boot down on her neck: 'You want to keep riding this gravy train? Don't fuck with my people.'"

"Wow," said Coleman. "Steve must really like you."

Serge nodded again. "It's great having a probate attorney as a friend. They're very loyal."

LATER THAT NIGHT

It always seems to be a full moon in the glades.

The sugarcane flowed like an ocean, waves of stalk in the wind. Million acres to the horizon in every direction. Whitecaps where the light reflected just right.

The lonely road south from the lake passed through a vacant crossroads called Okeelanta, Florida's version of the crop-duster scene from *North by Northwest*. Then emptiness. Just a long, desolate drive—one of the longest in the state—with no public turnoffs or safe harbor to pull over for three counties, unless you wanted to take your car swimming in a drainage canal.

Nothing but an elevated causeway of limestone and fill dirt that gave a nice crow's-nest view over the landscape, first the agricultural tracts, then the glades in full force. Just swamp and gators for another long run until hitting some truck stops on the outer outskirts of Miami.

It was cool and breezy up in the livestock bed of a cattle truck that crossed the railroad tracks in South Bay. Standing room only for the migrants packed in the back. They had to hold their bladders. Nobody spoke.

Up front in the cab, the driver turned on the radio, and the passenger turned it off.

"What's the deal?"

"Shut up," said the passenger. "I'm trying to think."

"About what was on TV today? The intercepted buses and raided clinic?"

No answer.

The driver stared ahead. "Maybe we should cool it until after the crackdown."

"You idiot," said the passenger. "How do you think the *policía* knew where to go?"

The driver shrugged.

The passenger simply held up an untraceable cell phone.

The driver did a double take. "*You* tipped off the cops? But why?"

"Those fucking hillbillies. This is our territory. They think they can just come down here and take what's ours?" He spit out the window.

"So you're trying to drive them out of business?"

"No, I want them in business."

The driver turned with a questioning look.

"As our customers," the passenger explained. "First I cut off their source. No more of this going straight to the clinics themselves and smuggling it out on buses. Then *we'll* be the only source, and they'll have to do business with us."

"I don't think they'll go for that."

"They won't have a choice. They'll have to pay a lot more, but they'll still make a bundle on the back end."

"But the police have been hitting our clinics, too."

"That's why we have to change tactics. They're looking for packed parking lots, and sending undercovers to look for lobbies jammed with people."

"Is that why we got those motel rooms on U.S. 1?"

"Don't talk anymore."

The passenger stared out the window at the moon. Gaspar Arroyo. Immigrant story. Crossed over at Laredo in '98, then hooked around the Gulf Coast from Louisiana to Biloxi. Worked the Florida farm circuit in Immokalee, then east to La Belle and Belle Glade. Nothing to show for it. The farms overcharged for food and claimed everything for housing, which was usually little more than a termite-ridden, clapboard barracks. It was either that or an INS jail cell awaiting deportation. The only migrant who made anything was the one whom the farm gringos deputized to keep each barracks in line however he saw fit. They picked the most sadistic.

Five years ago, Arroyo took his first beating from the barracks captain. The next morning, the captain couldn't be found. That afternoon he turned up in the blades of a harvesting machine. There was talk, but nothing more. The gringos put Arroyo in charge of the barracks. He wanted more.

Through a series of whispered circumstances, Arroyo became the only illegal immigrant with an executive's title and salary at one of the largest cane processors in Florida. He never went in the office, and everyone was happy about it.

Gaspar had bigger dreams as he gazed off the side of the causeway at the moonlit cane.

"Pull over," he told the driver. "I have to take a leak."

The truck stopped on the road, because there was no shoulder. Gaspar walked to the edge of the canal and trickled into the water. He zipped up. "José, get over here. I see something."

"What is it?" yelled the driver.

"I hope it's not what I think. Hurry!"

José hopped down from the cab and ran to the bank. "What's the tire iron for?"

"In case of snakes while I'm peeing."

José turned his head toward the swamp. "Where am I looking?"

"In the reeds on the other side of the canal." Gaspar crouched and pointed. "At the waterline."

"Still don't see it."

"Are you blind? It's right there."

José leaned closer. "You mean *that*? It's just an empty milk bottle bobbing."

"You're right," said Gaspar.

José straightened up. "This weird lighting played a trick on your eyes."

Gaspar stepped behind him. "No, I mean you were right about a lot of our clinics getting hit. Someone's been talking."

Gaspar swung the tire iron with all he had, smashing José at the base of his back and sending electric jolts both ways through his spinal cord.

A horrible, high-pitched scream emptied into the sugarcane.

José fell onto his back, limbs bent weird. "Oh God! I can't feel my legs!"

"That's the whole idea," said Gaspar, leaning over him and brandishing the iron. "You thought I wouldn't find out that you're ratting on me?"

"No, Gaspar! I can explain—"

The next swing hit José's right elbow. Another scream, then another elbow whack, and so on.

Gaspar finally dropped to his knees and rolled José onto his stomach. "This is what you get for fucking me!"

"Whatever you're thinking, please! . . . I still can't feel my legs . . ."

"Whatever I'm thinking? Here's what I'm thinking!" Gaspar gently caressed the back of José's neck. "I'm thinking of one of these cervical vertebrae. Then you'll forget about your legs. You won't feel anything, except your head. You'll be able to smile, frown, blink, even talk, except nothing will come out because your brain won't be able to tell your lungs to breathe . . . Consider it quiet time to mull over what you've done."

"No! Please—"

Wham.

The blow would have sounded like a dull thud to anyone standing around, but inside José's skull it was the sharp clap of a rifle shot. Then Gaspar rolled him over so he could face the night sky. His lips moved silently.

Gaspar stuck the tire iron in his belt and climbed the shoulder of the road. He looked up at the truck's bed. Everyone turned away. They were in the middle of forty same-looking miles. Even if they wanted to, there was no way anyone could pinpoint José's location before the alligators did their thing.

Gaspar climbed back in on the driver's side and resumed the trip to Fort Lauderdale.

He turned on the radio.

Back on the edge of the road, José heard a truck driving away as he watched the stars begin to dim.

Chapter Six

KEY LARGO

B rilliant colors screamed off a two-story concrete wall, where the mural of a giant angelfish directed visitors to nearby snorkeling pleasures.

A mile west, silverware jingled in a suitcase sitting on a kitchen table.

"Dang, the zipper's stuck," said Serge. He jerked the tab violently and cursed and slammed the luggage against the wall and jumped up and down on it. Ten minutes later: "Okay, that's not working. I'll try finesse . . . Just back the zipper up a little to free that tiny piece of fabric and there! Fixed in five seconds."

"Why didn't you just do that in the first place?" asked Coleman.

"Don't start talking crazy."

Coleman shrugged and took a seat at the table, painting a joint with hash oil.

Serge grabbed a chair on the other side. "I think our work here is done. You get all the lightbulbs?"

Coleman raised a shopping bag from beside his chair.

"Good." Serge opened the local morning newspaper. "Just let me read this, and we'll start loading the car."

Coleman torched the bone and exhaled a small cloud. "Why are you always reading when nobody's forcing you?"

Serge looked up and stared at Coleman a moment. "That question kind of answers itself." He looked back down.

Coleman tapped joint ash on the floor. "My teachers were always making me read. I'm talking about *books*. Shit. I swore when I got out, I'd never read another."

Serge kept his eyes on the paper. "You showed them."

Coleman took another hit. "Damn straight."

A rare moment of silence.

"Serge? I saw this cool bar up the street—"

"I'm trying to read. This is important."

"Why?"

"Because the way things are going, soon you'll only see newspapers in museums, like the Dead Sea Scrolls. Everyone now gets their data off the Internet."

"So? It's just a computer screen instead of paper."

"There's a bigger difference. On one hand, the *New York Times,* also known as the Old Gray Lady and the Paper of Record; on the other, Yahoo! headlines: 'Demi Moore's Style Showdown,' 'Best Cities for Cats to Live,' 'Ten Telltale Signs Nobody Likes You,' 'We Replace Half Our Friends Every Seven Years.' "

Coleman became worried. "I've known you for fifteen."

"Don't sweat it. You've got tenure." Serge turned a page. "Newspapers also provide the local lowdown that would never get on the net. That's how I learned about throwing rocks at cars down here, and cleaning your headlights before leaving bars."

"Cleaning what?"

"This one cop down here had like the record for DUI arrests before a ton of them got reversed." Serge flipped to the sports section. "He'd go to bars early in the evening and walk through the parking lot with a bar of soap, marking Xs on the headlights. Then, after midnight, if he saw some car with Xs, he pulled them over on some bullshit pretext. So after the news broke, people started checking their headlights. But you'd never know that if you weren't into newspapers."

"Wow," said Coleman. "Reading is cool! . . . Let me start with the funnies."

Serge whipped a page out of the paper and handed it across the table without looking.

Coleman haphazardly folded it over with an unending crinkling sound. "I can't believe I'm reading."

"The day the earth stood still," said Serge.

"They still have 'Family Circus,'" said Coleman. "Billy's running crazy all over the house again leaving a dotted line . . . I don't understand 'Doonesbury.'"

"Newspapers also help me line up takedown scores. They report the most devious, heartless scams perpetrated on the weak and the elderly, and since it's Florida, that's a lot of pages to fill. But it bird-dogs me straight to my pickin' of guilt-free heists. Like this one jackass here: Check out what he did to these retirees . . ." Serge turned the paper around and held it across the table.

Coleman leaned and squinted. "Jesus, that's terrible."

"See what I mean?" Serge turned another page. "I'd bum-rush these cowards for free. But usually they beg me to take them to an ATM."

"And then you give that money back to the victims?"

"If they happen to be walking by the ATM at that very moment, sure. But otherwise, no. I'm busy," said Serge. "And I want to go on the record here: Robin Hood fucked it up for everyone. Is it not enough that I'm punishing these miscreants while the law grinds like a toothless mouth? No, to be a charismatic criminal, I'm supposed to work for nothing?"

"Batman." Coleman pointed at the comics. "Bruce Wayne was already rich. No job, free cave."

"And they gave him a pass on all his shit—violated at least seven constitutional rights by my count, and that's just the Joker."

"It's not fair," said Coleman.

"But what are ya going to do? Dwell on the negative, or think about Catwoman?"

"That was my first boner," said Coleman.

"The first for everyone our age," said Serge. "And the rest of your life you're chasing that initial sensation, which is a recipe for disappointment, because even though you buy the most expensive Catwoman costume, the reaction's always the same: 'Get the hell away from me, you freak!' 'Wait! I was only six years old! I blame TV!'" Serge flipped to weather and the local crime report on the back page. "Ooooo! Here's a follow-up on the story of the year from the Keys. This woman was cruising down the Overseas Highway in a convertible and was arrested for distracted driving because she rear-ended someone while shaving her pussy."

Coleman dropped his comics and began coughing. He pounded his chest. "That's it. Fuck it. I'm definitely reading from now on . . . Please, tell me more!"

"Let's see, she was just convicted of DUI the previous day, and told the cops she wanted to look good for a date with her boyfriend; plus the passenger was her ex-husband, whom she had asked to take the wheel so she could shave, which means he's definitely not looking at the road either, and—here's the cherry on the sundae—a comment you will only hear from a cop in the Keys: It was the strangest traffic incident he'd seen on the Overseas Highway since pulling over that guy with four syringes sticking out of his arm—"

Thud, thud, thud . . .

Serge looked around. "What's that noise? Rats?"

"They'd have to be big." Coleman twisted the end of the jay in his mouth.

Thud, thud, thud . . .

"There it is again."

Thud, thud, thud . . .

Both of their heads turned slowly toward the closet.

"We completely forgot about him," said Coleman.

Serge reached in his pocket. "I guess our work here isn't done after all." He pulled out a tiny object and cupped it in his hand.

"A diamond-stud earring?" asked Coleman. "Did the dead guy who lived here have a wife or something?"

"No." Serge pointed the gem at the closet. "I pulled it off his ear in the trunk, remember?"

A muffled scream from the door.

Serge pocketed the jewelry. "And that's the same sound he made when I ripped it off his ear."

"I remember that now from the parking lot." Coleman took another giant hit and cracked a beer. "Still makes me cringe."

"Not my fault." Serge held up innocent hands. "He broke the rules of society at that bank branch, so I was involuntarily drafted into the War on Rudeness. If there's one thing I'm not, it's a draft dodger." He stopped and scratched the top of his head. "Although I could have enrolled in community college and gotten a deferment. But as John Fogarty sings, 'I ain't no senator's son.'"

"The guy was a little on the pushy side."

"No joke."

"Probably high on coke," said Coleman. "That's how you know if it's good coke. It makes you pushy."

"So keep it in the nightclubs," said Serge. "The clubs are specifically designated for people to work off their pushiness, just like gyms are made for exercise. But you don't see people lifting weights in the street."

"His ear was really bleeding."

"Couldn't be helped," said Serge. "You can't tear it off without that."

"Why tear it off at all?"

"If you're a gigantic prick, the diamond-stud earring is the exclamation point," said Serge. "It's like a huge, flashing neon frame around the prick picture."

"I didn't know you were prejudiced against guys wearing earrings."

"Just the opposite," said Serge. "It's all a question of what works. For most guys, it's pretty cool. But everybody simply has certain things that won't gel with their overall package, and it only emphasizes the fact you're trying too hard. For example, you won't see me strutting out of a hip-hop barbershop anytime soon with 'Don't Snitch' shaved into the side of my head. Clashes with the shape of my face. Four-hundred-pound guys shouldn't wear shirts with horizontal stripes, and pricks shouldn't wear diamond earrings. They're just fashion no-no's, like how certain people definitely shouldn't wear certain swimsuits to the beach—we all agree on this last point. It's the only concept that unites us as a nation."

"So have you decided what you're going to do with him?"

"I think I finally figured out my next science project."

WISCONSIN

A sink was running. Sounds of someone brushing his teeth.

Barbara McDougall was already in bed with a book. "You're not supposed to leave the sink running when you're brushing your teeth. We've told our students a million times."

"I always forget," said Patrick, turning a faucet.

He finished brushing and flicked off the bathroom light.

Barbara looked up from her book. "Don't forget to leave the sink running so the pipes don't freeze."

Patrick smiled and went back, giving the hot-water knob a quarter twist. He returned to the bedroom, pulled back the blanket and looked over at the cover of the thick book Bar had just started. An orange sunset over a sooty industrial skyline. "*Gravity's Rainbow?* How many times have you started that book?"

Bar looked over the top of reading glasses halfway down her nose. "Can't remember. Supposed to be a literary classic—all the people I respect say so. Except it's impenetrable to me."

"I've never gotten much farther than when he goes into the toilet and somehow wiggles through the pipes," said Pat. "Reminded me of that Scottish bathroom scene in *Trainspotting.*"

Her nose went back in the novel. "This time I'm determined. I'd hate to think I'm not smart enough."

"You're the smartest person I know."

A smile. "You're just saying that because you're married to me."

"It's *why* I married you—"

The phone rang. Patrick reached for the nightstand on his side. "Hello? . . . No, don't apologize. It's not too late . . . What's up? . . ."

Bar lowered the book and saved her spot with a finger. "Who is it?" she whispered.

Pat covered the receiver and whispered back. "Courtney's parents." He uncovered it. "Is she okay? . . . I see . . . Why don't you put her on the phone? . . . Hello, Courtney? It's me, Mr. McDougall. What seems to be the matter? . . . Courtney, just slow down and relax. I can't understand if you keep crying . . . That's better. No, everything's going to be all right. You haven't done anything wrong . . . I understand completely. Could you do me a favor and put your father back on the phone? . . ."

"What's going on?" asked Bar.

Pat held up a hand for her to wait. Then into the phone: "Jack, yeah, I know . . . Last night it was three A.M. before she settled down? She did seem a little exhausted in class today . . . Jack, you two can't blame yourselves. There's nothing you did to trigger it; I've read all the studies . . . What? Tonight she was crying so hard she gave herself a nosebleed? . . ." Pat pulled off the blanket and threw his legs over the side of the bed. "I'm coming over . . . Don't say not to. We're like family . . . Look, the longer we stay on the phone, the longer till I'm there . . . See you in a few."

He hung up.

Bar looked at the alarm clock. "You're going over to the Arsenaults' at this hour?"

"It's Courtney."

Bar threw off her covers.

"What are you doing?" asked Pat.

"Coming with you."

Pat pulled up his pants and buckled the belt. "She's not your student. Stay here and get your rest."

"I'm wide-awake," said Bar. "What am I going to do in an empty house? We can talk."

Pat slipped on a shirt, then pointed out the window in the general direction of a silo. "But I have to go to the school first, and that's in the opposite direction."

"You're going to the school *and* the Arsenaults'?"

"I know her favorite books. If I read to her . . ." said Pat. "A lot of driving; you don't want to go."

"Now I definitely want to go."

"Why?"

"So we can talk. I like it when we can talk."

A seventeen-year-old Geo Metro headed east out of Waunakee on Highway 19. It wasn't a typical car for a Wisconsin winter. Or even spring. But the drive was peaceful. No streetlights. A full moon lit up rolling hills of snow through dairy land. It was the only car they ever owned, which they bought slightly used just before getting married, which was twelve years ago.

They talked about early Hemingway, late Picasso, the Middle East, a new movie they were dying to see but would wait for the rental because money was tight. They realized they hadn't had Chinese food in a while. The kind of destination-free conversation that bounces all over the place when two people just enjoy each other's company. Still in love.

Forty minutes later, they pulled up at a shoveled-out driveway at a small farmhouse with all the lights burning.

"She's the sweetest child in the world," said Bar. "It's so sad."

"The good news is it's one of the mildest forms of autism," said Pat. "But since it mainly manifests in crying, it just tears at your heart."

They got out and walked up the front steps with their best game faces.

Jack Arsenault already had the door open. "Get in, you'll freeze."

He led Patrick to the bedroom. The women went in the kitchen. "Can I get you something? Danish, coffee?"

"I'm fine."

They both sat at the table and smiled, but their eyes were in another emotional room.

"You really didn't have to come," said Gabby Arsenault.

"Are you kidding?" said Bar. "We love Courtney."

"She's always talking about Patrick. You both have such a way with the students. You'd be great parents—" Gabby stopped. "I'm sorry. I didn't mean . . . I mean I forget."

"Don't worry about it . . ."

A half hour later, the men joined them in the kitchen. Gabby looked up. "How is she?"

"Asleep," said Patrick.

"I don't know how he does it," said Jack.

"You're the ones who do it all," said Pat. "She was practically asleep when we got here. I just gave the jar lid a final twist."

A heavy pause in the room. Jack formed tight lips. "Uh, I . . . me and Gabby, we want you to know that we feel absolutely horrible about what's going on with the teachers."

"Everything will work out." Pat smiled, and it was sincere.

"But I can't believe I voted for those greedy bastards." Jack shook his head. "It was supposed to be about government responsibility. Who knew they were going to raid the candy store?"

Bar got up from the table as Pat put a hand on Jack's shoulder. "The important thing is you have a wonderful daughter."

Chapter Seven

MEANWHILE . . .

It had been one of those killer Keys sunsets. Just a few hours earlier, a wavering scarlet ball melted into the Gulf of Mexico, silhouetting countless uninhabited mangrove islands scattered across the quiet water.

Then it was gone, but the show continued. Streaks of wispy clouds fanned out from a point in the distance, glowing rose and crimson underneath from the hidden sun. Below the clouds, drivers turned on headlights, creating a string of bright beads up U.S. 1. It was especially magical if you had a wide-angle view.

"Can we go now?" asked Coleman.

"I'm using my wide-angle," said Serge. "It's magical."

The final cloud faded to dark.

Serge tossed his camera in the '76 Gran Torino that was backed up in the driveway of a dead man's house on Key Largo.

Coleman followed him inside the residence. "The car's been packed for the last hour. You promised I could go to that bar."

Serge made a quick recon sweep for anything they might have forgotten. "We had to wait for night anyway."

A beer cracked. "What for?"

Serge gave him a "stupid question" look, then tilted his head across the room toward the closet.

"*Oh*, that." Coleman realized he now had an open beer in each hand. "But we're still going to that bar, right?"

"Of course." Serge checked wall sockets for left-behind electronics chargers. "You can't stop often enough in the old Florida bars because many will be converted into gentlemen's clubs before you know it."

"I like to go in those, too," said Coleman. "I can always spot them from the neon."

"Because that's the rule. They don't even need a sign. Any building with pink or purple neon: They're required to have strippers in quantity." Serge locked the front door and headed back through the dining room. "And I can't get enough of that name. Gentlemen's club. It's Orwellian for the new chivalry: 'Please, let me hold the door for you, right after I finish staring at your snatch for a dollar.' That's the exquisite psychology of advertising, like calling a fried-chicken buffet restaurant 'Skinny Boys.'"

"Or, you know, like partying," said Coleman, nodding and smiling.

"What do you mean?"

"You know, partying. Supposed to be birthday cards and brightly wrapped presents and pin the tail on the donkey. But, man, instead you're really getting seriously fucked up, completely hammered, ripped to the nuts, shit-faced and puking all over furniture and lawn statues, paralyzed, grabbing people—'What are these fucking frog statues doing here?'—but then you snort some radioactive coke and come back stronger than ever, man, first-string all-star team! More bong hits and lines and tequila, and you give each other shotguns with a real shotgun barrel until you're blind and forget how to speak and can't go to the bathroom right, like when you're a veteran and really know what you're doing." Coleman stopped and nodded again. "The word 'partying.' What you were just talking about. Get it?"

"Uh, yeah, that's exactly what I was talking about." Serge rolled his eyes. "Very insightful."

"So what are we doing now?"

"Road trip!" Serge walked over to the closet door.

"He's making those noises again," said Coleman.

"Probably heard me say 'road trip.' Some people get excited."

Serge turned the knob and pulled the door open quickly. "Ready to rock?"

A bound and gagged man slumped in the corner. A little smiley-face Band-Aid on an earlobe. Still scream- ing under the duct tape across his mouth.

Coleman finished the beer in his left hand. "I think he wants to say something."

"Probably itinerary requests for our trip." Serge leaned down and ripped the tape off.

"Owwww!"

"Where do you want to go?" asked Serge. "I can't make any promises because of my zany schedule. Unless they sell souvenirs. My weakness, but it could be worse. Actually it will be. Suggestions?"

"Please don't hurt me! I'm so sorry!"

Serge glanced at Coleman. "Haven't we heard that before?"

"Many times."

Crying now. "I'll give you money," said the man. "We can go to an ATM."

"Oooo, bad memories there," said Serge. "Remember last time?"

"I was wrong! I apologize!"

"You're just saying that now because you think I'm not a patient person." Serge grabbed a roll of duct tape and pulled out a long stretch. "But back when you thought I was patient, you took advantage and dumped all your negativity on me. And you knew it was going to stick in my stomach, and then my day's ruined. Not to mention the broader implications for the national fabric."

"I was just in a bad mood. I didn't mean it."

"Of course you did," said Serge. "You were still yelling as I patiently walked away, thinking you were home free. But that was just because ATMs have surveillance cameras. You never guessed that I'd outflank you to your car and wait. Because I'm patient."

"What are you going to do to me?"

"Stand up," said Serge.

"I think my kneecap's broken."

"You'll soon forget all about that. My promise to you."

"But I—"

Serge swiftly wrapped fresh duct tape across the captive's mouth. "Coleman, help me get him out to the car."

Moments later, the trunk slammed on the Gran Torino. The muscle car screeched backward out of the driveway and tore east on U.S. 1.

They reached Mile Marker 104. Coleman's head turned as they went by. "You're passing the bar."

"We'll be back." Serge pointed over his shoulder at the thuds coming from the trunk. "This one kicks a lot. I can't leave him in the saloon parking lot like some of the others who went limp. Banging sounds from trunks in parking lots tend to raise questions because some people don't have enough to do."

"Then where are we going?"

"It's a surprise."

It didn't take long. Around Mile Marker 107, just after the fork to Card Sound, Serge pulled onto an unmaintained dirt road and plunged into the darkness of the mangroves.

Soon the car stopped. Crickets and frogs.

The trunk popped open.

Serge reached in and sat the hostage up. "Surprise!"

Coleman fired a joint onshore, scanning the dark water. "So this is the surprise? *Lake* Surprise?"

"Good recall." Serge jerked his guest out of the car and threw him to the ground.

"He's shaking like crazy," said Coleman. "And just wet himself."

"Better now than later. Seriously."

"Why? Does that have something to do with what you're planning?"

"It always fits together." Serge swept an arm across the natural vista. "Everything's connected. The Hindus know all about this." He stood and slowed his breathing.

"Are you thinking of round things?"

"Yes. They're coming through like a vision. And I'm seeing . . . peanut butter cups? Hmm, the path to enlightenment isn't what I expected."

The hostage noisily flopped in the muck, attempting to escape like a landed fish trying to work its way off a dock.

Serge blinked rapidly a few times. "Damn, made me lose the peanut butter cups." He walked back to the trunk and began unloading supplies.

"Coleman, grab these ropes."

"What do I do with them?"

Serge seized the man by the hair and dragged him screaming back to the designated spot onshore. "Tie one stretch of rope to each hand and ankle."

More equipment came out of the car. Serge got down on his knees and hammered giant tent stakes.

"Serge, I finished tying the ropes." He stood proudly. "How did I do?"

Serge stared a moment with his mouth open. "Coleman, I meant *his* hands and ankles."

"Oh." Coleman looked down at his own wrists and feet. "But you didn't say that."

"Jesus Christ." Serge resumed hammering. "Him this time. And please ask any questions along the way."

Coleman loosened a knot. "Serge, why are you hammering?"

"Apparently for nothing." He stood up and looked around. "This muck is too soft. We'll have to lash him to the mangroves."

"Then what?" asked Coleman. "Alligators will eat him?"

"This is salt water."

"Little crabs will swarm and pick his bones clean?"

"Not the right species on this island."

"I was kind of hoping for crabs."

Serge found a large root of a red mangrove grabbing down into underwater silt. Tied a double hitch. "We won't be here to see anyway."

Coleman sagged. "I knew you were going to say that."

Serge secured another line. "What's with you always wanting to watch? I told you how sick and abnormal that is."

Under Coleman's breath: "You're the one waxing the dude."

"I heard that," said Serge. "We're not going to get into this discussion again."

Coleman stretched out his arms with dangling ropes. "I need a little help."

Serge sighed, then went over and untied his buddy. They connected the lines to the ones he had already fastened to the mangroves, and tied the captive spread-eagled on the bank.

Coleman fidgeted. "Is the part where we go to that bar coming up soon?"

Serge headed back to the trunk. "Almost there." He loaded up his arms and started walking back.

Coleman scratched his head. "How are those things going to kill him?"

Serge turned on his camcorder. "Patience."

CATFISH, PART II

After landing his prize horned owl, Catfish never got another whipping from Cecil and took up in his father's boot prints. A natural trajectory of local tradition. They were all God-fearing, hardworking people of the earth, good providers for their kin. But not slick like those eastern boys who made all the rules. So they navigated around them. First was the moonshine, then tobacco, which was legal unless you ducked taxes, which they did at every turn; then toward the end of Cecil's days, growing some of the wickedest bluegrass marijuana in the state. Until the next thing came along, which was just around the corner. They called it the Kentucky way.

Cecil died quietly around '83, and was buried under a lone oak on a bluff overlooking the gold dome of the state capitol in Frankfort. Cecil bought the plot thirty years back and told his son that Daniel Boone's tombstone was a rock's throw away. After the funeral, Catfish actually threw a rock, and his father was right.

The Kentucky State Police bought some new helicopters with fancy thermal-spotting equipment. Pot groves were set ablaze everywhere, and the growers burrowed deep into the hills. Catfish temporarily wrote off the weed trade as too risky, and eventually surfaced an hour north with a rusty single-wide wedged deep in Woodford County behind the vine-covered ruins of an eighteenth-century bourbon distillery. Deep thickets made the trailer invisible, which wasn't on the Realtors' list of high points. But it was on Catfish's. He began with the marijuana again, but low-key, only a few scattered plants in each location, which could be written off to nature because, well, it was a weed. The helicopters buzzed on by.

The old distillery lay ten miles northwest of Lexington and in another universe.

Extremes.

Appalachian poverty and international Thoroughbred wealth.

There were many such run-down trailers strewn about those hills, and people got used to the recreational, liquor-fueled gunfire at the moon that echoed across the horse pastures of many current and former Derby winners. Familiar names: Claiborne Farm and Calumet and Three Chimneys. Brookshire Farm had chandeliers in all the stables. The barns of a sheikh from the Arabian peninsula featured copper roofs, and a 747 jumbo jet with Arabic lettering sat on standby along a modest runway of the nearby Bluegrass Airport. A Florida connection would soon form in the hills around that airport, except there already had been one. Little known, but documented: In the immediate hours after the 9/11 attacks, when all aircraft in the nation were grounded, one small private plane was secretly in the air with the president's blessing—a flight into the Bluegrass Airport carrying young members of a royal family who were students in Tampa and who immediately boarded a well-guarded jet for their homeland. And that weekend, more bullets at the moon.

William Shatner lived there.

Catfish's trailer technically lay on the outskirts of a small hamlet called Versailles. But don't walk into a bar and pronounce it correctly like the French, or you'll be stared down as a damn communist or, worse, a fed. It always has and will be *Ver-sales*. The police found most of Catfish's pot plants and burned them in a big pile on a Saturday night and drank beer and stood close, but it didn't matter. The newspapers had already begun reporting emergency room ODs from some newfangled drug called Oxy. Catfish found two specific nuggets deep in one article. The pills were going for up to eighty dollars each on the street. And an unusual number of the prescriptions had been filled in Miami and Fort Lauderdale. He gassed up the Durango. Time to dip a toe in that raging river of tropical drug cash. It was the Kentucky way.

That was four years ago.

Back to live action: an anonymous motel room with the curtain pulled tight along U.S. Highway 1 in South Florida.

Catfish sat on the edge of the bed in deep thought as dozens of stranded Sterno bums wandered the beach in bib overalls. He was considered to be one of the top bosses in the Kentucky Mafia. Which didn't exist. But anytime three or more people of any ethnic or geographical group commit three or more crimes, it's the Polish Mafia, or Albanian Mafia, or Eskimo Mafia. And since the nicknames appeared in the newspaper, it had to be true.

The only other person in the motel room besides Catfish was his undependable right-hand man, Gooch Spivey, who had aspirations as a poker champ and used to stutter horribly as a youth until learning to overcome it with long pauses of intense concentration that appeared as if he were trying to levitate objects with his mind. It drove Catfish batshit.

"What are you . . . thinking about?"

"Can you not fucking do that?"

"Do . . . what?"

"Shut up!" Catfish ran both hands through his hair. At least the pauses came and went, and that gave him something to look forward to.

Gooch broke out a deck of airline playing cards to kill time.

Catfish looked up. "Gooch, why are you wearing mirrored sunglasses indoors. And a black cowboy hat?"

Gooch shuffled cards. "All the top TV champions dress like this on *Extreme . . . Poker.*"

Catfish tightly grabbed fistfuls of bedspread on each side of where he was sitting. "I'm going to have to kill myself."

" . . . Why?"

Teeth gnashed. Then a cartoon lightbulb came on. Catfish grabbed a notepad. "Forget Interstate 95.

That's history. We need to come up with something that moves unnoticed between Florida and Kentucky by another route. What does Florida have?"

"Oranges?"

Catfish shook his head. "Agriculture inspections . . . What else?"

Gooch cut his deck and shrugged.

Catfish rested the tip of his pen on the pad. "Let's look at it from the other direction. What does Kentucky have?"

"Bourbon?"

"No good. ATF. They can be worse than the DEA. What else?"

"Horses?"

"No, they—" Catfish stopped and grabbed a road map from his suitcase. "You might have something there." He traced up the spine of Florida with a finger. "That's it. That's how we're going to do it."

"We're going to put the drugs in horses?"

"Don't be stupid." Catfish began refilling a duffel bag with all the pills and cash on the table. "We need to get everything back in the Durango and clear out before they track us here. We'll be exposed for this one trip, but if we make it, we'll never have to worry again."

"How long will we be exposed?"

Catfish glanced toward the map he'd left open on top of the TV. A spot was circled a bit north of Disney. "I was never good with those mile scales. Two or three hours?"

A Dodge Durango rode through the night with little traffic. And no streetlights. That was the plan.

Catfish had picked up U.S. Highway 27 west of Plantation and headed north toward Lake Okeechokee. Just the moon and the emptiness of wind-flowing sugarcane fields that created a landscape from a movie where lost tourists fall victim. The only other rare vehicles were cattle trucks overloaded with migrant workers that raced past them next to the drainage canals full of fertilizer and gators. Route 27 was the spinal cord of Florida, practically vacant since the interstates, which took them up through towns with main streets that had the same early-evening closing hours since 1957. The only signs of life were the parking lights of local police cars on side streets, waiting for the local delinquents. Clewiston, Sebring, Clermont, Leesburg. An odd time to be passing through the sticks, but a Durango was the right vehicle to fit in.

Just after 2 A.M., Catfish pulled off 27 and turned into the countryside. Four-lane blacktop became a narrow, tree-canopied country road that dipped and rose across some of the few hills in all of Florida. Ten miles later, a wooden-plank fence began running along the side of the road. Painted white. The Durango gradually slowed and pulled onto the grass.

"What are you doing?" asked Gooch.

"Finding a quiet spot."

"Then what?"

"We go to sleep."

Chapter Eight

KEY LARGO

L oud music. Jukebox. Loud people. Bikers.
And others—locals, tourists, nomads—not exactly a melting pot but more like another of those polygonal tolerance zones common throughout the Keys.

A mug of draft beer tipped over.

"My bad," said Coleman.

"That's now a hat trick," said Serge. "I'll get more napkins."

"I'll get another beer."

He returned with a foamy draft in an ice-cold mug. "This bar rules," said Coleman. "People don't mess with you if you're just trying to enjoy yourself."

"You mean like that time you started howling at the top of your lungs, then took off your shirt, twirled it over your head, and danced like a drunken orangutan until they made you leave?"

"Exactly." Coleman wiped suds off his mouth with the back of an arm. "That bar was way too uptight."

"Coleman, it was a department store."

"What? Are you sure?"

"The lingerie section no less."

"So that's why so many chicks were around. I thought I was just popular."

"You did draw a crowd." Serge idly peeled the label off his bottle of water. "But you're right about one thing: This bar does rule. The Caribbean Club, established 1938 on the shore of Blackwater Sound by the great Florida pioneer Carl Fisher as a so-called poor man's fishing vacation camp. Last project before his death."

Coleman's head sagged over his beer with the neck posture of a vulture. "You're reading a newspaper again?"

Serge turned a page. "Correct. Next question."

"But you read the newspaper on Tuesday."

Another page turned. "They have a new one each day."

Coleman belched. "Are you making that up?"

"And I especially love reading papers in the Keys." Serge spread out the metro section. "It's the one place where most of the crime stories end with 'the suspect tried to escape police in a dinghy.' I always read the crime stuff first: Two perps culminated a burglary spree with thirty pounds of frozen chicken nuggets; woman seen burying a stolen purse on the beach; someone sitting on a bicycle attached to a car's roof in a transportation rack— while the vehicle was going over the Seven Mile Bridge. They're thinking alcohol might have been involved."

"I'll have to remember that one."

Another page. "But this isn't just entertainment. I'm working."

"Working."

"Learning new scams and lining up scores." Serge tapped a spot in the paper. "Like this dude. Got some address list of thousands of upscale restaurants in Florida, then mailed letters and a fake dry-cleaning bill for eleven dollars and fifty-three cents, saying a waiter spilled a drink on his jacket. It was such a small amount that most simply paid to avoid the fuss. Guy made twenty grand in three weeks."

"Good scam," said Coleman. "But you also mentioned scores."

"Roughly the same group of stories," said Serge. "Except I follow the old adage 'Shoot up, not down.' If you take advantage of people in higher tax brackets, I salute. Exploit the little people, and you go on my list for a late-night visit."

"To tell them it was wrong?"

"Might mention that in passing, but mainly I want money. My time's not free." Serge flipped a page to local bowling results. "Florida is the national scam capital, gorged with predators who target the weakest of the weak, especially old folks on fixed incomes. Newspapers are always reporting the arrests, but they're white-collar criminals with good lawyers and almost always make bail, which leaves their social calendar open for me."

"What do they do?"

"The list is endless," said Serge. "Like this one guy who drove around retirement communities and knocked on doors, holding a clipboard and wearing a short-sleeve dress shirt with an ID clipped to his pocket, which looked official because it was laminated. When some eighty-year-old woman answered, he'd start talking fast about roof problems he'd spotted from the street, and how you never noticed structural damage from leaks until the whole house fell on your head—he'd actually seen it, helping paramedics close the ambulance doors. But even if it didn't collapse right away, the code violations would add up faster than her

Social Security checks. And just as she was about to stroke out, he'd walk her to a chair inside, fetch a glass of water and say that lucky for her, he knew a crew in the area who could be there that afternoon before the big storm rolled in. Then he came back with a ladder, stomped around the roof for a half hour and drove off with a check for twelve thousand dollars."

"That's a good job," said Coleman.

"That's horrible," said Serge. "So when I read about his release from jail pending trial, it was an easy public records search to find his house. I figured it would only be neighborly to drop by to inspect *his* roof, which I thought was pretty magnanimous of me because it was two A.M. and he lived in a three-story mansion. And here's the thing I've learned about night visits. The people always start out pissed off because you woke them at some ungodly hour. But once you get a stranger up on the roof of a three-story building after midnight, they're suddenly your best friend: 'I'll do anything you ask.' Some people are prone to mood swings. So I said, 'But I haven't fixed your roof yet.' Didn't matter; he opened his safe right up and gave me all these gold coins and jewelry and bearer bonds. I thanked him and said I'd be following his trial closely and might come back to discuss defense strategy. Turns out he pled guilty and made full restitution with interest."

"Awfully nice of him."

"That's why I try not to judge."

Coleman nodded and looked around the inside of the bar. "Did they really shoot the movie *Key Largo* here like the sign says out front?"

"I wish, but that's for tourist consumption." Serge sat back as a waiter placed an iced coffee in front of him. "They'd have you believe Humphrey Bogart and Edward G. Robinson hashed it out right here where we're sitting so contentedly. But for the serious researcher, a depressing discovery that it was shot on a soundstage in Hollywood. Fact-checking cuts both ways."

"What do you mean?"

"See those tourists in the doorway?"

Coleman looked toward camera flashes. "Yeah, they seem happy. Kind of dazed, like starstruck."

"Because they don't know the truth. They think they're breathing Bogart's air." Serge's bottom lip pooched out. "But it's wrecked for me because I study history. I wish I could enjoy it the way they are . . ." He suddenly sat up straight. "And because I wish it, I will make it so . . . with the power of *coffee!*"

"Uh-oh. Here comes Underdog's Super Energy Pill."

Serge chugged his cup, placed his palms flat on the table and began vibrating with a sputtering noise.

"What are you doing?" asked Coleman.

"Rewinding the film in my brain. Looking for a loophole . . ." Serge pointed dramatically. "And there it is!"

Coleman's head swung around. "Where?"

"Inside my head. You'd have to watch the movie a hundred times, which luckily I have. There's some stock background footage they shot on this island to supplement the Hollywood reels. I'm now watching the aerial sequence during the black-and-white opening credits. A bus is heading up the Overseas Highway, past unmistakable geographical contours of this coastline." He waved a hand above the table. "Intrinsically speaking, this space was contained in celluloid frames of that 1948 classic. I have achieved bliss, Bogart's air, Hindus, round things, 'ride a painted pony, let the spinnin' wheel spin.'"

"Far out," said Coleman. He downed his mug. "I just remembered. What do you think our friend's doing back at Lake Surprise?"

Serge drained his bottled water and stood up from his stool. "Time to head for parts north until the heat cools down after the police find him."

"Why's that?" asked Coleman, gazing out the Caribbean Club's back windows at the rippling bay, where droplets began plopping into mild waves.

"Because it's starting to rain," Serge said with a smile. "Patience pays."

WISCONSIN

Earlier that morning, Patrick McDougall had stood in the front of his classroom, strumming an acoustic guitar like normal.

" . . . *Puff the Magic Dragon* . . ."

He couldn't stop yawning. Another late house call with one of his students' family.

The principal stuck his head in the door. "Pat, can I talk to you a second?"

"What is it?"

"In the hall . . ."

The principal looked terrible. "I feel terrible . . ." He gave Jack the news.

Change of plans. It affected all the dutiful teachers who had been laid off but decided to soldier on until the end of the school year. They now had to clear out their desks immediately, to make way for the new teachers who had just been hired because of the severe teacher shortage due to spending cuts.

At the other end of the hall, an assistant principal called Bar out of her classroom . . .

The McDougalls reached the staff parking lot at the same time. Pat stuffed his guitar in the back of the Geo. The beginning of the drive home was silent.

"What are we going to do?" asked Bar.

"Get other jobs."

"You say that like it's easy."

"We're blessed."

They parked in a crust of dirty snow. Pat was his typically buoyant self, like Bar usually was. But she seemed different now. He'd never seen her so stressed. The solution was obvious.

"You know what we need?" asked Pat. "To take a vacation."

"Okay, where do you want to go?"

"Florida."

"Florida?" said Bar. "I thought you meant like a quick weekend trip to Milwaukee."

"I mean a real vacation. We went to Milwaukee last year."

"I had fun," said Bar.

"I'm not saying that." Pat unlocked the front door and held it for his wife. "Just that we should really treat ourselves this time, a whole week, nice hotel, toes in the sand."

"Pat, I love the idea of getting away with you, but the timing couldn't be worse." Bar set her purse down. "We just walked in the door after losing both our jobs. And the heating bill's late. What about money?"

"Credit cards."

"I'd feel a lot more relaxed on vacation if we'd already secured our next jobs." She extended an arm toward the tundra outside the living-room window. "And with this economy, who knows how long that's going to take."

"That's why layoffs are the best time to take vacations."

"That doesn't make any sense," said Bar. "Just hit the road like a hobo? That's the responsibility level of a serial killer."

"Here's what's going to happen," said Pat. "We don't take this vacation, and then we easily get new jobs, become all caught up in that, and before we know it, it's another year and Milwaukee again. This is the perfect time to take that special trip we've always talked about. Spend some quality time together with no interruptions."

"Sounds expensive."

"We've been financially responsible our whole marriage." Pat walked over to the computer. "We even spent our honeymoon in Sandusky—and I'm not saying I didn't love it. It's just that we should do something extra nice for ourselves for once."

Bar could tell it would make her husband happy. And frankly her, too. She slowly began nodding. "Okay, I'm in. Let's do it."

"Now you're talking." Pat logged on to a travel Web site.

Bar leaned over his shoulder. "What part of Florida are you thinking about?"

Quick keystrokes. Photos of coconut palms. "I lived a few years near Fort Lauderdale. I remember it was beautiful, but you always take it for granted when you're a child."

"You told me your family moved up here when you were six."

"How much could it have changed?"

Bar pulled up a chair. They surfed the net together, talking a mile a minute, laughing and scrolling through chamber-of-commerce pitches. She was totally swayed. If it was this much fun just planning the vacation, imagine actually spending a week in paradise with Patrick.

"Here we are." Pat stopped on a page with pink and orange flowers. Mediterranean stucco, turquoise swimming pool. "This looks like a nice place."

"I can't really tell from the photos," said Bar. "They're all taken at weird angles like they're trying to hide something."

"The pictures looks great," said Pat. "And check out the price."

"That seems way too low." Bar narrowed here eyes. "There's got to be a catch."

"There is," said Pat. "Once the tourist season is over at the end of April, and the state starts heating up, most accommodations cut their rates. Sometimes in half."

"How hot?"

"Upper eighties, nineties."

"Sounds too hot."

"Listen, the place is on U.S. 1. That's right along the ocean." Pat leaned and typed. "Walk out of our room and we're splashing through the surf in ten seconds."

"I don't see the ocean in the pictures. You'd think they'd show that."

"Trust me." Pat entered a credit-card number on the reservation page. "I used to live there."

"Why is it called the Casablanca Inn?"

"They do that in Florida." More typing. "The Sands, the Dunes, the Sahara, the Algiers. It's a magnificent state in its own right, but some places think they also need an Arabian theme."

"Sounds more like a Vegas theme."

"Then there's the Polynesian, the Tahitian, the Hawaiian Tropic. That's the Pacific Ocean."

"I know."

Pat finished with their billing address, then moved his cursor over the "Submit Reservation" button. He turned to his wife and raised his eyebrows. "Your call. Say the word."

She smiled back. "Go for it!"

Click.

Chapter Nine

THE NEXT MORNING

D awn broke through the mangroves on an incoming tide.

The 911 call came from the cell phone of a fly fisherman working a shallow bank for snook.

The Key Largo police came in cars and boats, unspooling crime-scene tape and an orange berm in the water. Others high-stepped through the mangroves, collecting potential evidence in garbage bags, but mainly it was old beer cans and a few bleached Styrofoam crab-trap floats that had gotten loose and tangled in the roots.

The body was onshore, but only the feet and head were visible. Someone in a dress shirt leaned over the victim, taking photos of the undisturbed site. Then he gave a signal to the homicide guys that he had what he needed: disturb away.

"All right," said a lieutenant. "Start getting those things off him."

Investigators grunted as they strained to lift. No good way to get a grip; one slipped and sank a foot in the muck. Others in latex gloves snipped rope from mangrove roots, preserving the knots.

The lieutenant glanced sideways at the medical examiner standing next to him. "You might be able to make breakfast after all. Pretty obvious what we've got here."

"Yes and no."

"Why do you always have to say that?" asked the lieutenant. "This time it's more than clear: He was instantly crushed to death."

"No, he slowly suffocated."

"But look at all that weight. At least nine hundred pounds." He pointed at the growing pile the investigators had formed near the waterline. "How can you possibly say this was slow?"

The examiner looked up at the sky. "Because it rained last night."

"What's rain got to do with it?"

The examiner bent down and checked the capillaries in each eyeball. "He started with a maximum of forty pounds on him. Took several hours for it to reach nine hundred."

"Now I'm completely lost," said the lieutenant.

The examiner walked over to the pile and felt along a seam for a manufacturer's label. "These aren't regular sandbags. They're a newly developed type for easy, lightweight storage and transport. Two pounds each, dry, filled with special chemically reactive crystals that swell to a cement-hard thirty-five pounds when exposed to water." He looked at the sky again. "We're dealing with one of the worst kinds of killer."

"What kind's that?" asked the lieutenant.

"Patient."

THREE HUNDRED MILES NORTH

An hour before dawn, a mild, rhythmic thunder broke morning silence in the empty hills. The sound didn't originate from a stationary source, but swept by with Doppler effect. Then it was quiet again. Ten minutes later, the same thunder. And ten minutes after that. Perfectly spaced.

Eyelids fluttered open in a parked Durango.

Catfish sat up and shook his head to clear the cobwebs. Then he reached toward the passenger seat and poked a shoulder. "Gooch, wake up."

"Huh? What?"

Still not quite back among the living. Another poke. "Okay, I'm awake. Stop it." Gooch looked around the darkness. "What's that sound?"

Catfish pointed toward the other side of the wooden fence. The shape of a horse ran by, jockey standing high in the saddle.

Catfish could see the question on his subordinate's face. "It's morning warm-ups."

Gooch straightened the rest of the way. "What time is it? Where are we?"

"Six o'clock. Ocala."

Catfish started the Durango, drove fifty yards and turned up a private road. It went through a gate and under a giant wooden sign nailed up cockeyed on top of tall, crooked posts. An expensive sign company did that on purpose. It was from the bucolic section of its catalog. The sign's logo had an interlocking *D* and *G*.

Dry Gulch Farms.

"Isn't it kind of early to pay someone a visit?" asked Gooch.

"Not here. We actually overslept."

Five lengthy barns stood scattered across distant pastures. Lights already on. Catfish drove toward the nearest. A horse passed the car.

Gooch twisted all the way around in his seat. The farm went on in all directions beyond sight lines. "Look at the size of this spread! I didn't know there were places like this outside Kentucky."

"Most people don't," said Catfish. "But Ocala has one of the largest horse industries in the country with close to a thousand Thoroughbred farms. The Triple Crown hasn't been won for over thirty years, Affirmed in 1978, and he was raised right here in these hills."

"That's very interesting, but I don't know what it's got to do with our problems."

"Watch and learn."

The Durango pulled up to the barn and parked just outside the open stable doors.

A jockey trotted a horse inside, and Catfish followed.

The horse was greeted by a lanky man in jeans and a plaid shirt who took the reins from the jockey. He patted the horse on the side. The jockey removed the saddle, and the other person grabbed a thick, coarse blanket off a cedar bench near a stall and threw it over the back of the mare.

"Parsons! Parsons Gram! You son of a bitch!"

The man looked up and squinted into the darkness at the barn doors. "Catfish?"

Smiles broke out. They approached for a macho, back-slapping hug. Parsons held him out by the shoulders. "How long has it been? And what the hell are you doing here?"

"Thought I'd take me a little Florida vacation."

Parsons simultaneously pointed in opposite directions, east-west. "The beach is that way. And that."

"It's a working vacation."

"Uh-oh," said Parsons. "Here it comes now."

"I've got a business proposition."

Parsons shook his head. "I've heard this tune before. Look, I know we had some times—boy, did we. But I'm too old for that shit."

"Don't tell me you've settled down."

"Like Ward and June."

"At least hear me out."

Parsons folded his arms and smiled. "For entertainment value."

"What are you doing with your horse blankets these days?"

"Same as usual. Shipping them to Versailles."

"Versailles?" Gooch chimed in. "*Our* Versailles?"

"My manners," said Catfish, making way for his traveling companion to step forward. "This is Gooch Spivey, my assistant."

Parsons reached out and shook his hand. "Pleasure to meet."

"Why do you ship those blankets to Versailles?"

"For cleaning."

"But the shipping cost must be nuts," said Gooch.

Catfish and Parsons looked at each other and laughed.

Gooch glanced back and forth at the two. "Did I miss the joke?"

Parsons put a hand on his shoulder. "Son, these ain't regular horses. And those aren't regular blankets. Actually they are regular blankets, but you can't just clean them any old way . . ."

Catfish jumped in: "After morning warm-ups, you got to put blankets on the horses so they don't chill during the warm-down. And you can't transfer the blankets horse to horse because they could pick up parasites or skin diseases and such. It's just not done with Thoroughbreds."

"There are only a few places that can clean them right," said Parsons. "The shipping is nothing to protecting the investment."

"But who in Versailles?" asked Gooch.

"Remember our friend Bing, the firefighter who retired with partial disability?"

"Yeah?"

"He got an idea from the department," said Catfish. "After every blaze, they took the firefighters' bunker gear and mailed them to Chicago or Philly or some bullshit."

"Why?"

"Federal regulation. Potential carcinogens from burning building materials. They had to be cleaned according to very specific occupational standards before the department could put them back in use. Which means special washing machines that aren't very common, ten thousand a pop. So Bing bought one, and started doing his old department's gear for a lower price. Then other departments heard about it, and he bought a second machine and a third. Gear started coming in from Tennessee and Kansas. Ran the operation on the cheap out of an old gas station that had been shut down for leaky tanks."

"But what's that got to do with horses?" asked Gooch.

"Remember in the nineties when we had to lay low? The pot helicopters? And I had to do odd jobs in a stable?" said Catfish. "So I'm drinking margaritas one night in a Mexican restaurant in Lexington, and run into Bing and we catch up, and he tells me about the new business, and I'm like, you're sitting on a gold mine and don't even know it. He draws a blank, and I say, where are you living? Surrounded by horse farms. And I explained my work in the stables and the hassle with the blankets. His machines were perfect. More than perfect. Now he's got like thirty employees and a new big building near the Keeneland track. He owes me."

"I get it," said Gooch. "We ship all our problems in the horse blankets."

"Not a chance," said Parsons. "Whatever you're talking about shipping, count me out."

"But it will be like old times," said Catfish.

"I like the new times . . ."

A trotting sound outside the doors. A jockey brought in another stakes winner.

Parsons took the reins as the jockey dismounted. "Thanks, Eddie."

Catfish grabbed a second set of reins off an iron hook on the wall. He watched until the jockey was out of sight.

Then from behind, he wrapped the leather straps around Gooch's neck.

"Catfish!" yelled Parsons. "Have you lost your mind?"

Catfish was too busy with the reins; Gooch turned out to be stronger than he looked. He kicked backward and threw elbows. Eyes bugging out, gasping for breath, thrashing side to side. They crashed into a stable door and went down in the hay, Gooch on top.

Parsons grabbed a horseshoe and leaped. Bashing Gooch in the head over and over. The body went limp. Blood everywhere. Catfish released the reins and pushed the body off him. "Motherfucker!" He grabbed a hooked knife off a Peg-Board, repeatedly slashing Gooch's chest and stomach.

Parsons grabbed Catfish from behind. "He's dead, man. He's dead."

Catfish was still kicking and cursing the body as Parsons pulled him off. "Jesus Christ! What the hell's going on?"

"Let go of me!" Catfish jumped back down and ripped open Gooch's shirt. "They flipped him." He pulled a taped mini-microphone and wire off his chest."

"Oh my God!" Parsons grabbed his head. "They recorded all this?"

"Out of range." Catfish threw the listening device in a pail of water. "That's why I took these back roads, to make sure there was no tail."

Hoofbeats outside the barn.

"A jockey's coming!"

They quickly dragged the body into an empty stall just as another mare came in the stables.

Parsons took the reins. "Thanks, Willie."

The jockey dismounted tentatively, staring at blood spatter on their faces and shirts. "Are you okay?"

"A bird got trapped in here and was spooking the horses, but we got him."

The jockey didn't answer, just stared some more as he backed away.

A half hour later.

"The sun's already up," said Parsons.

"I'm digging as fast as I can," said Catfish. "You sure they're not going to develop this land?"

Parsons threw a shovel of dirt. "Been in the family forever. And I think there's some kind of historic horse designation . . . Duck."

Hoofbeats went by. They peered out of the woods as a jockey disappeared.

Catfish pulled something out of his pocket.

Parsons leaned against his shovel. "Why do you have smelling salts?"

"Because I just felt a pulse. Gooch is only unconscious." He waved the packet under his victim's nose. "Ain't no way I'm letting him sleep through this."

Gooch came out of it with a start and moan. "Ooooooo . . . What?" Thoughts of sitting up, but he was beaten too badly.

Catfish smashed the flat side of his shovel down on Gooch's nose. "Don't be passing out on me again! . . . After you stabbed me in the back, I'm going to enjoy every minute of this!"

"Ooooooo . . ." Gooch's head fell to the side and he instantly recognized the general dimensions of the rectangular hole they were digging. "Please! Catfish! Don't bury me!"

"Sucks to be you."

Parsons jabbed the spade back in the rich earth. "So you never told me what we're smuggling."

Catfish explained. "Had some problems lately with our I-95 pipeline."

"I saw those intercepted buses on the news." A shovel full of dirt went flying. "That was you?"

"We got a deal?"

"Sounds risky. And this ain't pot we're playing with."

"You know how many horse blankets are moving between Ocala and Kentucky? Nobody will ever suspect."

"I should have my head examined," said Parsons. "Okay, I'm in. When do you want to get started?"

"How about now? They didn't find our third bus." Catfish got on his hands and knees. "The goods are in my trunk."

They ducked again. The trotting sound went by and became faint.

Catfish looked up. "Shit, Gooch passed out again."

Another wave of the salts.

"Oooooo, where am I? . . ."

Parsons shook his head at Catfish. "A live burial and a life sentence of drugs in your car . . . Man, when you decide to drop in out of the blue, you *drop in*."

They rolled Gooch into the hole.

"Catfish! Stop! . . ."

"Shut up!" Catfish jumped down in the hole. "And you're just the kind of asshole who would pass out again. Well, I'm going to make sure you stay awake as long as possible, and then some." He violently crammed the smelling salts all the way up one of Gooch's nostrils.

"Ahhhh! Ahhhhhhhhhh!"

Catfish climbed out of the hole and picked up his shovel.

"No, Catfish! Don't throw dirt on me!"

He threw dirt on him.

Chapter Ten

A '76 Gran Torino cruised along Columbus Drive in West Tampa.

Serge finished off a large cup of 7-Eleven coffee. " . . . And another problem I have with Charles Manson. He created image problems with the British."

"Not the British again," said Coleman.

"Oh, yes," said Serge. "In jolly old England, a helter-skelter is a child's playground slide. Can you imagine what we'd think if some Liverpool mass-murder cult smeared their victims' blood on the walls to spell 'teeter-totter'?"

"It's just embarrassing," said Coleman.

"Manson is the gift that keeps on giving." Serge checked his rearview, then checked it again.

Coleman lowered his joint. "The police?"

"No, a Toyota. The driver's acting suspicious."

"How?" asked Coleman.

Serge looked back again. "Keeps checking his mirrors."

"He just changed lanes," said Coleman. "Coming up on our left."

"I've seen this movie before." Serge took his foot off the gas. "He's making sure there are no witnesses behind us."

"Carjacking?" asked Coleman.

"Nope, the classic Swoop-and-Squat."

The joint came back up. "What's that?"

"Tampa is now the national insurance-fraud champ. And one of the oldest but still effective methods is the Swoop-and-Squat. The scam artist targets a victim and tails him until conditions are optimal. Then he zooms past and cuts back in front of him and hits the brakes. It's nearly impossible to avoid a rear-end crash. And under Florida law, the person in back is automatically at fault in the accident because theoretically the person in front has no control over someone following too close. If you're lucky, they'll just go for collision damage; if not, they'll fake whiplash and jam you up for thousands in medical, pain and suffering . . . But I've developed a foolproof strategy to not only defeat this tactic, but punish the scofflaw and hopefully illuminate the error of his ways."

"He's racing past us," said Coleman.

"The Swoop."

"Now he cutting back in. He's hitting his brakes."

"The Squat." Serge was already applying his own brakes.

"Wow," said Coleman. "You were right. He *was* trying to make us crash."

"The fucker," said Serge. "It's like Manson all over again."

"You're really hung up on that."

"It's my conscience," said Serge. "I've never admitted this to anyone, but I secretly dug the Manson chicks."

"Really?" said Coleman. "Me, too."

"You're kidding," said Serge. "And all this time I've been thinking there was something wrong with me."

"No, those babes definitely had it going on." Coleman took a hit. "They smoked weed. Very hot."

"But only until they shaved their skulls and carved Xs in their foreheads," said Serge. "If you're on a dinner date with someone like that, your eyes just involuntarily drift upward."

"That's always awkward," said Coleman.

"Then you nervously fill up on bread sticks and don't have room for the T-bone."

"What about punishment?"

"I think some of the women got out of jail."

"No, I mean the guy in the Toyota." Coleman pointed at the windshield with his roach. "You said you were going to teach him a lesson."

"Oh, right," said Serge. "I'm still on it. I'm following him until I can employ my own patented maneuver: Serge's Squat-and-Scoot."

"What's that?"

"First I keep tailing him until we come to a red light with a bunch of other cars already waiting."

"That light up there just turned red," said Coleman. "The Toyota's stopping."

"And there are a bunch of cars in front of him," said Serge. "Now here's the Squat . . ."

The Gran Torino eased to a halt in front of a motel converted into an office complex.

"What about the Scoot?" asked Coleman.

" . . . And then I ease forward ever so gently until our bumpers are in contact."

"I just felt us touch."

"And now I give a quick burst of gas, followed by perfectly timed brakes . . ." Serge used both feet simultaneously on the pedals with coordinated heel-toe action. " . . . Sending the Toyota crashing into the rear of the car in front of him, but leaving us back here unscathed."

"And since he's the car in the rear?" said Coleman.

"He gets the blame—no insurance money." Serge cut the steering wheel. "And then we just back up and take a left to depart down this side street so the guy can't point fingers when the police arrive . . ."

Coleman turned around as they drove off. "He's grabbing his neck. I think he's screaming in pain."

Serge aimed his camcorder. "We don't even have to fake this."

A loud noise made Arnold Lip glance up from a patient folder and out the window of his examination room. A Toyota had rear-ended someone at a traffic light; a Gran Torino whipped down a side street.

Lip swung a rubber hammer.

"Ow! Bastard!"

Lip clicked his pen open. "Bruised eyeball."

Later that afternoon, an attorney with a Tour de France haircut knocked on the reception window.

Lip slid it open. "Oh, Hagman, glad you're here. Listen, I think I've got a patient who's actually injured. What do I do?"

The lawyer shook his head. "He *is* injured. One of our guys was pulling a Swoop-and-Squat and went and fucking rear-ended someone. Hurt him pretty bad. Is it too much to ask to drive well enough to cause a simple wreck?"

Lip pointed over his shoulder. "How'd the victim end up in here?"

"Luckily, the accident happened right outside our building, and I was able to run out there and tell the banged-up driver that I'd represent him and get some big bucks."

"You can get him a lot of money?"

"No, our guy's at fault. Make it go away."

Lip looked at the file. "The patient can't move his head, has second-degree facial burns from the air bag and is spitting up some blood."

"Tell the insurance company it's a pre-existing condition."

Lip made a notation. "You're the doctor." He began closing the reception window.

Hagman grabbed the edge to hold it open. "That's not why I came to see you. I've got another proposal . . ."

Arnold finished listening to the concept. "Isn't that illegal?"

"We're already at that dance," said the lawyer. "What's the difference?"

Arnold shrugged.

"Good," said the attorney. "We'll get started tomorrow. I know some people who will play ball . . ."

The next morning, Arnold and Hagman arrived at the same time in matching Porsche 955s. They parked in adjoining spaces and waved cheerfully at each other.

"Like your new lifestyle?" asked the lawyer.

The doctor buffed a spot on the hood with his sleeve. "Yes, thank you."

"There's a lot more where this came from."

"So when, uh, do you think we'll start seeing a return on what you mentioned yesterday?"

"It's going to be big, but it'll take some time . . ."

Before it had time:

Hagman Reed locked up his office at the end of the day and headed down to his coupe.

Arnold was waiting.

"You don't look so hot," said Hagman. "What's the matter?"

"I need a lawyer."

"Why?"

"I was indicted this afternoon. I need someone to represent me."

"That's legal stuff. I don't know any of that."

"What am I going to do?"

"First off, what did they indict you for?"

For greed. Arnold liked the car, and new clothes and champagne. He'd gotten the taste, and he wanted more. So he bought a second Porsche. He needed the second because he totaled the first after getting hold of a friend and staging their own little accident. Skidded into each other at a remote boat ramp and sank both vehicles. No small percentage of cash from someone else's wreck this time—they got to keep it all.

But here was the thing: When a two-car crash involves people who know each other, it's a major red flag to insurance investigators. Hagman had taught him that. So when the police accident investigators arrived at the scene, Arnold and his buddy said they'd never laid eyes on each other in their entire lives.

Then the cops started snooping around, just because both accident victims' driver's licenses listed addresses in the same apartment building. On the same floor.

"Really," said Arnold. "That's quite a coincidence . . . What do you mean, 'Do I still want to stick with my story?' We really don't know each other."

Then the detective confronted Arnold with Facebook photos they'd posted of themselves posing together at a Rays baseball game.

"Is that who that is?" Arnold asked the detectives. "Wow, what are the odds?"

And now Hagman and Arnold stood in conspiracy, whispering loudly between their Porches in the parking lot of a converted motel.

"Will you keep your voice down?" said the attorney. "They could be listening right now . . ." He twirled a finger over his head. " . . . With those parabolic microphones."

"But I can't go to jail," whimpered Arnold.

"You won't," said Hagman. "They just want to shut you down. So you'll lose your license in exchange for a plea to something that will get you a suspended sentence."

"Lose my license!" Arnold grabbed the hood of his car with both hands. "What will I do for money? I need food to live!"

"Don't piss yourself," said Hagman. "And put your hand over your mouth."

"What?" asked Arnold. He couldn't hear well because the attorney had a hand over his own mouth.

"I said put your hand over your mouth." Hagman twirled a finger again. "They have lip-readers with binoculars."

The doctor complied.

"You calm now?"

The doctor nodded.

"Good, because remember that other venture I mentioned? It's still on."

"With the police all over us?"

The attorney shook his head. "We'll just do what I did last time. When they cracked down on insurance fraud in Miami, I simply moved up to Tampa."

"But we're already in Tampa."

"You idiot! I'm talking about going back south." Hagman glanced left and right. "And here's the important part because I was depending on your medical license. But since you're now out of commission, do you know any other doctors who might play ball?"

Arnold nodded again.

"Are they any good?" asked Hagman.

"Not really."

"Excellent. Now I want you to follow my instructions very carefully . . ."

And the attorney laid it out point by point. When he was done, Arnold scratched his head. "I'm moving to Fort Lauderdale?"

"Live wherever you want down there. Fort Lauderdale, Boca Raton, a tree house, just get your ass moving."

"But I don't have the kind of money this requires—"

"I promised I'd stake you, remember? I'll wire all the cash we'll need to get started. You just make sure you come up with your doctor friends."

"Where will you be?"

"Right behind you," said Hagman. "You're the second doctor connected to me that's going down, so I'm not pressing my luck by sticking around here."

Crash.

Arnold looked toward the wreck in the street, then raised his eyebrows toward Hagman. "Our guys?"

The attorney unlocked his Porsche. "Let's get the hell out of here."

Chapter Eleven

A FEW DAYS LATER

Serge stood with his back flat against a wall. Eyes big with dread. His arms were spread wide, also plastered against the wall. He was outdoors, a hundred feet off the ground. The building was round. His feet inched sideways.

Coleman walked slowly behind him, hitting a secret flask and filming with the camcorder. "I didn't know you were afraid of heights."

"I'm not," said Serge, incrementally sliding along. "I'm reenacting my 1967 fear of heights. One of my earliest memories was my kindergarten teachers taking us up here on a field trip. It's the magnificent Jupiter Inlet Lighthouse, built on an Indian shell mound, her oil lamp lit for the first time on July tenth, 1860."

Coleman took a swig and aimed the camera over the railing. "We are pretty high up."

"It was a different era." Serge slid another step. "People weren't as obsessed with safety back then, like not making kids wear seat belts, or giving an entire class of five-year-olds a bunch of soda and sending them up to run around the balcony of a hundred-and-eight-foot lighthouse. I remember the other kids acting nuts and horsing around, and I'm thinking we're going to have a couple empty sleeping mats for nap time this afternoon. Of course, the adults were conscientious and told us to stay away from the railing. None of the other tykes listened, but I took their warning to the extreme, because that's where I live. So I pasted myself against the building like I'm doing now. I've got a long history of ultra-compliance with authority."

"*You?*"

"Don't say that like you're so surprised." Serge slid some more. "Another example: That same year there was a total solar eclipse. Huge deal, everyone talking about it for weeks. And they kept stressing the dangers of looking at the eclipse and the hundreds of people who went blind every time one came around. Except they didn't mention how long you had to look. So naturally I thought it was instant, like Lot's wife turning to salt."

Coleman took another swig. "Is it?"

"No, but I was only five. What did I know? Then the TV people gave tips on perfectly safe ways to view an eclipse, like poking holes in a shoe box. And I'm thinking: 'Risk going blind just to see a fuzzy image on a piece of cardboard? Fuck that.' But mainly I was worried that I'd simply forget when the eclipse was, because forgetting important stuff is a kid's main job, and then I'd be out riding my banana bike with training wheels and accidentally happen to look up, and after I finally feel my way back to the house: 'Mom, Dad, please don't be mad at me . . .' So I went in the carport and got the strongest piece of rope I could find, then I tied one end to a leg of the coffee table and the other to my ankle. Plus a backup rope in case I managed to pull free after forgetting why I had tied myself to the furniture, because my mind tended to jump around a lot back then. And I stayed inside all day and watched TV."

"What did your parents say when they came home?"

"Something like, 'What in the hell is going on in here?' I answered: 'Not staring at the sun.'"

"Your parents said *H-E*-double-hockey-sticks in front of a little kid?"

"Can't really blame them," said Serge. "Because we had these little lizards that ran all over our yard, and in the days leading up to the eclipse, I captured as many as I could, because I didn't want the lizards going blind. So in addition to walking into the room and seeing me lashed to the coffee table, dozens of lizards were tied up with kite string around their necks. You'll have to understand if my parents didn't see the logic right away."

"What did they do?"

"Sat me down for a calm talk, just like they did when I got confused about what 'allergic' meant. A month before, while we were finger-painting in kindergarten, I heard Susie Mapleton say she was allergic to bumblebee stings, and I thought it meant to be afraid. So then some of the other classmates added that they were allergic to peanuts and eggs and mold, and I start grabbing them by the shoulders and shaking hard: 'For God's sake, man, get a grip on yourself!' "

"Serge, you're moving so slow. I thought you said we were in a rush to get someplace."

"We are." Serge slid slowly. "Just keep filming."

"Got it." He pressed the viewfinder to his right eye.

Serge slid another step. "We have to begin my reality show in Jupiter because, as a child, this defined the northern limits of my global sphere of influence."

Coleman continued filming as Serge gradually circled the balcony. "Then why did we drive way up north of here on I-95, just to turn around and head south?"

"To experience driving down to Florida through the eyes of someone who's never been to Florida." Serge slithered along. "That's the theme of my reality show: I'm the Native Tourist. I'm going to track my life in Florida by roaming the coast and visiting all the great attractions."

"Why?"

"How many times have you heard the cliché 'I've lived in New York City my whole life but have never been up the Empire State Building,' or 'Born and raised in Possum Shoals but never seen that woman's goiter shaped like Wayne Newton.' I mean to change all that! Show people the possibilities of what's right under their noses each week by moving from town to town, getting into jams, meeting strangers, lending them help from the goodness of our hearts."

"Helping them how?"

"Out of the jams we've gotten them into. It's only polite."

"That was a pretty weird drive down the interstate. There must have been a million billboards for pain clinics. I wrote down the phone numbers."

"A relatively recent phenomenon." Serge scooted around to the east side of the tower. "We can now add to our list of visitors the OxyContin Tourists. And those billboards must be for legit operations because they're being pretty obvious, so imagine how many more are under the radar. Those signs start at the top of the state, between the population centers, facing north on the interstate, nestled among all the other billboards that are only designed to reach out-of-state travelers driving south into Florida. So now you got signs for truck stops, motels with free Wi-Fi, citrus stands, fast food, and pictures of car crashes with jagged red lettering to remind people that they might be in pain from something that happened in Cleveland. I mean how does that work? Are this many people suddenly making major medical decisions on vacation? When you're driving to Niagara Falls, do you see a hundred miles of billboards for joint-replacement surgery, 'Call 1-800-HIP-OUCH'? . . . Or is it an impulse thing: 'Let's see, I've been on the road for hours, so I need to stop for gas, use the restroom, get a Big Mac and develop a drug problem.' "

Coleman capped his flask and looked down at Serge's feet. "Why are you stopping?"

"To take in the view. It's spectacular!" Serge swept an arm across the horizon. "You've got a perfect day over the Atlantic, the inlet to the south with fishing boats motoring out of the Loxahatchee River and through those jetties. I've never seen it from this high up before."

"What?" said Coleman. "You never saw this before? But I thought you came up here on a kindergarten trip."

"Right, I came up here. But I kept my eyes closed tight the whole time I slithered around the top with my back against the wall."

"Why?"

"Because I was halfway up the lighthouse stairs with my class, and I suddenly wondered: 'Was that eclipse supposed to be today or tomorrow? Dang, I was busy playing with my turtle.' So to be on the safe side, I never opened my eyes up here." Serge resumed scooting again. "But that was typical during the Cold War. Kids today have it made, but growing up back then during our struggle with the Russians was a lot more intense. First, you had to learn how to hide under your desk in case a hydrogen bomb went off near the swing set. Then, one morning you're riding to kindergarten singing 'The wheels on the bus go round and round,' and the next minute they're running you through some rigorous stress test that involves not falling off a light-house during an eclipse. Back then they had to plan for every scenario."

"Your kindergarten teachers did that on purpose?"

"Definitely, because they pulled me aside when we got back from the field trip." Serge finished circling the top and reached the door. "They wanted to know why I was behaving so differently from everyone else on top of the lighthouse, because clearly I was the only kid getting it right. So I told them everything, even rounding up lizards for their eyesight, and that's prob-ably the first time they realized I was more advanced than the other children because they sent me to see a special doctor." Serge began heading down the light-house's corkscrew staircase at a rapid clip. "We'll have to move fast now to make up for all the time we wasted up there. Our reality show is running up some hefty production costs. But our conversation on the balcony gave me some ideas. This whole pain-clinic deal got me thinking. Don't ask me how I know, but I just have this vibe that something big is about to go down in that area. And it might involve a large payday for us."

"Money," said Coleman. "Cool." They reached the bottom of the lighthouse and headed for the gift shop.

"But what ever happened when the kindergarten teachers sent you to see that doctor?"

"He said he was going to put me on some special pills, which I assume were to make me more advanced. Then he asked me if I was allergic to anything, and I said, 'Just grizzly bears, sharks, eclipses, atomic bombs and Old Man Clancy down the street with the cloudy eye. But that's it; nothing ridiculous.'"

FORT LAUDERDALE

A Porsche 955 pulled into a strip mall on U.S. Highway 1.

A lawyer with a Lance Armstrong haircut looked for a parking slot but had to keep driving. "Holy Jesus, look at all these cars!"

After parking behind a lawn-ornament store on the next block and walking back in the heat, Hagman Reed entered a newly opened pain clinic that looked a lot like the insurance-fraud clinics back in Tampa. Chock-full of patients, neck braces, old magazines with candid fat photos of the stars on vacation. Hagman went straight down the hall.

"Sir?" a receptionist called after him. *"Sir! You can't just—"*

He ignored her and walked past a row of doctor's offices, peeking inside each, diplomas on the walls from Guyana, Cancún, the Caymans, French Guyana. The diplomas had regal crests with toucans and tree frogs. Hagman reached a final, closed door at the end of the hall and opened it.

Arnold Lip sat behind his desk, playing a video game pitting farm animals against fighter jets.

Hagman plopped down in a chair without invitation. "Damn, when you said this place was hopping . . ."

A chicken exploded. Arnold wiggled the joystick. "Can hardly keep up with demand."

"Are the other three clinics the same?"

"Four clinics," said Arnold.

"Four? And all in this short amount of time? I can't believe it!"

"No, wait, three," said Arnold. "No, four. No . . . fuck it, I can't remember."

"You don't know how many clinics we have?"

"First, one got raided, then we opened two more, then another got raided . . ."

"But you're doing everything I said to firewall us, right? All the legal precautions?"

Arnold nodded.

"Including that window?"

Arnold looked back over his shoulder, then nodded again.

"Good." Hagman relaxed in his chair. "I see you're still hanging your diploma despite losing your license."

Arnold looked back at the framed parchment. "I still graduated."

Hagman glanced upward in mild condescension. "Whatever gets you off . . . But where'd you go to school? The thing looks like a sweepstakes entry form."

"It *is* a sweepstakes entry form. I lost my diploma. Most of the patients can't read English anyway. Half are migrant day laborers who only speak Spanish; the rest are Kentucky day laborers who spit a lot."

"Kentucky?"

"Who would have thought?" said Arnold. "They fill up buses and run them down. Apparently there's a huge OxyContin market in that area. West Virginia, southern Ohio."

"But where do these bums get the money to pay for their trips and doctor visits?"

"It's the other way around," said Arnold. "*They're* paid. Then as soon as they fill the prescriptions, the trips' organizers confiscate the pills and stash them in steel lockboxes in the luggage compartment—I've seen it—an outrageous pile of these orange plastic vials. The cops know what's going on, and they're always going on TV after the latest raid, claiming that they're winning the war. But it's like a tidal wave; they're completely outmatched. As long as we have the will to keep opening clinics"—the ex-doctor pushed a ledger book across the desk—" . . . there's no way we can lose."

Hagman whistled at the numbers. "I heard this was big, but I had no idea."

"Neither did I."

"But how'd you get so many doctors so quickly? I know you knew people in Tampa, but down here?"

Arnold pressed a button on top of the joystick. "I knew one guy who had a cousin over here, who knew two more guys, and it just snowballed. Everyone had heard about the clinics and couldn't wait to get in."

Hagman pointed at the video screen. "The goat."

Boom.

"What do I do now?" asked Arnold.

"The pig on the hill."

"No, I mean I'm bored." A stealth bomber swooped over a barn. "I lost my license, so all I do is sit back here the whole day."

Hagman pointed north. "I'm opening a new law practice up the street."

"You're going to practice law?"

"Not a chance. I'm going to the beach," said Hagman. "But I'll still be your attorney."

"Cool," said Arnold. "So I can call you if I get in any trouble with the pain clinics?"

"No, only call me if you're not in trouble. But anything to do with the pain clinics, stay as far the fuck away from me as you can. Just because I'm your attorney, don't assume you can come to me with problems."

"I'm thinking of opening another business."

"Bad idea," said Hagman. "We're getting a big enough profile with this operation; we don't need to press our luck with a second scheme."

"Not another scheme. A totally legal business."

"Oh, I understand now. Then you set fire to the building."

"No, I mean really legit. An honest operation."

Hagman thought a moment, then shook his head. "How is that supposed to make any money? Sounds suspicious."

"I don't know." Arnold twisted the joystick. "But I've heard about such places."

"I think that's an urban myth."

"Maybe I'll just invest with someone already running something," said Arnold. "See how it's supposed to work from someone with experience."

The attorney sat back and ruminated on the concept. Then his thoughts drifted to the Kentucky bus pipeline. Inside his brain: A financial model rotated in 3-D.

Lasers crisscrossed and connected dots. He tapped his chin. "You know, I think there's a way to squeeze some more money out of this. A lot more."

A dairy cow launched a shoulder-mounted rocket. "What do you have in mind?"

"Okay . . ." Hagman leaned against the front of the desk. "Here's my plan. I know these guys who work the sugarcane fields—"

From down the hall: *"Raid!"*

"Quick!" yelled the lawyer. "The window!"

Arnold pulled a lever, and special springs jettisoned the glass. They crawled out through the hole.

Chapter Twelve

PALM BEACH COUNTY

A thumb pressed the record button on a camcorder. Coleman's nose filled the viewfinder screen.

"Serge? How can I tell what I'm filming?"

"By turning the camera around the right way."

"I'll try it," said Coleman. "Hey, I can see stuff now."

The '76 Gran Torino headed south on U.S. 1 and took a right at Indiantown Road.

Coleman filmed across a small drawbridge. "You promised we'd hit a bar right after climbing that lighthouse."

"And we will." Serge made a right. "This is the pilot of my reality show. I'm continuing to trace the touchstones of my childhood and getting misty-eyed. Reality shows require crying or almost crying."

"I've seen that." Coleman zoomed in on Serge's profile. "This one chick was competing to become a restaurant cook and fucked up the gravy. Completely lost her mind, and the camera crew's banging on the bathroom door for her to come out, and she's screaming, 'No, leave me the fuck alone! I just want to die.' I was thermonuclear stoned, thinking: 'Gravy is intense.'"

"Then wait till you see my show." The Gran Torino made another left. "There's our first stop, 113 Center Street, Ralph's Stand Up Bar."

"You went to bars as a child?"

"No, but this is my home county, and Ralph's is the oldest bar. I need to set up the backstory for my reality show from the time before my birth. They do it in all biography specials that start with century-old movie footage of people walking comically fast outside steel factories, fish markets and Chinese opium dens full of wrinkled old women with encouraging grins passing long pipes to the white man. And suddenly a baby's born that makes everyone own a phonograph."

"I think it's the same story every time."

"It is." Serge cut the wheel. "Here we are."

"I see a bunch of Harleys parked out front." Coleman raised the camcorder. "*Only* Harleys."

"And now a Gran Torino . . . Make sure to get plenty of stock exterior shots."

Coleman panned across a plain tan concrete building with plain black letters announcing the bar's name. The only distinguishing feature was a life-size silhouette next to the door of a cowhand leaning against a post.

"What do you do in Ralph's Stand Up?"

"Stand up. That's why I love Ralph's. You stand up at the bar like it's a Wild West saloon."

"But all the motorcycles," said Coleman. "Is it safe?"

"Of course," said Serge. "But it never hurts to hedge bets in a local bikers' bar." He popped open the trunk and grabbed a pair of shirts, tossing one to Coleman. "That's why I always wear black biker T-shirts to fit in. Of course, the shorts and sneakers make you not fit in, so the key is to constantly attract attention to your upper body."

"How do you do that?"

"By waving your arms over your head and pointing at your upper body."

Coleman removed his current T-shirt of a marijuana leaf over a quote: "I like skinny chicks, but never turn down a fattie." He pulled the new black shirt over his arms and popped his head up through the neck hole, then looked down at the front. A classic skull and crossbones with wings coming off the sides of the head in the shape of Florida. A pirate banner over the top: SERGE'S DISCIPLES. Below, a motto: "I follow nobody."

Coleman looked up. "Where'd you get these?"

"A gift from some codependents I met in the Keys. They started tailing me, thinking I had the answers. I do, but you can only take codependents in small doses for reasons obvious in their name."

"But 'Disciples'? 'Follow nobody'?" said Coleman. "That doesn't make any sense."

"It's existential. The bikers will get it. They're road philosophers." Serge pointed toward the intersection. "Here comes one now."

The signature thunder of a Harley Twin-Cam 88 Fathead growled up the street. The rider pulled into a slot and dismounted. Barrel chest, American-flag head scarf, leather jacket and crusty jeans. His boots jangled with spurs.

He walked toward Serge and squinted at his T-shirt, then looked down more oddly at his shorts and shoes.

"Up here!" said Serge, waving arms in the air. "I seek acceptance of the road philosophers."

The biker stared at the T-shirt again. " 'Disciples'? 'Follow nobody'? That doesn't make any sense."

"So you get it!" said Serge. "To Kierkegaard." He held his hand out for a fist bump that never came. The biker went inside.

Serge turned to Coleman. "Now that I've officially been accepted, it's time to seal the deal by entering the bar with the swagger of total confidence."

"But that guy didn't swagger."

"Because he's a real biker." Serge practiced by pacing in front of the building. "How am I doing?"

"Looks like you have jock itch."

"That means I've perfected my swagger. Let's rock. And because it's a locals bar, keep your presence as low-key as possible to show ultimate respect. Our goal is to minimize their staring."

Serge walked inside, loping bowlegged and dangling arms over his head like a chimpanzee.

He bellied up to the counter. "I love these joints at this time of day. Blazing hot and bright outside; in here, dark and breezy cool with the door open to remind you of the difference. Venerable wooden walls and graffiti."

"It's a bar," said Coleman.

The bartender came over and took their order.

Coleman's face was a question mark. "You didn't order water. You always order a bottle of water."

"Except in a local bikers' bar. You never know. So I order a Diet Coke, and the bartender comes over with a rocks glass. The regulars are sipping beer and thinking, 'Who is this mysterious stranger drinking hard liquor in the morning? Maybe that swagger really wasn't fungus.' "

"Serge, they have chairs."

"It's better to stand."

The bartender came back with a shot of bourbon for Coleman. He placed an empty plastic cup in front of Serge, along with a can of Diet Coke.

"Serge, he brought the can. And he didn't even pop the top."

"A public-relations nightmare. Quick, call attention to your upper body."

Coleman waved his arms. Serge turned his back and furtively poured the soda.

"Now, if I can just get rid of this can before anyone else sees . . ." He jump-shotted it toward a wastebasket behind the bar. It clanged off the wall and the rim of the garbage can.

"Serge, it's still bouncing on the floor and making a lot of noise."

"Not the mystique I was going for." He placed a small canvas pouch on the bar and pulled a zipper.

"What's that?" asked Coleman.

"A Bible cover."

"But it's camouflaged."

"For evangelical campers." Serge unfolded it on the counter. "There's a compass on one of the pouches in which I can store my harvest of matchbooks, souvenir pins and poker chips. I must buy anything with a compass, even though I don't need one in Florida unless I'm performing renegade survey work. Bible covers are the perfect size for my notebooks and guides and pens. We need to write our first script."

"Scripting reality?"

Serge leaned over with a ballpoint. "My show will distinguish itself with lists."

"What kind of lists?"

"You know: best of, worst of, one hundred reasons why making lists prevents you from doing something meaningful. Let's start . . ."

"But why does your show need them?"

"Because reality TV needs controversy, and the whole purpose of lists is to start fights. People always argue over them, ever since the beginning of time. You know the first list?"

Coleman knocked back a shot of whiskey and shook his head.

"The Seven Wonders of the Ancient World. Largely credited to Philo of Byzantium. But since it was compiled in the third century BC, I'm guessing he called it the Seven Wonders of the *Modern* World. And even back then it pissed people off."

"Why?"

"Because Philo did his research at the largest library of the time in Alexandria. And some people got the notion that the fix was in. At the top of the list, the Great Pyramid of Giza in Egypt—no argument there—and at the bottom, the lighthouse at Alexandria. The early Persians are like, 'I thought we outgrew this hometown bullshit in the Neolithic. I mean, you can't be serious. *That* lighthouse? When we've got the Apadana Palace of Persepolis? What are we, fucking Mesopotamians over here?'"

"What are your lists going to be?"

"Everything! Best beaches, best bars, best lighthouses—and I'm putting the one we just climbed ahead of Alexandria. That should start some fistfights. My list, my call."

Coleman looked over Serge's shoulder. "What are you writing now?"

"List of best things to do at a beach. Number one: build sand castles with real cannons on the walls. Number two: play water hockey except with special gloves and live jellyfish. Number three: line up lucrative scores to take down, potentially involving pain clinics . . ." He clicked the pen shut.

"Why did you stop writing?" asked Coleman.

"This reads like all the other mainstream beach lists. I need inspiration." He zipped his Bible case closed.

"And we've got some driving ahead. A lot of golf country to clear before we hit the landing zone, so better get a move on."

"Do we need to do anything careful leaving the bar like when we came in?"

"No," said Serge. "First impressions are important, but so is efficiency. That's the whole key to life: Fuck what people think when you're leaving the room."

Serge backed out of the bar, taking a dozen photos, then sprinted down the sidewalk as an incoming jet roared overhead.

The jet was a southbound flight descending from thirty-five thousand and buffeting through a heavy bank of cotton-ball clouds.

"I never want to connect out of Atlanta again," said Barbara McDougall.

"We'll remember for next time," said Patrick.

The airplane broke into the clear at ten thousand and banked over the Palm Beaches, following the coastline south.

Both their faces filled the oval window. Below: tiny yachts with little white wakes. More white foam where waves rolled into the sand.

"Look at all the condos," said Bar.

"I don't remember this," said Pat.

"What's the huge place on the water with the golf course?"

"The Breakers. That I remember."

A tap on Pat's shoulder. He turned around. "Yes?"

It was the flight attendant. "I'm sorry, but the seat-belt sign is on. We're preparing to land."

Before they knew it, the Boeing 737 had touched down at Fort Lauderdale International and was guided toward the gate by a man with a pair of orange batons.

As the McDougalls stepped from the plane onto the jetway, a blast of scorching hot air came through a seam in the accordion arm.

"We're definitely in Florida," said Pat.

If they weren't sure, the air-side was a gauntlet of tiny shops selling tropical T-shirts, key chains, refrigerator magnets and citrus candy. Bar stopped and picked up a coffee mug with her name spelled in palm trees. "Should I get something?"

"We have all week. And it's twice as expensive in here."

"Look, key-lime marmalade."

"We need to get to the luggage before someone steals our stuff."

"Is crime that bad here?"

"No," said Pat. "It's just good to be careful."

Chapter Thirteen

U.S. 1

The '76 Gran Torino sped away from Ralph's Stand Up Bar and cruised south from Jupiter, down through the most golf-rich terrain in the country, where top-flight courses take up as much real estate as the homes. Mirasol, Old Marsh, Turtle Creek, Frenchman's Creek, River Bend, Tequesta, Loxahatchee, and the granddaddy of them all, PGA National.

"I used to play golf," said Serge. "It's a frightening game. Forget football or even NASCAR." He whistled in awe. "Golf takes it to the brink."

"That bad?"

"It's the mental component. They try to hush it up, but the game can destroy the strongest men. Every year, dozens of ugly psychotic breaks. Frustration builds over a lifetime until a tee shot lands in the water of a sadistic island hole, and then a hedge-fund manager hurls all his clubs like tomahawks at the other guys in plaid knickers before stripping off all his clothes and making 'snow angels' in a sand trap, prompting a special unit from the pro shop to hustle him away through secret underground doors. Fortunately, I have the perfect emotional composition to excel at golf."

"You don't seem the golf type," said Coleman.

"That's what the other players said until they saw me in action." Serge uncapped a thermos of coffee and chugged. "Let's face it, golf is a slow sport. Which isn't good for my constitution, so I tried to spice it up. First, since it's called a sport, I'd run all the time, sprinting up fairways, hurdling small water hazards, hitting a nine iron and racing the ball to the pin, until they asked me not to run. So I got a golf cart and hung out the side with my club, playing like polo, but they didn't dig that either. Finally I decided to aim for all the sand traps, because they're like beaches and blasting out of one is the most dramatic shot in golf, but I made it even more dramatic. Instead of a sand wedge, I used a driver, just exploding with this massive one wood like an artillery shell had hit the trap. Of course, it took me seven or eight shots since it was the wrong club, and then they asked me to leave because I was allegedly 'putting an insane amount of sand on our greens.' See, that's the thing about golf, a lot of technical rules you'd never think of."

"Why'd you quit?"

"Because I love Florida golf courses too much." Serge took a left on PGA Boulevard and swigged more coffee. "We're different from clubs everywhere else in the world. Even if you don't play the sport, do yourself a favor and fork over the fees just to walk our great courses, especially the ones that incorporate the state's raw beauty. I was constantly dizzy from natural intoxication: All manner of palms and palmettos and banyans, birds of paradise, crape myrtles, water lilies in the wetlands, reeds, and alligators, coral snakes, newts, geckos . . ."

"Serge . . ."

" . . . Different geckos, herons, spoonbills, ibis feeding in the rough, gopher tortoises crossing cart paths . . ."

"Serge?"

"What?"

"Sounds like the opposite of a reason to quit."

"That's the thing about obsessive disorders." He finished the coffee and capped the thermos. "Either all focus or none. Take basketball, no problem. I excelled because I could practice the same shot a hundred thousand times in a row. No distractions: just me, the ball, the basket, the sun repeatedly setting and rising. But golf, the majesty of the landscape, too much competition for my attention. Take that cloud, for example . . ." He pointed up through the windshield. "Shaped like Hemingway, but from the back. I didn't realize how dirty this windshield was, but beach season is also love-bug season. My advice? Don't let them bake on or it could eat the paint, so scrub gently with fabric-softener squares you throw in clothes dryers, which won't scratch the coating of your vehicle." Serge nodded to himself.

Coleman blinked a few times. "What about golf?"

"What? Oh, right. Golf is like falling asleep," said Serge. "You can never pinpoint the exact moment it happens. One minute I'm chopping away in a sand trap, and the next I'm wandering the woods following a cute little rabbit. Other golfers thought I was looking for a lost ball, but then I climbed down from a cart bridge and started skipping stones across the pond and catching lizards, and they sent one of the staff after me: 'Are you catching lizards?' 'Who? Me?' Then I opened my hand and there was a lizard. 'Sorry, got a little distracted.' So I climbed back up to the course and grabbed a club.

Played a little golf, chased a couple lizards, some more golf, saw a *really* cool butterfly, and by the way, I've met a lot of butterflies. But the staff was understanding and gave me a ride back to the clubhouse, even though I'd come screaming out of the woods: 'Guys! You've got to see this fucking butterfly!' . . . For some reason, I've never been able to finish a round."

"Remember the one time you took me golfing?"

"Unfortunately."

"Can't believe you're still sore about that," said Coleman. "A lot of the rich dudes were drinking, too. And right out in the open, big bottles of Johnnie Walker in their carts."

"Coleman, it wasn't just that you were drunk. You snapped the flag stick in half on number seven."

"But nobody else saw me," said Coleman. "I was able to toss the bottom part in the lake and stick the rest of the flag back in the hole."

"Coleman, you didn't think they'd get suspicious?"

"Was it that noticeable?"

"The flag was knee-high, like miniature golf."

Coleman shrugged and uncapped a pint of Jim Beam. "Your fault. You told me to tend the flag while you were hitting out of another sand trap. But I warned you my balance was playing tricks on me again. Maybe I should have my ears checked."

"It wasn't just the flag," said Serge. "Remember the stunt you pulled when we caught up to that foursome on the twelfth tee?"

"That was supposed to be a joke." Coleman took a slug of whiskey. "After all, they called that thing a ball washer. Get it?"

Serge placed a hand over his eyes. "I was so embarrassed. Nobody should ever have to see something as disturbing as that."

"I thought it was funny."

"Run it by me first next time."

Coleman stared out the passenger window. "Look at that freakin' guard shack. It's like a military base."

"Landmark alert," said Serge. "That's Lost Tree Village, home of the legend and adopted Florida favorite son Jack Nicklaus."

"Jack Nicklaus lives back there?" said Coleman. "I wonder what his house is like."

"Ask me."

"You've seen photos?"

"Negative," said Serge. "I've been inside."

"No way," said Coleman.

"Way," said Serge. "The foyer's got these floor-to-ceiling glass cases flanking both sides with all his trophies, and one shelf is just the Masters, a whole row of sterling silver replicas of the Augusta clubhouse that look like a bunch of shiny Howard Johnsons."

"When the hell were you inside Jack Nicklaus's house?"

"When I was a kid, his oldest son and I were in the same golf league. My friend Kenny also lived in Lost Tree and got me into the car pool, and they were totally regular folks, Jack's wife driving us around in a station wagon, taking us to McDonald's afterward, and then we'd spend the afternoons playing pool in the den and watching Jack's cable movies, which was a big deal back then."

"Wow, you actually played golf with Jack Nicklaus's son?"

"No, I said I carpooled," replied Serge. "There were eight divisions in the youth league based on talent. His son was in the first; I was in the last."

"So where to now?"

"We obviously need to stop in my hometown of Riviera Beach, and then on to our score in Fort Lauderdale.

"Fort Lauderdale?"

"I just have this weird feeling," said Serge. "But here's my favorite part about golf: It's got some of the greatest nicknames in all of sports. The Golden Bear, the King, the Goose, Lefty, Merry Mex, Champagne Tony. Even my youth league had nicknames."

"What was yours?"

"Lizard Catcher."

FORT LAUDERDALE

"We need to hurry," said Pat, running for the escalator at the end of the terminal.

"I needed to get something for my stomach." Bar hurried and munched from a bag of chips. "All they had on the plane were those little peanuts."

"I know," said Pat. "I just don't want our luggage to be sitting there out in the open."

"I thought you said crime wasn't bad?"

"It isn't." Pat walked down the steps of the moving escalator. "You know my overcautious paranoia."

They hopped off at the bottom in baggage claim. Giant, framed posters on the walls of beach attractions being enjoyed by tanned people with perfect teeth. The McDougalls jogged past carousels of moving luggage from Pittsburgh, Memphis and Birmingham. The rest of the passengers from their flight were already waiting at the last station. A buzzer sounded and a red light blinked. There was a mild bubbling of impolite human nature as people aggressively jockeyed to get near the front of the belt because it was unimportant.

"See?" said Bar. "The bags are just starting to come out."

Big ones, little ones, hard-shell cases for golf clubs and musical instruments, cardboard boxes wrapped with twine, backpacks, identical duffel bags for a college softball team. A lot of the luggage had colorful ribbons tied to the handles to avoid confusion. A small woman tried to grab an extra-heavy bag that was already past her, and it pulled her onto the belt. So she had to let it go for another lap. An announcement on the PA: "Many bags look alike . . ."

The crowd began thinning as people wheeled belongings toward ground transportation.

"There's one," said Bar.

"Got it," said Pat, hoisting it off the belt.

"There's another . . ."

They stood with two bags by their feet. Watching the belt go round and round.

Half the people from their flight were already gone. Then it was down to a dozen. Then just the McDougalls and an empty, rotating belt. A buzzer sounded, and the belt stopped.

Patrick's mouth fell open, and his hands went out helplessly. "Where's the rest of our stuff?"

"I'm sure it's coming along," said Bar.

"The belt's stopped."

"That doesn't necessarily mean anything."

"It means the belt's stopped."

"Maybe they're just delayed," said Bar.

"But we brought three more bags," said Pat. "I only got the smallest two. And that's just because we checked these at the gate because they said the overhead bins would be full. There's just toiletries and travel books and my laptop in these. We're stuck with the clothes on our back. This could ruin our vacation."

"Please try not to worry so much," said Bar. "We always talk about blessings."

"You're right," said Pat, pressing a spring-loaded button and extending the telescoping handle on a tiny carry-on. "I just wanted everything on this trip to be perfect for you."

"It is. We're together." She snuggled into his arm. "There's the luggage information office . . ."

They walked inside.

"Our luggage didn't come off the belt," said Patrick. "And then the belt stopped."

They were given forms. They filled them out.

"Thank you," said the attendant, making marks on the form in the grayed-out, official-use-only corner. "We'll send the bags to your room when they arrive . . . Where are you staying?"

"The Casablanca Inn."

The attendant reflexively looked up and stared.

"Something wrong?" asked Pat.

"Uh, no." She looked back down. "Is this your cell-phone number?"

"Yes," said Pat. "When do you think we'll know when our bags are here?"

"Probably already on the next flight in from Atlanta."

" 'Probably'?" said Pat. "Don't you scan bar codes on the bags? Can't you tell exactly where they are right now?"

"Yes," said the woman. "But my computer is down."

"Is your phone down, too?"

"What's your point?"

"Can you call someone whose computer isn't down and see if they know where our bags are?"

"Yes."

"So can you pick up the phone?"

"No." She picked up her purse. "Office hours just ended. Please step outside while I lock up."

Chapter Fourteen

RIVIERA BEACH

The Gran Torino wound south on Singer Island along Jack Nicklaus Drive. They passed through John D. MacArthur Beach State Park, a prime loggerhead-turtle nesting ground, and emerged along a thin mangrove isthmus overlooking Lake Worth.

"This is the A-drive," said Serge. "Most people take Blue Heron Boulevard over to the island, but this back road is one of the state's hidden jewels, thanks to John D., who donated the park. Coleman disagrees, of course, but screw that drooling pothead stupidness . . ."

Coleman rolled a joint in his lap. "Hey!" He looked up and saw Serge filming himself with the camcorder. "Oh, our fake feud. Cool." He looked back down.

"So for those of you playing at home: Remember to take PGA east from U.S. 1. Peace out."

"Finally," said Coleman. "The beach."

"Coleman, grab the camcorder and start filming to capture the return of the native. My mom used to set up my playpen right out there." The Torino slid into a parking slot on Ocean Avenue. The pair got out as Serge pointed north. "And over there is where all the surfers used to catch radical breaks off the wreck of the *Amaryllis*, which ran aground during Hurricane Betsy in 1965—"

From behind:

"Coleman!"

The pair turned around.

A gang of skater punks zipped toward them on large boards. "Is that you, Coleman?"

Coleman nodded.

"Righteous!" said a sandy blond. "Hey, dudes. It's Coleman!"

The skaters took turns high-fiving him. "You're my hero." "I want to be just like you." "It's an honor." "You give us hope . . ."

"Uh, thanks?" said Coleman.

Serge whispered sideways. "What's going on?"

Coleman shrugged. "No freakin' idea."

One of the skaters kicked up his board and tucked it under his arm. "Listen, man, I know you're mega-busy and all laying down your scene, but could you slide me a piece of advice from the mountain?"

Coleman shrugged again. "Why not? What do you need?"

"Okay, man, like we got this killer Tallahassee weed that's resin-city, except it's way too sticky, but we don't want to dry it out and make it brittle."

"Obviously," said Coleman. "That unbalances the equilibrium from the nuanced high of a fresh bud."

"Man, like I *knew* you'd say that! So the problem is we're not getting a full blaze in the bowl and there's a big waste factor of a lot of blackened, slow-burn shit left over. The weed is a buck-twenty for a one-finger bag, except we cop four and sell three so our shit's free, but still our sweat . . . Coleman, please tell us: What can we possibly do?"

"Got you covered." Coleman stepped forward and gestured as he held court. "First, go to any of the finer men's fashion stores. The cotton on the collars of expensive dress shirts gets worn and frayed from dry cleaners, so they sell these special fabric shavers that smooth it down. But be specific because even a lot of longtime workers at these places don't know about them. The devices have removable collection compartments inside to capture the blowby, so just shave down your buds, which retains resin but renders a fine, more smokable yield. And these devices are battery-powered to conveniently pursue the stoner lifestyle while taking the higher road."

"Oh, thank you, man! Like fuckin' radical genius, man! Nobody would have fuckin' thought of that but you!"

The next skater asked for Coleman's autograph on his board. "Like you're The Man, man!"

They finished their good-byes and the kids rolled away, an enthusiastic conversation trailing off:

"That was so excellent."

"I know, man. But where do you buy a dress shirt?"

"I don't know."

"Should we go back and ask him?"

"No, man, it's Coleman. He's a very busy dude . . ."

Serge raised his eyebrows toward his sidekick. "You've never met these guys before?"

"Not that I remember." Coleman raised a paper bag to his mouth. "But that doesn't mean anything in the drug culture. This happens all the time."

"Strangers come up and call you a genius?"

"No, but there's a universal recognition among my people, and yet a lack of *specific* recognition, even if you grew up together, if that makes any sense."

"I'm with you." Serge popped the trunk and pulled out a heavy orange canvas bag from Home Depot. "To the beach! . . . Are you filming?"

Coleman pressed a red button. "I don't see my nose this time."

Serge began trudging through the sand barefoot with a load over his shoulder. He glanced back at a row of uniformly tasteful pastel structures with Key West awnings and new Old Town light posts. "When did these buildings pop up on the beach strip? I can remember two generations back: They replaced the buildings that *replaced* the buildings when I was a tyke. There was this one little hot-dog shack with a wind meter on the roof—you know, those three-ice-cream-scoop things spinning like a propeller. And Coca-Cola in bottles and everyone with something new called a transistor radio, playing Beatles—"

Serge's canvas bag suddenly went flying. He was knocked hard, blindsided in the ribs, taking him off his feet. He adjusted, midair, like a cat, and did a somer-sault to bleed off the landing impact.

Coleman ran over. "You okay?"

Serge propped himself up to assess the cause of his tumble.

A young but unusually large muscle-boy smirked and tossed a football up and down in his palm. Huge pecs from daily workouts and an anabolic needle. Blond crew cut. "Watch where you're going, Pops. You could get hurt."

"Me?" said Serge.

"Yeah, you got in my way. Just be more careful."

A second such youth took off running in the sand along the shore.

"Joey!" he yelled back to the first guy. "Post pattern!" He waved a hand in the air as he ran past bikini bunnies. "I'm open! Hit me!"

The quarterback slapped the ball with his free hand, then unleashed a perfect Doug Flutie spiral for the end zone.

Serge stood next to Coleman, watching the ball sail in an exquisite arc. "Why do I feel like I'm in a Charles Atlas comic-book ad from the fifties?"

"Because you are?"

"Keep filming."

The receiver left his feet, making a circus fingertip catch but clipping the corner of a playpen with his knee. Fortunately, it was empty. The mother hustled her children away, and the father folded up their umbrella.

"That could have been my playpen," said Serge.

Coleman fetched the orange Home Depot bag. "This is pretty heavy." He pulled out a steel masonry trowel. "What's all this stuff for?"

"Our reality show." Serge reached in the bag and pulled out an industrial-strength trenching tool. "The number one item on our beach activity list: build a sand castle."

Coleman handed Serge the bag and filmed as they continued toward the water. "I thought building sand castles used plastic children's buckets and shovels. Bright red and yellow, and plastic castle forms."

"That's amateur hour." Serge handed Coleman a bundle of surveyor's stakes. "This is Xtreme sand castles! Which means aiming for the very top. And in Florida, that can mean only one thing!" He swung dramatically toward the camera.

Coleman tightened the view on his face. " . . . You don't mean . . . !"

"That's right!" Serge dropped the bag in the sand and fell to his knees. "Castillo de San Marcos!"

Serge lay stomach-flat on the beach, squinting in concentration with one eye closed and his tongue sticking out of the corner of his mouth like an eight-year-old with a slingshot. "The seventeenth-century Spanish fort is the quintessential Florida structure for anyone working in sand. If you're going to build, *build* . . . Coleman, to the left . . ."

Coleman moved a tiny stick with an orange ribbon to the right.

"Your other left," said Serge, aiming his Jesus-camping compass from his Bible cover.

Coleman obliged.

"Perfect! . . . Hammer it in."

They repeated three more times, and Serge stood up, admiring a perfectly square, magnetically oriented outline of twine that roped off forty geometric yards on the beach at Singer Island.

The trenching tool dug a deep cut down to the shallow water table for the moat. Serge scooped up beach mud to sculpt a corner fortification. "These bastions are most important, in case the French from Fort Caroline lay siege, then you can shoot back at the ladders they place on the outer walls. Castillo doesn't have a moat, but it should—"

A disturbance up the beach.

"What's that shrieking sound?" asked Coleman.

"A toddler crying."

"But it's super-loud like an air horn," said Coleman. "I didn't know small kids were capable of that kind of noise."

"Unless they're behind you on an airplane." Serge set down his tools and stood up. "Something must be highly wrong."

"Look," said Coleman. "It's those young studs passing the football."

"One of them trampled the child's sand castle. He's not even apologizing, just flirting with the underage girls on the next blanket."

"The father's saying something about it." Coleman pointed. "The bigger stud is coming back. He's standing chest to chest with the dad, glaring down at him . . . Now the dad's retreating and packing up his stuff."

"The stud's mocking the dad to the giggling beach girls." Serge shook his head. "And in front of the man's wife and older children no less, but the father just has to take it in silence because it's the responsible move for the sake of the family. Except that dick has wounded the dad's image in their eyes."

"That's wrong," said Coleman.

Serge resumed work on his Spanish fort. "I knew I should have bought those cannons ahead of time."

FORT LAUDERDALE

An almost empty cattle truck pulled through the parking lot of a strip mall on U.S. 1. Three men hopped down from the rear bed without waiting for the truck to stop. Three other migrants waiting in front of a store chased the truck across the lot and dove in back. The vehicle sped up again.

Gaspar Arroyo drove a quick half mile and turned into another parking lot.

The truck stopped in front of a twenty-nine-dollar motel room. Gaspar and the others went inside. A couple dozen additional men were already waiting. They all shut up when Arroyo entered.

TV on: *"Breaking news at this hour as another South Florida pill mill has been raided in the latest sweep of prescription-drug trafficking. We take you live to the scene . . ."*

The image on the tube switched to a small shopping center, much like the one the cattle truck had just visited. In the middle of the building, sandwiched between two businesses that sold billiard equipment and shampooed dogs, sat a store with no sign and blacked-out windows. A police public-relations officer stepped in front of the cameras. *"Our coordinated multiagency crackdown of illegal pain clinics is clearly yielding results, as such operations are becoming harder and harder to come by. However, there is still much work to be done, as we've received information that some OxyContin dealers are simply switching tactics. Up until now, we've been able to locate many clinics from anonymous tips of inexplicably full parking lots and heavy pedestrian traffic. In today's raid, for example, there were none of the usual telltale signs, and the break came when patrol* cars spotted a large number of men loitering in the breezeway of an abandoned office building. Further surveillance revealed that organizers were receiving alerts by cell phone and then ferrying groups of three or four to the clinic to avoid detection. It's the same technique used in the overflow waiting area of popular restaurants where they give you a blinking cocktail coaster . . ."

A cell phone rang. A hand turned down the volume on the TV.

"Speak . . ."

Gaspar listened briefly, hung up and selected three of the men. They followed him out to the cattle truck.

Chapter Fifteen

RIVIERA BEACH

Coleman sipped a bottle of Dr Pepper spiked with vodka. "What are you doing now to your sand castle?"

Serge delicately applied wet sand with a trowel. "Notching the parapets to thwart French aggression—"

Another interruption.

"Hey, Coleman!"

Serge kept his head down in the sand. "Are those guys back?"

"No, new guys."

"Coleman? Is that really you?"

Coleman took another swig. "All day long."

"Dig it, guys, it's Coleman!"

Three surfers dropped their boards and sat cross-legged at his feet. "Man, I can't believe we're actually talking to you in person."

Coleman placed a hand over his stomach and held up a finger for them to wait a second—"Don't feel too good"—then he jackknifed over and threw up on the fort's parapets.

Serge knelt motionless, staring down at his sand castle, then up at Coleman in silence. He sighed deeply and began troweling Coleman's lunch off the cannon deck. "French aggression takes many forms."

The surfers were beside themselves. "We got to see Coleman vomit!" "The dude knows no limits!" "Nonstop balls to the walls!"

Coleman wiped his mouth and washed his hand in the sand, making it look like a breaded cutlet.

"Coleman? . . . May we call you Coleman?"

He nodded and sat down in front of them.

"Coleman, we've been having a debate. To Bogart or not to Bogart? Your thoughts?"

"Well," said Coleman. "There's no hard-and-fast weed etiquette on the subject. More of a sliding scale predicated upon a Keynesian economic model. If there's plenty of herb on the market, go for it. But if it's been seriously dry, definitely don't Bogart."

"What would constitute such a drought?"

"Phone records," said Coleman. "Everyone making lots of calls to people they've lost touch with since the last drought. And to follow the pot-politeness rule, you don't bring it up for the first two minutes, making small talk. ' . . . No particular reason, just thought I'd call to see how you were doing . . . Why do you think we barely knew each other? . . . Yeah, I'm still living with my parents . . . So how are you and Linda getting along? . . . She broke up with you three years ago, haven't seen her since? . . . Wow, that's really a bummer and do you have any pot?' "

The surfers nodded solemnly. "We rode out those mothers."

They began getting up. "Here's a twistie for you." He palmed the joint as they waved good-bye. "Thanks, Coleman!" "Never change, dude!" "Just knowing that you're out there doing your thing keeps us all going! . . ."

Coleman returned to inspect Serge's construction techniques.

Serge grabbed an aluminum-handled floater. "What was that all about?"

"I haven't the slightest idea," said Coleman. "Something really weird is going on . . . What are you doing now?"

Serge ran the tool sideways at the end of a wall. "San Marcos was an exquisite example of 'star fort' architecture unique to its era. The design first appeared in Italy and was even adopted by Michelangelo before the Spanish imported it to the New World at St. Augustine. The defining feature of the 'star' was the pointed bastions at the corners, which allowed complete covering fire, unlike the previously rounded bastions that created defenseless 'dead areas' on the outer curves and were exploited by assailing forces." Serge grabbed the trowel again for a finishing touch on the diamond-sharp point of the final battlement. He stood and dusted sand off his palms, then kissed his fingertips. "Masterpiece! The fort is finished. Completely impenetrable to my enemies."

"*Joey! I'm open, I'm open! Hit me!*"

A football spiraled high through the air on a perfect timing pattern.

A beach stud ran underneath and made a lunging catch.

Coleman looked down at a flattened castle. "That's fucked up."

The stud raised his arms in the air and did a touchdown dance for the bikini babes, then spiked the football over his shoulder behind him.

"He just smashed the last bastion," said Serge.

"I thought your fort was impenetrable," said Coleman.

"In its time," said Serge. "But modern aggression has obviously rendered its defenses obsolete."

The stud began trotting back for another pass pattern.

"Excuse me?" Serge called after him. "Could I have a word?"

The young man turned around. "Oh, it's Pops again." He walked back. "What do you want now?"

"You severely damaged my fort."

"It was in my way."

"Look at the surveyor stakes. I was clearly here first."

"A grown man playing in the sand? What a faggot!"

"I'm going to skip that one for now because it's a nonstarter," said Serge. "Why begin in the emergency room, right? And I perfectly understand that when you go into the military fort business, you accept that you'll be performing a certain amount of repairs. That's the whole reason we need forts: assholes. But you and I are Americans." He interlaced his fingers. "We need to pull together. The fabric of the republic. Spacious skies, amber waves of grain. I'm sure you've heard of them in passing."

"What's your friggin' problem?" The stud bounced the football off Serge's forehead and caught it. "Are you crazy or something?"

"Crazy about promoting understanding," said Serge. "And I've been dialoguing very politely, so it's only reasonable that you reciprocate. Maybe kick it off with: 'I'm sorry for destroying your sixteenth-century star-pointed bastions that provided covering fire at the mouth of the Matanzas River in St. Augustine.' It doesn't have to be an exact quote."

The stud bounced the football off Serge's forehead again.

Serge rubbed the red spot. "That's not exactly the same as 'I'm sorry,' but maybe among your tribe . . ."

The ball bounced off his forehead again.

"Okay," said Serge. "We're going backward now. But I have to warn you: I saw what happened earlier to that small child's sand castle. Of course, it wasn't as nice as mine because, after all, whose ever is? But I'm sure that tot gave it her best."

The ball bounced again.

"I may not look strong, but I'm wiry," said Serge. "And into patience. Which cuts both ways. Right now patience is why we're still in negotiations. But if our path-to-peace talks break down, I've been known to fight unfair. Sorry, it's a character flaw."

The ball went to bounce off his forehead again, but Serge caught it.

The stud was momentarily taken off guard at the speed of Serge's reflexes. "Give me my ball back!"

"Apologize."

"Give it to me or you'll regret it!"

"The smallest sign of respect will do."

The stud snatched the ball and shoved Serge to the ground. "Go fuck yourself!" He stomped away.

"I must learn more about your tribe," Serge yelled after him. "Something's getting lost in the translation."

Coleman helped Serge up into a sitting position. "Jesus, you really are dedicated to patience."

Serge assessed the damage to his fort.

"You going to make repairs?" asked Coleman.

"Yes, but I'll need to make another trip to Home Depot first. It's clear that protecting the national fabric requires more advanced defensive systems."

FORT LAUDERDALE

A rented Chevy Impala cruised south on U.S. Highway 1.

Pawnshops, pain clinics, ethnic grocery stores with burglar cages on the windows.

"Are you sure this is the correct way?" asked Barbara McDougall.

"I've got the address right here." Patrick held up a street map with scribbled notes across the top. "We're on U.S. 1."

Bar looked around at people loitering outside a boarded-up gas station. "I thought you said U.S. 1 ran right along the ocean."

"I think I got it mixed up with A1A."

"We're in the urban section of the city, not the vacation part."

"Sorry," said Pat. "I was only six years old."

A half dozen blocks later, a long, two-story building needed a pressure washing that it would never receive. Moroccan architecture. A sign with a rock through it.

CASABLANCA.

Pat pulled into the parking lot. "Here we are."

Only two other cars. Someone in a white T-shirt sat on a milk crate outside one of the rooms, smoking a thin cigar. A cat, all ribs, licked water from a rain gutter.

"Doesn't look like the photos," said Bar.

"The view from the street always appears worse." Pat got out and headed for the office. "The pool area's probably great."

Pat rang the bell on the reception desk. They heard noises in back, so they knew someone was there. He rang it again. A terrible, racking cough. Then a hocking sound. Water ran. Something fell on the floor. Sneezing. More coughs again.

Pat and Bar glanced at each other.

It became quiet. Footsteps in the back room like someone was on their way out. Coughing resumed. A retching noise. *Splat.* A scream. Coughing and burping. Another hock. *"Is that blood?"* Cough, cough. Sneeze, retch. An extra-big cough that caused a simultaneous fart.

Bar stared at the floor. Pat looked at the ceiling and tapped his fingers on the counter.

Some final spitting and a violent clearing of the throat.

A jaundiced man in a soiled bowling shirt appeared from the back room, wiping his mouth on the back of his arm. "What do you want?"

"A room," said Pat. "We have a reservation. The name's McDougall."

"Do you have a reservation?"

"Yes."

"What's your name again?"

Pat took a deep breath. "McDougall."

The clerk pulled out a sheet of paper with three names. He ran his finger down the page. "Nope, not on here."

Pat leaned over the counter and tapped the middle name on the page.

The clerk looked up at him oddly. "But that says McDougall."

"That's our name."

"Then why did you just give me a different one?"

Bar looked at her husband. "Maybe we should stay somewhere else."

Pat looked at the clerk. "We think we'll stay somewhere else."

"No problem." The clerk headed toward the back room.

"Uh, excuse me," said Pat. "But our card won't be charged, right?"

The bowling shirt turned around. "We already ran it through. To hold the room."

"Can we get a refund?"

"You'll have to talk to the owner about that."

"Okay, we'd like to talk to the owner."

The clerk stared at them.

"The owner?" asked Pat.

"What about him?"

"We'd like to talk to him."

"You already said that."

"And?" asked Pat.

"And what? You didn't ask a question. You made a statement: 'We'd like to talk to the owner.' Good for you."

Patrick took a deep breath. "Is the owner here?"

"No."

"Can you call him?"

"No."

"Why?"

"Don't know his number."

"Where is he?"

"Probably at his house."

"Where's that?"

"Somewhere in Sri Lanka."

"When's he coming back?"

"I've never seen him."

"Is there any other way to get a refund?"

"Maybe at some other place."

"Do people ever ask you for refunds?" said Pat.

"All the time," said the clerk.

"What do you do?"

"Wait for them to go away. Then sometimes I watch TV. Or get something to eat if I'm hungry, maybe call my girlfriend. But why are you curious about my girlfriend?"

Bar looked at her husband. "That's payment for seven nights. We can't afford to lose it. We'll have to go back home."

"What are you suggesting?" asked Pat. "Stay here and hope for the best?"

"Why not?" Bar said reluctantly. "We'll commute to the beach. Plus, this is where we told the airline to deliver our luggage."

Pat turned back to the clerk. "Okay, we'll stay here."

"Can I see your driver's license and credit card?"

"Sure . . ." Pat pulled two plastic cards from his wallet and slid them across the counter.

The clerk made a Xerox of the license, then swiped the credit card through a magnetic slide. A printout spit from a machine. He handed Pat a nineteen-cent ballpoint pen. "Sign here and put the make and model of your car."

Pat scribbled. "Why did you need to swipe my card just then?"

"To charge it."

"You said before that my card was charged when we booked the reservation."

"That was only to hold the room in case of late arrival," said the clerk. "But you were early. Here are your keys. Number seventeen."

"Wait. So until a minute ago, my card was never charged," said Pat. "I didn't actually need a refund."

"That's right."

"Since it was just a minute ago, can we get a refund?"

"You'll have to talk to the owner."

Pat snatched the keys off the counter and looked at his wife. "Let's just go."

"Hey, buddy, what are you trying to pull?"

"What?" said Pat.

The clerk pointed. "My pen."

Pat handed it back, and the couple left with brass room keys.

The clerk waited until the door closed and shook his head. "What's with the customers in this place? . . ." Then he picked up the phone. "Zzmükhan, it's Mo. Yeah, just got another bunch. Drop on by."

A trail of black smoke came up the highway, and a thirty-year-old purple Cadillac Fleetwood pulled into the motel. Its windows decoratively trimmed with mariachi sombrero balls. A gypsy cab.

The driver entered the office.

"Zzmükhan," said the clerk, tossing him a thumb drive from his laptop.

The driver was lanky, with an untucked button-up shirt and long dreadlocks that fell down his back from under a floppy, knitted cap in the national colors of Jamaica. The whites of his eyes were a baleful yellow. Empty. He handed the motel manager three hundred dollars without speaking, and left the office with even less fanfare. Then he went back to his motel room six blocks away and plugged the thumb drive into his own computer, where data from the magnetic strips of fifty credit cards zipped through microprocessors to a special machine that cloned the information onto the magnetic strips of fifty stolen blank credit cards, which went back out to the gypsy cab and three blocks north on U.S. 1 to a boarded-up gas station, where a loose, roaming group of life's leftovers quickly formed a line of loyal customers, each forking over sixty dollars to respectively become Casey Windsor, Octavio Reyes, Danforth Hill, Molina Pomeroy, Hideki Yokomota and Patrick McDougall.

Chapter Sixteen

RIVIERA BEACH

The sun had gone down. Coleman stood at the edge of the surf, surrounded by a group of sunburned kids with salt-water-bleached hair.

"Shhhhh!" said one of the boys. "Coleman's about to speak."

"Here's a foolproof way not to get arrested while blowing doobies." Coleman turned his back against a sea breeze and cupped his hands to fire up a number. He exhaled the hit and began strolling as small waves rolled over his toes. The others followed. "You walk along the edge of the ocean after dark, making sure nobody else is within a comfort bubble of twenty yards, just in case there's an undercover narc on the beach.

And here's the most critical part: Make sure your stash is *stashed*. Nothing on your person except the jay in your hand. Then just smoke it like a regular cigarette; no clutching or thumb-toking. The beach wind should take care of the smell, and if it doesn't, or if some narc makes a move for other reasons, the twenty-yard buffer gives you plenty of cushion so he can't snatch the evidence from your hand, and you just dive in the ocean and roll it apart in your fingers underwater."

"Wow," one of the kids said to another. "Coleman's, like, got his act completely together, man. His mind is working on so many levels at the same time . . ."

"He didn't just pull that shit out his ass," said another. "It took some stone-serious planning, man . . ." His hands cut through the air like slow-motion karate. " . . . Seeing all the angles before anyone else could even dream of them . . ."

"Thank you, Coleman . . ."

"Right on, Coleman. Don't ever give up the fight, man! . . ."

Fists of solidarity went into the air as the group walked away.

Serge approached from the opposite direction. "Who *are* all these people?"

"I have no idea," said Coleman. "You think something odd is going on?"

"You mean the part about lots of strangers coming up out of the blue and acting like you hold an endowed chair at Oxford? Gee, I wonder." Serge headed back up the beach, past his sand fort.

Coleman followed and pointed down. "Are you going to finish repairing that?"

Serge shook his head and continued plodding through cool night sand. "It's gotten way too dark. I'll resume reconstruction in the morning." He shifted the strap of the canvas bag on his shoulder. "Meanwhile, back to the beach activities list . . . *Ding, ding, ding!* . . . That's the surprise beach-list Daily Double!"

"What's that?"

"Read cheesy magazines you'd otherwise never touch, and they're all in unusually heavy supply at beach convenience stores. I saw one over there on the strip."

They finished trudging back through the sand and crossed the street. Someone over at the public beach showers threw a hand in the air. *"Coleman! Power party!"*

Coleman waved back. "Thank you very much."

The pair reached the doors of the convenience store. Some babes came out. They covered their mouths and whispered. *"It's Coleman!"* *"Are you sure?"* *"I'm getting an autograph . . . Coleman, can you sign my breast? . . ."*

Serge watched dumbstruck as Coleman capped a pen and belatedly came through the doors. "We've definitely fallen through some kind of flux port in the universe." They wandered into the magazine aisle and began riffling issues.

"Here's a motorcycle magazine with hot chicks on choppers," said Coleman. "And a fishing magazine with a hot chick in one of those deep-sea rod holders right over her snatch, and a hunting magazine with a chick in a T-back straddling a moose head . . ."

"I love convenience-store periodical sections." Serge picked up a magazine dedicated to bodybuilding and dirt bikes. "Completely different from the rest of the world."

"Here's one that must be for women. Check out their main feature article: 'Call Him or Text Him?' I say blow him."

"Coleman, that's offensive."

"But it's the right answer."

"Of course it's the right answer, but you can't just put that on a magazine cover."

"Because chicks will get upset?"

"I don't know about them, but I'll get upset." Serge unfurled a centerfold of a swamp buggy. "Word like that getting out? Women apparently don't know it yet, but if they all coordinated on the Internet, they could rule the world in forty-eight hours."

"Holy shit!" said Coleman.

"Relax. I don't think it's going to happen anytime soon."

"No," said Coleman. "They got the new issue of *High Tides!*"

"What's that?"

"It's like the Florida version of *High Times.*" Coleman waved the magazine at the clerk behind the register. "When did these come out?"

"Just delivered this morning."

Serge grabbed a wrestling magazine with blood-streaked faces. "I don't see why you're getting so excited. I'm sure you already know everything in there."

"It's not that," said Coleman. "Look!"

"Holy shit!" said Serge.

"I'm on the cover," said Coleman. "Lenny, too."

They went silent and read the headline on its glossy front: "The Bong Brothers! Can their records ever be broken?"

Serge quickly flipped through pages. "But what—? . . . How—? . . . Why—? . . ."

"These magazines are always asking for reader photos," said Coleman. "So Lenny and me sent in everything we had. Then someone called his mom's house in Pompano while we were there. Lenny thought the request for an interview was a hoax, but played along anyway as a goof."

"So that's what all this nonsense with those kids on the beach has been about."

Coleman carried ten copies to the register and plopped them on the counter. "It's the happiest day of my life . . ."

They came out of the store. From across the parking lot: "Coleman! Rock steady!"

Coleman returned the power salute.

A two-stroke engine gunned.

"Great," said Serge. "It's my new friend again. The quarterback."

"He's on a motorcycle," said Coleman.

"No shirt, no shoes, swim trunks. If there was a photo of flunking an IQ test . . ."

"A bunch of bikini babes are gathering around him."

"Christ," said Serge. "They're just encouraging his ego . . . Now he's offering a ride and they're all raising their hands and hopping up and down."

"He picked the blonde in the skimpiest suit," said Coleman. "She's climbing on the back of his bike."

"This is sickening," said Serge. "The most perfect specimens of each gender from the whole beach. It's

like the fucking master race on that bike. And absolutely everyone else is staring in envy . . . Come on,
America. Don't buy into surface flash."

"I'd do her," said Coleman.

"Thank you for your support."

"He's gunning the engine again. They're about to
take off . . ."

A final fuel injection of the V-twin.

The stud patched out to impress everyone. When he
did, it was like a magician pulling the tablecloth from
under his passenger, and she fell to the ground in a sitting position, skidding a few feet down the road on her
bottom.

"Oooooo!" Coleman covered his eyes. "Ass rash. I
can't look . . . And she was so hot just a second ago."

Serge looked. His eyes locked twenty yards up
the road, where the stud had stopped his bike.
"Unbelievable. He's too embarrassed to come back and
be a man, so he's compensating by arrogantly making
fun of the girl with his brain-dead buddy."

Serge darted out into the road and offered a hand.
"Let me help you up . . . are you okay?"

Tears. "It hurts."

"That's the worst part," said Serge. "I think you're
fine, but it's definitely going to tickle for a while." He
peeked behind her to gauge the injury and winced.

"Here, put your weight on me. Let's get you some first aid."

"Look," said Coleman.

"Oh, *now* he's coming," said Serge.

"What's the deal?" said the stud. "You trying to make me look bad?"

"You already have your arms all the way around that job."

"Let her go."

"So you can help her?"

"No, you're showing me up. If the bitch is too stupid to hang on, she deserves what she gets."

"Coleman," said Serge. "Take her arm." Then back to the crew cut: "I was pussyfooting around before with the sand castle, but seriously, what is your malfunction?"

"*You're* going to have a malfunction!"

"Listen, king of the comebacks, the girl's too young for you to begin with, then you injure her and offer insults instead of assistance. So you need to step off of me right now or we're going round and round."

The stud instead took a step forward. "You're telling me to step off?"

Serge took his own step forward, putting them chest to chest. "Not really. That was just another IQ test. And there's the buzzer. Sorry, but we have some lovely consolation prizes backstage, like a new set of knuckle guards for when you drag them."

"That's it!"

A lifeguard, who was in pretty good shape himself, ran over with a medic bag and wedged himself between the two. "Break it up, guys, or I'm calling the beach patrol."

The pair continued steaming and glaring like boxers being introduced by the ring announcer. Serge finally turned to more important matters. "Got a bottle of hydrogen peroxide in that bag?" he asked the lifeguard. "And some triple-antibiotic cream? . . ."

BROWARD COUNTY

An early evening on U.S. Highway 1. Modest traffic.

But along one block just below the county line, an untypical amount of honking horns, even for South Florida. All directed at one vehicle.

A gold Oldsmobile with curb feelers drove through the intersection at eleven miles an hour before finally turning into a parking lot, its undercarriage grinding the curb in excruciating slow motion. It was a '91 Cutlass Supreme, and it had ten thousand miles on the odometer. The front seat was all the way forward so the driver could see out from under the steering wheel.

The parking lot ran in front of a strip mall anchored by a pain clinic. All the storefronts appeared more or less the same, except one. It had a row of reinforced cement pylons at the curb to prevent drivers from plowing into the place. Which usually meant a liquor store.

But not this time. On the glass behind the pylons, in an arc of elegant silver lettering: WOLFGANG'S DANCE STUDIO. And underneath: *Classic ballroom instruction.*

The Oldsmobile continued across the parking lot. Other cars that had started backing out quickly pulled back in. The Cutlass approached the studio, slowing to three miles an hour, then two. When the front bumper hit a pylon, it was the signal for the driver to turn off the engine.

The car door opened. Five minutes later, the front door of the studio opened. Bells jingled.

A dashing man in a tuxedo turned around at the sound. Sixty-three years old, conspicuously dyed hair and a gleaming smile of the whitest, most obvious dentures, like a game-show host on a cruise ship. He spread his arms. "Coco! Coco Farina!"

"Wolfgang!" said the shuffling old woman, eyeing the other women in the room. "Don't be buttering up those tramps."

Wolfgang rushed to her. "Always the character! Full of moxie!" He bent down to kiss her hand.

"Moxie, schmoxie. I'm completely serious," said Coco. "They're sluts. Especially Mabel over there, with her new permanent, thinking sunshine beams from her twat—"

Wolfgang intentionally interrupted with a hearty, nervous laugh—"Ha! Ha! Ha!"—then looked back at a cadaverous woman snoring in a chair. He reached deep for his best Clark Gable and gazed into Coco's eyes. "Mabel's a lovely woman, but not half as exquisite as you!"

Coco gazed back. "How come nobody's ever snagged you? Hubba hubba!"

"Who wants to get married?" Another kiss on the hand. "When I can instead spend so much time with all you great gals at the studio."

And it was a nice enough studio. Fake parquet floor, full mirrors on all the walls, waist-high wooden hand-rails. The sound system was a boom box from Walmart that sat in the corner on a bar stool. But the main attraction was Wolfgang.

Wolfgang Finch.

Suave as they come for the silver set. He clapped his hands loudly for attention, then placed a hand over his heart. "What a stunning vision of beauty. You're even more radiant than last time . . . Now, if you will all take your places, we can begin today's lesson."

Eventually. The women began moving, or so it seemed. Slippers slid across the dance floor. There were a few canes, a couple of walkers with yellow tennis-ball feet and a wheelchair.

The studio had a total of five daily classes, each numbering twelve to fifteen students, depending on doctor's appointments and memory. Several times a week, they migrated to the strip mall and mustered up in the usual three lines. Then most would slowly dance by themselves to the sounds of Glenn Miller— keeping eager eyes on Wolfgang as he moved one by one through the group for personal instruction. Which is why they came. And it was why, when they fell in line each session, there was the usual dust-up at the front of the first row. Because that's where Wolfgang started, and if there was enough time, those were the gals most likely to squeeze in an extra dance.

"Bitch!"

"Coco," said Wolfgang, waving a benevolent finger. "Play nice with others."

"But I was here first."

"Just slide over one space. I promise I'll give you an extra dance."

Coco snarled sideways at Mabel.

Wolfgang stood in the corner, his thumb on a boom-box button. "Ready?" He pressed it. The opening notes of "In the Mood" drifted through the room.

He took Mabel's hand and began swaying, careful never to take his eyes off hers. "You look more exquisite every time. Are you getting younger? . . ." The compliments kept flowing for the entire personal session, which lasted the standard lap-dance three-minute limit. Finally, the all-important departing peck on the cheek. Then on to Coco, and Stella, and Gertrude, and the rest of the gals, endlessly repeating the same business model of a congressman: eye contact, bullshit, kiss.

The class took necessary fatigue breaks every ten minutes, and then, after an hour, the music stopped. The women began working their way toward the door with melancholy afterglow. Outside, waiting cabs and a line of Buicks pressed against concrete pylons.

The studio was empty again. Almost. Three of the women sat in a short row of chairs against the wall just outside Wolfgang's office. This was the rest of the business model.

He came to the doorway. "Mrs. Goldstein, you wanted to see me? Come on in."

"Oh, thank you." She pushed herself up with a cane. "I know you're very busy."

"Nonsense, I'll always have time for you."

She went inside. Wolfgang smiled back at the other two women, then closed the door. They all liked the fact that he closed the door: makes the others wonder. He walked around and took a seat behind his desk, then opened a business ledger and made a precise notation. He looked up with a reassuring countenance. "What's on your mind?"

"My podiatrist . . . I don't know. I shouldn't say anything." She leaned forward and idly placed a hand on the desk. It's what they all came for.

Wolfgang took his cue. He leaned forward and placed his own hand on top of hers. "I'm sure it's important. Please, tell me all about it."

"Okay . . ." And she did.

A clock on the wall ticked.

" . . . Then I got this bunion . . ."

Wolfgang continued holding her hand.

" . . . And my son-in-law has this esophagus thing where he has to cut his food in really small bites. But what are you going to do? . . ."

He dialed in that smile and eye contact, thinking about the Jaguar he test-drove last weekend.

" . . . My daughter hates me. I can't complain . . ."

At the half-hour mark, he slowly began to stand, signaling the end of their time but easing the impact by taking her hand this time in *both* of his. After opening the door for Mrs. Goldstein, he stuck his head in the hall. "Mrs. Marconi?"

He went back behind his desk again, making another notation in his ledger.

" . . . I brought you something to eat . . ." She unwrapped a casserole. Then looked at the framed photo prominently displayed on his desk. "I know you miss your wife since the volcano accident. But that was five years ago. You deserve to find somebody nice. You look too thin."

Wolfgang stared at the photo with sorrow. He had never married. It was a picture he clipped from a magazine. He shook his head with glassy eyes. "Nobody can replace Beth."

"You're a keeper," said Mrs. Marconi.

Wolfgang leaned and warmly placed a hand on top of hers. "Did you bring your bank statements? I just want to make sure nobody's taking advantage of you."

She pulled envelopes from her purse. "You're so kind looking out for us."

A half hour later, his head popped back into the hall. "Mrs. Farina? . . ."

She came in and took a seat. "They don't want me to drive anymore."

"Who?"

"Everyone."

Wolfgang checked his ledger. Two previous dates in his office, now three. Which meant it was time.

His smile dissolved to a tight mouth of concern.

"What's the matter?" asked Coco. "Something I said?"

"I'm sorry about that." He shook his head. "You came here to talk to me. I don't need to bother you with my own worries."

"No, really, what is it?" asked Coco.

"My foundation."

"You mean Ballroom Preservation?"

He nodded. "We're having trouble with the bills. I'm afraid it looks bad."

Coco edged closer. "Is there anything I can do?"

"Well . . ." He quickly pulled out a glossy brochure and handed it across the desk. "As I believe you already know, the foundation is supported entirely by the contributions of generous benefactors who belong to my gold membership."

Coco scanned the brochure, given to each dance student upon their third office visit, and again after every three subsequent visits, upping their membership status to platinum and diamond. She unhesitatingly whipped out her checkbook, like most. They'd seen what had happened to the others who held back.

Sitting outside on their fourth visit and getting skipped over, again and again, finally the only one left in the hall, Wolfgang grabbing his coat: "Sorry, in a hurry to see someone at the hospital."

Cut off.

Everyone knew there were no hospital visits, and they all blamed their frozen-out classmate for being selfish. She deserved it for not helping such a kind soul in his ballroom foundation's time of need. He was the lonely hearts club's one-stop shopping for all their emotional and spiritual needs.

Coco squinted at her checkbook. "How much do you need?"

He slid a piece of paper with a number across the table. Not what he needed; what she could afford. He'd seen the bank statements.

She finished writing and ripped out the check. "Here you go."

Twenty-four thousand.

That number ain't fiction. And Wolfgang wasn't alone. All across the state, every day. Age demographics helped Florida corner the market on debonair geriatric gurus. Some woman in Fort Myers was taken for eighty-nine thousand before her children noticed the electric company had turned off her lights. It made the papers, as did the other cases, handfuls every month—dance instructors, nutritionists, home health workers—but their customers still kept writing those checks. Happily.

Wolfgang himself had gone through his own brush with authorities after an estate planner discovered a widow from Boynton had cashed all her CDs.

They handcuffed him right in the studio.

"Booo!" "Leave him alone!" "Fascists!" Coco even spit on one of the officers as they led him away. But all charges were quickly dropped when the victim said she wanted to give him more money for legal bills.

He'd found his calling.

And things couldn't be going better for Wolfgang. In addition to a bustling clientele with loose checkbooks, he had just gone into partnership with a major new investor. Someone he became acquainted with from the strip mall. More specifically, the pain clinic. Wolfgang had already begun milking him for information with eventual plans to rip him off as well. He now had a new partner, a defrocked doctor from Tampa named Arnold Lip.

Chapter Seventeen

SINGER ISLAND

S ky and ocean blended together in the black night. The rim of the horizon became defined by a yellowish glow and a preview of the coming moonrise.

Two Floridians stared out over the tranquil Atlantic.

"Now, this is a bar," said Coleman, downing a double of Jack on the rocks.

"It's definitely going on the list." Serge bent over his notebook. "Top O' Spray, on the Palm Beach Shores side of Singer Island. Not only is it on the beach, but it's got an elevated view from the top of a motel with lots of glass. Plus it's a *real* bar: old decor and old school, genuine people with quiet class who don't whoop it up to call attention to themselves during fertility runs at genetically engineered beach joints like Coconuts or Rumrunners or 'World Famous Tiki Bar.'"

"Don't the people up north know there's like a thousand of those famous tikis."

"Amazingly, they're like kids going to see Santa Claus at the mall and always think they've found the only one: 'Look, Velma, the sign says "World Famous," so we're forced to go inside.'"

Coleman knocked on the ancient counter under his drink. "But how'd you find this place? It's so out of the way."

"My hometown," said Serge. "During return visits, I'd stay here when it was a Best Western. Then I'd stare out the back windows of this bar and pretend I was a contestant on *Treasure Isle.*"

"What's that?"

"Believe it or not, they used to shoot a nationally televised game show right out on that very shore. I can see it all like it was just yesterday . . ." Hands waved in the air over his bottled water. " . . . The year was 1967, the network: ABC! Couples paddling little toy boats across a man-made lagoon behind the landmark Colonnades Hotel, digging in the sand for clues to solve the puzzle, urged to hurry by the booming voice of host John Bartholomew Tucker until the familiar strains of Herb Albert's 'Tijuana Taxi' signaled that 'we've run out of time again,' and then they'd all gather and wave to the camera. It was a magic era."

"I remember it now," said Coleman. "The show that was like *The Newlywed Game* on the beach."

"I was just a little kid sitting too close to the TV and ruining my eyes, thinking, 'This is just a few miles away but being broadcast to the entire country. That must be really important!' Then I ran around the house yelling hysterically, 'Mom! Mom! Take me to sit in the live audience!' 'I'm making dinner.' And I'd stomp my feet and point toward the ocean, screaming falsetto: 'But they're paddling in the lagoon right now!' . . . We never did go, and then it got canceled in 1968, and years later I realized it was just a bunch of silliness."

"If it was silly," said Coleman, "then why did you make us stop before coming to this bar and dig a lot of holes out on the beach?"

"Because when they cancel a show, the staff doesn't give a shit. Do you think they actually made sure they dug up all the leftover clues? Who knows what it could be worth to solve an unfinished puzzle?"

"That beach cop who questioned us wasn't very polite."

"I generally have universal respect for law enforcement, but some can be deliberately obtuse, and he comes over with his flashlight: 'Hey, what do you two fellas think you're doing out here?' 'Digging for clues. Solving puzzles.' 'Clues?' 'When they cancel a show, the staff doesn't give a shit.' "

Coleman raised his drink. "He acted like something bizarre was going on."

"He'll never make detective." Serge chugged his water. "Let me see that magazine again. I can't believe you made the cover of one before I did."

"Where do I pick up my fan mail?"

Serge flipped inside to the feature article. "Look at this. I'm so jealous. They even have a time line of your career, like they're tracing the ice ages in North America. Here's your 'early bong period,' and then the advent of your unforgettable chicken hookah . . ."

"You use what you have on hand."

" . . . And the time you and Lenny made a bong from a hundred-gallon aquarium, which this magazine says silenced even the most jaded cynics."

Coleman tapped a spot farther down the graph. "That's where we lost our crown to the Australians, who used silicone caulk to seal up one of those red British phone booths . . ."

"They're saying it was like the America's Cup . . ."

"And here's where we finally won it back." Coleman tapped another spot. "That should keep the title in the States for a while."

"Where was I during all this?"

Coleman just shrugged. "Me and Lenny were hanging out in this college bar. And we met some stoners from the physics department, and one of the grads was a teaching assistant who had a key, so we went in after midnight . . ."

Serge incredulously held the magazine closer to his face. "You made a bong from a super-collider?"

Coleman downed a drink and smiled offhand. "A bong has to be airtight, and those collider things can't be having little particles getting loose."

Serge closed the magazine and patted Coleman on the back. "Drink up."

"But we just got here."

Serge climbed off his stool. "Have to find a home improvement store before they close, then get to bed early for plenty of rest."

"Why?"

"I need to repair a Spanish fort."

OCALA

Six A.M. Shadows. Hoofbeats.

No lights except the horse barns. Electric faux lanterns. Parsons Gram folded a used horse blanket and placed it on a stack in the back of the stables. Then he lifted the entire bundle and lowered it into a heavy-gauge corrugated shipping box.

Clip-clop, clip-clop. A jockey guided a filly up the paved driveway into the barn.

Parsons took the reins.

"Thanks, Dominic."

He threw a blanket over the horse and returned to sealing up his mailing container. Must have gone through a half roll of strapping tape. No way he was going to let this thing bust open in transit.

Clip-clop, clip-clop, clip-clop.

Parsons stayed bent over his box. He could tell it was two horses. He tore off a last length of tape and pressed it firmly over the flaps. Then stood up and turned around.

"Who the hell are you?" said Gram. "And what are you doing in my barn?"

A pair of Latinos in straw cowboy hats climbed down from the mares. Smiling.

"We have a business proposition."

"Where's Eddie and Willie?"

"Taking a smoke break."

Parsons pulled out his cell phone. "I'm calling the police."

"I wouldn't do that. Unless you want them to search the barn. You'd be amazed how fast we can make this a crime scene."

Parsons hung up. He glanced toward some tools leaning against a stable door. Ax, pitchfork, shovel.

The other Mexican stuck a hand in his jacket and smiled with gold teeth. "You're not that fast."

"Look, I don't know how you got this address or what you're up to, but this is a mistake. You've got the wrong place."

Gold Teeth looked at his partner. "Pablo, you think we might have gotten the wrong place?"

Pablo looked around the barn and up at the truss supports in the vaulted ceiling. "Seems like a nice enough place to me."

Gold Teeth turned toward Parsons again. "Pablo said he likes this place. I do, too."

"You want money?" said the horse rancher. He pointed in the general direction of an unseen farmhouse on the back of the property. "I have a safe. Some jewelry, too."

Pablo shook his head. "We want the Oxy."

"Oxy?" said Parsons. "What's that?"

Gold Teeth gave Pablo a disappointed look. "And I thought we could have a friendly business discussion." Back to Parsons, no-nonsense time: "Where's the shipment?"

"What shipment?"

"It's in the box, isn't it?"

"What, that?" Parsons turned around. "They're just horse blankets."

"It's in the box . . ."

Five minutes later, Parsons pushed himself up in the hay, bloody and bruised. He watched his two attackers stroll out of the barn with a pile of horse blankets. He punched up a number on his cell. " . . . Catfish, it's me, Parsons . . . Yes, I know what time it is. That's why I'm calling. I've got some bad news . . . I lost the shipment . . . Not police. It was a drug rip-off, two Latin guys with guns. I think they were Mexican . . ."

On the other end of the line: "Something's not right," said Catfish. "If this was just a rip-off, you wouldn't be talking to me. You wouldn't be talking to anyone, ever again . . . But why did they beat the shit out of you? You think they were sending some kind of message . . . What do you mean, they wanted information? What did you give them? . . . I see . . . Hold on, I got another call coming in. I'll get back to you . . ." He punched a couple buttons. "Hello? . . . Yeah, I had a strong feeling who it might be, judging from the odd hour and the fact that two assholes just beat this phone number out of a close friend of mine. I don't know your name yet, but I'll call you a dead man . . . What? Could you repeat that last part? . . . You want to give back the shipment? Then why'd you take it in the first place? . . . You do

realize there are other ways to get someone's attention
. . . You want a meeting? Sure, we can have a meeting
. . . Alone? Absolutely. I won't bring another soul . . .
I got a pen; give me that address . . . Right, see you at
three o'clock . . . And, uh, since we're going into business together, one question, if you don't mind: How'd
you know about the horse barn? . . . What? Last week
you followed my buses from a pain clinic and saw I was
the trail vehicle and then I stopped at a gas station . . ."
Catfish closed his eyes tight. "No, I already know the
rest . . . Right, I'll be there at three." He hung up and
walked out into the parking lot toward the Durango.

His fingers felt around under the back bumper until
they stopped against something that wasn't factory
equipment, attached by a sturdy magnet. He pulled
the GPS homing device free—"son of a bitch"—and
smashed it to small electronic bits on the ground.

Chapter Eighteen

RIVIERA BEACH

Coleman stood on the shore of Singer Island with a Schlitz in his hand, watching the sun rise out of the Atlantic.

"It's dawn. I win another beer." *Pop.*

Serge was on his knees, patting down the courtyard of his fort. He made one last swipe of his trowel over a turret and stood up. "Castillo de San Marcos is completely repaired and ready for the French, possibly Italians."

"What do we do now?"

"Be patient."

"Can I drink beer?"

"Beer drinking is the wayward child of patience."

They headed fifty yards away and reclined in a pair of beach chairs. Coleman reached in their canvas beach bag for another cold one.

Morning broke over the shore.

"Look, it's Coleman! I can't believe it! . . ."

The morning wore on.

"Can I get your autograph?"

The sun tacked across the sky.

"First," said Coleman. "Never use your driver's license to de-seed dope. Cops notice the dirty edge, and now they can even run tests."

"Far out . . ."

Into the afternoon.

Coleman posed for photos. A ring of people with cell phones hit buttons. *Click, click, click . . .*

"Yo! Jackie-O!" said Serge. He stood up as he noticed something down the beach. "We're in business."

Coleman finished signing a ceramic wizard bong and turned around. "What's up?"

"My pal over there just kicked in all my bastions. Knew he couldn't resist." Serge reached into the beach bag and pulled out his latest novelty.

"That's the football you were messing around with last night," said Coleman. "Except it's smaller and bright orange."

"Because it's a special Nerf beach football. The vortex foam model with tail fins." Serge reached back and froze in a classic Dan Marino stance. "It's a gift for him. I'm going to speak real nice, my way of trying to bridge understanding."

"I get it now," said Coleman. "The football is a bomb. You're going to get him to play catch."

"These babies fly so much farther than regular balls that he won't be able to resist showing off for the bubbleheads." Serge took a hike from an invisible center and dropped back in the pocket. "But no, it's not a bomb."

"So it really is a present? You're actually going to be nice to that dick?"

"Speaking nice and being nice are two different things." Serge scrambled in the backfield, eluding make-believe tacklers. "I initially considered the idea of a football bomb, but that would irresponsible because there are too many people around. What if my pass is off target or he tips it and I accidentally blow up some people from Michigan? Imagine the headlines in Detroit. So my scenario demands a pinpoint surgical strike . . . The ball isn't a bomb, but there is a surprise inside."

"Is that what you were doing in the motel room last night, slicing the ball open with a razor blade, then gluing the halves back together?"

"And therein lies the rub . . . Let's see if I can get his attention." Serge stuck two fingers in his mouth and whistled loud.

The muscle-boy turned around.

"Hey, homey!" Serge yelled down the beach. "Got you a present!"

"Go fuck yourself."

"No, really." Serge held it high over his head. "It's the vortex football. Flies forever."

"Am I going to have to come over there and beat your ass in front of everyone?"

"Only if you're afraid my arm's too strong, and you can't handle a simple hitch-and-go pattern."

"I can do hitches in my sleep," the stud shouted back. "And I can definitely deal with anything your scrawny arm can sling."

"Then we're on." Serge stepped up to the line. "Fourth down, trailing by five! Three seconds left! No time-outs! The stadium is going wild! . . ."

The crew cut crouched with a hand on his knee, ready to blast off.

" . . . Storms is in the shotgun, but the crowd's too loud! He steps under center! . . . Hut, hut, ninety-two, forty-six, slant-blue, thirty-eight, hut, sweep-red, twenty-seventy, trap-yellow, seventy-one, whiskey-tango . . ."

The stud took his hand off his knee and stood up.

" . . . Hut, fifteen, box-red, blue-light special, double-A batteries, eleven herbs and spices, fifty ways to leave your lover . . ."

The crew cut placed his hands on his hips in frustration. "Come on! Throw the fucking thing!"

" . . . Jackson Five! Three Dog Night! Turn your head to the side and cough! Hut! Hut! Hike!"

Serge took the snap and faded back in a three-step drop. The stud sprinted down the beach.

" . . . It's a blitz! Storms is forced to scramble! . . ." Serge dodged left and right. " . . . He's flushed out of the pocket! . . ." Serge ran in a circle. " . . . His tight end picked up the linebacker! . . ." More scrambling . . .

The stud stopped running. *"Throw it!"*

" . . . He's got Janofski on his back! . . ." Serge ducked as a phantom player sailed over him. " . . . I don't see how he's staying on his feet! . . . The crowd is losing its mind! . . ."

"Throw it!"

" . . . He's pressured toward the sideline! Here it is! The money play! He reaches back! He releases! Here's your ball game, folks! . . ."

The Nerf flew up in a tight spiral. The stud took off again. The ball arced higher into the blue. The stud picked up speed, now looking back over his shoulder as the ball began its ballistic descent.

"I got it! I got it!"

He continued sprinting on a perfect intersecting path with the ball's trajectory.

"I got it!"

The ball fell into his fingers just as he reached Serge's sand-castle fort.

He stopped in the middle of the fort's courtyard and raised the ball high over his head in triumph. "I told you I'd get it—"

Boom.

The sound concussion got everyone's attention. A huge plume of sand flew into the air like Singer Island was under naval bombardment.

"Where'd he go?" asked Coleman.

"I'm not sure."

Coleman pointed with his beer. "Red stuff's raining down into the water."

"That's him."

Everyone started running. Lifeguards toward the explosion; everyone else in the other direction.

Coleman calmly finished his Schlitz. "I thought you said there wasn't a bomb in the football."

"There wasn't," said Serge, picking up the canvas beach bag. "I told you: too many innocent bystanders around. And in addition to the other reasons, the football would have been an above-ground detonation, which means shrapnel and other hazards could fly out sideways toward families and children. On the other hand, if a device was underground . . ."

"Like buried beneath your sand fort?"

"Hypothetically. Then the blast is vectored upward, eliminating lateral damage and only imperiling that which is directly above."

"Now I understand." Coleman nodded. "He stepped on a makeshift land mine."

"Still too risky," said Serge. "What if a toddler wandered over and stepped on it first before I could scramble out of the pocket? My top priority is public safety."

Behind them, people stampeded away from the black smoke rising out of the crater.

Coleman reached in the bag hanging from Serge's shoulder and came out with another beer. "Then how'd you blow him up?"

"Hypothetically again, what if some rascal had glued a garage-door opener inside the football? With the button taped down in the on position? Those things have a fairly limited range."

"You wanted to open a garage door?"

"No, unimaginative people might want to use it to trigger the actuator on a garage door and park their car for the night." A fire engine raced by. "But what if a certain person decided that instead of wiring the receiver to a garage-door motor, he attached it to a blasting cap under a Spanish sand fort? Oh, and some very small sticks of dynamite that went missing from a limestone quarry west of Miami."

Coleman tossed a beer can in the trash. "So you threw the football to lead him to the fort, and when the garage-door opener got within range . . . I like it. Spanish forts are cool."

Serge grabbed the door handle of the Torino. "History doesn't have to be boring."

U.S. 1

A canvas beach bag sat on a motel bed, brimming with sunscreen, towels, flip-flops and a throwaway camera.

Patrick McDougall stood on a chair and pushed up a ceiling tile.

Bar opened a dresser drawer. "What are you doing?"

Patrick reached into unseen dust. "Hiding my wallet."

"Why?"

"Because people keep knocking on our door."

"When was this?"

"You were in the bathroom getting ready. And also before you woke up. Three so far."

"What did they want?"

"First they acted like they had the wrong room." Pat fit the ceiling panel back in place over his head.

"Then they acted like it was the right room, and asked for a cigarette and said I could listen to their radio. I'm not familiar with the local customs, so I didn't know where it was leading."

"All three said the same thing?"

"No, the last was a woman who told me she was locked out of her room."

"Why is she coming to our room instead of the manager's office," said Bar. "We don't have her keys."

"I pointed that out." Pat hopped down from the chair. "She said she wanted to use my phone so she could call the people inside the room to open up for her."

"What about knocking on her own door?"

"I mentioned that, too," said Pat. "I think something else was going on."

"My Sherlock Holmes."

Pat pointed up at the ceiling. "That's why I'm taking steps."

"Do you think we're in any danger from those people?" asked Bar. "They could come back."

"I don't think so," said Pat. "I watched through the curtains after the woman left. Wanted to see if she tried knocking on her room or went to the manager's office."

"Did she?"

"No, she went across the parking lot and around behind a Dumpster. Then she ducked down."

"Did you see her again?"

"About five minutes later, her head popped up behind the trash bin like a woodchuck. Then back down. It happened a couple more times before I got tired of watching."

Bar looked toward the ceiling. "With your wallet in there, what are you bringing to the beach?"

Pat went over to the nightstand. "My backup wallet." He displayed a cheap fabric billfold. "I transferred just a little cash and an ATM card, because nobody can use it without the PIN number. In the other compartment is my reserve driver's license."

"Reserve?"

"A couple years ago I read a travel tip: Always have a reserve photo ID packed separately on vacation in case you lose the first one. Otherwise you can't clear security and get on the plane for home. So I paid ten bucks for a duplicate license I told them I'd lost."

"You lied?"

"I fibbed. Don't say anything. It was the travel tip."

"Sometimes you worry too much." She jammed a box of Ritz Crackers in the beach bag. "I'm not criticizing; just don't want you to lose your hair."

"Remember when we locked ourselves out of the house, but instead of breaking a window, I'd buried a key in the yard?" Pat tapped a finger on his temple. "Worrying can also have benefits."

"What will you do with the backup wallet while we're swimming?"

"Leave it onshore with our beach blanket, hidden inside my shoe."

Bar unzipped a suitcase. "Isn't the shoe where everybody puts it?"

"I've never heard that."

She stood silent, staring down into the dresser drawer.

Pat slipped into his swim trunks. "What's the matter?"

"These drawers are disgusting. The room doesn't look like the photos."

"We'll barely be in the room."

"But where am I going to unpack?" She walked gingerly across the soiled rug, keeping her arms tight to her body, just as she had ever since they'd gotten inside and fastened all the locks. "Ick, the closet's worse. There's something splattered on the wall." She reached down and pulled a small butter-white square from the nap of the carpet. "Is this what they call crack?"

"I don't know," said Pat, tying off the strings hanging from the front of his swim trunks. "But better put it down. Maybe you can get high from just touching it."

"Doubt it," said Bar. "I'll just throw it in the waste-basket." She stood over their luggage with her hands on her hips. "Where am I going to store our stuff?"

Pat peeled open a power bar. "Maybe just leave it in the bags. We only got the two smallest suitcases."

"Thanks to the airline." She opened her cell phone. "Which reminds me."

Pat got back up on the chair.

"What are you doing?" asked Bar.

"Making sure I remember where my wallet is."

Someone came on the line. Bar pulled the cell close to her ear. "Yes . . . I'm calling to check on some lost luggage . . ." She gave the baggage specialist all the particulars, then became silent.

Pat replaced a ceiling tile. "What's going on?"

Bar covered the phone. "She's checking her computer." Bar uncovered the phone. "Yes, I'm still here . . . Cincinnati?"

Pat jumped down from the chair. "What's Cincinnati got to do with anything?"

Bar held up a hand so she could hear the person on the phone. "What are our bags doing in Cincinnati? . . . I see . . . But you're sure they're going to be on the very next flight down here? . . . Four o'clock? . . . Okay, thank you." She hung up. "Unbelievable. It's one thing if they lose your bags on the flight home, and you've got all your other stuff in the house, but it really affects a short vacation."

"Honey," said Pat. "They told you they were on the next flight. That's just until this afternoon. We'll be at the beach until then."

"But I won't feel comfortable until they're in hand."

"You're the one who always talks about not worrying," said Pat. "Besides, think of it another way: Every vacation has a glitch, and we've just gotten ours out of the way."

"I thought this motel was the glitch."

"Okay, two glitches," said Pat. "What are the chances? That means it can only get better from here."

"I don't know . . ."

"Just look out the window. It's an absolutely beautiful day." Pat grabbed a tiny cooler of generic soda they'd bought at Publix. Then he took her in his arms and gave her a kiss. "This is our special time. We'll only be here so long, and there are only so many hours of great weather to catch. Our luggage will be sitting here or in the motel office when we get back."

"I guess you're right." She grabbed sunglasses off the top of the TV. "But what about my purse?"

Pat climbed up on a chair and raised a ceiling tile. "Hand it to me . . ."

Soon a rented Impala turned east off U.S. 1 and headed down a desolate road of wild marsh vegetation. Except for one unusually large building with an athlete painted on the side, swinging a curved basket.

"What's that?" asked Bar.

"The fronton," said Pat. "I remember it from when I was kid. Let's go watch jai alai tonight."

"What do they do?"

"It's like racquetball, except faster and Spanish."

Their car finally reached the Atlantic Ocean and turned south.

"Now, *this* is A1A," said Pat. "Welcome to Dania Beach."

"It's beautiful," said Bar. "Was it like this when you were young?"

"No, we used to be able to find a place to park."

A half hour later, the Impala drove under a low-hanging yellow iron bar and angled up a ramp.

"A parking garage on the beach?" asked Bar.

"Not what I remember." Pat reached the fourth level before he could find a slot.

Voices and footsteps echoed through the deck as Pat fed money into a machine that spit out a windshield ticket giving them until 5:41 P.M. Eastern Time. It was a half block to the beach. Snack counters, burger shacks, a shaded seating area with a giant plastic ice-cream cone, a beach bar with someone playing three-chord Chicago blues in French. Bicycle rentals, scooter rentals, cabana rentals, no refunds, no parking, no dogs allowed on beach, no wet suits inside, bathrooms for customers only.

"Don't feed the birds!" someone yelled from a pizza window.

Bar quickly jumped out of the way as an oiled-up man zipped by on Rollerblades, checking a cardio monitor strapped to his arm. Someone else furiously pedaled a recumbent bicycle.

Bar turned as they went by. "I thought the beach was for relaxation."

"I was only six."

The couple strolled hand in hand across a vast expanse of shore, covered with bright umbrellas in primary colors and a hundred shoes with wallets. They spread out a Green Bay Packers blanket on the sand and just dropped everything. The water awaited. Off they ran. Pat had oversize trunks with football helmets; Bar's one-piece suit was sexier than most bikinis. They splashed in together, still holding hands. Perfect temperature. They waded out until they were neck-deep and fifty yards from the nearest kid screaming on a raft. Bar climbed on Pat's back and wrapped her arms around his neck. A kiss on the side of the head. "I love you."

"Love you, too."

"I've never seen water this color. Look how it changes with the depth."

"It ain't Lake Erie."

"The motel threw me at first," Bar confessed. "But you were right. This vacation is just what we needed."

"W-what are you doing?"

"What?" A coy smile.

"Bar!" Pat glanced around quickly to see if anyone was watching. Then he looked down in the water at her purposeful hands. "What's gotten into you?"

"What are you talking about?" The smile widened.

They sank to chin level and slowly began a pirouette without speaking. Just a gaze into each other's eyes that they'd never lost.

Another slow romantic turn in the water. The water was at the top of their necks. Bar raised her chin above a wave. "Are you crouching down?"

"No," said Pat. "The water's getting deeper."

Bar smiled at a playful angle. "Are you fooling around?"

Pat shook his head. "I'm on my tiptoes . . . Now I'm not on my tiptoes. I can't feel the bottom."

"You're treading water?"

"I think it's the tide or something. We should swim in to shallower water."

"Okay."

They released each other and began dog-paddling. Two minutes went by.

"I still can't feel the bottom," said Bar. "Are we getting closer to shore?"

"No," said Pat, paddling harder. "In fact, we're farther."

"How can you tell?"

"Those buoys marking the end of the swimming area used to be behind us, and now they're in front . . . We better swim faster."

They both broke into an all-out freestyle stroke. Five minutes later, Bar stopped and came up sputtering and gasping. "I'm all out of breath . . . Wait . . . Have to rest . . . How much farther . . . do we have to go? . . ."

"Hold on . . . Give me a second . . ." Patrick did his own hyperventilating and came up coughing as a wave crashed over them. "Looks like we're even farther . . ."

"But how is that possible? . . . We've exhausted ourselves . . . swimming . . . for five minutes."

"I don't know . . . but the buoys . . . are now . . . way back there."

"Pat," said Bar. "On the beach . . . A guy's waving at us."

"It's the lifeguard . . . He's got a megaphone . . ."

"I can't make out what he's saying . . . Sounds like 'riptide.'"

They timed the next wave and held their breaths so they wouldn't choke. Their heads popped back up. "What's a riptide?"

"Beats me," said Bar. "But now a whole bunch of other people are standing at the edge of the water and waving."

"They're all motioning to the left," said Pat. "And the lifeguard is saying something else in his megaphone."

"I think he's telling us to swim parallel to the beach."

"Why would we want to do that?"

"I don't know," said Bar. "But he's got a megaphone, so he must know what he's talking about."

"Okay, ready when you are," said Pat, taking a few last deep breaths. "Just stay ahead of me so if you're tiring out again, I'll know . . ."

They took off splashing again.

Three minutes later, Bar stopped and grabbed Pat's arm. "Need to rest again . . . Do we keep swimming this way?"

"I don't think so," said Pat. "The people on the beach are waving us toward them . . . And there's a lifeguard on a paddleboard coming out. He's pulling a spare board."

The couple headed toward shore at a much slower rate, but making progress this time. Halfway back, they met the lifeguard. "Grab this paddleboard side by side and kick with your feet."

The couple stretched their arms over the top of the waxed board and began splashing toward shore. "What just happened?" asked Bar.

"You got caught in a riptide," said the lifeguard.

"A what?"

"Lots of tourists don't know, but sometimes underwater channels form in the sand, and when waves go back out, their speed is greatly increased because of the depth and added volume the channel can accommodate."

"We were over one of those channels?" asked Pat.

"Must have been," said the lifeguard. "The suction is deceptively strong, and a lot of people drown because they follow natural instinct and try to fight it by swimming straight for shore, but that only takes them farther out and exhausts them."

"Is that why everyone was waving for us to swim sideways?" asked Pat. "So we would clear the channel and then come in?"

"That's the picture," said the lifeguard. "You're a couple of the lucky ones."

"This is getting ridiculous," said Bar. "First luggage, then the motel, and now this."

"But the lifeguard said we were lucky." Pat grinned. "So it evens out."

"My math says three glitches."

"Exactly," said Pat. "The odds must be astronomical. We're now due for the best vacation ever."

Paddling continued. "Uh, Pat," said Bar. "What's that guy onshore doing?"

"Which one?"

"The one standing on our beach blanket holding your shoe."

Pat sighed. "At least it was just my backup wallet."

"Four glitches," said Bar. "And don't say it's only going to get better from here."

Pat kept kicking. "But how can it not?"

"Excuse me," said the lifeguard. "Can you stop kicking?"

"Why?"

"And just let me move my board around behind yours . . ." The lifeguard slid over to their backside and pulled out a small baton that was clipped to his waist. He swung it down hard into the water, landing the end on a moist snout.

There was an explosive thrash in the surf, before a dorsal fin quickly knifed away.

Pat looked up dubiously at the lifeguard. "Was that a shark?"

"The chamber of commerce would prefer you didn't say anything."

Chapter Nineteen

BROWARD COUNTY

The boom box played the kind of optimistic Benny Goodman tune that made everyone want to go out and buy war bonds.

Three rows of retired women lined up on cue.

"Ladies, you look even more exquisite than last time! I am one lucky man. Let's get started." Wolfgang walked to the end of the first row. "Mildred, shall we?"

They began swaying to the music.

The front door opened. A bellowing voice. "I absolutely *love* ballroom dancing!"

Wolfgang stopped swaying. "Sir, we just started a class. Please."

"Then I'm right on time," said Serge. "Come on, Coleman."

Wolfgang forced a smile toward the rest of the group. "Excuse me a moment. Just continue."

He rushed over. "Please, this is a private class. Now, if you wouldn't mind . . ."

Serge pulled a wad of bills from his pocket. "Does this open it?"

He'd found Wolfgang's soft spot. "Two-fifty," said the instructor.

"Let's make it an even three," said Serge, peeling off hundreds.

Wolfgang looked suspiciously over at Coleman, who grinned and raised a can of Pabst Blue Ribbon in salute. "Dancing's cool."

"Don't worry about him," said Serge. "He'll be my partner."

Oh, they're partners, thought Wolfgang. *That explains it.* He felt more at ease as he pocketed the cash. "Okay, take a spot in the back." Then he walked to the front. "As we were . . ." He took Mildred's hand.

Everyone moved gracefully to the big-band music. Except Serge, who manically jitterbugged out of tempo with the melody, twirling Coleman around and around.

Wolfgang rolled his eyes. After three minutes, he moved to his next partner.

Suddenly, from the rear of the room: "Whoa! Dizzy! . . ." Coleman staggered sideways and crashed into a mirror.

Everyone stopped and stared.

Serge smiled back. "Sorry, must have twirled him too much . . . Coleman, straighten up. You're attracting attention." Coleman gripped the sides of a plastic wastebasket, his head all the way down inside, retching. Serge smiled again at the others. "It's his first time. Stage nerves."

Coleman grabbed a stool on the side and took a time-out for the duration. Wolfgang worked his way along a series of partners in the front row, and Serge worked along the back. "Agnes, you're a natural!"

An hour later, they were done. The students thanked Wolfgang as usual and shuffled out the front door. Except those who decided to stay behind for additional, personal attention.

Wolfgang stuck his head out his office door and looked at the chairs lined up against the wall. Gertrude, Rita, Phoebe . . . and Serge and Coleman.

He took a deep breath and called the first woman in.

The afternoon went by. None of the ladies were left. Wolfgang stepped out of his office and conspicuously jingled keys. "Sorry, guys, have to lock up for the day."

Serge jumped to his feet. "What? But we didn't get to talk!"

"I've got an important appointment."

Serge pulled out the roll of cash again. "And I've got a business proposition. It'll just take a minute."

Wolfgang couldn't take his eyes off the dough. "Okay, but just one minute."

They went back inside and took seats.

Serge gestured with the hand that held the cash. "Let's get money out of the way first."

"Fine by me," said Wolfgang. "How much are we talking about?"

"All of it."

"All of it?" said Wolfgang. Wow, it was a big roll. "What's your proposition?"

"I want you to give back all the money that you fleeced from these wonderful, trusting women. In exchange, you'll never see me again. Believe me, it's a bargain. Ask around." He sat back and folded his arms with a big smile.

Wolfgang reached for the phone. "I'm calling the police."

"And have them go through your financials again? You just got lucky last time when the woman stood up for you and they had to drop the charges. Only cowards prey on the most vulnerable."

Wolfgang withdrew his hand. "Who *are* you?"

"Serge A. Storms. And I'm just crazy about reading newspapers, every word every day, starting with the funnies and ending with articles about scams so I can line up scores. Maybe you can answer this: How come Blondie's eyes don't have any pupils? It creeps me out." Serge shook at the thought.

"You're nuts! Get out of my office!"

"I see you've accepted my terms." Serge stood and unfolded two pieces of paper on the desk. "Just sign on the dotted lines. And give back my three hundred and anything you've got in the safe . . ."

"Out!"

" . . . This first form redistributes your profits. And the second is your revised will that leaves everything to your students. But that's just a fail-safe, like a John Garfield clause, in the unlikely event that something unfortunate should happen to you before the first document can be executed."

"I'm not signing anything!"

Serge reached under his shirt, and pressed a .44 between Wolfgang's eyes.

"Where's my pen?"

"That's better," said Serge.

Moments later, Wolfgang was on his knees in front of an open office safe. "This is all of it."

Serge finished stuffing the contents into his pockets. "Now, that wasn't so hard." He pulled the gun again and motioned toward the door. "Let's take a little ride."

"But I thought we had a deal."

"I never signed anything." Serge turned. "Coleman, did I sign anything?"

Coleman shook his head.

Serge shrugged at Wolfgang. "You should always get everything in writing . . . Now, get up."

"Wait!" Wolfgang threw out his hands in a pleading gesture. "I know where you can get a lot more money. Thousands. *Tens* of thousands!"

"That's fear talking," said Serge. "Fear's a bullshit artist."

"This is real, I swear," said Wolfgang. "The dance studio just got a new investor. Another guy in this strip mall. He runs a pain clinic . . ."

Serge scratched his chin with the end of the gun, then sat back down. "Tell me more."

"He's got at least five offices now. They work with these Mexicans who are trying to corner the market as the local wholesaler."

And he laid out the whole pipeline plan, cradle to grave. Including the Kentucky customers.

"Interesting," said Serge. "And they always use the same motel?"

"I don't know. I think so."

"You've done great," said Serge. "Now let's go for that ride."

U.S. 1

Patrick stood outside their room at the Casablanca. "My face is on fire."

"You're severely sunburned." Bar reached into a drugstore bag and removed an aerosol can. "You shouldn't have fallen asleep on the beach while I was window-shopping."

"But I was tired from the riptide."

Bar uncapped the Solarcaine. "Close your eyes and hold still."

A hissing sound.

"Why are we outside?" asked Pat.

"Because this really musts up the air if you spray indoors."

"Can I open my eyes now?"

Bar replaced the cap. "All done."

Pat felt his face. "This is definitely going to peel."

"No, it's not," said Bar. "Your face will just feel hot tonight."

A voice behind them from in front of the next room: "Can I borrow some of that?"

"Sure." She handed over the can.

The man uncapped it again, spraying heavily into a brown paper bag, then placing the mouth of the bag over his face and inhaling deeply. His eyes rolled back in his head as he crashed back through the door of his room, the can of Solarcaine clanking across the parking lot.

Bar quickly opened their own door, and the couple rushed inside.

"What was the deal with that guy?" said Bar, grabbing dry clothes.

Pat leaned with his face three inches from the mirror, staring and slowly running fingers over his eyebrows. "I fell asleep on the beach with my sunglasses on. I look like a raccoon."

"Just wear sunglasses whenever we go out until it fades."

Patrick climbed up on a chair. "It's definitely going to peel."

"What do you want to do about dinner?"

"Maybe the Mai-Kai?" said Pat. "My parents used to rave about it when I was a kid." He pushed back a ceiling tile and felt around in the dust. "Where's my wallet? Someone stole my wallet."

"Wonderful," said Bar. "Did they also steal my purse?"

"No, here it is." Pat reached deep into the ceiling. "Whoever stole my wallet probably didn't find it because it was pushed back farther." As he retrieved the handbag, his fingers found something else.

"What's that?" asked his wife.

Pat held the discovery in front of his face. "Looks like a joint from those drug-education slide shows at our school. Someone else must have been up here in the ceiling before me." He replaced the tile and jumped down from the chair. "Told you it was a good place to hide stuff."

Bar slipped on denim shorts. "Is the whole state like this?"

"You're stereotyping based on a few random glitches."

"So we've lost a specific glitch count now?"

"It's just a weird run. There's no way it can continue—"

A knock at the door.

Bar raised her eyebrows.

"Odds on our side," said Pat, walking past and opening the door. "Hello?"

"I'm locked out of my room," said a woman. *"Can I use your phone?"*

"Pat," Bar yelled from behind. "Is she the same one?"

"No, another." He faced the woman again. "I'll bet I can help. You know that thing you just did with your knuckles on this door to get me to come and open it? Try that."

He closed the door.

"Why are you smiling?" asked Bar.

"I think I'm getting the hang of this."

"I think we might consider going home early."

"But the airline will hammer us with charges for the flight change. I told you: It's just been a quirky twenty-four hours. Nothing else can possibly—"

A cell phone rang.

"Nobody calls your phone," said Bar. "We only have it for road emergencies."

"Then let's answer it." Pat dug it out of a pocket on his suitcase and flipped it open. "Hello? . . . Fraud unit? Who is this— . . . Our credit-card company? . . . Do we have our cards in our possession? . . . Uh, that's hard to say . . . Because it's a big ceiling with a lot of dust and I don't want to jump to conclusions until I can get back up there with a flashlight . . . No, it was a travel tip . . ."

"What's the matter?" asked Bar.

"They want to know if we have our credit cards."

Bar fished in her purse. "I found mine."

Pat got back on the phone. "Half accounted for . . . And I'll bet if I had a flashlight— Are you sure some-one's running up charges? . . . I see. Well, they must have gotten our number off a receipt or something . . . What? They actually presented a card with a valid magnetic strip? But how is that possible? . . . Computers? I don't mean to be critical, but this is very disconcerting . . . Sure, I can verify recent transactions . . . Could you repeat that? . . . All fifteen of those were for an even hundred dollars at a department store? To the penny? . . . Uh-huh, I see. The thieves often go on a spree and buy a bunch of gift cards before the account is turned off . . . That makes sense. I shop at that store all the time near our home in Wisconsin. Someone must have gotten it there . . . What do you mean 'not Wisconsin'? . . . South Florida? What's the address? . . ." Pat clicked open a pen and grabbed something to write on. "But that's just a few blocks from our motel . . . What? There's one last transaction? Forty-three dollars and sixty-two cents? The Oasis Inn? . . ." Pat walked to the window and peeked through the curtains. On the other side of U.S. 1, a lighted motel sign with camels and date palms. "That's right across the street! Call the cops! . . . What do you mean your job is just to document fraudulent activity? They just made the charge on our account! And it's a motel, not a store. They're probably in there right now, maybe even sleeping! You can break the case! . . ." Pat listened some more to the phone, then quietly hung up.

"What's the matter?" asked Bar.

"The good news is we're not responsible for any charges."

"The bad news?"

"They turned off our cards."

"What!" Bar stood up rod straight. "But we need them for our vacation. We're practically stranded here without them."

"They said that they would immediately issue replacements."

Bar relaxed. "Okay, where do we pick them up?"

"They can only mail them to our billing address."

"Wisconsin?"

"For our security," said Pat.

"At least we still have our ATM cards. Or one card. Your shoe."

"Except there's not enough money in the account."

"Don't forget the two hundred in cash we brought with us," said Bar. "It'll just about cover . . ."

"Except half of that was also in my shoe."

"This is getting old fast."

Ringgggg!

It was the room's old rotary phone.

The couple stared at it in silence.

Ringgggg!

"Who do you think is calling us?" asked Bar.

"Nobody knows we're here," said Pat.

Ringgggg!

"Are you going to answer it?"

Pat tentatively picked up the receiver. " . . . Hello? . . ."

Bar watched intently.

Pat finished listening. "No." He hung up.

"Who was that?" asked Bar.

"Woman says she's still locked out of her room and would like to use our phone." Pat walked to the window and pulled the curtains open a foot. "This really pisses me off."

"Honey," said Bar. "You never get mad. And you never say 'pissed off.' "

"I know." Pat took a measured breath and squinted across the street at the blue neon strip under the overhang along the front of the Oasis Inn. "It's just that there are some people staying in one of those rooms who are ruining our special vacation, and the credit-card company won't even call the police about them . . . Maybe I should call."

"What good will that do?"

"If they're arrested, maybe the credit-card company will turn our cards back on."

"I don't think it works that way," said Bar.

"I don't care anymore," said Pat. "My face feels hot again."

"Put on more Solarcaine."

"I've had it with what's happening to the country. First those politicians and their layoffs, now these criminals." Pat glared out the window. "I'm not going to stand idly this time."

Bar came up from behind. She put her arms around his waist and her head on the back of his shoulder. "Honey, don't scare me. I've never seen you this upset. These people . . . we don't know what they're capable of. What if they retaliate?"

"They can't if we call the anonymous tip line."

"But we don't know who they are," said Bar. "Or even what room they're staying in."

"Already thought of that," said Pat. "And we actually do know their names."

He took a seat on the bed and grabbed a thick phone book from the bottom of the nightstand. Pages heavily curled at the top right. A big chunk missing in the middle. Dated six years ago. Pat flipped to *Hotels and Motels* and ran a finger down to the *O*s. "Got it!"

"Pat . . ." Bar sat down on the bed next to him. "Please don't do anything rash."

Pat stopped and took her hands in his. "Baby, I'd never do anything to put you in harm's way. My face is still hot, but I'm thinking straight now."

"Are you sure?"

"Positive. Sometimes private citizens just have to step off the sidelines and take action for the betterment of society." He dialed his cell phone. "Hello? Is this the Oasis Inn? . . . Could I have the room number of Patrick McDougall? . . . You're not allowed to give out information on guests? Then could you ring his room for me? . . . Thanks . . ."

Bar snapped a whisper: "What are you doing?"

"*Shhhhh!* . . . Hello? . . . Yes, I'm also staying at the Oasis and we were just leaving the parking lot and I thought I saw a dropped wallet outside your room with a lot of money blowing out of it, but we were really late for something and couldn't stick around . . . Who is this? . . . I can't hear you; you're breaking up." Pat held the phone out at arm's length and clapped it shut.

"What's going on?" asked Bar.

"To the window!" said Pat.

Bar joined him, heads side by side in the curtains. "This is actually exciting."

Pat's nose was almost against the glass. "And it's totally safe behind this window, like it's all happening out there on TV—"

"A door's opening!" said Bar. "Hide!"

They pulled the curtains tight to their faces, so each only had one eyeball's view.

Two people came out. A woman in sparkling hot pants and a halter top, bare feet, with a tall blond wig that looked like it was kept in a sock drawer. The man weighed half as much, wearing orange paisley boxers and a LeBron James jersey that was inside out. They scanned the ground in front of the room. Even crouched down to peek under cars for fluttering currency. Then she kicked him in the ass, literally, and chased him back into the room . . .

Back across the street, Patrick McDougall wrote "113" on a notepad and held it up. "Is that the right room number?"

"It's the one I saw," said Bar.

Pat grabbed his cell phone, then thought about it and put it down. He picked up the rotary phone on the nightstand—and thought about that, too. He hung up.

After years of marriage, it was telepathy. "Pat," said Bar. "I saw a pay phone at the corner. They can't trace the anonymous tip call to us or the room."

Pat ran out the door, rooting around in his pocket for change. He dialed 911. "Hello, yes, my emergency is that someone is staying in room 113 of the Oasis Inn with a stolen credit card . . . How is that an emergency? Because if you hurry, you can catch them! . . . My name? . . ." He hung up.

Bar was waiting when he got back. "What did the police say?"

"They're sending someone, but I got the feeling it wasn't a top priority."

"But they stole from us."

Pat shrugged. Then they watched out the window. And watched.

"They're not coming," said Bar.

"But they're supposed to," said Pat.

The couple got tired of peeking outside and made sandwiches from their cooler. They watched some tube, local news. Drifter arrested in slaying, police ask public's help in identifying torso, man charged with groping Minnie Mouse at Disney, vacationers carjacked in a rental from airport. They decided not to watch the tube.

Pat stretched and yawned. They checked the window one last time to see if the police had come, then went to bed.

Chapter Twenty

JUST AFTER MIDNIGHT

Another full moon rose above the trees.

A key went into the trunk of a Gran Torino. The hood popped. Wolfgang Finch raised his hands. "Please don't kill me."

"That's entirely up to you."

"I'll do anything," said Wolfgang.

"I know you will," said Serge. "Let me give you a hand out of there since you're tied up."

"Hey." Wolfgang looked back up the road. "That's my car."

"Coleman drove it over behind us." Serge grabbed him roughly by the collar and began walking him down the street, where the front of a black car sat even with a white line painted across the pavement. "And a nice ride it is, classic BMW, the best old ladies' money could buy."

"I'm so sorry about that! You don't have to do anything to me."

"Maybe." Serge opened the driver's door. "But I'm concerned that if I let you off easy, I'll be gypping you out of a free self-improvement lesson . . . Get in."

Wolfgang looked both ways. A long, empty road in both directions, surrounded by woods. Nowhere to run. "You realize that somebody could drive by any minute. You'll get caught."

"I don't think so." Serge pushed Wolfgang's head down and shoved him into the coupe. Then he stuck his own face inside. "Before I opened my trunk to let you out, I borrowed some barricades and detour signs from a nearby road construction site. They've got a million of them—never miss a few. And I set them up at both ends of the street so nobody will inadvertently drive by, because this might get embarrassing if you start crying. I respect your dignity."

A beer can popped. "Serge," said Coleman. "Where are we?"

"Glad you asked!" Serge turned on his camcorder and handed it to his buddy. "We're in Lake Wales. Spook Hill to be specific. So renowned locally that the nearby school is named Spook Hill Elementary, and its mascot is Casper the Friendly Ghost . . . But what's spooky about this hill? you ask. I'll tell you! Ancient lore has it that this was an old Indian settlement, and the biggest granddaddy gator of them all used to raid its residents. The brave chief set out alone into the marsh to vanquish their foe in single-handed combat. The chief prevailed, but the struggle was so fierce it left a depression massive enough that the next rainy season created a lake." Serge laughed heartily and elbowed Wolfgang. "The wacky stories we have in our state's history! That's why I love this place!"

"But, Serge," asked Coleman, "what's the spooky part?"

"It's also been said that this hill is haunted, either by the gator seeking revenge, or the chief protecting his land. The ghost wasn't clear on that." Serge ran back to his car and returned with coils of thick rope. He reached into the BMW. "Now hold still."

"No! Stop!" Wild wiggling. "Not that! Oh God, I know what you're going to do! I'm begging you!"

"Shut up!" Serge socked him in the jaw, then lowered his voice. "Can you let a man concentrate while he's working?"

Serge continued his task until he was finished with a series of intricate knots. He'd pushed the driver's seat all the way back and left Wolfgang sitting cross-legged on the floorboards, hands bound and neck tied securely to the bottom of the steering wheel. Wolfgang's nose pressed hard against the blue-and-white BMW emblem in the center of the wheel.

Serge made another supply run and wedged a pair of bricks under the brake pedal. "Ain't no way those are coming loose. Stay there—I'll be right back."

Serge retrieved a cooler from the Gran Torino and set it beside the Beemer. Then he ran into the woods. Wolfgang heard a scraping sound and tried to turn his head to see. Serge dragged another barricade scraping across the street and around to the open driver's door.

"We're almost ready." Serge patted the top of the barricade with a flashing amber light. "This is the last detail and then it's all up to our contestant. I promised I'd give you the chance to decide your fate."

"We're almost ready to do what?" asked Wolfgang.

"Stage a car accident." Serge spread his arms. "I'm sure your new investor told you all about it, so the odds are in your favor, right?" He opened the cooler and held an ice block in his captive's face. "Got three more of these. I'm going to place them in front of the front tires and behind the rear tires." He ran around the car and came back.

"Serge," said Coleman. "The air bag is going to break his neck."

"That's what he was thinking during all that screaming a few minutes ago."

"Reminds me of what Jim Davenport did to that
carjacker."

"That was different." Serge reached inside the car
and threw the gearshift in neutral. "But it was the
kernel of this concept." He faced Wolfgang again and
rubbed his palms together impishly. "Ready to play?"

The answer was uncontrolled sobbing.

"Here's the deal," said Serge. "It's hot as hell out
tonight, so that ice is going to melt pretty fast on this
pavement. And when it does, since the car's in neutral,
this baby will begin rolling either forward or backward. So you just tell me which way you think it will
go, and I'll set the barricade up on the other end of the
car. If you're right, the BMW will harmlessly roll to a
stop. If you're wrong, you hit the barricade, and the air
bag goes off, and yuck . . . you can figure it out."

Wolfgang just stared sideways with his nose mashed
into leather.

"Which is it going to be?" asked Serge.

"Is this a trick question?" asked Wolfgang.

"I don't know. Is it?"

Wolfgang twisted his head slightly. "Obviously that
way."

"Which way?"

"Backward," said Wolfgang. "Downhill."

"Excellent!" Serge dragged the barricade and set it up an appropriate distance in front of the car. He returned—"Let the games begin!"—and slammed the driver's door.

They retreated to the opposite side of the road as Coleman raised the camcorder and filmed little rivers of water trickling from under the tires. "That ice is melting fast like you said. It's almost gone . . . But I don't get it. You usually never give assholes such an easy chance to get away."

"Look again."

"At what?"

"The ice water."

"Hey, it's trickling the wrong way." His head swung toward Serge. "But how is that possible?"

"This hill is what's known as a gravity hill, also known as a magnetic hill . . ."

"The ice is gone," said Coleman. "The car is starting to roll . . . *uphill?*"

"Actually an optical illusion of the landscape, because the human mind prioritizes visual cues over internal equilibrium." The coupe continued picking up speed. "Early settlers first discovered it when they noticed horses increasing their labor when they were supposed to be going downhill."

Hysterical screaming from the luxury sedan as it crossed the final distance and crashed into the barricade.

Bang.

The pair winced and puckered their butts.

Coleman turned off the camera. "Spook Hill sure is spooky."

Serge slapped him on the back. "I love keeping legends alive."

MEANWHILE . . .

Two A.M.

Pat woke up. He looked at the digital alarm clock as the number flipped over. 2:01. Then he looked the other way. Bar's eyes were open, staring back at him.

"How long have you been awake?" asked Pat.

"I just woke up."

"Me, too."

"Did something wake us?" Bar sat up in bed. "Maybe a sound in our sleep?"

"What was that loud noise just now?"

"Sounded like a firecracker," said Bar. "I've been hearing them ever since we checked in . . . What are you doing?"

Pat was out of bed. "Turning on the TV to block the noise so we can sleep."

They closed their eyes again.

They opened them. Bar was staring again. "Did you put on a police show?"

"No, those are real sirens."

They both threw off the blankets and ran to the window.

Across the street, a patrol car jumped the curb and screeched to a stop, high beams blazing on the door of room 113 at the Oasis Inn.

"Well, what do you know," said Pat. "They're finally responding to our call."

"It's about time."

The officer drew his weapon and took up a defensive position in the parking lot, shielded by the open door of his car. More cruisers converged from both directions on U.S. 1 until six units were angled in the parking lot, all headlights on the room. More officers behind doors with large guns.

Bar looked back at her husband. "I thought you said this credit-card thing wasn't a priority."

"Looks like they changed their minds."

One officer made a series of silent signals, and the K-9 unit led the charge. They kicked in the door and poured through.

Pat tore open another granola bar. "This is almost worth getting our credit card stolen."

Bar looked at him.

Back out the window: The K-9 unit emerged and gave the remaining troops the all clear. Then typical aftermath. Ambulances arrived. A supervisor's unmarked car. The TV trucks. One officer began unrolling yellow crime-scene tape.

The locals slowly began creeping forward to form the required sidewalk gallery of onlookers.

Pat slipped into his pants.

"What are you doing?"

"Going outside to see what's happening."

"Wait for me . . ."

The police took statements and drank coffee. Onlookers swapped gossip, gestured in every direction and floated various theories involving drugs, sex slaves, black helicopters and another face-eating zombie.

Paramedics appeared in the doorway, wheeling out a stretcher.

Bar nudged her husband. "Looks like they had a fight. One of them's hurt."

Small wheels wobbled as the paramedics pushed the stretcher toward the back of an ambulance.

"I think he's more than hurt," said Pat. "The sheet's covering the entire body."

"He's dead?" said Bar.

"From what I've seen on TV shows."

More paramedics came out. Another stretcher.

"They're both dead?" said Bar.

"And I just talked to them a few hours ago," added Pat.

"You're saying that like you knew them."

"Ooooo, there's a lot of blood on that sheet. It's near the head."

"That's horrible."

One of the ranking officers called a small meeting on the opposite curb. "Get those shell casings to forensics, dump the motel's phone for all calls incoming and outgoing, and"—he made a twirling gesture in the air with his finger—"canvass five blocks. Make sure to check all the Dumpsters and storm drains."

The officers respectfully nodded and dispersed. Eventually, so did the onlookers. A few at first, until the McDougalls felt slightly conspicuous.

"Let's get back inside," said Pat. "We don't want to be the only ones out here."

A last officer: " . . . And check that pay phone at the corner."

Chapter Twenty-One

THE NEXT MORNING

Rush-hour traffic stacked up on I-95 near the Pompano exit.

Rubberneckers.

But no wreck. Just another roadside altercation, where a couple of motorists screamed in each other's face on the highway shoulder that sloped into the palmettos and a ranch fence. A more common sight in South Florida than a flat tire.

Vehicles slowed even more as the entertainment increased. It had come to blows. Rabbit punches and roundhouse haymakers. Someone got thrown over the hood. The other had sand and gravel thrown in his face. They tangled up good, rolling on the ground, pulling hair. The taller one finally broke free and ran back to his car.

A gun came out.

That made half the other drivers duck and speed away. The other half stopped completely.

The unarmed combatant was back on his feet, holding out his arms, begging and pleading as the gunman approached.

Before the witnesses could digest what they were seeing, two large-caliber shots rang out. But unlike the movies, when a victim's body jerks as slugs strike, the unfortunate person simply slumped straight down to the ground like an electric toy being unplugged.

There was an immediate string of rear-enders. Then more crashes as the crazed assailant swept his gun at their cars—"*What are you looking at, mother-fuckers?*" The gunman finally tucked the pistol in his waistband, grabbed his victim under the armpits and dragged him back to his car, where he pushed the body into the backseat and took off for the exit.

Halfway down the ramp, Coleman sat up in the backseat of the '76 Gran Torino and looked out the rear window. "Those people are really acting jumpy. They're all standing outside their cars on cell phones . . . I guess those blanks in your gun sounded pretty real."

"America loves fake disputes!" said Serge, reloading in his lap with live bullets. "This is going to be the best reality show ever!"

"Where to now?"

"The beach," said Serge. "At some point, our show has to capture a real crime in progress or we face criticism from CNN's *Showbiz Tonight*. Hand me the camcorder so I can change the tape."

Coleman turned around and reached behind the backseat, toward the middle of the carpeted ledge under the rear window, where the video camera was duct-taped in place and aimed out the rear of the muscle car to film the previous action. "What kind of crime? . . ."

U.S. 1

Nine A.M.

Patrick McDougall's eyes fluttered open in room 17 of the Casablanca Inn.

Bar opened hers, too.

"Some noise again?" asked Pat.

"I don't know. I was asleep."

A sharp knock on the door.

"Don't answer it," said Bar. "Probably that woman."

Another hard knock. *"Police. Is anyone in there?"*

Pat jumped out of bed. "I better answer it."

He opened the door. Two men in suits flashed badges. "Patrick McDougall?"

Pat rubbed his eyes. "Is this about the credit card?"

"I don't know," said the detective on the left. "Is it?"

Moments later, all the lights in the room were blazing. The detectives preferred to stand. One wrote in a notebook and glared. Pat and Bar sat on the edge of the bed, clutching their legs together and holding their arms close to their chests, trying to make themselves small.

The first detective looked up from his notebook. "We've got two different Patrick McDougalls staying in motel rooms across the street from each other."

"That's a pretty big coincidence," said the second.

"Except now there's only one," said the first.

"That's pretty convenient," said the second.

"How do we know the other guy wasn't the real Patrick McDougall?" asked the first. "And you stole *his* identity?"

"Why is your face peeling all over?" asked the second.

Pat held out innocent hands. "But I really am Patrick McDougall."

"He is!" said Bar. "They stole *our* credit card."

The detectives maintained steely eyes on Pat. "Do you have any photo identification to prove who you are?"

"Absolutely." Pat started to stand. "I . . . no. My driver's license was stolen from my shoe."

"Shoe?"

"And my primary wallet with my second driver's license was stolen from the room while we were gone."

"How did you have a second license?" asked the other detective.

"I paid for one at motor vehicles. Told them it was lost."

"Was it lost?"

"Not really."

"So you lied under oath?"

"It was a travel tip. The book told me to."

"What else have you been lying about?"

Bar reached for her purse. "I have my license. Will that help?"

"Stop!" said the first detective. "Take your hands out. I'll get your wallet."

The other detective: "So you're saying that you have no idea who those people across the street were, and you'd never met them. Is that your story?"

Pat nodded emphatically. "That's right. We really don't have anything to hide."

The other detective flipped pages in his notebook. "Then why did we trace a phone call from your cell to their room?"

"Oh, the call," said Pat. "I can explain. I was trying to draw them into the parking lot."

"Do you make a habit of that?"

"No, look . . ." Pat clutched the sheets on each side of him. "The credit-card company notified us about fraud, but they said they wouldn't call the police."

"So you talked them out of calling the police?"

"No, no, no, it's the other way," said Pat. "It's very complicated."

"It seems to be."

The other detective pointed out the window. "Why did you hang up when the police asked you your name?"

"What?"

"Are you denying that you called 911 from the pay phone down at the corner?"

"Oh, that," said Pat. "Yes, I made that call."

"You're changing your statement?" asked the second detective.

"No!"

"So you're going back to denying it?"

"Yes, no, huh?"

"You've been making a lot of phone calls for someone who has nothing to hide."

Bar mustered courage and stood. "What happened across the street last night? Maybe if you tell us, we might be able to help you clear this up."

"Major drug rip-off," said the first detective. "There was a lot of cocaine moving out of that room. Except we didn't find any. The place was totally ransacked, so the shooter apparently didn't get what he came for."

The second detective jotted in his notebook. "How do we know it wasn't *you* who was moving a lot of cocaine out of *this* room?"

"I don't know," said Pat. "I mean, no. Definitely no . . . I'm confused."

"That happens when you can't keep your lies straight."

The other detective reached in a wastebasket. "Is this your crack?"

"No," said Pat. "My wife put it there."

"Your wife smokes crack?"

The second detective stared down at the carpet. A fresh sprinkling of plaster dust. He looked up at an ill-fitting ceiling tile. "Have you been in the ceiling lately?"

"I was hiding stuff."

"I thought you had nothing to hide."

The other detective pointed with his pen. "I'll ask you again: Why did you hang up when the police asked your name?"

"I didn't want the people across the street to recognize who called."

"I thought you said you didn't know them."

"We don't," said Pat. "It was just we were trying to be cautious. Ever since we got here, lots of people have been knocking on our door."

One detective looked at the other. "Drug activity."

"There's no drug activity in this room," protested Pat.

The other detective reached in the wastebasket again. "Is this your joint?"

"What? No, I threw it away."

"I thought you said there were no drugs in here."

"Except for that," said Pat. "And the crack."

"So all these people are knocking on your door just because you're popular?"

"It's not what it seems," said Pat. "Like these women keep knocking and asking to use the phone to call people and let them back in the room they locked themselves out of."

"That doesn't make any sense," said the first detective. "You want us to believe people keep knocking on your door who don't know how to knock on other doors?"

"I—"

A cell rang. The detective held up a hand for Pat to stop. "Store that thought." He reached inside his jacket and flipped open his phone. "Benson here . . . Really? They check out? The credit-card company and their airline confirmed everything? . . . Even the school board in Wisconsin? . . . No, actually the story they're giving us is totally shaky, but I think we can attribute that to the fact they've been holed up in this room smoking crack, joints and PCP—"

"There's no PCP," said Pat.

" . . . Now he's claiming just crack and marijuana . . . Yeah, real paranoid. They were even up in the ceiling . . . Tell me about it . . . But it's the Casablanca, so it all fits . . . No, just a small rock and dusty joint in the wastebasket. Not enough to hold up in court . . . Yeah, we can always charge them later if we think they might lead us to bigger fish. But it's such a tragedy that they work around children. You might want to alert the education department back in Wisconsin—"

"No!" the couple yelled in unison.

The detective finally hung up. "Well, it looks like you're in the clear. But I strongly suggest you get some help for your problem."

"But we don't have a problem."

The detectives exchanged a knowing glance. "Then you're just going to have to hit rock bottom before you see the light . . ."

The pair headed for the door.

"Wait!" said Pat. "So that's it? You're completely done with us now?"

"We are."

"What's that supposed to mean?" asked Bar.

The first detective looked out the window at the Oasis Inn across the street. "I can't get into specifics about injuries sustained by the bodies, because we're withholding certain details from the public . . ."

" . . . That's how we verify confessions," said the other detective. "You've seen TV . . ."

" . . . But based on the level of torture, it would appear the victims didn't have any product or information. That means there's a very unsatisfied individual still on the streets, which could lead to another problem. We've seen it a hundred times before."

"What kind of problem?" asked Pat.

"Mistaken identity," said the first detective.

"Someone definitely has a bone to pick with a Patrick McDougall," said the second.

Pat's cell phone rang. Pat jumped.

The first detective reached toward the sound. "I'll get that if you don't mind . . . Hello? . . . I see . . . I see . . . Thanks." He hung up.

"What was it?" asked Pat.

The detectives headed out the door. "Your luggage is in Baltimore."

Chapter Twenty-Two

HOLLYWOOD BEACH

"The ocean!" yelled Serge, whipping an empty coffee cup into the trash. "And there's one of those big-ass beach stores that sells bikinis, water toys, alligator-shaped bottle openers and T-shirts with coded messages about penises. Let's shop!"

Serge raced around the aisles like it was a game show. Moments later, he plopped his purchases on the counter. "Okay, last chance to spin around where I'm standing in case I forgot something essential. Do I need batteries? Nose plugs? Eye protection? First-aid kit? Frisbee? Badminton racquet? Swim noodles? Temporary tattoo? Shot glass? Pez-like condom dispenser? Live hermit crab in a pet cage? Dead baby shark in a jar? Plastic pirate sword? Super Soaker that I can fill with gasoline? This coffee mug saying 'Tell Your Boobs to Stop Staring at My Eyes'? . . . What's that strange expression you're giving me, Mr. Clerk? . . ."

Serge pushed open the door to the parking lot. "Some people don't acclimate well to the heat."

They reached the sand.

"It's Coleman! . . ."

"Way to go! . . ."

"Thanks for bringing the title back to America! . . ."

Coleman acknowledged the applause with a courteous wave.

Soon they found the perfect spot between a lifeguard stand and a large family that was from Pennsylvania and told you so.

Serge knelt in the sand, pulling stuff out of a canvas beach bag. He tossed a bottle to Coleman. "There's your sunscreen, SPF 30 with aloe, apply liberally."

Coleman squirted white liquid on his arm. "The label has a young chick wearing a fruit hat and kissing a toad."

"Because that bottle contains everything you now want in a sun-protection formula, which is designed to moisturize your skin like an amphibian, reverse the aging process and make you smell like a kiwi."

Serge stood and shook out a large, colorful piece of fabric. "My new beach blanket!" When it was completely unfurled, he flapped it out horizontally, letting the wind catch beneath, and gently lowered it to the sand.

Coleman rubbed his arms and chest. "Looks like a flag."

"State flag of Florida." Serge smoothed out lumpy spots. "Not that you've been living here any amount of time." He stood and proudly admired the design. "I just love the selection of blankets in beach stores. And always the same: unicorn, Budweiser, Corvette, Grateful Dead skull, pirate flag, Confederate flag, peace sign, happy face, kittens, Hank Williams Jr., the local sports team, motorcycles, Bruce Lee, hundred-dollar bill, *Dark Side of the Moon* prism and a picture of people lying on beach blankets."

"That last one fucks with me when I'm stoned," said Coleman. He pooched out his lower lip. "I wish *I* had a beach blanket."

Serge smiled big and reached back in the bag. "Here you go!"

A balled-up towel hit Coleman in the stomach. "A present? For me?" He unfolded it. "Bob Marley! How'd you know?"

"Took a wild stab." Serge returned to rooting through his bag. "And I'll just hide my wallet down in the toe of my shoe, grab my underwater disposable camera . . ."

They got the feeling someone was staring at them. They turned around.

Three youths stood before them in silence, politely folding their hands at their waists. Knee-length swim trunks, designer flip-flops, shaggy hair. Somewhere in a parking lot was a van with bad springs and an air-brushed mural of a Yes album cover.

"Can we help you?" asked Serge.

"We don't want to bother Coleman," said the tallest. "It's enough just to watch him in action."

Serge reorganized his canvas bag. "He's applying sunscreen."

The tallest glanced at the others. "Dig it."

Another youth cleared his throat. "Uh, Coleman, we know how busy you are doing all that you do . . ."

Coleman poured rum in a Coke can. "It is a heavy load."

"Can we get your advice?"

Coleman took a big sip. "Go for it."

"Okay, with all the new laws, it's getting harder to find the one-point-five rolling papers for a proper thick one. So we often have to settle for regular tobacco single wides from grocery stores. Please tell us, what are we to do?"

"It's an increasingly common conundrum afflicting our people." Coleman set the soda can down and held his fingertips together. "What you do is tear one of the singles lengthwise, lick the gummed edge and attach it to the non-adhesive side of a full sheet, and you've got the common man's one-point-five. But the key is to first roll each paper empty and render it supple, which facilitates the torque of the twist-up because the seam you've created is a lateral weak point."

The youths glanced at one another in awe. "Amazing . . ."

"I never would have thought of that . . ."

"Gee, thanks, Coleman . . ."

"Yeah, Coleman, with all your success, you're so down-to-earth . . ."

Serge rolled his eyes.

Coleman shrugged and picked up his soda can. "No biggie." Then he noticed something resting in the sand at the feet of the young trio. "Now, that is severely cool."

The three exchanged looks again. "Coleman approves of us!"

The tallest stepped forward. "You think it's cool? It's yours, man. Just a small token of appreciation."

The three young men departed, exchanging a series of complex celebratory handshakes.

Serge examined the gift. "That *is* cool. I'm jealous."

"Borrow it anytime you want."

"No," said Serge, continuing his preparations for the water. "It's definitely more you."

Coleman glanced up from his present. "Serge, your legs look weird."

"I'm wearing panty hose." He unbuttoned his tropical shirt.

"What's with your chest?"

"I cut up other panty hose and fashioned them into a vest. And now I'm cutting another pair in half and slipping one leg onto each arm."

Coleman sipped from the Coke can. "Why?"

"Because I want to be taken seriously as an athlete." He snapped the nylon over his left hand. "Let's go swimming."

Serge grabbed one more item out of the beach bag, then sprinted down the shore and splashed into the water. *"Cowabunga!!!!!!!"*

Coleman slowly waded out until he was chest-deep next to Serge. He took a sip of rum from his soda can.

They took a moment to enjoy the moment, soaking in the postcard-perfect scenery. The next lolling wave rose up to their necks and washed over Coleman's soda can. The wave passed. Coleman took a sip of Bacardi-flavored ocean water and nodded. "This is sophisticated."

Serge began slowly waving his arms across the surface of the ocean. "Coleman, get behind me."

"Why?"

"Take my word. You want to do it."

"What are those things on your hands? I mean over the panty hose."

Serge scrutinized incoming waves. "Oven mitts. Or actually those thick rubber oven gloves you wear when cleaning out the appliance with that aggressive foam . . . Note to self: oven foam, alternate use . . ."

"But, Serge, why are you wearing any gloves at all?"

"You know how they now have all these weird Olympics for extreme sports that should really be called extremely made-up sports?" Serge got a water rhythm going with his arms. "I'm bringing those games to the beach!"

"What's this game?"

"Jellyfish hockey." Serge spread his stance in the underwater sand. "And I'm the goalie."

"What am I?"

"The net."

"Serge!"

U.S. 1

Three Dodge pickups followed a Durango down Federal Highway. They parked behind a used car lot with barbed wire and easy financing. Everyone got out to huddle near the fence.

"There's the motel where this Gaspar character called the meeting." Catfish pointed two blocks up the street. "If I don't come out, take them all."

"How long?" asked one of his men.

"How long till what?" said Catfish.

"Until we burst in shooting."

"No, you don't burst in shooting," said Catfish. "You wait until I come out."

"Then we start shooting?"

"No," said Catfish. "If I *don't* come out."

"So if you don't come out, we don't shoot."

"Okay, look, it's really simple," said Catfish. "If you see all of them come out and I'm not with them, or if I come out with them and I'm at gunpoint and they're about to kidnap me in one of their Jeeps . . ."

"Then we burst in shooting."

Catfish sighed. "The room will be empty then."

"So why do you want us to shoot it up?"

"Stop. Forget everything up to now," said Catfish. "I'll make it simple: Protect me."

"We're changing the plan?"

Catfish closed his eyes. "Let's just go."

The men split up and headed south on both sides of the street. The last two took an alley.

Catfish walked alone out in the open on the east side of U.S. 1. He stopped at the corner, casually looking around as his backup team took positions behind trash bins and parked vehicles. He checked his watch— five till three—then his eyes lifted across the street at a second-story window. The closed curtain opened briefly, then closed again. He took a deep breath and stepped off the curb.

Some of the old U.S. 1 motels make do with an occasional splash of high-gloss white paint and some tropical pastel shade of trim. This time it was turquoise.

Catfish trotted up the bare concrete steps and knocked on a door.

It opened. He walked in with his hands up.

The room was crowded. Five men standing with MAC-10 machine guns. One let his weapon hang by its shoulder sling as he frisked their visitor. Catfish looked toward the only person sitting. "You must be Gaspar."

"Have a seat."

"I like to stand."

There was an old painting of a beach scene on the wall. Three people sagged in canvas chairs, staring out at the rolling surf.

"Suit yourself," said Gaspar. "Here's the deal: There are strict antitrust laws in this country, so your vertical integration is history. From now on, no more going directly to the clinics. I'm your exclusive wholesaler."

"Why would I want to do that?"

"Because this is our territory, and we make the rules." Gaspar nodded toward one of the gunmen.

He placed a suitcase on the bed.

Gaspar smiled. "Your missing shipment. You're lucky we recovered it for you. No need to thank."

"How much?" asked Catfish.

"Seventy-five thousand."

"Sure," said Catfish. "Let me just pull that kind of money out of my pockets."

"Aren't you going to open it?"

Catfish stared a moment, then flipped the latches and raised the lid. Thousands of name-brand tablets, tightly packed in Ziplocs. He looked up again. "Is this a joke?"

"No joke," said Gaspar. "I promised on the phone I'd return it, and I always keep my word."

"But this is only a fraction of what I had."

"I figured you wouldn't be prepared to carry that kind of money, seeing as it might catch most by surprise for us to visit their horse barns before dawn." Gaspar stopped and lit a thick black Honduran cigar. He puffed toward the ceiling. The cigar had a gold band. "I'm fronting you part of your shipment so you can sell it back home and raise the cash for the rest of your wares—and the next shipment that we'll have ready when you come back. It doesn't do me any good to put my best customer out of business."

"I'm not your customer." Catfish slammed the lid. "And you're crazy if you think I'll pay seventy-five for what's already mine."

Silence. Cigar smoke swirled toward a wooden ceiling fan. A cockroach scurried up the wall and under the beach painting. The painting had been done in 1966 near Lantana by a broke artist using live subjects. The people were from Michigan. They didn't know they were being painted.

Another big cigar puff. "Everybody wins," said Gaspar. "In case you haven't heard, they're cracking down. But we know the turf and the techniques, and I've got an endless supply of men to outlast all their roundups."

"So do I," said Catfish. "Why should I pay you?"

"Because you've been losing buses."

"Someone's been calling in tips," said Catfish.

"I can't control the phone company," said Gaspar. "And I understand your sticker shock at seventy-five. But you've been getting by on the cheap. It's a dynamic, changing labor market down here. And you'll find our price is a bargain compared to the fortune you'll make when you unload it back in Kentucky. We both get rich."

"So I just pay you all this money out of the goodness of my heart? For nothing?"

"Not nothing." Gaspar tapped ash onto the floor. "Here's what you get: We take all the risk with the raids, from the clinics to the pharmacies, and you've got secured transport to the motel of your choice. Any losses come out of my end. From there, it's a cake-walk. You save the entire travel expense of shipping your crew down, plus my price is lower than otherwise because we were able to persuade the clinics to accept our group health insurance rates."

The people in the beach painting were not speaking to each other at the time it was painted. Their daughter was dating a man suspected of being against the Vietnam War and Puerto Rican. Their vacation ended early when the mother suffered a bout of sensitive gums. The next year they put a new roof on the house and received word that a distant cousin wasn't actually related.

Gaspar blew smoke rings and overstated a gesture with his right arm. "If you prefer, I'll even buy a horse trailer and guarantee transport all the way to Ocala. For a modest fee, of course."

"What if I say no?"

"You will never leave this room."

"Two can play." Catfish smirked. "Then nobody leaves this room."

Gaspar tapped more ash. "One thing you should know: I love American movies. And you've got a pair of big ones coming in here alone. But you're not stupid. If I was in your shoes, I'd have a posse waiting outside with instructions to eliminate all of us if you didn't come out of the room. Or if you came out under duress, like a gun in your back. Was that the plan?"

The door opened. Catfish turned around. His men were marched into the room with guns in their backs. One of them looked at Catfish. "What was the plan if they brought us inside?"

Gaspar stood up and stubbed out the stogie. "Seven days. Same room if that's agreeable to you. One-fifty for two shipments. The rest of this and the next . . . I'll take that as a yes. Now go."

Catfish grabbed the briefcase and led his men back into the sunshine.

The people in the beach painting were all dead now.

Chapter Twenty-Three

MEANWHILE . . .

The sun was high and bright over the strip on U.S. 1. People continued going about their business loitering at boarded-up gas stations.

A curtain parted a slit in room 17 at the Casablanca Inn.

"You can't keep peeking out the window," said Patrick McDougall.

"Why not?" asked Bar, secretly watching black Jeeps and a Durango.

"Because it's not healthy," said Pat.

Barbara's eyeballs rotated the other way. "Nothing about this vacation is healthy."

"But we've stayed cooped up in this room for hours ever since the police left."

"Baltimore!"

"Forget about the luggage," said Pat. "We need to get out of this room."

"There's no way I'm unlocking that door!"

"Let's go to the beach."

"How can you think about the beach at a time like this?"

"Because it's better than staying crammed in here letting our thoughts feed on themselves."

Bar let the curtain close and turned around. "You're really serious about going to the beach?"

"It's the best thing in every way." Pat grabbed their canvas bag. "We get out of this room and its negative energy, as well as all of U.S. 1. Then we relax at the beach and maybe start seeing things more clearly."

"But the police . . ." She pointed at the curtains. "Last night at the Oasis."

"When you think about it, the whole thing's crazy," said Pat. "It's probably just random weird stuff. You've read the articles about Florida. We're probably letting our imaginations run wild."

"Everyone out there's insane." She opened the curtains again. "Look at that guy with the space helmet."

Pat came up from behind and gave his wife a shoulder rub. "Bar, you know we're the worrying types. It's because we're responsible. But most likely all that business across the street was nothing. So we can either enjoy the beach, and have great stories when we get back, or we can stress out in this room and always have regrets."

She turned around and hugged him. "I guess you're right. Let's go to the beach."

"Now you're talking." Pat headed for the bathroom and his toothbrush. "Should I take a shower?"

"We're going swimming."

"Good point." Pat pulled up his swim trunks and grabbed a chair.

Bar stood by the door. "I'm ready."

"One more second." Pat stuck her purse up in the ceiling. "Hey, I found my stolen wallet."

"You mean your *lost* wallet?"

"That's what I meant." He grabbed it and hopped down. "Now we can go."

The rented Impala took the same road east back to the beach. Bar's head turned as a large building went by. "We never got to jai alai last night."

"We'll go this evening."

"Sorry for being a drag back in the room." Bar put on dark, movie-star sunglasses. "I guess I'm not cut out to live here."

Pat took a hand off the steering wheel and placed it on top of hers. "Don't ever say you're a drag. It was a perfectly normal reaction, which is why we're such a great team. Remember yesterday when I started to unravel after the fraud call from the credit-card people? And you talked sense into me?"

"I love you." Bar leaned and snuggled into his arm. "Let's go have a nice romantic date . . . Watch out!"

Screeeeeech.

Pat swerved back into his own lane and grabbed his heart. "Jesus, we almost had a head-on!"

"Oh, honey, I'm so sorry," said Bar. "It's all my fault for grabbing your arm."

"Don't blame yourself," said Pat. "But maybe we should just focus until we turn the car off at the beach."

HOLLYWOOD BEACH

"Serge! Watch out!"

"Piece of cake." Serge grabbed the first jellyfish in an oven mitt and flung it through the air, tentacles trailing in an aerodynamic arc. "Nothing gets by me: slap shots, one-timers, wraparounds, screens, rebounds, deflections." Another jellyfish went sailing.

Coleman crouched precariously behind Serge's left shoulder. "The gloves I get, but what's with the rest of the getup?"

Fling. "My goalie uniform. Most people have no idea the degree of jellyfish protection that simple panty hose provides because they think, hey, water can get through panty hose. But a jellyfish sting isn't like a surface burn: Its tentacles release teensy-weensy nematocysts that pierce the skin and inject venom." He raised an arm to illustrate. "But women's leg wear thwarts their invertebrate designs!"

Coleman watched another translucent orb go flying. "What's with that electrical bolt you drew in Magic Marker across your panty-hose vest?"

"For the Tampa Bay Lightning." Serge corralled another jelly. "So my goalie uniform will be traditional."

"Look at that next wave," said Coleman. "There's a whole bunch more."

"It's called a bloom," said Serge. "Just stay down behind me."

"How'd you know it would be here?"

"Because the chamber of commerce said it wouldn't." Two more globs went airborne. "But I follow the scientific Web sites. So in addition to protecting you, I'm also the final defense of the tourist swimming public." Another flying jellyfish launched with gusto. "And preventing unproductive headlines back up north."

"Michigan?"

Serge nodded. "The last ice age carved out five big lakes, and we've never stopped hearing how *great* they are."

"They're living in the past."

"Fuck glaciers." Serge looked at his hands. "And what the hell am I doing?"

"I thought you were inventing a new sport."

"Changed my mind. I'm covered in panty hose. That's ridiculous." Serge blinked hard. "I need to filter out some of these ideas that pop into my head, but there are so many, like you know that mega-sporting-goods store called Outdoor World? Except the whole store is indoors. Your head will explode if you don't learn how to let that kind of stuff go."

A tap on his shoulder. "Serge."

"What?"

Coleman pointed backward. "There's a dude up on the beach hanging around our stuff. He looks suspicious."

"Good," said Serge. "I was waiting for him."

"How do you know who it is if you aren't even looking?"

"I *don't* know who it is." Serge turned around. "But I know his type. And I knew he'd finally come. You think this was just about jellyfish hockey?"

"What is it about?"

"Fighting crime. For some reason, robbery really makes tourists gabby."

"But how can you fight crime way out here in the water?"

"Observe as the Master Plan unfolds."

"But I thought you already had a Master Plan."

"The number one directive of any decent Master Plan is unlimited sub–Master Plans."

Coleman gazed toward the beach. "I was right. He's deliberately trying to act casual, but really checking out our shit."

Serge gazed off to admire clouds. "Is he going for my shoe yet?"

"As a matter of fact, reaching for it right now."

"He's going for my wallet. Excellent."

"But then he'll steal it. How is that good?"

"Because it's my backup wallet. You always take your backup wallet to the beach, containing just the bare essentials: driver's license, one credit card, fifty in cash."

"But he's still stealing that stuff. Aren't you mad?"

Serge shook his head. "My backup wallet doesn't contain any of that. It stands alone among backup wallets everywhere."

"How does it stand alone?"

A horrible scream from the beach.

Serge smiled. "That's how."

A man grabbed his face, running in hysterical circles, trampling others' blankets.

"He'll soon be paying us a visit," said Serge.

"How do you know?"

"Because jumping in the water is the natural reaction," said Serge. "I got a small piece of string and rigged my wallet so that when you open it, a tiny keychain canister of pepper gas is activated."

Coleman pointed. "Here he comes now. Right toward us."

"Let's give him a hand."

The thief splashed out toward them and dunked his head. He rubbed his eyes and dunked again. The screaming stopped. Another dunk. He opened his eyes to slits, blood-red, puffing up. But at least the discomfort was fading.

"Are you all right?" asked Serge, splashing forward and reaching the bandit. "Maybe I can help."

Serge steadied the unsteady man by holding him around the ribs with a pair of rubber oven gloves.

A two-second delay.

The thief's eyes flew open wide from the searing agony across his chest. He dashed back toward the beach, screaming even louder.

"Ooops," said Serge, turning his hands over. "I forgot that my gloves are full of nematocysts. And since I handled so many of the little buggers, it's like that poor guy got stung all at once by at least twenty jellyfish."

"Look at him run," said Coleman.

"It is a motivator." Serge marched toward shallow water. "I'm getting hungry."

They returned to their personal space in the sand. Coleman began rolling up his beach towel. Serge stood over a trash can, carefully peeling off gloves.

Whispers behind them. Three different youths.

"It's Coleman! . . ."

"Quiet, he's working . . ."

"I just knew he'd have a Bob Marley towel . . ."

Coleman looked up. "What's happening, dudes?"

"We don't want to bother you . . ."

Coleman mixed another rum and Coke. "Nothing's really going on right now."

A man ran screaming across the towels.

Coleman chugged from the can. "How can I help you?"

"Do you have a tip that can impress our friends? Something nobody else knows?"

"Let's see . . ." Coleman looked at the sky and tapped his chin. He finally raised a single finger of epiphany. "I got it." He crawled across the sand and pulled a bottle from the beach bag. "If you've procured some primo 'shrooms or peyote buttons, select the type of sunscreen that has an amphibious moisturizing agent, which retards porous excretion, hence retaining the psychoactive ingredient for a more prolonged and potent ride."

"Whoa, that is so cutting edge," said one of the young men. Then he looked in Serge's direction. "Do panty hose work on the same principle?"

"No," said Coleman. "He was playing hockey."

"But tell us," asked another youth. "How did you know about the excretion concept?"

Coleman finished off his rum and burped. "It's the same reason that heroin addicts don't take showers before spiking." He then pointed at them in earnest. "But don't do heroin. Even though it created some really great music, the Big H is still a heartbreak."

The trio nodded. "I think we got it."

"Repeat it back," said Coleman.

"Use sunscreen; don't do heroin."

Coleman nodded. "Carry on."

The trio walked away in delight.

Serge stepped up next to his buddy and watched the kids leave. " 'Use sunscreen; don't do heroin.' . . . If you could give the entire human race only one sentence of advice, I think you've just nailed it."

Coleman stuffed Bob Marley in the canvas bag. "I'm ready."

"Me, too." Serge looked down at the special gift Coleman had received from his earlier students. "I guess we'll now get to see how that thing works. And for the record, I'm still jealous. It even has special wheels for traction in the sand."

A man grabbing his face and chest ran by screaming.

Coleman leaned down and flicked a switch. "Let's rock."

Serge began walking back to the parking lot, and Coleman drove along beside him on an electric riding beer cooler. "What happens now?"

Serge pulled out his beach checklist. "Get caught in a riptide."

Coleman looked up from his riding cooler. "Aren't you supposed to avoid a riptide?"

"Those people are amateurs," said Serge. "But it's like a free theme-park ride, and perfectly safe if you're a Floridian who knows how to bust a move in the middle of one."

"You do?"

"An aquatic dance step I invented." Serge picked up a shell and skipped it across the water. "The Riptide Ultra-Glide."

A rented Impala proceeded through another marathon search for parking, which ended when the McDougalls spotted the brake lights of a departing Corvette.

"See?" said Pat. "Our fortune's changing."

Bar stopped on the sidewalk and stared at the ocean. "It's even more beautiful than yesterday."

"Told you. Our ship's come in," said Pat, watching someone ride a beer cooler down the sidewalk. "Nothing else can go wrong."

They trudged through sand again and laid out the Packers blanket.

The sound of screaming from the water.

Bar turned. "What the—"

A man splashed out of the surf and onto the beach, eyes swollen shut, hands rubbing his skin raw. On his chest, blotchy, bright red jellyfish stings in the shape of two large palm prints. He took off blind and crashed headfirst into the side of a lifeguard stand. Then he got up again and sprinted across the sand toward the McDougalls.

Just before reaching their blanket, he was tackled by paramedics from the beach patrol. A lifeguard ran up and cracked open a first-aid kit.

"What's the matter with him?" asked Bar.

"Only got stung by jellyfish," said the lifeguard. "Hurts at first, but it's nothing. He'll be fine."

A crowd of onlookers gathered around. "Is there any way we can help? We're from Pennsylvania."

"I got it," said the lifeguard. A few more minutes of work. "There. Almost good as new."

"But the beach *is* safe?" asked Pat. "We can go swimming, right?"

"Oh, absolutely. That guy probably got tagged by a stray."

"Very rare," added one of the paramedics. "Please enjoy yourselves."

They loaded the victim into the beach-patrol cart and drove him backstage.

Bar rubbed Coppertone down her left arm. "Pat, what are you doing?"

Pat was digging a hole in the sand. "Burying my wallet and marking the spot with my shoe."

Then they stopped and looked at each other. All the built-up psychotic tension broke loose in boomerang reaction: Giddy smiles broke out. Bar took off running and laughing, and Pat chased her into the water, until she let herself be caught. They splashed over sideways in each other's arms, then slowly waded out as they had the day before, but remembering to check first for any unusually strong extra currents. They sank neck-deep, romantic privacy.

Bar nuzzled him from behind. "Sorry about back at the motel. We're really going to enjoy the rest of this week together."

"Me, too. I love you so much."

Bar swung around in front of him. Hands dropped from his neck and into the water.

"What are you doing?" asked Pat.

Her mischievous smile returned. "I'm not doing anything . . ."

Pat glanced around again to see if anyone was looking. His expression changed. "Oh, man, don't you just hate people who litter?"

"What brought that up?" asked Bar.

"I can't believe it." He pointed. "This is such pristine nature, and jerks still have to dump their garbage on the rest of us."

"What is it?"

"Looks like a sandwich baggie someone tossed off a boat or something."

The compulsively responsible environmentalists in them took over. "We should pitch in," said Bar.

Pat let go of his wife. "Hold on a second. I'll just stick it in the pocket of my trunks and throw it in a garbage can when we get back on shore."

"Must be one of the Ziploc baggies," said Bar. "Still got air in it and floating . . ."

Five minutes later:

"Ahhhhh! Ahhhhh! Jesus! . . ."

"Just hold still," one of the paramedics told Patrick, lying flat on his beach blanket. "And keep your eyes closed while I dab this."

Bar crouched over in concern. "Is he going to be okay?"

"Good as new in no time, except it'll leave some nasty-looking marks for a bit." The lifeguard handed the paramedic another swab. "But why would he deliberately pick up a jellyfish?"

"We thought it was a baggie," said Bar.

"We're from Wisconsin," said Pat.

They finished patching him up. "You can use vinegar," said the lifeguard, snapping the first-aid box shut. "But not freshwater, which could release more toxins . . . Unfortunately it's a little worse than usual because your face was already completely peeled from a sunburn."

Pat sat up on the blanket, and Bar consoled him with a gentle hand on his unaffected shoulder. "Honey, I'm so sorry. I should have yelled 'jellyfish' earlier."

"It's not your fault." Pat turned to her with one eye swollen closed like a baseball. "How does my face look?"

She pretended he didn't have a dozen cherry-red stripes across his cheek, forehead and left ear, where the tentacles had slapped his face when he spazzed out in the water.

"Handsome as ever."

Pat scanned the ground near their blanket. "Where are my shoes?"

"I stacked them over there by the bag. The paramedics needed to clear some space when they laid you out."

"Oh jeez, no . . ."

"Pat, your shoes are still here. I just told you."

He got on his hands and knees and began flinging sand between his legs like a golden retriever.

"What's going on?" asked Bar.

Pat eventually stood up in the middle of what looked like a bombing range. Twenty holes of varying depth. His head sank. In defeat: "My wallet . . ."

The lifeguard suddenly raised his megaphone toward two people way out in the surf. "Riptide! Swim parallel to shore!"

"*We know! . . .*" yelled a faint voice from far beyond the swim area. "*Woooooo! Ultra-Glide! . . .*"

The lifeguard saw something else and yelled into his megaphone. "Shark!"

In the distance, a fist splashed down hard. "*Thanks, got him . . . Riptide! Woooooo! . . .*"

Barbara tried consoling her husband by stroking the back of his head. "Honey, it's just a wallet, material possessions. If there's one thing that this week has taught us, it's to put things in perspective. Our lives are perfect."

A ring tone from their beach bag: "Blowing in the Wind."

"I got it," said Pat. He flipped the phone open. "Hello?"

"*I want my fucking cocaine! Don't think you fooled me with that couple in the Oasis Inn, and don't think you can get away!*"

A cell phone fell in the sand.

Chapter Twenty-Four

ACROSS TOWN

A Dodge Durango parked outside a motel room near Sunrise Boulevard. Next to it sat a horse trailer that was empty except for some hay and the blankets. The motel sign had a pirate resting a boot on an overflowing treasure chest. The pirate's hat had a lot of bird shit.

Inside room number two, Catfish Stump unzipped a common piece of carry-on luggage.

Someone over his shoulder: "So that's what a hundred and fifty grand looks like."

"Not for your amusement." Catfish zipped it closed and sat quietly on the end of a bed, staring in thought at the wall. The wall had a beach painting, but there were no people in the picture. Just a radiant sunset that cast an orange glow on foaming waves. Four people were sitting just to the left of the picture when it was painted. They had objected when they noticed the artist painting them, and made him move over.

"How'd you get the money so fast?" asked his top lieutenant.

"Had Bing wire it to me from Versailles."

"But I thought we were going to wait and sell the front product back in Kentucky, and then return."

Catfish shook his head. "Sign of weakness if we take the crumbs he throws us just to peddle and fork over the profits. I want to be done with this stupid deal. Clean break. Then we start fresh on an equal plane and see if this fucker can be trusted . . ." His voice trailed off in distraction.

"What are you thinking about?" asked the lieutenant.

Catfish closed his eyes and pinched the bridge of his nose. "Whether to go through with this fool's errand."

"You don't trust them?"

"That's a given." Catfish stood up. "The question is *how* I don't trust them. The most obvious: an outright rip-off."

"But he said he needed you for future business."

"Please. You know how many other hillbillies are waiting in line? They need us like a third tit." Catfish picked up the suitcase and idly gauged its weight. "Then there was that body found in the drainage canal south of Okeechobee."

"What body?"

"It made the papers. José Medina, numerous pain-clinic arrests. But it didn't mention any convictions. That means he was cooperating."

"Looks like Gaspar shut him up for good," said the lieutenant.

"Maybe," said Catfish. "Or maybe something else. Maybe his tips to intercept our trucks weren't so anonymous. We could be walking into a sting . . . On the other hand, it could be totally legit. That's three outcomes, and two are bad."

"So let's not go," said the subordinate.

"There's always a fourth outcome." Catfish pulled a Beretta nine-millimeter pistol from under his shirt and checked the chamber. "We could always rip *him* off."

"But you always said you'd never rip anyone off in a deal. That a man's word was everything."

"It is." Catfish tucked the pistol back in his pants. "But this already is our shit—they ripped it off from us. The main question is, what benefits them more: us as customers, or eliminated competition?"

The subordinate checked his watch. "It's two thirty. Shouldn't we be going?"

Catfish nodded and turned toward the rest of the room. "Okay, all you swingin' dicks, look like you got some. This could be a live one."

Clicking mechanical sounds from a variety of weapon activity, loading bullets and clips, racking slides. They headed out the door and down the stairs toward the Durango. The lieutenant trotted behind Catfish. "So what's your decision?"

"Haven't made it yet."

Four Jeeps with fog-light racks sat in front of a bright white motel with turquoise trim.

In a second-floor window, curtains parted slightly. Then closed again.

"Stay away from the window and stop pacing," said Gaspar Arroyo. "You're getting on my nerves."

"You think they came up with one-fifty?" asked a goon lugging a MAC-10.

"Who knows?" said Gaspar, sitting on the far side of the room and puffing a thick cigar.

"You don't seem so sure of these guys."

"I'm not," said Gaspar. "It's a little suspicious they suddenly call and say they already have the money, without even going back to Kentucky."

"What do you think they're up to?"

"Could be a rip-off," said Gaspar. "We put the arm on them, so they kill two birds with one rock: get the

Oxy for free, and eliminate a middleman who's standing between them and doing direct business with the clinics again."

"But you said they were a pushover. Our guys could squash them at any time like bugs."

"Did some additional checking," said Gaspar. "These hombres got tougher hides than I thought. Some enemies of theirs are missing up north. I'd say we're about evenly matched. They call them the Kentucky Mafia."

"Who calls them that?"

"It was in the newspaper," said Gaspar. "So it must be true."

"Do we plan like they're coming to boost us?"

"Unless it's a sting," said Gaspar. "Did you see TV last night? Some kids in Ocala were playing in the woods with their dog, and it dug up a shallow grave. Identified the body as Gooch Spivey."

"Who's that?"

"Catfish's former right-hand man," said Gaspar. "The reporter mentioned several possession-with-intent arrests. That's a dime in the pen minimum, yet he was out breathing free air. Which can only mean he was a confidential informant."

"That's probably why Catfish had him iced."

"Probably. But if someone else was behind it, who's to say Catfish also isn't wired for sound? He was in Ocala at the same time."

"Then which do you think, a sting or a rip-off?"

Gaspar stared off in thought.

"What are you looking at?" asked the goon. He turned around and saw a beach painting on the wall.

"Nothing," said Gaspar, shaking his head to snap him back into the moment. "I could be over-thinking all of this. It might be a legitimate milk run. If he shows up with the whole count, we know it's not a sting because no police agency ever approves that kind of buy money. And if it's a rip-off, the money will never enter the room. That'll be the sign which way this thing's sliding."

"And if the money shows?"

"We might rip them off."

"But you said it was against your code to double-cross. Your honor was life."

"Except in self-defense," said Gaspar. "The objective is survival."

"So the plan is? . . ."

"Start by conducting a regular deal." Gaspar checked his Rolex. Three o'clock. "I haven't made up my mind yet."

Another goon parted the curtains again. "Here they come."

"Everyone get ready," said Gaspar. "But put them at ease. If they're planning something, I want them to think we have our guard down . . ."

FORT LAUDERDALE
INTERNATIONAL AIRPORT

Incoming jets cleared I-95 at ninety-second intervals. Horns honked curbside. Luggage and beeping electric carts rolled through terminals. A PA announcement: *"Please report any suspicious or unusual behavior . . . Do not accept bags . . ."*

Two people sprinted at top speed for the ticket counter. Patrick McDougall collapsed out of breath against the desk. "We want to go home!"

The chipper attendant wore a sky-blue bonnet and a robotic smile. The smile quickly faded. "Good God, what happened to your face?"

"I picked up a jellyfish," said Pat. "But it was already peeling."

"We're from Wisconsin," said Bar.

"We'd like to go back there now, please."

The attendant's fingers addressed a keyboard. "Do you have a reservation?"

"Yes, but it's not till Sunday," said Pat.

"We want to leave now," said Bar. "The name's McDougall, connecting to Madison."

"No problem. I can change that for you." Fingers began typing. "But you understand there will be a rebooking fee."

"We'll pay it."

"Here we go," said the attendant. "I have something tomorrow morning."

"Nothing today?"

"All flights are booked. Earliest is seven A.M."

"We'll take it!"

More typing. "I'll just need to see your driver's licenses."

Bar went to grab hers, then remembered. "I left my purse in the room because we went to the beach."

The attendant nodded. "As long as you have it when you board. Meanwhile, I can process the tickets under your husband's name." Fingers continued clattering on the keyboard. "Sir, may I have your license?"

"Uh, I don't have it," said Pat. "My wallet was stolen at the beach yesterday. And I buried my other wallet but the shoe got moved."

Typing stopped. "You don't have a driver's license?"

"But I buy tickets online all the time without a license."

"No," said the attendant. "I mean without a license or other official photo ID, the Federal Aviation Administration won't let you on any airplane in America. Especially at our current heightened level of security."

Pat turned to his wife and smacked the side of his head. "That's right. It was the whole reason for the backup wallet." He faced the desk again. "But then I'm stuck in Florida. This has to have come up before. Isn't there some kind of emergency procedure?"

"There is one thing." The woman got out a paper and pen. "If you can reach your home state's motor vehicle department and give them this number . . ." She handed Pat the scrap of paper. "That's our central security office in Omaha. They'll ask to be faxed certain documents and other verifications, then they'll forward a special numbered certificate back to us to get you through security."

"Great. Thanks," said Pat. "And could you do me a small favor and look up motor vehicles in Wisconsin?"

"Don't have full Internet." She glanced across the terminal. "Information booth should be able to help."

Soon Pat had the number and was on his cell. And soon he was transferred, again and again, by people who never heard of the procedure. Finally, a bureaucratic accident: "Yes, I can help you with that. What is your name?"

"Oh, thank you! It's Patrick McDougall, Madison."

"Patrick *M.* McDougall?"

"That's right."

"I'm afraid I can't honor your request."

"Why?" asked Pat.

"Your license has been suspended. So we can't issue any travel waivers."

"Suspended?"

"There's a hold on your file pending the receipt of clarifying documents from South Florida."

"Documents?"

"We received an alert from the education department that you were driving while smoking crack and PCP."

"Because that's all a big communication mistake," said Pat. "It shouldn't have said driving. And no PCP, just crack."

"You were only smoking crack? I'll make a note in your file."

"No, that's not what I meant. Don't touch anything."

"I'm sorry, it's already in the system. Can I help you with anything else today."

Pat hung up.

The phone rang. Patrick answered it.

"I want my fucking cocaine—"

Pat hung up.

"Is something the matter?" asked the attendant. "You don't look too well."

Pat just stared.

The receptionist smiled again and looked down at her computer screen. "I do have some good news for you. Your luggage is now in Nashville."

"Nashville?" said Bar.

The woman nodded. "It just landed."

"How is that good news?"

"Because it's moving closer," said the attendant. "In fact, it should be here this afternoon."

Chapter Twenty-Five

JUST OUTSIDE THE AIRPORT

A Gran Torino cruised south on U.S. Highway 1.

"It's just like Alec Baldwin said in *Miami Blues:* 'The problem is I can be anything I want.'" Serge made a wild gesture out the driver's window with his left arm. "I just can't make up my mind."

Coleman lit a joint. "Example?"

"Internationally acclaimed interior designer." Another cavalier fling of his arm. "Here's the key: Take all indoor furniture—sofas and loungers covered in white linen—and lug it outdoors. Then grab all the outdoor furniture—wicker, bamboo, postmodern aluminum tubing—and bring it indoors. Now I'm a fucking genius. All the Ian Schrager hotels want to hire me."

"They do?"

"Unless the South Beach techno-dance clubs outbid them. They don't have live bands, just DJs up in a booth. And the DJs are now celebrities like Mick Jagger, with their own dance-mix followers who make pilgrimages club to club to hear them turn on the music. When did a stereo become a musical instrument?" Serge leaned forward and clicked on the car radio. "There, I'm an artist. Thousands of women on ecstasy now want to have three-ways with me."

"You get chick double action just for turning on the car radio?"

"Who could have seen this trend coming?"

"What about me?" Coleman exhaled a hit out the window. "What should I do?"

"Just be yourself," said Serge, gesturing again out his window. "You're like the guy in those Dos Equis beer ads: 'He is the most interesting man in the world . . . Children's tearless shampoo still makes him cry.'"

"It always has made me cry," said Coleman. "What's wrong with that shit?"

"I think it's you, Coleman." Serge checked his watch and sped up to make a yellow light. "Every time you take a shower, I hear this grief-stricken weeping from the bathroom like you're having a breakdown or something. At first I thought it was the smorgasbord of psychedelics you were taking, and your unborn soul was being ripped from the abyss and forced traumatically into the material world like you were giving birth to yourself."

"I *was* giving birth to myself, but shampoo makes it more intense."

"Maybe you should stop taking LSD before showers."

"No, it's the shampoo," said Coleman. "That's how they plan it."

Another arm flung out the driver's window, this one dismissive. "Next subject."

Coleman turned around in his seat. "Cars are scattering. Both sides of the road."

"They have the worst drivers down here."

"I think it's because of the arm you keep waving out the window," said Coleman. "It has the gun."

"The gun's under the seat," said Serge.

"No, it isn't. Look."

"Okay, to humor you . . . Yow! When did that happen?"

"You got it out a few blocks back when you were screaming about instant replay ruining croquet. Just like you got it out the other day and didn't know it. Keeps happening more and more. Sometimes you even shoot it."

"I do? Who am I shooting at?"

"Not aiming at anyone, not on purpose."

Serge tucked the gun back under his seat. "I'll have to watch that . . . How's traffic doing back there?"

Coleman turned around again. "Still parked in the middle of the road and on sidewalks."

"They must have anxiety conditions. It's this crazy pace of modern society." Serge checked his wristwatch again.

"What time is it?"

"A couple minutes before three." Serge looked out his window as they went through an intersection. "And there's the Swashbuckler Motel."

Coleman saw a two-story, whitewashed place with turquoise trim. "Some guys are heading up the stairs."

"Right on time." Serge hit his blinker and turned into a parking lot with a horse trailer. "Just like that ballroom scam artist told us . . ."

Across the street at the Swashbuckler Motel: three evenly spaced knocks on the door of room 213.

It opened.

Catfish and an associate entered with hands raised again, and turned around for the frisk.

"They're both clean," said one of the goons.

Gaspar set a cigar in the ashtray and rubbed his hands together. "You got the money?"

"Yeah, I got the money," said Catfish. "You got the stuff?"

"Yeah, I got the stuff," said Gaspar, picking up the cigar. "Where is the money?"

"Oh, it's not with me," said Catfish.

"No?"

Catfish shook his head. "But it's nearby . . . What about the stuff?"

"I don't have the stuff either."

"You don't?"

Gaspar shook his head. "No, but it's also nearby . . ." He broke into a smile and pointed with the cigar. "The money's in the car, isn't it?"

Catfish shook his head again. "No, it's not in the car."

"So what part of Kentucky are you originally from—"

"Why don't I come back in and we start all over again," said Catfish.

"What's the rush?" asked Gaspar. "I like to get to know people I do business with."

"You'll get to know me when you stop jerking off and start doing fucking business with me!"

Everyone tensed, itchy fingers on triggers.

The door suddenly opened. Everyone jumped. Gaspar's outside detail marched three of Catfish's men into the room.

Gaspar stood. "Did you find the Durango?"

One of the gunmen nodded. "No sign of the money."

Catfish's head snapped toward Gaspar. "So this *is* a rip-off! I should have known!"

"Rip-off?" said Gaspar. "You didn't bring the money in the room! You're the one who came to rip *me* off!"

The rest of the two gangs glanced side to side, shifting weight on their feet. Gaspar's goons tightened the grip on their weapons. Catfish's men moved their hands slightly to be closer to their hidden backup pieces tucked in the smalls of their backs and strapped to their ankles.

"What about Gooch Spivey?" yelled Gaspar.

"How'd you know about Gooch?" Catfish shot back. "What about José Medina?"

Simultaneously: "You're working with the feds!"

"Open your shirt!" Catfish yelled at Gaspar. "You're wired up, aren't you?"

"You're a motherless dog for even saying that!" Gaspar turned. "Guys, check him out."

Catfish backed up. "Get the fuck away from me. You're not laying a hand . . ."

The goons grabbed him anyway. One ripped the buttons halfway down his shirt. Catfish twisted and pushed one, stumbling backward off balance. He grabbed the other by the arm and swung him into the wall. His Kentucky crew used the confusion to pull their backup pieces. The others swung their MAC-10s and aimed.

Gaspar saw the future: a mass suicide from the criss-crossed trajectories in the tight room. Just as everyone was about to start firing, he jumped into the middle. "Stop! Stop! Stop!"

"Hold your fire!" yelled Catfish. "But keep those guns up and cocked."

"Keep 'em aimed!" yelled Gaspar. He took a deep breath and wiped his forehead.

"How can I trust you?" asked Catfish. "You ambushed my men outside again."

"They were lying in wait again. What the hell was that about?"

"I still don't see any drugs!"

"I don't see any money!"

"This is bullshit!"

"Easy," said Gaspar, holding out open palms. "We're just making it worse. Let's everyone dial it down a notch. It's not a sting, that's for sure. And if we all kill each other, nobody makes any money."

So they were left in a motionless circle of aimed, high-caliber firepower. Nobody wanting to give an inch or advantage.

"How do we defuse this?" asked Catfish.

"Have your boys put down their guns."

"Not a chance. You toss yours."

"Like hell."

"So much for defusing," said Catfish. "How about not escalating until we figure this out?"

"Fine," said Gaspar. "What about this: Nobody fires on either side unless they get a specific order from either me or you. Deal?"

"I can live with that."

They both looked around at their men and nodded for them to accept the terms.

Catfish faced Gaspar again.

"Now what?"

A Gran Torino sat pointed out of an alley.

Serge zoomed his camcorder on an upstairs motel room across the street. "I'd give anything to be a fly on the wall."

"What do you think's going on?" asked Coleman.

"I don't know," said Serge. "This footage sucks."

"But you were able to film those Mexicans ambushing the hillbillies and marching them up into the room."

"That was minutes ago," said Serge. "The TV audience is increasingly restless. It's all: What have you done for me lately?"

"I'm getting bored," said Coleman.

"So is my audience." Serge handed the video camera to Coleman. "By now they've gotten up to make popcorn or take a much-anticipated dump."

"What are you doing?" asked Coleman.

Serge opened his door and popped the trunk. He came around to the passenger side, holding the handle of a heavy-gauge molded-plastic case that looked like it could hold a trombone.

"What's that?" asked Coleman.

"Sometimes reality needs a catalyst to jump-start the action." He began heading across the street. "Whatever you do, don't stop filming!"

Coleman didn't. The camera followed Serge as he tiptoed up the stairs and opened the case on the balcony. Then Serge grabbed a rubber handle attached to a rope and pulled. He pulled again, and again. Something wasn't working. He pulled again . . .

Coleman pressed the viewfinder harder against his eye. "What in the living—"

Serge pulled a final time and was satisfied. He ran back down the stairs . . .

Inside room 213 of the Swashbuckler Motel, everyone suddenly turned toward the sound coming from outside on the balcony. Reminded them of a high-rpm lawn mower.

Gaspar motioned. "Benito, check it out."

Benito opened the door. The two-stroke gas engine got louder. "Someone left this outside." He walked back into the room with a still-running chain saw.

Everyone clenched up.

"What the fuck?" said Catfish.

"Turn it off!" yelled Gaspar.

"Where's the switch?" asked Benito, unwittingly stepping farther into the room.

Someone backed up and bumped into a nightstand. A lamp crashed to the floor.

Benito started and turned with the chain saw, slicing a gash in the shoulder of a hillbilly.

Trigger fingers spasmed. A shot rang out. Nobody knew who fired, but the bullet went through the beach painting on the wall, taking out the mother.

Then everyone let loose in a deafening fusillade.

It was the second Mexican-American War. Except it wasn't fought over Texas. It was waged between Mexico and Kentucky. In South Florida.

And it didn't last nearly as long. All the shooting took less than ten seconds. Everyone toppled over like a bowling strike.

Quiet again. The room filled with a choking haze of smoke.

Then it was aftermath.

The number of dead wasn't known. But nobody on either side was law-enforcement-trained in marksmanship. Which meant injuries. The moaning started. People tried to roll over and push themselves up. The less wounded looked around the floor for scattered weapons.

Finally, someone was able to crawl. He reached up from his knees and grabbed the doorknob. It opened.

Then a delayed gunshot. It hit the man in the back and he fell forward out the door, dead on the balcony.

Gaspar glanced around from behind the cover of the nightstand. He had gone down like the others; but decided to do it preemptively and not wait for the help of bullets.

Now he moved quickly on hands and knees, along the edge of the bed, peeking over the top. He got to the end. Catfish lay dead on the floor in front of the dresser. Gaspar scrambled past.

Something seized his ankle. Nope, Catfish was just playin' possum. "You son of a bitch!"

Gaspar looked back and kicked him in the face, freeing his leg. He scurried the rest of the way to the door and got up. Luckily, he tripped over the body on the balcony and crashed into the railing, just as Catfish's shot from behind sailed over his head.

"You're a dead man!" shouted the Kentuckian. "I'll kill you if it's the last thing I do! . . ."

Gaspar sprinted to the landing and down the stairs.

Chapter Twenty-Six

SOUTH FLORIDA

In the pool supply stores and Cuban restaurants and pain clinics and traffic up and down U.S. 1, everybody heard the gunfire. But the echoes from the canyon of concrete along the highway threw the sound all over the place. Nine-one-one operators were flooded with calls, placing the shoot-out everywhere along a ten-block stretch.

Serge had taken over the video camera again, filming through the windshield from his driver's seat. He'd already gotten the first guy falling out the door, then Gaspar tumbling over his body and dashing down the steps, followed by Catfish, who looked both ways over the railing before sprinting for the opposite stairwell.

Now it was mop-up time. A triaged sequence of men spilled out of the room, starting with the flesh wounds, then the through-and-through shots still able to walk, and, bringing up the rear, the middle-luck souls who could only manage to flop out the door into a pile and wait for paramedics.

Serge pumped a fist with his free hand. "This is definitely going to be the series pilot!"

In a parking lot two blocks away, a ruddy man in a plaid shirt moved indecisively, a couple of panicked steps in one direction, then another, then back. He had been left to guard the suitcase of cash in the horse trailer, and he had heard the shots. What to do?

Moments before, he'd finished a lengthy daydream about the vast amount of money an arm's length away. Temptation whipsawed. Proverbial devil and angel on his shoulders. Then he thought about the floating rumor concerning Catfish and Gooch, and *poof!*—his shoulders were lighter.

But now . . . There had been way too many gunshots. A lot of people weren't coming back. And even if Catfish did make it, well, he was sure to understand that the responsible thing to do after everything went south was to get the horse trailer out of there before the police sealed everything off. At least that was the story he'd be sticking to.

His name was Skeeter.

Skeeter jumped in the cab of the pickup towing the trailer and high-tailed it north on U.S. 1.

Back up the street, Serge lowered the camera from its view of the motel balcony. "I think that's the last of them."

"Where to now?" asked Coleman.

"Let's consult the Master Plan." Serge gritted his teeth in thought, then slapped the dashboard like he was buzzing in on *Jeopardy!* "I got it! Follow the money!"

"But where do you think the payoff for the drugs is?"

"Odds against that room." He pointed. "Because after that kind of shoot-out, one of the most able-bodied would be carrying a briefcase or duffel."

"All their hands were empty," said Coleman.

"So the money was stashed at a nearby location as a precaution against a rip-off." Serge bit his lower lip. "But where?"

"I hear sirens." Coleman took a big hit and talked without letting out any breath. "Good dope."

"I hear them, too," said Serge, changing tapes in his camera. "How's my power charge on this thing holding up?"

Sirens grew louder.

The electric meter on his camera showed an icon of a half-full battery. He nodded. "That should last."

Coleman exhaled out the window as the first police cruiser raced by, overshooting to one of the inaccurate phoned-in locations.

The pair sat relaxed and stared toward U.S. 1 at nothing in particular.

Coleman rested his joint on the edge of the window and popped a beer. "This is the life."

"You said it, buddy." Serge uncapped a bottle of water. "Florida, a full tank of gas, and no appointments."

Another siren went by.

"Doesn't get any better," said Coleman.

They shared a toast, tapping an aluminum can and a plastic water bottle. "To travel with friends."

The pair sat and idly watched traffic. "Watching traffic is soothing," said Serge. "I used to think that those old codgers were weird."

"Which ones were weird?"

"The guys in the lawn chairs on the side of the road, wearing World War Two vet baseball caps and watching cars go by like a basset hound staring forever at an empty food bowl. But now I get it."

"I got it a long time ago. But I had a head start because I smoke weed."

They sat and watched some more.

"There's a few sedans, and a city bus," said Serge. "A restored Charger—I love those—an exterminator company's car with fake whiskers and rat ears on the roof, another police car . . ."

Coleman paused. "What were we talking about before?"

"I don't remember . . . a taxicab, a livery, UPS truck, a horse trailer . . ."

"A horse trailer?" said Coleman.

At the same time their faces snapped toward each other: "The money!"

Serge threw the Gran Torino in gear. The car began speeding from the cover of the alley.

Out of nowhere, a screech of tires and a factory-fresh Jeep Cherokee blasted from beneath the shade of a royal poinciana.

Serge slammed on his brakes with both feet. The nose of the Torino lurched to a stop just out of the alley. The Jeep swerved with inches to spare.

"Hey!" Coleman pointed at the tinted windows and Gaspar Arroyo. "That's one of the guys who made it out of the room. Was he sitting under that tree this whole time?"

"I don't know," said Serge. "We were drifting there a bit."

"What's he doing now?"

"Skidding around the corner to chase the horse trailer." Serge hit the gas and brakes, spinning tires in an eruption of smoke. He let off his left foot and sling-shotted out of the alley like a dragster, skidding around the same corner as he tossed the camera to Coleman. "Maybe you should film because I probably need to concentrate on driving."

FORT LAUDERDALE
INTERNATIONAL AIRPORT

Patrick McDougall walked up to the airline counter again, as he had done every ten minutes for the last two hours. "When is our luggage supposed to arrive?"

The baggage-service attendant looked from her computer screen and smiled patiently. "Still four o'clock."

"Are you sure?" said Pat. "Did it make it on the plane? What if it's going somewhere else? Maybe we're tracking the wrong suitcases? Is there anything I'm missing? Cleveland?"

"Sir, everything's fine," the attendant said with another smile. "And as I already told you, we'd be more than happy to deliver the bags to your motel room when they arrive."

"No," said Pat. "That's just another chance for something to go wrong. Once they get here, I'm not letting them out of my sight."

"I understand," she said, but didn't.

Pat pointed behind him. "I'm going to go sit over there."

She smiled and nodded and tapped computer keys.

Pat returned to his wife.

"What did she say?" asked Bar.

"Still four o'clock." Pat took a seat.

"That's forever," said Bar, glancing around nervously.

"It's only a half hour," said Pat. "And we couldn't be in a safer place. Even if the guy who called my cell finds us, there are lots of people around and a ton of security. Nothing bad can happen as long as we stay here."

U.S. 1

Seven different car chases were currently under way in the greater Fort Lauderdale area, which was below average for the afternoon. One involved the police and a stolen Mercedes; the rest were between private citizens for a variety of unresolved personal matters. A cheating spouse, a repo man, road rage, a street race, a drug rip-off over a small amount of marijuana and another concerning a suitcase with $150,000.

The last was taking place on U.S. 1 north of Hallandale. It was a slow chase through stop-and-go traffic, but difficult to lose track of a horse trailer.

"I lost him," said Coleman, bringing his head back in through the passenger window.

"Coleman, you're my spotter," said Serge. "How could you lose him?"

"That big bus got in between." He opened a Schlitz.

Serge glanced over in disapproval. "Beer during a chase?"

"Keeps me focused."

"How can it do that?"

"Otherwise I'll be thinking about beer."

A black Jeep with a fog-light rack crossed into the oncoming lanes and blew by Serge's window.

Coleman pointed with his can. "How'd the Jeep get behind us?"

"That's a different Jeep," said Serge. "The first is still up there. My guess is he called in fresh troops."

Something else tried to pass the Torino, but had to pull back to avoid an oncoming delivery truck. Serge looked up in the mirror. "And there's the Durango. Everyone's at the party."

The motorcade crawled through maddening traffic lights at Hollywood, Sheridan, Sterling Road and Dania Beach Boulevard. A shot was fired from the Durango, past the Gran Torino, at one of the Jeeps.

"I'm getting terrible gas mileage," said Serge.

After Griffin Road, the pursuit quickly picked up steam as the pavement curved east. The Durango blew by. A loud roar overhead.

Coleman aimed the camcorder out the window. Another loud roar. "The horse trailer's taking an exit."

"That's what I'd do," said Serge. "He going to try to lose them at Fort Lauderdale International. And there's a ton of security around, so no violence. Hopefully."

Serge eased the wheel left around another broad bend, watching the first Jeep exit, then the second, and finally the Durango. He hit his blinker and took the ramp.

Merging traffic. Signs for rental-car drop-off and long-term parking. Departures, United, American, Southwest, Lufthansa.

"Serge," said Coleman. "He's heading for arrivals. Is he picking someone up?"

"Just keep filming."

They entered another ultra-slow zone. Cars along the curb. Drivers double-parked with flashers. Cops waving people through and knocking on windows.

Luggage thrown in the trunks. Travelers urgently smoking after long flights.

The horse trailer was already parked at the last skycap. The first Jeep pulled up, then the others. People jumped out and ran through various automatic doors. Serge stopped in the second lane and jumped out. "Coleman, slide over and take the wheel."

"Where am I going?"

"Just drive in circles and keep making passes by here until you see me come back out."

He ran inside the airport.

Chapter Twenty-Seven

BAGGAGE CLAIM

Some chases are easy to follow because of all the running. Except at airports. Despite heightened security designed to detect suspicious behaviors, running is not one of them. People are late.

Serge stood between a pair of rotating baggage carousels from Cleveland and Kansas City, looking both ways, trying to filter through all the galloping customers. A family from Little Rock ran by pushing an overloaded luggage cart like a dogsled race. Serge's eyes stopped at the west end of the terminal.

Skeeter dashed hell-bent through the terminal, followed closely by four Mexicans. A single, non-automatic door flew open, and Skeeter ran back outside into the sun. The door closed. The Mexicans threw it open and ran out.

Serge took off in a sprint, weaving through chauffeurs holding cardboard signs. Then he stopped. Because someone else had.

Up ahead, Gaspar Arroyo stood watching one particular carousel as the crowd around it thinned out.

Serge scratched the top of his head. "What's he stopping for?" Then his brain went in rewind mode: The guy being chased out the door was empty-handed. Serge smiled and moved over to a wall of courtesy phones, folding his arms.

Gaspar continued his vigil of the luggage carousel. Serge made a reflexive sweep of the surroundings. More families, baggage handlers, someone driving a beeping cart containing a passenger with two arm casts, flight attendants with smartly packed luggage, a guy carrying snow skis with misplaced confidence. Serge's eyes backed up. The hall to the restrooms. A second smile slowly spread across his face.

Standing around the corner, visible to Serge but out of sight from the other direction: the man Serge had first filmed trotting up the stairs at the Swashbuckler Motel.

Catfish pretended to be resetting his wristwatch for the time zone, but he kept peeking around the corner at Gaspar.

Another beeping cart cruised down the terminal. *"Coming through . . ."* In the rear seat were the
McDougalls. Pat had become increasingly unhinged
back in the luggage office, asking every five minutes,
and the attendant decided he needed some personal
service. A cart was called up and a grinning man in a
visor gestured for Pat and Barb to get in. "I'll take you
to your luggage, and then load it in your rental. Sorry
for all the inconvenience . . ."

And now the cart beeped its way through people not
paying attention, finally stopping at the carousel for a
just-arrived flight from Nashville. "Just point out your
bags," said the driver.

"There's one," said Pat. "I can't believe it's finally
here."

"And there are the other two," said Bar.

"I got 'em," said the driver, snatching suitcases off
the belt and tossing them in the back of the cart. He
drove off toward short-term parking.

Serge remained in the shadows, keeping a close eye
on Gaspar and Catfish. The score became clear: The
man being chased through the terminal had needed to
ditch the suitcase of money, and since there were no
lockers anymore, options were limited. But his choice
was clever. Hide it in plain sight. Set it on a baggage
belt and return later to unclaimed luggage. It had

almost worked, except Gaspar had apparently noticed the drop, and Catfish had noticed Gaspar.

They all waited patiently in the background of the Nashville carousel for the process of elimination. More and more passengers wheeled away luggage until, finally, no more people were left. A lone bag made another lap and rotated again through the hanging rubber strips. Gaspar casually grabbed the handle as it went by. He headed for the automatic doors and back into the heat. Serge looked the other way. Catfish was on the move. He went toward a different set of doors, for surveillance separation on Gaspar, and strolled outside. Serge burst through door number three.

At the curb, it was a banner day for the towing company. A pickup and horse trailer were already being driven off. Then one of the Jeeps. They started hooking up the Durango, but Catfish didn't make a move to avoid alerting his adversary. Up the line, Gaspar had his wallet open, negotiating a bribe with a tow driver.

Serge began to fidget. "Come on, Coleman, now's the time. Pull on up . . ."

Gaspar climbed in his Jeep and attempted to ease out, but the traffic was thick. Catfish ran the other way toward the taxi stand.

Serge picked his nails. "Okay, Coleman, any day now . . ."

A break opened up between cars, and Gaspar nosed the Jeep out of its parking space. Serge looked the other way. Catfish climbed into a tropical cab.

"Coleman, dammit!" Serge stared intensely at the lanes leading into the arrival area, trying to use sheer will to make the Gran Torino appear. Instead, Catfish's taxi drove by, tailing a Jeep out of the pickup zone.

Serge continued staring. No Gran Torino. "God, please don't do this to me—"

Suddenly from the opposite direction, a symphony of blaring horns and profanity. Serge turned around. A Gran Torino was driving the wrong way, in through the exit of the arrival zone. Everything clogged to a stop. Serge ran onto the road and sprinted up between lanes of brake lights. He raced past Catfish's taxi and then a Jeep with Gaspar hanging out the window: "What the fuck is going on up there? . . ."

Parking cops began converging from other directions, but Serge reached the wayward car first. He yanked the driver's door open. "Move over!"

Coleman scooted. "Serge, everyone is driving the wrong way."

"Shut up and film!"

The cops were almost to the car when Serge executed a swift three-point turn and sped out the exit. "At least you held up the people I was trying to follow."

A Jeep flew by on one side, and a Durango on the other. "Sometimes it's better to be lucky than good."

"Wait a minute," said Coleman, twisting the end of a joint in his lips. "Are you saying that *I* was the one going in the wrong direction?"

"No, Coleman, we're in a mirror universe." Serge shook his head. "But how is it even possible to come up that road in the other direction?"

"Wasn't even trying," said Coleman. "I just got confused and it worked out."

Serge followed the other vehicles as they retraced their route south on U.S. 1. Just past Dania, the Jeep pulled into an empty motel with a sombrero on a sign that said they had color TV.

The cab drove past the motel and dropped Catfish at the next intersection. He crossed the street and doubled back. Serge went an additional block and made a U-turn so he could follow Catfish on the way to Gaspar's motel room.

"Serge?" asked Coleman.

"Yes, camera number one?"

"I know you're very busy, but I don't have any idea what's going on anymore."

"I think I can help," said Serge. "We're hurtling through space on a blue planet with a thick layer of nitrogen and oxygen, where single-cell life spawned from a primordial soup billions of years ago and continued to develop until we could text each other. Then we decay, releasing tiny amounts of radiation according to Einstein until we die. Following that, there's either no afterlife, or I've got some serious explaining to do: 'Sorry, I thought death was the end. This is really kind of embarrassing, especially if you could see me masturbating all those times.'"

"No," said Coleman. "I mean about this chase we're on. I've lost track of the players."

"Oh," said Serge, gradually slowing down. "I thought this was like the time you were tripping and asked me to help orient you, and I gave our location and the date, and you said 'back up,' so I recapped our steps over the last week, but you kept saying 'back up,' and I went further and further until I got to the hurtling planet we call Earth, but you still said 'back up,' so I kept going until we reached the big bang, and you said 'back up,' and I said, 'Coleman, that's it. That's as far as it goes.' You stared in my eyes a couple minutes and said, 'Fuck me!' Then you went in the shower and cried."

Serge drove slowly through a shopping-center parking lot so he wouldn't overrun Catfish walking up the sidewalk.

"Like that guy," said Coleman. "Who's he?"

"I'm guessing one of the Kentucky gang, probably the leader . . ."

Catfish sat down on a bus-stop bench across the street from the Acapulco Motel.

" . . . He's staking out the room of the Mexican gang's leader."

"That's a pretty nice Jeep," said Coleman. "Why is he staying in such a dump?"

"I don't think he is." Serge grabbed the camera from Coleman. "Probably just picked a random motel for a few minutes of privacy with that suitcase."

"Suitcase?" asked Coleman.

"Saw it back in the airport," said Serge. "After the shooting started at that other motel, it became a rugby scrum for the buy money, and it appears our friend with the Jeep was the lucky winner."

"What now?"

"Wait," said Serge. "The hillbilly looks like he's figuring out a way to ambush. Then when they get busy with each other, we might be able to turn the confusion to our advantage."

Coleman raised a beer can. "The door's opening."

Serge swung the camera to room number five. "That's strange. He's getting back in his Jeep. But he doesn't have the suitcase. He's driving away."

"It must still be in the room," said Coleman.

The camera swung the other way. "That's what our Kentucky friend thinks. He's abandoning thoughts of ambush and running across the street for the motel . . . But why on earth would the other dude leave a suitcase full of cash in that kind of joint? It's an awfully big risk."

"The second one's jimmying the door," said Coleman. "He's going inside."

"Now I'm definitely curious," said Serge. "And you know me when it comes to curious. I've got the perfect temperament to reassemble the debris of a downed jetliner to find which rivets came loose at thirty thousand and sucked the stockbroker out the lavatory roof. That really happened, but they turned me down for the reassembly team. I'm curious why."

"The motel door's opening again," said Coleman.

"So fast?" said Serge.

"He's coming out," said Coleman. "He doesn't have the suitcase either. He's leaving the parking lot . . . Why aren't you following them?"

"Change of plans," said Serge.

Serge started the Gran Torino and sped to the parking lot of the Acapulco Motel, skidding into a parking space previously occupied by the Jeep.

He jumped out and ran to the building, then glanced around for witnesses as he slipped a flathead screwdriver from his pocket. Every room had been jimmied so many times that there was already a convenient slot in the doorframe for his tool. It popped without effort.

They ran inside and stopped in disbelief when they saw that the suitcase was just sitting there. Lying unguarded on one of the beds. Zippered top flipped open.

Serge stood over it for a prolonged pause. Now he was really confused. He reached inside and removed a handful. "Women's underwear? . . . Must be camouflage." He dug deeper. Just more female apparel.

"Can I have those black panties?" asked Coleman.

"Quiet." Serge stared down. "I'm trying to think . . . Okay, the first guy came in and left, and then the second one. And they both seem to have departed with purpose."

"What happened to the money?"

"Maybe there's a clue in the suitcase." They began searching through the contents, wantonly casting stuff on the floor.

"Here's a makeup case," said Coleman. "But just the usual crap inside."

Serge threw a bra over his shoulder. "Keep looking."

They reached the bottom.

"Serge, there's nothing in here but this chick's stuff."

"I can't figure this." Serge turned the suitcase upside down and shook vigorously.

"I'm pretty sure it's empty," said Coleman.

"This really pisses me off." Continued shaking, even harder.

"Serge, your face is turning purple again."

Serge shook the suitcase even harder until the stitching on one of the handles started to pull out. "Motherfucker!"

Coleman pointed. "Look!"

Serge stopped shaking luggage. "Huh?"

A small rectangle of card stock fluttered down onto the bedspread. Serge picked it up.

"What is it?" asked Coleman.

"One of those suitcase identification cards that people fill out so the airlines know where to deliver your bags after they tour the country." He held the card closer. "It's got a Wisconsin address. This is important."

"Why?" asked Coleman.

"Because I'm betting the two previous characters in this room found other forms of identification, but left this card behind. The officials are always harping at the airport that a lot of bags look similar."

"So what?" said Coleman. "Just means that those guys we've been following picked up the wrong suitcase."

"Which means someone's got the right suitcase."

"Any idea?"

Serge held the card to his friend's face.

Coleman read it and looked up. "Who the hell are the McDougalls?"

ONE MILE AWAY

A rented Impala raced south on U.S. 1.

"What are we going to do?" asked Pat.

"Get the rest of our stuff out of the room as fast as we can and clear out of town."

"And go where?"

"Who cares?" Pat ran a red light. "We'll just drive until money and gas run out. Wherever we end up will be better than this."

A ringing sound.

Pat jumped.

"It's our cell phone," said Bar. "Aren't you going to answer it?"

"It's probably that guy."

Bar checked the numeric display. "I don't think it is."

"I'm not answering it."

"But what if it's the police?" She opened it and held it to her husband's head.

He shot her a glance, then grabbed the phone. "Hello?"

"Is this Patrick McDougall?"

Pat covered the phone and turned to his wife. "You're right, it's a different voice." Then back into the phone. "Yes, this is Pat."

"Patrick McDougall from Madison, Wisconsin?"

"Who's this?"

"My sincere apologies. It's all my fault," said the voice on the other end. "I believe I picked up one of your suitcases by accident at the airport a few minutes ago."

"But we have all our suitcases."

"I know," said the voice. "One of them is mine."

"Hold on just a minute." Pat covered the phone again. "Honey, do we know if we have all the right bags?"

"Of course, I—" She stopped and remembered. "Actually, the driver of the beeping cart grabbed them off the carousel and put them in our trunk. I never got a good look."

Pat nodded and uncovered the phone. "We might have it, but we'll have to check."

"Really appreciate it. And again my apologies."

"It's nothing," said Pat. "If we've got it, I'll call you back and leave it in our motel office."

"I'd rather meet in person and give you a reward, a little something for your trouble," said the voice. "What room are you staying in?"

"We're really in a rush," said Pat.

"So am I. Let me come by your room."

"I don't want to," said Pat.

"It's very important to me."

A beeping tone on the phone. "Excuse me," said Pat. "I have another incoming call."

"Don't put me on hold—"

Click. Pat put him on hold. "Hello? . . ."

"Give me my fucking cocaine!"

Pat hung up and switched back to the first call. "Sorry about that . . ."

"Give me my fucking suitcase!"

Pat threw the phone out the window.

Chapter Twenty-Eight

PARADISE INTERRUPTED

A rented Impala raced through another red light on U.S. 1.

"Maybe you should slow down," said Bar.

"I ain't slowing down until we're out of that motel and hit the Georgia line."

Bar kept checking the mirrors. "Why don't we just call the police? That's what any local person would do."

"Call the police? You heard them in the motel room during the interview: They might charge us later if it leads to bigger fish. So, like, I just get back in contact and ask them to protect us from someone who wants his cocaine back? They'll book us for sure. I'm not pressing my luck by calling any cops around here."

"Let's just get on the interstate."

"I wouldn't go back to the room if we didn't absolutely have to." Pat checked his own mirrors with a newly developed twitch. "But our ATM's tapped out, our credit card's turned off, and the only money we have for gas is some emergency cash I hid in a side pocket of one of our suitcases."

"But what about those guys on the phone?" Bar twisted all the way around in her seat like a radar dish. "One of them mentioned the people from the Oasis Inn. They could be waiting back there right now to ambush us."

"Then they wouldn't have called. They would have just jumped us when we got back to the room." Pat leaned over the wheel as the speedometer hit sixty. "The fact that they called means they don't know where we're staying—yet."

"What do you mean 'yet'?"

Pat pointed. "There's the Casablanca now."

"Let's be quick," said Bar.

"Don't worry," said Pat. "It's almost over. A few more minutes and we'll be home free."

The Impala jumped the curb in front of the motel and skidded diagonally up to room 17. Pat grabbed the door handle. "I'll be back in a second."

He ran inside, and true to his word, he was out in a flash. He started getting in the car, then stopped. "Uh, honey?"

Bar looked up. "Oh my God!"

A gun was pressed to the back of her husband's head. *"Where's my fucking cocaine!"*

"I don't have it! You got the wrong person!"

"I'll blow your fucking head off!"

The finger on the trigger was connected to a meth-thin ex-con with a teardrop tattoo next to one eye. Teeth so bad it looked like he was wearing novelty teeth. He swung his sunken eyes, and then the gun, toward Barbara's head. "What about your wife? Ready to talk now?"

"Don't point that gun at her!"

"So I found your soft spot?"

Pat grabbed the pistol. But not to wrestle it away; he took the barrel and pressed it back against his own head. "Leave her out of it. There's been a mix-up, but maybe I can help you figure it out."

"Here's the mix-up," said the coke dealer. "You got my shit hidden in your room. But I spent an hour in there and couldn't find it. So you're going to come in and help me. *Both* of you." He stepped back and motioned at Bar with the gun. "Now out of the car!"

Bar complied and stood together with her husband.

The gunman thought of something. Where hadn't he looked? He eyed the Impala's trunk. "Toss me the keys!"

Pat did. The gunman kept his eyes on them as he popped the rear hood. "Don't move! I'm throwing this luggage in the room in case you stashed it in one of those bags."

The last suitcase flew through the open door. Another wave of the gun. "Now get in there!"

A block away, a screech of tires as another vehicle whipped around the corner.

The gunman turned to see a black Jeep Cherokee with a rack of fog lights. "Shit!" He yanked Pat out of the room. "Back in the car! I'm driving!"

Pat quickly crowded toward his wife in the front seat as the man jumped behind the wheel.

"What's going on?" asked Pat.

No answer. The assailant threw the Impala in gear and hit the gas.

A shot rang out. Just missed the back end of the rental and shattered the window of room 23. The Impala scraped over the curb and bottomed out with sparks. The driver cut the wheel hard and took off south on U.S. 1.

Pat and Bar clung to each other, eyes locked on the man behind the wheel. Time slowed down, volume dropped out; details grew large. The beads of sweat rolling down their driver's cheek magnified his pores in sharp focus.

There was a quiet *pock* sound, like someone accidentally dropping an egg on a tile floor. It went unnoticed, but not the tiny hole in the windshield surrounded by a circle of cracks.

The driver fell forward on the steering wheel. The horn blared, blood squirting from his head, keeping beat with his fading heart.

Then time swung the other way, fast motion. The driver's limp head rotated the steering wheel left, and the Impala swerved over the centerline. Oncoming cars swerved and honked, until a Nissan clipped the front bumper. Both cars spun out and the McDougalls were thrown against the passenger door in a mad teacup ride. Other drivers scattered and slammed brakes. Some found safe spots to crash; others found other cars.

There was a brief intermission of stillness while everyone tried to recalibrate their brains.

They didn't get to finish.

More information followed: The driver's window of the Impala exploded from automatic-weapon fire. All cars emptied, everyone diving into shops, behind trees, under bus benches. Except Pat and Bar, who spilled out their door and froze on the pavement, bullets riddling fenders on the opposite side.

Everyone stayed crouched wherever they landed. People peeked out store windows like extras in a western gunfight. The Impala remained alone, sideways in the middle of U.S. 1 with all the windows blown out. The broad, open, six-lane highway around it bathed in sunlight, a death zone, easy pickings for the ammunition continuing to rake the road and kick up chunks of pavement that pinged against cars and street signs. A shotgun blast blew open the trunk.

Pat and Bar held each other tight, eyes closed, leaning against the rear tire.

Something made their eyes open. The tire wasn't wide enough. It got hit and went flat. Other bullets began skipping under the car. One tore through Pat's left pants pocket. Then he felt a moist pool of fluid spreading around him. Pat checked himself for blood. Then realized it was seeping out from under the car. He recognized the rainbow in the liquid.

"Gasoline!"

A decision was needed. Fear made it for them.

The couple began scrambling on hands and knees down the center of U.S. 1 on the opposite side of the car from the gunfire. They'd barely made it twenty yards when a flash of heat seared up their backs and a concussion wave knocked them flat on the ground. The fireball from the Impala mushroomed into blackness above the coconuts and Canary Island date palms. More bullets now, but less accurate because of the obstructing flames and smoke. The shots came from the occupants of the Jeep Cherokee, which was forced to skid to a stop behind the crashed Nissan. Heavily armed men poured out in cowboy hats and plaid shirts. Stray rounds hit storefronts and newspaper boxes. Twenty witnesses on the phone to police.

Pat veered Bar right in the road—"Over that way! There are less bullets"—he wasn't correct. New gunfire came from a silver Ford Explorer and a Durango, both with Kentucky plates, that had cut through a Citgo station and landed over the curb at a drugstore. More armed men, this time blue jeans and rawhide boots. They took turns firing at the McDougalls and the gang from the Cherokee, who returned the gesture. Men from both sides took hits. A police helicopter swooped in, the spotter on the radio with a crackling voice and whapping rhythm in the background:

"Two civilians on Federal Highway at One Hundred and Fifteenth, taking fire . . ."

The first responding officer raced north up the center of the cleared-out highway, siren echoing off the concrete storefronts. His windshield cracked. Not gunfire. A dislodged chunk of road that flew up. Two innocent people appeared ahead in the middle of the street, through mirage waves coming off the hot pavement.

They would be dead any second. The cruiser hit ninety. No time to think. Only option was to kick out the back tires in a combination of gas and brake, then steer into the skid. If everything went right, the patrol car would come to a stop just past the couple, shielding them in a kind of modern breastwork. If it went the other way, the cruiser would leave a big McDougall stain in the road and prop the officer up as an easy target behind his driver's window.

Pat and Bar looked down the road.

"It's the police!" said Pat.

"He's coming right at us."

They closed their eyes and ducked.

A ripping screech as brakes locked up in the patrol car.

Pat and Bar felt the wind of the cruiser going by.

They opened their eyes. They were still alive.

Bullets immediately riddled the cruiser's door panels.

The couple looked back. A police officer knelt outside his car, holding the back door open and waving wildly for them to join his position. They didn't waste time.

"Get in!" yelled the officer.

Bar reached the cruiser first and began climbing into the backseat. A well-aimed salvo from the Jeep blew out two of the patrol car's tires and most of the windows.

"Get out!"

The cop pulled her from the car, and he covered the couple on the ground.

"What do we do?" asked Bar.

The officer pointed at a copy shop. "We need to get around the corner and into that alley."

"I feel safer here," said Pat.

"We're dead here," said the cop. "Some of those rounds are armor piercing."

Bar's instinct said to move, but it couldn't get through to her body. "I can't do it."

A bullet came through the door of the police car and hit the pavement near her head. Bar took off like a track star, bullets kicking up dust around her shoes. The men weren't far behind.

Chapter Twenty-Nine

ONE MINUTE LATER

The McDougalls survived the gauntlet and ran around the side of the building into the alley. The officer pushed them behind him, then flattened against the wall. He reached for his shoulder radio to report their position.

"What on earth's going on?" asked Pat.

"Probably find out on the news tonight." The officer looked at both of them. "Do you know any of those people?"

They shook their heads. "Never seen them before."

"What about the dead driver in your car?"

"He highjacked us from our motel, the Casablanca."

"The Casablanca?" said the officer, appraising their intelligence level. "Why the hell would you do something crazy like stay there?"

"We're from Wisconsin."

"Just remain put." The officer crept to the corner of the building, holding his pistol upright at the side of his head. He took a quick peek around the edge. Lead and plaster dust exploded by.

He retreated to the couple and grabbed his radio mike again. "Where's that backup?"

"What did you see?" asked Pat.

"They're advancing."

"Advancing?"

"Military tactic. They've reached your car." He turned around and looked down their alley, which dead-ended against a junkyard fence topped with razor wire. Then into his radio again: "Need backup now! Taking fire, location vulnerable."

"Are we going to be okay?" asked Pat.

"We'll be fine," lied the officer.

More rounds hit the corner of the copy shop and the end of the sidewalk, which meant their position was known. The officer didn't risk his head this time, just reached the pistol around the corner and fired blindly. Not to hit anything, just slow 'em down.

The cop glanced quickly at the McDougalls. The obvious targets of the melee. It wasn't adding up. You never knew about some people, but others you did. And these definitely weren't the type to get mixed up in this. The officer didn't know why they were wanted dead, and he didn't care. But he knew why he'd become a cop. He was now a one-man Thin Blue Line. They weren't getting at this couple except through him.

His training said the shots were less than a block away, maybe half. He pulled out his wallet for a quick look at some family photos, then tucked it away and got on one knee. Shooting stance. "No matter what, stay behind me."

The McDougalls complied and dropped to their own knees.

"But don't grab my shoulder," said the officer.

"Sorry," said Bar.

Weapons grew louder. Almost there. The officer's finger put a couple pounds' pull on the trigger, so his first shot wouldn't take much more.

Even louder fire. Then *more* fire. But a different echo, meaning different origin. And different caliber. M16s. Standard SWAT-team issue.

Cavalry time. The officer's backup made a big splash, led by an armored police assault vehicle. In no time, they easily swept the street of bad guys like they were brushing off a case of fleas.

The cop holstered his gun, turned around to the couple and tried to hide a body-racking wave of relief.

But the McDougalls were still shaken, staring toward the empty street and trying to imagine the unseen violence that had transpired around the corner. Pat looked down at an engraved rectangle of plastic over the cop's pocket.

"Thank you, Officer Garcia."

"No problem. And we're going to check you out at the hospital, if for nothing else, give you something to help you sleep after all that."

"Does this happen often?" asked Bar.

"It was pretty common back in the early eighties, but now something like this is a five-year event. Guess it was your lucky time for a vacation." Garcia pulled out a pad and pen. "Need to get a preliminary statement from you."

"Sure, anything to cooperate. I mean I think you just saved our lives, right?"

"Do you have any idea what that was all about? Seems to be a little more involved than a simple carjacking."

"I think it has something to do with a suitcase. Or cocaine. Or both."

"What suitcase?"

"I don't know, but the guy who forced his way into our car had been making threatening phone calls," said Pat. "And another caller claimed we had mistakenly picked up his suitcase at the airport."

The officer stopped writing. "That's it."

"What's it?"

"You're in South Florida. Do you have any idea how many pieces of luggage and briefcases are floating around? Undeclared cash, heroin, uncut diamonds?"

Pat and Bar shook their heads.

"Well, it's a lot," said the officer. "Mostly they stay with the right people, but with the sheer volume out there, a few are bound to get away from time to time . . . Where is this suitcase?"

"Probably back in our room right now," said Bar.

"Probably?" said the officer. "You wouldn't recognize big piles of money or drugs?"

"We haven't had time to look in all our bags," said Pat. "The airline lost them for a while."

The officer had a chance to pause for the first time. "What's wrong with your face?"

"Jellyfish. And sunburn."

"Do you think you could take me to your luggage now?" asked Officer Garcia.

"Sure," said Pat. "We're not doing anything else."

They headed out of the alley.

An unmarked Crown Vic with a blue light on the dashboard came bouncing around the corner into the alley. The driver's window rolled down. Dark sunglasses. "What have we got here? These the victims?"

The couple could tell by the way Officer Garcia stood straight that this was someone a few pay grades higher. So far up the chain of command that Garcia had never seen him before. But if anything could bring out this level of rank, it would be the mess still sitting out on U.S. 1.

"Sir," said Garcia. "I believe I know what triggered our altercation."

"Altercation? It's a goddamn shooting gallery out there."

"Yes, sir."

"As you were saying?"

"I strongly believe that this visiting couple—" He looked over at them. "Names?"

"Pat," said Pat. "Pat and Bar McDougall."

Garcia faced the brass again. " . . . That the McDougalls accidentally picked up a suitcase of contraband at Fort Lauderdale International. Some competing interests tracked them to their motel, where they got caught in the middle."

Dark sunglasses studied the officer a moment. "You already got that whole cluster-fuck in the street figured out? All by yourself? Jesus, I can still smell cordite."

"Yes, sir."

The supervisor shook his head. "I'm not making any promises . . . Forget that. I *am* making promises. Start clearing wall space at home for an attractive plaque."

"Thank you, sir. And you should know that they were just about to take me to the suitcase right now."

"Who else knows about this?"

"Nobody, sir."

"Then don't you think we ought to get the hell over there pretty fast before any more bad guys can show up first and grab whatever the fuck it is?"

"Yes, sir."

The driver of the Crown Vic hit the unlock button. "Okay, everybody get in."

A nine-millimeter pistol came out the window. Silencer.

Officer Garcia looked down in disbelief at the gunshot wound in the middle of his chest. Then up at the supervisor in the window of the Crown Vic, before slumping lifelessly against the wall of the copy shop.

The driver got out of the car.

"Holy shit!" said Pat, jumping back a step. "You shot Officer Garcia! You shot another cop!"

"Whoever said I was a cop?" He waved at them with the pistol. "Now get in."

They didn't move. It wasn't from courage. They were paralyzed.

"Look," said the driver. "I'm not going to kill you. Then I'd never find out what room you're staying in at the Casablanca—and never get the suitcase."

Movement returned to Pat's body. "Garcia never mentioned the Casablanca. How'd you know where we're staying?"

"It's my job."

"Who *are* you?"

"The guy who found your travel itinerary, including this motel, in your luggage. You seemed awfully anxious to get back to Wisconsin. And I'm shocked that you were smoking crack."

"So the guy who carjacked us? He was working with you?"

"No, I don't know what that was about. But I recognized him. He's a low-level coke dealer. Or was."

A flash of understanding hit Pat. "You're the one who shot him through the windshield!"

"I couldn't let him get away and do something terrible to you guys. And as you saw, I took great pains to make sure you weren't hit, so you can trust me." A motion with the gun. "Get in."

"You're just going to kill us right after you get the suitcase," said Pat.

"If you keep pissing me off." The man extended his shooting arm. "Now get in!"

"You're Mexican."

"What are you, prejudiced?" A more urgent gun gesture. "No more stalling! Get the fuck in!"

Pat turned to his wife. "If we get in that car, we're dead. But as long as we stay here, he won't shoot us because he needs the room number."

"You're priceless." The man laughed behind the dark sunglasses. "This isn't a TV show. You think you can compete with me in this game? This is chess, and you're playing tic-tac-toe."

"See," Pat told his wife. "He needs the room number."

"Here's the game: There are two of you, and I only need one alive." He stiffened his arms and held the gun firmly with both hands. "Checkmate. Please get in the car."

The couple froze again with mouths open.

"You're seriously beginning to hack me off." He aimed the gun at one, then the other. "You have exactly five seconds to get in the car, or who will it be?"

They still didn't move.

"Have it your way." He swung the gun back and forth between husband and wife as he counted off. "Eenie, meenie, miney, moe . . ."

The McDougalls closed their eyes.

Bang.

They opened their eyes.

"Motherfucker!" yelled Gaspar Arroyo, wincing and grabbing his bloody shoulder where the bullet had torn through and sent his pistol flying.

Then the couple looked down at the bottom of the alley, where Officer Garcia remained slumped against the wall, his arm barely strong enough to hold up the just-fired gun. Then it fell by his side and his head sagged for good.

Pat grabbed Bar's arm. "Run! . . ."

Chapter Thirty

BACK AT THE CASABLANCA . . .

"Cut! Print!" yelled Serge, standing on the second-floor balcony. He turned off his camcorder and headed for the stairs. "This reality show is turning out better than I ever expected. I got the whole shooting sequence, and it was dumb luck. I just had the camera running for stock footage of a carjacking when all hell broke loose."

"How'd you know to follow those tourists?"

"I didn't. I was following everyone else. After discovering that ID card in the suitcase, we just drove up and down until I saw a Jeep and then a Durango staking out this motel, and the rest fell in place."

Coleman ran after him. "Where to now?"

"The copy shop up the street." Serge bounded down the steps two at a time. "I want to interview those tourists while their memory is fresh. After such a traumatic experience, they could be highly quotable. Or they could be shitting themselves in terror and begging for us to get them out of Florida. Either way, great television."

Coleman reached the street just behind Serge and struggled to keep up on the sidewalk. "But what do you think all that shooting was about?"

"It's U.S. 1," said Serge. "So it doesn't have to be about anything. But this time it was about a suitcase full of cash from that other shoot-out this afternoon—the indoors one at the pirate motel. That luggage was like a basketball rebound that gets tipped in the air over and over and nobody can quite get a handle on it. This could make the whole series! And depending upon their camera presence, we might require them to ride along with us at least a week—for their own good—to film a three-to-five-show arc. Even if they initially resist, they'll come around."

"How do you know?"

"Have you seen the audition lines for *American Idol*? Everyone wants to be on television."

Serge picked up the pace, checking battery life on his video camera. "There's the copy shop." He clicked on the camcorder. "We need to be filming when we come around the corner to catch them in their natural state. And just in case they've calmed down from all the action, we'll need to jump out and scream like wild maniacs to remind them of their panic. You're a witness in case someone calls it a breach of journalism ethics."

"It isn't?"

"Not if we really scare them."

"Here's the corner," said Coleman.

"Ready? . . . Now!"

Serge and Coleman leaped out into the end of the alley, jumping and waving their arms.

"Booga! Booga! . . ."

Then Coleman yelled for real. *"Ahhhhhhhhhhh!"*

Tires squealed.

"Watch out!" yelled Serge, tackling his buddy and knocking him to the ground on the other side of the tight corridor. A Crown Vic with tinted windows blasted by them and made a skidding turn south on U.S. 1.

Serge rose to his knees and filmed the unmarked car as it disappeared, then swung the camera down at his pal's face.

"Holy Jesus!" said Coleman. "That guy almost killed me! My heart!"

Serge zoomed in tighter. He made a beckoning motion with his free hand. "More freak-out! Give me more freak-out!"

"But, Serge, I really am freaking out."

"I love it!" The free hand formed into a fist. "Now fake it for real! . . ."

"*Ahhhhhhhhhhhh!*"

"Man, you really can act. I never knew . . ."

"No, Serge. Look!"

The camera swung. "It's a cop! He's been shot!"

Serge ran over and felt for a pulse.

"Is he alive?"

Serge shook his head, eyes following a separate trail of blood to where the Crown Vic had been parked.

"Think it was the tourists?" asked Coleman.

"Unlikely." Serge stood back up. "And that guy who almost hit us was driving an unmarked police car, probably wounded. This isn't normal. We need to find that couple. But first we need to get out of this alley before we're unfairly blamed again."

Serge raced around the corner and took off down the sidewalk.

"Wait up!" yelled Coleman. "Where do you think they went?"

"Who knows?" Serge stopped at an intersection. "But I know where they might be going. They were carjacked after pulling into the parking lot of the Casablanca, so that's where they're probably staying."

"Why do you think they'll come back after all this?"

"Because they left their stuff," said Serge. "It's a fifty-fifty proposition. Maybe they'll abandon it and split, or maybe they need something from that room in order to get out of town."

"So what now?"

"Go back to the motel like nothing's happened, and if they do return, we pounce for the ambush interview." Serge began running again with an enthusiastic spring in his step. "Everyone loves the ambush interview!"

SIX BLOCKS AWAY

Behind a scratch-and-dent patio-furniture outlet.

Pat McDougall poked his head out around the edge of the store. His wife tightly clutched the back of his shirt. "See anything?"

"No."

"Maybe we should try calling the police."

"I told you, we can't. We don't know who's on what side. That guy threatening us at gunpoint in the alley was a cop."

"He told us he wasn't," said Bar.

"He shot another cop! But lying's beneath him? . . . And by now he's probably pinned that murder on us. Our prints are all over the alley."

"What are we going to do?"

"Get out of Florida. Then we find some police we know we can trust and explain everything."

"But how can we leave?" said Bar. "We're broke, no credit cards, and now we don't even have a car."

"That's why we need to go back to the room."

"Go back? Have you lost your mind?" said his wife. "After everything that just happened?"

"Especially after everything that just happened," said Pat. "We don't have a choice. We're helpless street people now until we get in there and grab the emergency cash in my suitcase . . . Duck!"

They crouched behind a hedge on the side of the building.

"What was it?" asked Bar.

"Police car. But not the guy from the alley."

"How are we going to get in our room? Someone might be watching it."

"So we also watch it," said Pat, peering around the corner again. "We go back after dark and hang out across the street until we're absolutely sure it's clear. If anything's suspicious, we leave."

"Then what?"

"Figure something else out." Pat reached down and touched his leg. He held up his palm.

"You're bleeding," said Bar.

"Skinned my knee when I tripped getting out of that alley." He grabbed his left sleeve. "And my shirt's ripped."

Bar looked down at herself, then at her husband. "We're completely filthy from crawling around bushes for the last mile."

"That's the least of our problems." He raised a dirty foot that had lost a shoe. It was bloody, too.

"How long till dark?"

"At least seven or eight hours . . . Duck."

They crouched again as another squad car went by.

"What do we do until then?"

"Stay out of sight."

"I'm hungry," said Bar. "I didn't eat lunch. And only had a bite for breakfast. I'm thirsty."

"What do you want me to say?"

"Sometimes they give free samples in the grocery store," said Bar. "There's one up the street."

"I don't think they give samples to people looking like us," said Pat. "In fact, I think they have procedures to deal with people like us . . . And we won't be out of sight."

"Eight hours?"

Pat felt something in his stomach. Not hunger. Frustration at being unable to take care of the woman he loved. "Don't worry. I'll get you something."

"Where?"

He looked around. "That strip mall next door. It's got a couple restaurants."

"They're not giving away free food."

"Not that." He pointed. "The Dumpsters out back."

"Oh God, I just lost my appetite."

"Baby, how many times have we seen people leave half a plate of perfectly good food? Restaurants also throw out unserved stuff that's just a little old. We're not in a position to be picky."

"I'd rather hold out," said Bar. "Let's sit down and rest."

They reclined in the bushes.

Two hours later:

Snoring. An incredibly deep nap from exhaustion.

Something woke them up.

"Bastards!" Pat grimaced and scratched welts running down both arms. "What the heck kind of ants do they have down here in the bushes?"

"Apparently big red ones," said Bar, rubbing her own arms. Then she heard her stomach growl. "I guess it wouldn't hurt to take a *look* in a Dumpster."

They went in the alley behind the strip mall. The search was tentative at first. They stood back with folded arms, afraid to even make contact with the metal lip. Then Pat found a stick and began moving trash around. "I see half a bagel."

"Grab it."

He reached over the edge and retrieved the baked good. Then brushed off some coffee grounds and handed it to his wife.

She sniffed it, and pointed back in the trash bin. "Is that an egg roll?"

"I think so," said Pat. He hung farther over the side and snagged it. "You were right."

"Trade?"

They swapped and ate like they'd just crossed the Sahara.

A police car drove by. And kept going.

The couple dove for cover after the fact.

"Dammit," said Pat. "Our guard was down. We were so busy digging for food that we forgot to stay alert and hide."

"I think we *are* hiding." Bar munched the egg roll. "Not bad."

"What do you mean we're hiding?"

"Look at us." Bar held out her arms. "Look what we've become. I'd cross the street if I saw us coming."

"We do look kind of homeless," said Pat.

"I think we've just turned invisible," said Bar. "And technically we *are* homeless."

"You might have something there."

Bar got on her tiptoes and hinged at the waist, leaning deep into the trash bin. "I think it's a sticky bun. I can't reach it."

"Let me help."

"Just give me a boost. I'm almost there."

Bar's fingertips brushed the pastry. "A little more . . ."

Suddenly the garbage in the bottom of the bin erupted. Napkins and old lettuce flew.

The couple screamed and fell back on the ground.

A head popped out of the Dumpster. "Oooo, don't feel so good. What day is it?" The head looked left and right. Then down. "Hey there. How's it going?"

"Who are you?" asked Pat.

"Lawrence." He disappeared back into the bin. Heavy rustling sounds. Pat and Bar looked oddly at each other.

The head popped back up again. An arm raised an uncapped bottle of Boone's Farm. "My lucky day. A little left at the bottom." He held it over the side. "Want some?"

"We'll pass."

Lawrence shrugged and climbed out of the bin.

He smiled, then a different look. "Good Lord, what happened to you?" he asked Pat. "You look awful."

"Is it that noticeable?" said Pat.

"Your face is all blotched and peeling with a bunch of red streaks," said the stranger. "I've seen a lot of guys living out here, but you must have been on the streets forever."

"Just this afternoon."

"Jesus, man, pace yourself."

"We're on vacation."

"Me, too," said Lawrence, staring at the welts on their arms. "Don't you know about fire ants?"

"We're from Wisconsin."

"That's why I don't recognize you."

"It's been a bad couple days."

"Been there myself." Lawrence drained the bottle and chucked it over his shoulder into the bin. "You'll be back on your feet in no time. Just look at me."

They did.

"I'm a hedge-fund manager," said Lawrence. "Or used to be."

"The economy?" asked Pat.

Lawrence shook his head. "Big misunderstanding with human resources. Falsely accused of smoking crack. Okay, I smoked crack, but they made a big deal like I was a long-term addict when I just smoked a whole bunch in a short amount of time."

A police car drove by. The couple flinched.

Lawrence cracked a smile. "I get it now. You've had your own little misunderstanding with the law."

"We just need a place to stay low until after dark," said Pat. "When we can sneak back to our motel room."

Lawrence gestured behind himself at the trash bin as he walked away. "You can stay at my place. I'm not expecting company."

Chapter Thirty-One

A FEW HOURS LATER

The sun went down, and night fell over U.S. Highway 1.

A Dumpster stood beside a strip mall. Two heads popped up. One of the dirt-smudged faces looked at the other.

"Bar, you're shaking like a leaf."

"I'm scared witless to go back in that motel room after everything that's happened." She wiped her nose on the back of her arm. "What if someone's waiting inside?"

"They may know the motel," said Pat. "But not the room number."

Bar glanced up and down the street. "What if they're hiding somewhere around here like we are, waiting for us to show back up and see what room we go in?"

"That's why we've been moving around these alleys. To make sure nobody's watching the motel. And it looks like nobody is."

"They wouldn't be obvious," said Bar.

"They can't watch forever," said Pat. "And for all we know, they probably think we split and are three states away by now. I mean who in their right mind would go back to the room?"

"Precisely."

"We have to do this," said Pat. "Can't go to the police in this town since that business in the alley. We just need enough money for gas and food. Our only path of survival is through that room."

"I'm just so terrified."

"Then stay here," said Pat. "That would actually be better. It's dark, and they're looking for a couple. A single silhouette might go unnoticed."

"No way," said Bar. "Anywhere you're going, I'm going. I love you."

"Love you, too," said Pat. "Okay, here's the plan. We'll loop around and come in from the rear, and once we're in that room, we're as good as back to Wisconsin. The most dangerous time is the exposure from when we leave this hiding spot until we reach the door. You sure you want to do this?"

She suppressed a panic attack and nodded.

"Let's go . . ."

They dashed across the highway two blocks down from the hotel and worked their way along a street behind the buildings. The first five minutes seemed like an hour.

Bar stopped by a chain-link fence. "I can barely get my legs to move. They're not doing what I tell them."

"We have to keep going," said Pat. "It's not safe to stay in one place."

They finally reached the edge of the Casablanca Inn on an unlit side street. Pat peeked around the corner. "Looks clear."

"I don't think I can do it." Bar grabbed her racing heart. "We'll have to walk out in the light, in front of all those other rooms, until we get to ours. We'll be completely naked—it can't get any more dangerous."

"Too late to worry about that now. The longer we remain—"

"I know, I know," said Bar. "Let's look around one more time."

"Okay."

Two pairs of eyes made a slow, 180-degree sweep of the street, checking for any movement or out-of-place characters.

"I think we're good," said Pat. "Walk fast, but don't break into a run . . . Now."

The couple strolled briskly. Pat got out his brass key and started inserting it into the knob.

Bar's head jerked around, looking behind them.

Clang.

"Damn, I dropped the key."

"I got it." Bar picked it up and unlocked the door.

They darted inside and slammed the door.

"Where's the light switch?"

"I think it's over here," said Bar. "I found it."

She turned on the lights.

They froze.

Then slowly looked at each other. "I can't believe we made it," said Bar.

"Got to move fast," said Pat. "They may have missed us on the way in, but it could be hairy getting out. Grab just what we need."

Clothes flew. Pat found the suitcase pocket with the emergency money.

"Pat?"

"What is it?" He grabbed another suitcase and ripped through its contents.

"Pat?"

Without looking: "What?" Socks and underwear hit the wall. Something was off. Pat stopped, realizing there wasn't any sound or movement from his wife's direction. "Honey, what's the—"

She just stared down at an unzipped suitcase just delivered from Nashville.

"Holy shit!" said Pat. "Look at all that money!"

"So that's what this is about. We grabbed the wrong suitcase at the airport . . . Or rather that baggage guy did."

"Zip it up," said Pat.

"Why?"

"We're taking it with us."

"Have you lost your mind? I've never known you to be greedy."

"Bar, that might be the only thing keeping us alive," said Pat. "It's our bargaining chip."

From behind: "You're right."

The couple spun around. "Who are you?" said Pat. "How'd you get in here?"

"You forgot to lock the door. Happens a lot with these old joints that don't automatically latch . . . And to answer your first question, most people call me Gaspar. You can, too."

They weren't looking at his face. The gun in his hand meant he wanted to control their movements. The silencer meant something else.

"Wait," said Pat. "I recognize you. Except without the hat and sunglasses. You're the cop who shot the other cop in the alley."

"Take the money," said Bar.

"I will," said Gaspar.

They got the message.

"Let her go," said Pat. "There's no point—"

"Shut up and walk backward toward me."

Moments later, the couple knelt side by side, facing the back of the room. Mouths taped, hands bound behind their waists with plastic wrist straps.

Knees buckled. Tears streamed. Stomachs now heaved with tremors. Out of the corner of her eye, Bar saw the end of the silencer pressed against the back of her husband's head. A muffled scream came from under her tape.

Suddenly the bathroom door flew open.

Two people jumped out with a camcorder.

"Surprise!"

Gaspar looked up. "What the—?" He raised his pistol quickly and fired.

Pfffft.

The camcorder flew out of Serge's hand. He and Coleman dove back in the bathroom.

"Serge, I thought you said everyone loved the ambush interview."

"Tough room." Serge pulled his own pistol from under his shirt and stuck it around the corner, firing a blind, high shot.

Bang.

Pffft, pfftt.

"What are we going to do?" asked Coleman.

"The element of surprise is lost, so I'll settle for a regular interview." He fired again around the corner.

Then from the other side of the room:

Bang.

Coleman looked at Serge. "I thought that guy had a silencer."

"He did." Serge fired another shot for cover before looking around the corner.

The McDougalls wisely decided to flatten themselves on the ground. Gaspar had his back to them, ducking behind a dresser and exchanging shots with someone taking cover just outside the door of the room.

Gaspar fired again, spraying plaster. "Catfish! You moron! We can split this!"

"Fuck you!"

Bang.

Coleman turned. "Catfish?"

Serge shrugged, then jumped out of the bathroom. "Drop it!"

Gaspar turned around and squeezed off a wild shot. Serge jumped back in the bathroom.

Bang.

Catfish caught Gaspar in the left thigh while he was facing the other way. "Son of a bitch!" Gaspar fired another pair of shots in both directions to buy time.

It wasn't like the movies. Most people think a close-quarters firefight leaves carnage, but reality is the opposite. Just watch a few convenience-store surveillance videos. People too busy ducking to aim, then fleeing at the first chance. Over in seconds.

The Mexican was pinned in a crossfire and made the instinctive decision to attempt a limping charge toward the exit, blasting his way out. Serge stepped from the bathroom and fired at Gaspar's back. He missed but hit Catfish just as he stepped out to take his own shot. The bullet struck his elbow and sent his gun skittering across the parking lot.

Gaspar made it to the door and split stage right. Catfish was already high-tailing the other way.

Serge grabbed Pat by an arm and jerked him up to his feet. "We have to get going . . ." He helped Bar up and shouted sideways: "Coleman, grab that suitcase of cash. I'll get the video camera. We're rockin' . . ."

They all ran out the door for the Gran Torino.

Street people on the sidewalk watched as Serge shoved the bound and gagged couple into the back-seat. Then they went on with their lives. The Torino patched out.

"Coleman, my Swiss Army knife in the glove compartment. Cut them loose . . ." Serge glanced over his shoulder. "You're safe now."

Coleman sliced plastic straps. Pat briefly rubbed his wrists, then pulled the tape off both their mouths. "Thank you! Oh, thank you! You don't know what we've been through."

"Actually I do," said Serge. "You accidentally got caught in the middle of a big case."

Bar rubbed her own wrists. "You're not local police, are you?"

"I can honestly answer no," said Serge. "And you made a smart move not to go to them."

"Then who are you with?" asked Pat.

"It's better you don't know." Serge made a skidding left onto Hollywood Boulevard.

Bar looked at her husband. "Probably federal."

Pat nodded. "Investigating local corruption."

"Just doing my job," said Serge.

They crossed the bridge to the beach.

"So where are we going?" asked Bar.

"A special place." Serge made another squealing left north on A1A. "It's cool."

The couple breathed a heavy sigh and fell back into their seats.

In practically no time, they were getting out of the Torino in a jammed parking lot. The foursome walked through overgrown tropical foliage and past a bunch of discarded toilets with houseplants sprouting from the bowls.

Bar whispered as they walked behind Serge. "What's going on?"

"Must be some remote place that the feds use."

"I'm not so sure," said Bar.

"Honey, this is a side of life we've never seen before. We have no clue what's normal or not."

"You might be right," said Bar. "He saved our lives, so he must know what he's doing."

Serge waved for them to keep up. "Follow me."

They threaded their way through an old rustic bar crammed with crab-trap floats, fishing nets, license plates, a stuffed marlin, a pool table, a bathtub, international flags and more toilets. Claustrophobic like a submarine: a multilevel labyrinth of sturdy old boards and intimate bench seating squirreled into corners. Windows open all around to the night breeze off the water.

Serge finally reached the end of the building and gestured at the last bench. "Here we are."

They all sat down. Pat hunched toward Serge with a low voice. "What happens now? I guess we'll have to give a statement."

"Definitely." Serge turned on a camcorder. "I want you to tell me everything."

The couple nodded at each other. "We can do that," said Bar. "Are you meeting some backup people here?"

"No, it's just me and Coleman." Serge raised his hand for the bartender and ordered an iced coffee. "We travel fast and light. Or at least I do. Mornings start a little slow for my partner."

"If we're not meeting anyone, then why did we come here?" asked Bar.

"Because it's Le Tub, but most tourists miss it."

The coffee arrived and Serge chugged it. "Ever watch that great new TV show *The Glades*?"

"Heard of it," said Pat. "Why?"

"In the second episode, Matt Passmore interviewed a suspect on this very bench, right by that window overlooking the Intracoastal." Serge began rocking back and forth. "Isn't that priceless?" He slapped Pat on the back. "Are you getting fuckin' jazzed?"

"Am I what?" asked Pat.

"Jazzed," said Coleman, slamming back a shot of whiskey. "He's a Mort Sahl fan."

The bartender was already on his way over with a refill for Coleman.

Pat pulled his head back. "Should you be drinking so much at a time like this?"

"Why?" Coleman downed the second drink. "You want some weed?"

"What?"

Serge snapped his finger in front of Pat's face. "Pay attention. Things will start happening quickly. I didn't invent coffee; I just do what it tells me. We're heading to the band shell now. It's Hollywood, Florida, so naturally they had to have the Hollywood Bowl. It's not as big as the other one, but they did film *Body Heat* there. I'll play the part of William Hurt, and your wife can be Kathleen Turner for linear tension." He pulled out a digital camera. "Smile!"

Flash.

Serge looked at the preview screen on his camera. "Both your mouths are open like Mr. Bill on *Saturday Night Live* . . . Let's try again."

Flash.

"You're not photogenic. Fuck it, we're behind schedule . . ."

Bar nudged her husband. "I don't think they're with the government."

"Oh, I'm with the government all right," said Serge. "But when I say 'with,' I mean in the context of I'm in favor of it because otherwise there are no streets or postage stamps, and everyone wanders the woods carrying their own mail and looking at the sun to know when to eat until there's an eclipse and everyone's blind. That's why you should vote."

Whispers. "We need to get away from them . . ."

"I know . . ."

"I heard that," said Serge. "To the car! . . ."

The Wisconsin couple clutched each other and glanced around as they deliberately fell farther behind Serge.

"Now!" said Pat. They took off in the opposite direction and burst through a tall hedge on the side of A1A.

"Hey!" yelled Serge. "The car's this way. Stop fooling around."

The McDougalls hit the sidewalk and suddenly dug in their heels. A Jeep with fog lights went by. "It's that Mexican," said Bar. "He followed us."

They crashed back through the hedge, ran across the lot and dove into Serge's car.

"Are you feeling okay?"

The couple kept their heads down in the backseat. "Just drive."

"Glad to see you're with the program, because I was beginning to wonder." Serge sped off down the street and hooked east toward the beach.

Five minutes later:

"We're at the band shell. Smile!"

Flash.

"Mouths still open. Work on that . . . And this the famous Hollywood boardwalk, and this thatched-roof bar was the fictional joint Cancun in another *Glades* episode . . . Smile!"

Flash.

"Back to the car! . . . Hey, you're running the wrong way again!"

Pat stopped and grabbed his wife by the arm.

"What's the matter?" asked Bar.

Pat nodded ahead. "That guy at the take-out pizza counter."

"Looks like he's showing photos to the staff."

"Isn't he the other guy who was shooting from the doorway of our motel room? . . ."

Serge watched as the couple sprinted past him and jumped in his car. He followed them at a more casual pace and climbed in.

Pat McDougall peeked out the Torino's rear window. "Hurry up and drive!"

"Man," said Serge. "I thought *I* was exhausting to be around. But it means I picked the right stars for my show."

Bar tugged her husband's sleeve and pointed. A black Jeep with fog lights. They bonked each other's head ducking again. "Just get out of here! I think we're being followed!"

"Relax, audition's over," said Serge. "You already got the part."

Chapter Thirty-Two

The Gran Torino whipped back onto A1A. Coleman turned around in his seat. "Here's your weed."

"What?"

"Your joint. Take it."

"You mean pot?" said Pat. "We don't do drugs."

"Then why'd you ask for some back at the bar?"

"We didn't," said Bar. "You must have misunderstood."

Coleman pointed with the unlit twistie. "Okay, but that's entrapment if you're The Man . . ."

"We're not."

Coleman settled back into his seat. "Serge, I think they're narcs. Are you going to kill them?"

"No!" snapped Serge. "I never harm law enforcement."

"What if they're just civilian informants trying to work off a beef? Then will you kill them?"

"What's gotten into you?"

Coleman fired up the joint. "It's trippy watching you waste dudes, like that guy you left in the mangroves."

"Keep your voice down." Serge jerked a thumb over his shoulder. "I think they can hear you. See? They don't look like they're having a good time."

"I offered them weed."

Pat raised a hand.

"Yes?" said Serge, glancing in the rearview.

"We'd like to get out of the car now, please."

"But you're in a bad area," said Serge.

"Don't think we're not thankful," said Pat.

"Yes," said Bar. "We totally appreciate all you've done for us, especially the shooting."

Serge held up a modest hand for them to stop. "Say no more. If you want to thank us, please tell your friends after you get home."

"Tell them what?"

"That a trusty travel guide is essential for the total Florida experience. This is a word-of-mouth industry."

Coleman grinned in the rearview and waved a joint. "Don't forget to mention our reality show."

"What?"

Serge looked in the mirror again. "Can you have a marital spat? Just a fake one to boost our ratings. Maybe hold a knife to his dick, but don't cut if off because this is a family show."

Coleman offered the joint again. "This will help with those ant bites. That's what Willem Dafoe told Charlie Sheen in *Platoon*."

"I'm impressed," said Serge. "How were you able to remember that?"

"Classic weed moment in cinema." Coleman pointed at the couple. "But they're refusing to toke up. I think they're narcs."

A hand raised in the backseat. "We would like to get out of the car."

"You're fixating," said Serge. "Sit back and enjoy your life."

"Serge," said Coleman, looking out the back window. "I think they were right about us being followed. I see a Jeep with fog lights and maybe a Durango."

"Excellent," said Serge. "Hang on."

The Gran Torino swerved left and right through narrow streets, the McDougalls sliding side to side with each turn.

Serge reached U.S. 1 and sped north. "What about our tail?"

"Still back there," said Coleman.

Serge hit the gas and wove through traffic. "Okay, everyone, timing is going to be tight. If the schedule in my head is correct, we'll only have a few precious seconds. Just hope Captain Loogie isn't running behind."

"Loogie?" asked Pat.

"His real name's Chris Brennan, but it doesn't have that ring."

Serge ran a yellow light and made another screeching turn between two honking trucks. The couple in back covered their eyes.

Serge glanced at his side mirror. "How's it looking?"

"Both got held up at the light," said Coleman.

"Perfect. Just the time cushion we'll need." He raced east on Seventeenth Street, past Pier 66 and the Yankee Clipper, then a final hard left before skidding up at the fire station.

"Everyone out!"

Serge tossed the cash-crammed suitcase in the trunk, then led everyone running down to the water. A boat was about to cast off. An odd-looking narrow vessel with a domed cover, like the offspring of an Italian gondola and the Beatles' Yellow Submarine.

"Captain Loogie!" yelled Serge. "Wait up! We got four more!"

The man held the last line as the engine idled. The out-of-breath quartet scrambled aboard.

"Thanks," said Serge. "I owe you."

"But I'll never get paid." He undid the line's knot. "Dang it, you always do this. Why can't you just slow down and be prompt for once?"

"Hurry up," said Serge, watching a Jeep and a Durango roll up next to the fire station. "We're being followed."

"As usual." The man went up front and pulled away from the dock.

Serge turned and smiled at the McDougalls. "Everything's fine now. We're in Captain Loogie's hands. Don't be thrown by his long-haired, friend-of-the-earth hippie appearance. In a pinch, he can knock out local history with the best. That's why I picked him to be our guide for this segment of the tour."

"Guide?"

Serge took a seat next to them and swept an arm around the vessel's interior. "This is one of the world-famous Fort Lauderdale water taxis. But why do they even need water taxis? I'll tell you! Fort Lauderdale has more canals than Venice, so they call it the Venice of America, even though there's another city in Florida actually called Venice, which is known for prehistoric shark teeth on the beach and not Italians. Next question?"

"Is this the best way to escape?" asked Pat.

"No, the boat's going way too slow. They should easily be able to follow us from land . . ." Serge hummed merrily and gazed off the port side. "Check out those ridiculous mansions and their massive docks. Fort Lauderdale has forty-two thousand yachts. We're cruising the Intracoastal Waterway. They also got a bunch of Ferrari and other exotic car dealerships that followed the wealth up here during Anglo flight from Miami-Dade, which is now sixty-seven percent Latin. You might want to write some of this down . . ."

Pat and Bar clutched each other as they watched a Jeep and a Durango race along the shore.

" . . . And now we're turning up the New River," said Serge. "On the left is the historic 1902 Stranahan House, built by Fort Lauderdale founder Frank Stranahan. Dig how it's this little old joint dwarfed by all the surrounding downtown buildings. Carl Hiaasen grew up in this county, and it's where he got the name of protagonist Mick Stranahan in his bestseller *Skin Tight* . . ."

It sounded like an echo. Up on the bow, an annoyed Captain Loogie stood with a microphone, his own history lecture almost a verbatim, half-second delay of Serge's rant.

Serge wildly waved a hand in the air. "Ooooo! Ooooo! Captain Loogie! Do you take requests?"

Loogie slowly lowered his microphone in exasperation. "What?"

"Tell them about the Japanese fish!"

The captain unenthusiastically raised his mike and continued in a monotone. "A rich guy lived in that mansion on your left, and he threw a birthday party for his five-year-old daughter, who wanted their swimming pool filled with fish, so he bought fifteen thousand dollars' worth of Japanese koi, and in the middle of the party, a flock of brown pelicans dive-bombed the pool, eating all the fish and making the children cry."

Serge turned and grinned at the McDougalls. "Always a heartwarmer . . . Everyone up!"

"What for?" asked Pat.

"The river runs along the popular Las Olas entertainment district with lots of people eating veal on sidewalks. And lots of bars, so there's plenty of taxis. Plus the streets are tricky around here with all the canals. We need to grab a cab fast before our adversaries can figure out their way back around to the landing . . ."

The boat pulled up to a larger dock. Serge jumped off before it came to a stop, running out from behind a waterfront pub and waving down a cab. He didn't have to tell the others to keep up.

Three people dove into the backseat, and Serge climbed in up front.

The driver was a laid-back immigrant from the Ivory Coast. "Where to?"

"Just take off," said Serge, handing the man a hundred. "We're being followed. I'll give directions on the way. And there'll be another C-note at the end if we survive."

The cabbie grinned and nodded.

A tap on Serge's shoulder from the backseat. "Where are we going?"

"Drimmer's. That's all I can say right now without spoiling the surprise. You're going to love this!"

The taxi headed north through bright city traffic. Following Serge's directions, the driver peeled off the main drag and wound through a dim residential neighborhood. "There's the house." Serge fished another hundred from his wallet.

They all got out and Serge stuck his head back into the passenger window. "When you leave, drive crazy like we're still in the car."

"What?"

Serge raised his shirt to display the pistol tucked in his pants. "For your own safety."

The taxi drove off crazy.

Serge put his wallet away. "They're so cooperative down here." He ran up to the front door and rang the bell. No answer. He darted around the back of the house with the others close behind. A man was hosing something off a dock.

"Dave!" yelled Serge. "I need your keys! Fast!"

The man peered into the darkness at the forms rushing across the lawn toward him. "Serge? Is that you?"

Serge clomped down the dock. "No time to explain." He made an urgent gesture of rubbing a thumb and index finger together. "The keys!"

"Dammit, Serge!" The man fished in his pocket. "Do you ever think of calling?"

"We're being followed."

"What a shock." Dave slapped the keys in Serge's hand. "Just don't wreck it."

Serge looked back and waved. "Everyone aboard."

They followed Serge through an oval hatch on the side of a giant metal tube.

The McDougalls looked around the walls and ceiling. "Is this thing really a boat?"

"It is now." Serge ran up front to the cockpit and climbed into a pilot's chair. He cranked the engine and pulled away from the pier. One mooring line had been forgotten, and it tore off a dock cleat and a couple of planks.

From back on the dark shore: *"Dammit, Serge!..."*

The tube picked up speed and motored out of the canal.

"Pat!" Serge called over his shoulder. "Come up here and take the copilot's seat. You'll never get this chance again."

Pat nervously eased himself down into the chair.

Serge turned and smiled like a kid on Christmas. "Go ahead and play with the antique levers. They don't work anymore anyway. See? I'm doing it. Loads of fun . . ."

"But, Serge, I don't think this is the right—"

"Play with the fucking levers!"

"Okay, okay." Pat reached for the aircraft-style console. "I'm throwing levers . . . Now, what is this thing we're riding in?"

"Howard Hughes's private plane, Boeing B-307." Serge slowly turned the yoke and cornered another canal. "After being retired, she was stripped down to just the fuselage, fitted with propellers, and converted into a houseboat. But here's the best part! Jimmy Buffett was hanging out down here and saw this peculiar craft tooling through the water and it became the inspiration for the *Cosmic Muffin*"—Serge pointed up toward blue lettering at the top of the cockpit —"in his *Joe Merchant* novel, and further immortalized with his song 'Desdemona's Building a Rocket Ship' from the dynamite *Banana Wind* album. I wish I had my boom box . . ."

Pat looked out the side window of the cockpit. He sat back quickly with shallow breaths and glanced at Serge.

Serge smiled back. "I was hoping you wouldn't notice them following us again onshore." He threw some useless overhead levers that he hadn't gotten to yet. "Don't worry: We're taking this baby out in the ocean where they can't keep up."

"Is this boat seaworthy enough?"

"Not remotely." More levers. "I hope you're having as good a time as I am."

Ten minutes later. Pat and Bar held each other tight in the back of the *Cosmic Muffin*. Waves crashed the side of the fuselage, rolling it to forty-five degrees and back again. Serge played with an instrument dial. "Look at the stars! . . ."

Coleman worked his way up front. He had been drinking heavily and was staggering like he'd fall down any second. Between that and the rocking of the boat, he walked a straight line. "Serge, I don't think this baby's going to make it. We need to get it docked."

"Working on it." He increased the throttle, running parallel to land. "Been watching landmarks onshore. There's Bahia Mar and the Clipper, with Friday-evening mermaid shows." Serge turned the wheel. "We'll beach there between the two, then run across the sand, and our car should be waiting right where we left it to catch the water taxi." He brought her around ninety degrees.

The new direction toward land created a new challenge; the moonlit waves caught the back of the boat, then rolled up underneath and raised the cockpit to a sharp angle before crashing it down again.

Onshore, a few curious night strollers began pointing at the strange ship emerging from the Atlantic. They cautiously approached. As it grew larger, word spread through the bars and restaurants. More and more onlookers worked their way onto the beach until it became a mob. With the courage of their numbers, the audience slowly moved forward until they reached the edge of the surf.

"*Hey!*" someone yelled. "*It's the* Cosmic Muffin*! . . .*"

"*Desdemona's Rocket Ship! . . .*"

"*Buffett for president! . . .*"

With a helpful push of the waves, Serge nosed the boat a last fifty yards and landed it. A hatch opened. "Everyone out!" He jumped down in a foot of water and trudged ashore like MacArthur.

"I know that guy!" came another voice from the crowd. *"He's famous!"*

"Thank you," Serge said with humility.

A few others in the crowd were wearing custom T-shirts with a fleshy face on the front, over the quote: "Use sunscreen; don't do heroin."

They charged past Serge. *"It's Coleman! . . ."*

"I should have known he rolls in the Cosmic Muffin*! . . ."*

"Coleman, are you going to make the Muffin *a bong? . . ."*

Coleman came ashore signing autographs.

The crowd swarmed around them as they crossed the sand toward A1A.

"Coleman, stop with the Paris Hilton shit," said Serge. "We got company."

Coleman handed back a pen. "Where?"

"That way," said Serge, looking to his right, where Gaspar was getting out of a black Jeep. Serge turned in the other direction toward a Durango. "And over there."

Coleman grabbed Serge by the arm. "What do we do? There's no place to go."

"*Is something the matter, Coleman?*"

"Yes, those guys are after us."

"*Who?*" asked someone else in the crowd.

"Those two," said Coleman. "The Mexican in the dark shirt and that second one in the jeans."

"*Are they out to steal your record?*"

"Exactly," said Serge. "And they cheat. They want to break Coleman's kneecap like Nancy Kerrigan."

"*Son of a bitch! . . .*"

"*We won't let you down, Coleman! . . .*"

The two assailants approached the crowd from opposite directions.

Then the crowd turned and approached *them.*

The pair were so preoccupied trying to spot their prey that they didn't notice a shift in the mass of people. The going got rougher until they couldn't proceed at all.

"Out of the way!" yelled Gaspar.

"Move it!" said Catfish.

"*Fuck you!*"

Gaspar raised a pistol in the air and fired. That usually scattered crowds. This time they just plucked the gun away. Then the mob collapsed inward around the two, like the natives seizing Captain Willard in *Apocalypse Now.*

"Get your hands off me!" shouted Catfish.

They were both quickly pinned. A skateboard punk looked up. "Coleman, what do you want us to do with them?"

Serge smiled at his pal. "Tell them to bring 'em to our car. I'll go on ahead and open the trunk . . ."

THE CASABLANCA INN, ROOM 17

Six people crowded inside.

Patrick McDougall paced. "I don't like this."

Serge sat on the edge of one bed, aiming a pistol at two men sitting on the other, wrists bound behind their backs with plastic ties. "What? I should let them kill you?"

"But this isn't right," said Pat.

"You're saying that because you're a good man." Serge shifted his weight and got a better grip on the gun. "That's why this is my business. My hands are already dirty . . . Why don't you take your wife and go in the bathroom until this is over."

Bar gently grabbed his arm. "Let's do like he says."

"No!" asserted Pat. "I'm not going to let him murder them in cold blood."

"You have my word," said Serge. "Nothing will happen to them as long as we're in this room."

Bar tugged his arm. "Come on, honey."

Pat relented, and they went in the bathroom.

"Now, where were we?" asked Serge.

"You better kill me," said Catfish. "Otherwise you're a dead man."

Gaspar spit on the floor. *"Mierda!"*

Serge crossed his legs and leaned casually. "Tell me a little about yourselves, as long as we're going to be sitting here. You like sports? Indie films?"

"Kiss my ass!"

Serge cracked Catfish on the side of his head with the barrel of his gun, then smashed Gaspar in the nose with its butt. "I just want some conversation partners. Is that too much to ask?" He raised the gun again. "Why don't you tell me a funny story from when you were growing up? . . ."

TWO HOURS LATER

Small waves from an incoming tide lapped a seawall. The moon had gone down, leaving Serge to work in the privacy of near-total darkness.

"Serge, you don't have to do this," said Pat.

"What? You mean borrow another boat?"

Coleman threw the end of a joint in the water with a sizzle. "Borrow? Didn't you steal it?"

"This is no time to parse words." Serge tied a final knot in clear, thin monofilament. "There, done." He brushed his palms together.

"It's not too late," said Pat.

"It's *real* late." Serge climbed back up on the landing. "Almost dawn."

"You don't have to kill them!"

"I'm not going to kill them, although I can't prevent every accident."

"Serge, I'm begging—"

"Don't you want to know what I've rigged up here?"

"No!"

Serge looked down into the aluminum dinghy. "I'll bet *they* want to know. Their mouths are taped shut, but I can always tell by the eyes." He took a seat on the edge of the concrete wall and let his legs dangle over the side. "Catfish, that was quite a childhood story you told me back at the motel about how you got that nickname. So in your honor, I shopped for a brand-new frog-darter lure, but I couldn't find one because apparently they're super-rare. It's the thought that counts. So instead I went with live bait. I put a good-size fish on the hook because there's no point in this unless you're going for large game! . . . See that line moving around in the water? That's your bait swimming around right now. As you can tell, the line is attached to that fishing pole

in the rod holder, and whenever you leave a pole unattended, you need a bell or some other alarm system to
let you know when you got a bite. Because you wouldn't
want your first big one getting away, right? The bait is
big enough so that it's making the tip of the pole twitch
slightly. Don't worry: not enough to set off the alarm
. . . But I know your next question: What kind of alarm
has ol' Serge rigged to my pole? Believe me, you won't
miss it." He pointed at the running camcorder in his
other hand. "To share the memories . . . Well, off you
go! . . ."

Serge reached down with a foot and pushed the
dinghy out into the middle of the water. "We probably
need to stand back. Way back."

He led the gang along the seawall to the edge of
some grass.

"What's going to happen?" asked Pat.

"Hopefully they'll catch a fish."

"Then what?"

"The alarm system." Serge clicked on a flashlight
and aimed the beam. "I put some drag on the line
so when the big one hits, it'll start running out a few
yards. Unless it's a really big hit, then the line will just
fly. And when it does, I've got a piece of string running
from the reel to the alarm."

"I can't make it out," said Pat.

Serge moved the flashlight's beam. "Hard to see in this light, but it's that tiny condiment packet. I'm sure you've tried Tabasco sauce. Great stuff. It's balanced at the top of the cut-open heating pouch for an in-the-field military meal."

"I remember," said Coleman. "Like that guy from West Point started a fire during survival training. But you left it on the gas tank."

"What tank?" asked Serge.

"That one." Coleman pointed at the spot illuminated by the flashlight. "The big red metal thing with a rag coming out the mouth where the cap should be."

"Did I do that?" Serge whistled. "A clear safety violation. But I loved the part of Catfish's tale where he tied the owl to the gas tank because, if nothing else, I want to be relevant."

Coleman looked around. "How'd you find this place?"

"We're in the backyard of one of those ridiculous waterfront mansions on the New River," said Serge. "Captain Loogie tipped me off which ones were unoccupied. This guy was indicted for emptying retirement accounts. *Another* one. Get out your scorecard."

"But don't mansions like this have outrageous security systems?" asked Coleman.

"The best," said Serge. "But they're mainly designed to prevent burglars breaking into the house, not someone minding his own business and seeking backyard access to the water."

Coleman squinted toward a circular ripple in the water where the fishing line went in. "That bait really is swimming."

"Should catch something in no time." Serge pressed an eye to the viewfinder.

"Please!" Pat pleaded. "There's still time to stop!"

"And let the big one get away?" said Serge. "Not a chance. This is for Santiago, from *The Old Man and the Sea*."

"Uh, Serge," said Coleman. "I think there's a problem. I don't know how they're going to catch anything where they are."

"What do you mean?" asked Serge.

Coleman pointed in another direction away from the backyard. "Shouldn't they be in that other body of water?"

"You mean the New River on the opposite side of the seawall? No, I specifically meant to place them exactly where they are." Serge slapped himself on the forehead. "But I left out a critical step. Follow me . . ."

They walked to the back of the mansion, where Serge found an electrical switch near the gazebo.

He threw it.

Tranquil, muted waves of light danced up the back wall of the house, as the entire backyard lit up in the emerald glow of a palatial swimming pool. With a dinghy floating in the middle. And lots of aquatic movement under the surface.

"There," said Serge. "Now they can see it."

"Who can see it?" asked Coleman.

The first one splashed into the water like a cannon-ball. Then another, and another, drawn to the bright rectangle that was a beacon in the otherwise dark night.

The pelicans kept dive-bombing the pool, feasting on dozens of Japanese koi fish that swam around a hill-billy and a Mexican.

Coleman took a big toke on his joint. "This is some far-out shit."

"I didn't invent nature," said Serge. "I just like to rearrange it."

The splashing became continuous until the pool was a froth.

"Look!" Coleman dramatically stretched out an arm. "One of them ate the bait fish! He's flying away! The line's in the air!"

"So it is," said Serge.

"The Tabasco tipped," said Coleman. "There's a little flicker in the heating pouch. And now the rag is starting to—"

Boom.

The light and heat forced everyone back a step. A fireball went up, and flaming pieces of fishing equipment splashed down in the water.

"But what about the pelican?" asked Coleman.

"I used an environmentally friendly hook that will dissolve in a few days, so no animals would be harmed in this production, with obvious exceptions . . . Better turn this off." Serge stepped back to the gazebo and flicked the switch.

The backyard went dark, and the flames in the boat faded until there was just the burning outline of two human forms.

Coleman scratched his head. "Didn't we leave a guy burning in a boat at night last year?"

"Yes," said Serge. "That oil asshole in the Gulf of Mexico. But it never gets old."

Epilogue

Serge turned off the video camera. "Okay, show's over, back to the car . . ."

They walked to the side of the mansion, where the Gran Torino sat far up a long brick driveway, out of view from the street.

Bar cried inconsolably.

"What's eating her?" said Serge.

Pat just gave him a stare.

"Oh, I get it," said Serge. "A marriage fight."

"Can you give me a couple minutes alone with her?" asked Pat. "We'll be right along."

"No problem," said Serge. "Except those are police sirens we're hearing. It's coming from the other bank, but still a good idea not to dawdle . . . Come on, Coleman."

They walked back to the Gran Torino and leaned against the driver's side.

"Serge, maybe you shouldn't have let them see that." Coleman fired up his predawn jay. "She's a wreck."

"You live, you learn."

A cell phone rang.

Serge looked at his sidekick.

"What?" said Coleman. "Aren't you going to get that?"

"It's not my ring tone."

Coleman looked in the back window. "Where's it coming from?"

"I don't know." He opened a door.

"There," said Coleman. "The wife's purse in the backseat."

Serge reached inside the handbag and pulled it out. The ringing got louder. He flipped it open.

"Hello? . . . Uh, the McDougalls? Yes, they're right here, but I don't think they can come to the phone. They're indisposed, so I'll just discreetly leave it at that because they're having a marriage fight about sexual role-playing, probably costumes . . . What? Could you repeat that last part? But it's not possible! . . ."

Coleman tapped his arm. "What is it?"

Serge swatted the air for him to keep quiet. "But how can *you* be the McDougalls when they're here with me? . . . Listen, I gotta run." He clapped the phone shut. "Pat, Bar, where'd you get those guns?"

"Hands up and move away from the car."

"What's going on?"

"You just helped us eliminate the competition," said the woman.

"I . . . but . . ." Serge held up the phone. "These people said *they* were the McDougalls."

"They are," said the man. "We grabbed them from the side of the motel just before they were about to return to the room. We'd been following them since the shoot-out until we could take their place."

Serge smacked himself on the forehead. "Of course, I only previously saw you at long distance, so I wouldn't have noticed." Then his eyes narrowed. "What have you done with them?"

"Relax, they're completely safe." The man stepped forward and relieved Serge of the gun under his shirt and the keys in his pocket. "We put them up in a suite at the Ambassador and told them to stay put until a special agent came by to escort them."

"Is an agent coming by?" asked Serge.

"No. They'll just wait in the room until they get bored and realize nobody's going to show up. It's bad business to hurt civilians. Only attracts attention."

"But all this . . ." Serge gestured back at the canal. "Why?"

"We were working with Gaspar Arroyo to eliminate a pesky rival."

"So that whole business at the Casablanca was a trap for Catfish?" asked Serge. "It was a mock execution?"

The man nodded. "But we didn't count on you being in the bathroom. Which actually turned out to be a big break in our favor."

"But then why did you let me kill Gaspar in that boat back there?"

"Because Gaspar *thought* we were working together." The woman motioned with her gun for Serge and Coleman to start walking. "We were just using him to get to Catfish, then take care of Gaspar as well because the real objective was to eliminate both of them. That's where you fit in very nicely."

"I get it." Serge whistled. "Man, have I been a dupe. You're working for a third party that's muscling in."

"Let's just say that certain more sophisticated executive elements back in Kentucky saw how lucrative Catfish's operation had become."

Serge smiled. "And the big boys are clearing a space at the trough?"

"Something like that." The man removed a suitcase of cash from the trunk of the Gran Torino.

Headlights approached from the end of the residential street. The lights went out, and a Mercedes swung up the brick driveway in the dark.

The man turned around. "That's our ride."

"So now you shoot us?" asked Serge.

"Don't be ridiculous. You're worth far more to us alive than dead. As long as you're out there roaming around doing whatever the hell it is you call this, the police will be chasing your trail and leaving us alone. And, of course, we'll be calling in some tips about the boat fire."

"And what if *I* call the police on you? Huh?" said Serge. "Did you think about that?"

"Who's going to believe you? You're insane."

"Touché."

"Been nice working with you."

They climbed in the sedan. Door slammed. The Mercedes backed away without headlights.

THE NEXT MORNING

Knock, knock, knock!

"Honey, someone's at the door."

"I got it."

Three more hard knocks on room 1151 of the Ambassador Hotel.

"Coming! . . ." Pat McDougall checked the peephole, then opened the door on the chain. "Yes?"

A gold badge came through the crack.

Pat undid the door and opened up the rest of the way. "Thought you'd never arrive."

From the other side of the room: "Who is it, honey?"

Pat looked back at his wife. "It's the special agent who's going to escort us."

The visitor pocketed his badge. "We don't have much time. Please gather your belongings."

"Thank God," said Pat. "This has been the craziest vacation. So the nightmare is finally over?"

"Yes," Serge said with an effervescent smile. "Now let's get in the car!"

THE NEW LUXURY IN READING

We hope you enjoyed reading
our new, comfortable print size and found it
an experience you would like to repeat.

Well – you're in luck!

HarperLuxe offers the finest in fiction and
nonfiction books in this same larger print size and
paperback format. Light and easy to read, HarperLuxe
paperbacks are for book lovers who want to see
what they are reading without the strain.

For a full listing of titles and
new releases to come, please visit our website:

www.HarperLuxe.com